BASH

BASH

A NOVEL

MIKE BARTOS

Library of Congress Control Number: 2012914672
ISBN: Hardcover   978-1-4771-5892-0
                 Softcover   978-1-4771-5891-3
                 Ebook   978-1-4771-5893-7

To order additional copies of this book, contact:
Xlibris Corporation
1-888-795-4274
www.Xlibris.com
Orders@Xlibris.com
116584

ACKNOWLEDGEMENTS

Many people lent their hand in helping create this story. First and foremost is my wife Jody, who in addition to being my muse, performed tireless editing and content review of the early drafts, putting aside her own creative projects to help make this work possible. She had to use a river of red ink to get my attention. Jody also gets props for the author photo and design.

The reading team provided invaluable content review and feedback on character development. The members of the team included Lanetta Smyth who was fearless in her critique, Tom Sabo, Ned Moore, and Sam Klein.

Thanks also go out to Bruce Hopkins, illustrator extrordinaire, who took the ideas from my head and was able to depict them just the way I envisioned them. He patiently dealt with my indecisiveness and difficulties maneuvering around computer files.

Jay Shore, former publisher and editor, was my inspiration to create the Charley Town newspaper during the time I lived in Charleston. Charley Town was never actually published, but it finally came to life as part of the BASH story.

Mike Bartos
Napa, California
September 2012

Call me Doc. Everyone calls me Doc. My former wives call me Doc. My mother calls me Doc. My golden retriever, Grover, can't quite get it out, but he comes close. Officially, I'm Dr. Patrick Michael Kerrigan, psychiatrist at the illustrious Bay Area State Hospital. When I'm not ministering to the criminally insane, I might be analyzing a glass of Irish whiskey straight up, playing some down home bebop and blues, and if I'm lucky, enjoying the company of a beautiful woman.

This is the story of events that changed my life, as well as the lives of some of my friends and a few of my adversaries. Sometimes you can't alter circumstances, but you can always pay attention, listen, and learn. As my friend and colleague Scotty Powell likes to say, "We're all students until the day we die."

The old joke is that psychiatrists are doctors who can't stand the sight of blood. Maybe they can't stand it, but if they work where I work, they damn well better get used to it.

At least surgeons and prizefighters get to wear gloves.

Eleven years ago, while having a long drink from a whiskey bottle in a brown paper bag and enjoying the view while seated on the concrete base of a light pole in the outlet mall parking lot in McMurtree, South Carolina, Tyler Goode overheard two teenage boys, as he put it, "talkin' trash about my momma." They were unlocking their car as Tyler approached them and asked not so calmly why they were "talkin' shit." One of the young kids was startled and momentarily speechless. He didn't have a satisfactory answer, as if there could possibly be one, so Tyler belted the teen upside the head with the bottle. He was about to nail him again when the other young man, a high school varsity lineman, tackled Tyler, who ended up having a broken collarbone.

After a police-escorted trip to the emergency room, Tyler was booked into the Bay County jail, arm in sling. He was a frequent flier at the county jail; but this time, the ticket back to the street would not be arriving in time for a convenient spring release date.

According to the jury, Tyler was not in his right mind; and although no one ever denied he was somewhat of a violent fellow, the final decision came down to whether he knew right from wrong. Apparently, striking and injuring people who (he imagines) insult his mother is not a wrong thing, at least in Tyler's mind, but it is a wrong thing in the town of McMurtree and the state of South Carolina.

The court sentenced Tyler to the custody of the state Department of Behavioral Health Services until he could be restored to sanity and was no longer dangerous. In Tyler's case, that was not a trivial task, as his condition was one that tends to worsen with age despite treatment.

For over a decade, Tyler wandered the hallways of the old Bay Area State Hospital, mumbling, grumbling, talking to unseen antagonizers, cursing, sometimes smiling, and sometimes offering a pleasant "Good day, sir" to the doctor.

Even though Tyler walked slowly from the medication, he had hard, fast fists that could catch a younger man by surprise. He was known to knock a fellow patient to the floor with one unannounced swift punch to the face. After spending fifteen minutes in the "quiet room" for his offense and getting a small dose of tranquilizer, Tyler would return to his normal routine of pacing the hallway, conversing and negotiating in a world that was filled with hostile people who existed primarily to disrespect his mother. Was he sorry? "No, but that little punk learned a lesson. I had to straighten him out, just like those other young punks."

This was Tyler Goode's day in court. Every year for the past eleven years, Tyler had his day in court. He could waive his hearing and spare Bay County the expense of a jury trial, the purpose of which was to determine whether or not he could leave the Bay Area State Hospital and return to the community at age forty-five, but neither Tyler nor his public defender would hear of it.

If the jury decided in his favor, found that he was no longer mentally ill and dangerous, he would live among free men. The "community" in state hospital and prison parlance is basically anywhere that isn't in some kind of institution. Like, "Mr. Goode, how do you propose to take care of yourself in the community?" Mr. Goode would take the stand and proudly announce that he actually owned the Bay Area State Hospital and was worth many millions of dollars.

On this day, his treating psychiatrist, one Morton Frizell, would testify that in no way shape or form should Mr. Tyler Goode be loosed on the good people of South Carolina. Morty was a New York transplant who fell in love with Charleston and started to adopt Southern ways and accent. Every day he made the drive from Charleston down to Bay County, the location of the Bay Area State Hospital, to tend to his flock of lambs, or wolves, depending on the day.

The Honorable Judge DeWitt Gaillard of the probate court would be hearing this case. For the defense, the petitioner actually, was Ms. Leticia Andover Gibbs, a true believer in the evils of psychiatric commitment. Such commitment was even more egregious when applied to a brother who was railroaded into a mental institution for many years longer than he would have served in jail for hitting a seventeen-year-old white kid on the head with a whiskey bottle.

Tyler Goode sat in the courtroom, wearing a crisp white shirt and dress slacks, much different from the hospital "blues" that patients were required to wear. His often unruly thinning hair was slicked down and combed straight back, and his face was clear of the usual stubble. He wore drug store reading glasses that made him look somewhat studious. He may have arrived in the courthouse in his hospital blues, but today he appeared transformed. Maybe the jury might think all the years of treatment have had some salubrious effect.

The courtroom was in need of a new carpet, as years of humidity and closed windows left a distinct musty smell which the attorneys carried home on their suits. Paint was peeling from the ceiling, and the upholstered chairs in the jury box were cracked and torn. The air-conditioning worked but was weak, needing supplementation from three ceiling fans. Courtroom 1A had distinctive mahogany paneling on the walls; and although the wood was faded, a little refinishing could restore the rich luster. Upgrading the courthouse was on the county supervisors' list of projects, but was way down on that list.

Tyler was seated next to his attorney, Ms. Andover Gibbs, who was looking through copious notes on yellow legal pads. Articles were stacked on the petitioner's table and more were in file boxes on the floor. This was not a Supreme Court case; but to Attorney Andover Gibbs, each mental health case she represented before the court was a matter of pride and striving for the greater good and dignity of mental patients.

Dr. Frizell was dressed in a charcoal gray suit with a smart blue tie, his usual attire for a day in court. He was tall and slender, with curly dark hair that seemed to explode off his head. Wire-rim glasses were perched on the tip of his nose. He looked like what the layman would expect of a psychiatrist. Judge Gaillard, a distinguished black man in his mid fifties, was prompt as usual. The attorney for the state, an experienced, silver-haired assistant DA by the name of Hilton Breuer, was ready to match wits with his friend and adversary, Ms. Andover Gibbs, once again.

Judge Gaillard liked to keep things casual. When the bailiff announced, "All rise," the good judge motioned for all to stay seated. However, everyone in the courtroom, including the judge, stood respectfully, honoring the jurors as they filed in.

Mr. Breuer called his first and only witness for the People, Dr. Frizell.

He questioned his witness, age forty-seven, graduate of NYU and Einstein Medical School, with psychiatry training at Bellevue and all the other necessary requisites. The judge agreed, as he had several times before, that Dr. Frizell was indeed a psychiatric expert.

Mr. Breuer continued, "So, Doctor, have you had a chance to evaluate Mr. Goode, and do you have an opinion as to whether or not he suffers from a mental illness?"

"Yes, I have," he answered, not giving any extra information.

"And what have you concluded?"

"He does indeed suffer from a mental illness."

"And what is your diagnosis?"

"Chronic paranoid schizophrenia."

The ritual continued.

"Can you explain to the jury exactly what that diagnosis means?"

"Surely, Mr. Goode has a mental condition characterized by delusions. That is, he believes things that aren't real, things that he imagines, even if bizarre, are true in his world. To him they are facts indisputable." Dr. Frizell swiveled in his chair to face the jury, focusing on the blonde in the back row. "For example, he believes he invented the computer, even though he has no idea how to use one. Then he claims the computer companies send him a million dollars a week."

"Go on, Doctor."

"I asked him where all that money is, and he said, 'Well, I ain't gonna tell you.'"

There was some low level chuckling in the courtroom but no gavel.

"What else?"

"He says he was an astronaut."

"Okay, what about the paranoid part?"

"He believes people everywhere are talking about him or somehow disrespecting his mother. He hears this from people on the wards, from patients, from staff, from anyone who happens to be nearby, seen or unseen."

Tyler blurted out from the defense table, "That's damn right, y'all tell 'em to shut up." Ms. Andover Gibbs shushed him and patted him on the shoulder. He turned and looked at her. "Ain't that right, Sister?"

The doctor continued, "Sometimes he accuses staff or patients of stealing his underwear and switching it for their own. When I ask him why anyone would do that, he replies with something like 'Cuz they put me in this hospital with all these crazy people.'"

Mr. Breuer continued, "So just because he believes these things makes him a danger?"

"No, what makes him a danger is because he hits people."

Tyler's counselor leapt to her feet. "Objection, the doctor is testifying to facts not in evidence."

After some whispered debate in front of the bench, the objection was overruled, as she knew it would be—just trying to make a point.

Mr. Breuer asked the psychiatrist to continue.

"He's belted a few patients. And last month, he threw a plate at a cafeteria worker."

"Why did he do that?"

"He said something about getting the wrong kind of sandwich."

The silver-maned assistant DA continued, "So your patient gets easily frustrated and doesn't act appropriately when dealing with everyday stressors that anyone and everyone experiences in the community." This was exactly the point Dr. Frizell was trying to make. It felt good to have logic and reasoning on his side. Yes, it's the job of the psychiatrist to bring crystal clear thinking to the table.

"That's right. It doesn't even have to be a real stress. Often it's just one that he imagines. I don't believe he's really improved that much since he hit that young man in the parking lot a dozen years ago. He'll probably slug somebody again if he's out walking the streets. He still hears people insulting his mother even though she's been dead six years."

Tyler started to rise from his seat. "Lying sumbitch, kick yo muthafuckin' ass."

The bailiff took a few steps toward the table, but Ms. Andover Gibbs had her client under good control with a gentle hand to the shoulder, guiding him back into his seat. This seemed like the opportune moment for the assistant DA to declare, "No further questions."

Ms. Andover Gibbs was out of her seat like a jackrabbit and waving papers in the air. For her, it wasn't always about winning the case—well, it was somewhat—but she was a true believer about the massive fraud that is psychiatry and the hubris of psychiatrists, just like the one who was sitting on the witness stand.

"What do you mean he hits people?" It seemed like a stupid question; but in front of a jury, they say there are no stupid questions. They could be wrong. The good doctor sighed and refrained from rolling his eyes.

"Well, he punches other patients especially when he thinks they're talking about him or his mother. That's how he ended up at BASH in the first place."

"BASH?"

"That's what they call the Bay Area State Hospital."

"Is that some kind of a joke?" It was. She already knew that.

"No, Counselor, that's just what they call it."

"So, Doctor"—*doctor* as often said by opposing council with a flavor of derision and contempt—"how long has it been since Mr. Goode hit anybody?"

"Oh, maybe a month or six weeks."

"Did you see him hit anyone?"

"Not personally, no."

"No? So how do you know he hit anyone?"

"It's in the nursing notes and we talked about it at the team meeting and there was an incident report."

"Who wrote the incident report?"

"I don't remember."

"So your opinion that my client is a dangerous man is based on something you didn't see happen and reported by some staff member you can't remember who it is."

"Those are pretty reliable documents, and it happens fairly routinely."

"You mean something supposedly happens that you don't see and you don't remember who told you?"

"No, that Tyler gets angry easily and acts out."

Ms. Andover Gibbs sneered, "*Doctor*, would you get angry if you were locked up in an old decrepit facility with three roommates, all of whom are mentally ill?"

"Maybe I would, but I wouldn't imagine people are talking about my mother."

"Do you know as a fact that people aren't talking about his mother?"

"Well, it's not likely."

"Not likely, Doctor, not likely? Well, maybe you don't come from where I come from, but where I come from, people are always saying stuff like 'Yeah, yo mama' or 'Yo mama's fat" or 'Yo mama needs a shave.' Like that's the way some people talk in a community like Mr. Goode's. Were you aware of that, Doctor?"

"I guess I've heard that."

"And how many patients on this ward that Mr. Goode lives on are African American?"

"Maybe about half."

"Oh, maybe about half, maaaybeee about half. So there's a good chance that from time to time, somebody is actually saying something inappropriate about mothers?"

"It's possible."

"Oh, possible. How about likely?"

"I can't say for sure."

"Well, Doctor," she continued, spitting out the title again, "weren't you just sitting here just a few minutes ago, saying how in your pro-fesh-i-nal opinion my client is delusional and should stay locked up?"

"Well, not exactly . . ."

"I can have the stenographer read back your statements."

"Uh, that's not necessary. Keep in mind he threatened me right here in front of this court just a few minutes ago."

"Did he hurt you? You know, I'm a little lady, half his size, and he just calmed down when I asked him to."

"Well, apparently he trusts you and feels you're on his side."

"Oh, you're his doctor, aren't *you* supposed to be on his side? Did you ever think that what Mr. Goode needs is someone to trust, offer him a gentle hand, instead shooting him up with whatever drugs some pharmaceutical company bribes you into prescribing?"

"Objection!" shouted vigorously by Mr. Breuer.

Judge Gaillard gave Ms. Andover Gibbs a warning. She apologized and withdrew the question. The damage was done. She knew just about how much she could get away with.

She continued, "So you say he was an astronaut?"

"No, Counselor, he said he was an astronaut."

"Did you ever hear him say that?"

"As a matter of fact, he personally told me that several times—said he's been to the moon."

"Do you know for a fact that he wasn't an astronaut?"

"I think we would all know about that if that were the case."

"Why would he say that?"

"Well, Counselor, as I said, he's delusional—he's not normal."

This was the trigger that either set off Ms. Andover Gibbs or perhaps the one she was waiting for. "Normal? You want to talk about normal? Who are you to say who's normal? Maybe you're not normal. You know, a lot of people think psychiatrists aren't normal."

Dr. Frizell was caught off guard. "I think anyone imagining such a fantastic situation isn't normal," he said, throwing gasoline on the fire.

"He's a poor man, lived in poverty all his life, so he imagines or fantasizes a more glamorous life than the crappy one he's had. Maybe that's something you don't do, Doctor, and maybe it's something I don't do, but people do it. People dream about winning the lottery. Grown men go to fantasy baseball or football camp. Little boys imagine they're Superman and little girls dream about being a fairy princess. Should we lock them up too?"

"That's not what I'm saying."

"Well, praise the Lord."

Mr. Breuer: "Objection!"

"I withdraw my comment."

Judge Gaillard checked his watch. "I think it's time for lunch."

CHAPTER 2

Burton Peals sat handcuffed in the backseat of Bay County Sheriff BD Harmon's cruiser, riding from BASH to be delivered to the Charleston County courthouse. His muscular arms were shackled to his waist. He was a clean-cut, good-looking, light-skinned black man in his early thirties. He could have been an athlete or a cop or a teacher. Maybe if he wore a pin-striped suit and minus the shackles, he might be a lawyer. But Burton Peals was none of these things. Unlike his colleague, Tyler Goode, he wasn't going to be cut loose by a sympathetic jury. His crime eleven years ago occurred about the same time Tyler was hitting teenagers with a whiskey bottle.

While on a prolonged amphetamine binge, he had been parked in a hotel room in North Charleston with a lady of the evening. She was a tired looking woman, about thirty-five, with platinum blond hair and a resigned joylessness for the task she was being paid to perform. However, Burton was rockin', hoppin', and buzzin' with the drug coursing through his nervous system. He sat naked on the edge of the motel room bed, preparing to watch the prostitute shed her clothing, when he noticed an intense yellow glow emanating from her eyes. He thought, *She's looking right through me.*

He cocked his head to one side and dropped his jaw. The woman asked, "What's wrong, honey? You don't like what you see?"

He didn't like it, not at all. She smiled at him, trying to calm him down. She had seen the meth freaks before, even within the past week. The meth was everywhere, including some in her own little purse. He focused on her with an ominous glassy stare.

Oh shit, she thought, *this dude is freakin' out on me right now.* As she reached for her skimpy clothing thrown across the chipped desk chair, he grabbed her wrist and yanked her toward him. She tried to pull away, but his grasp was too strong. Burton was convinced he had hooked up with a demon who was going to suck out his soul. He had to save himself. The woman screamed, but only for a moment before his large hands clenched like a vice around her throat. Guests in the neighboring rooms heard pounding and thumping against the wall, a little more than the usual level of disruption at this particular establishment.

When the police arrived and kicked in the door, they saw Burton naked, kneeling on the floor with his hands still clamped around the motionless woman's neck. The last thing Burton said before being tased was "She's still growling. Do something."

The amphetamine had done its dirty work, tipping a chronic user into a paranoid psychotic killer. It took about a year at BASH, but Burton mostly recovered from his descent into madness. He remained on a modest dose of medication that kept the paranoia under control. Treatment appeared to be successful. He stayed clean and sober and attended the mandated groups over and over again, but he wasn't going anywhere, at least that's what everybody seemed to think.

Every year, when it was time for a release hearing, his psychiatrist would appear in court and beam about what an exemplary patient Burton was. Then the DA would present his case as to why Burton should remain in the hospital. There was little logic but a lot of emotion at every trial, year after year. The jurors were treated to the details of the crime, glossy photos of the strangled prostitute, copies of the original police report, psychologist reports from the time of arrest, and angry cross-examinations of the doctor.

"Doctor, can you guarantee this patient will not repeat his crime?"

"Doctor, do you know for a fact that Mr. Peals will continue his medication?"

"Doctor, are you willing to be personally responsible for any repeat of the tragedy that befell Mr. Peals' first victim?"

The jury usually did not take long to reach the conclusion that "based upon the preponderance of the evidence," society would best be served by having Mr. Peals receive another year of treatment at the Bay Area State Hospital.

ON THIS DAY of his annual hearing, he was dressed in casual street clothes, a tan polo shirt and dark slacks. He was patted down before leaving the facility; but as most of the residents knew, the cops didn't get really intimate with the procedure. In each shoe, he had about five hundred dollars, in as high of denomination as possible. He wore shoes a half size larger than his normal size, with what he considered really comfortable arch supports.

He "earned" his money over the past year through what was referred to in the hospital as "wheeling and dealing." Throw that in with gambling and a dash of strong arm intimidation and he realized his goal of a thousand bucks. He managed to swap out small bills for larger ones with other patients and

MIKE BARTOS

an occasional staff member who would receive a small commission for the service.

Burton was an absolutely charming passenger in the sheriff's cruiser, discussing groups at the hospital, the virtues of the substance recovery program, and his favorite verses from the Bible. Sheriff Harmon, a veteran of twenty years of law enforcement, was at ease with Burton as they pulled into the Charleston County municipal garage. He guided the cruiser into the "official vehicles only" space. Together they walked up the echoing stairway.

The courthouse had several security guards at the entrance with a metal scanner and conveyor belt with x-ray. The sheriff and his prisoner were able to bypass the scanner and entrance security. The side door simply opened with a key and then latched shut. Burton stood with his hands cuffed to a waist chain and looked at the somewhat overweight sheriff. "Hey, Sheriff, I need to visit the rest room. Could you . . . ?"

"No problem, son. I'll show you the way." Harmon removed the chain and cuffs as he would be required to do before escorting his prisoner into the courtroom. The men's room had bars over the window. Burton was a cooperative, pleasant fellow. Besides, he was a patient, not a correctional inmate, and they were in the courthouse, where there were deputies and security guards up the wazoo.

Burton entered the bathroom stall and closed the door while the sheriff waited a few feet away. Burton sat on the john and removed his shoes, stuffed the twenties, fifties, and a few hundreds into his previously empty wallet.

Sheriff Harmon looked at his watch—five minutes. He thought he'd give him just a little more time. After one or two more minutes, Harmon shouted through the stall door, "Son, we gotta get movin', you don't wanna piss off the judge, do ya?" Harmon pulled the cuffs off his belt and readied them. He stood right in front of the stall as Burton stood up and flushed the toilet. The sheriff anticipated Burton's reappearance when—wham—Burton gave a full-thrust kick to the stall door, smacking the sheriff square in the face. He was momentarily stunned before Burton's muscular arm propelled his hard fist square into the sheriff's jaw. The overweight Harmon went down to the floor. Burton, standing over his fallen custodian, looked down—"Sorry, Sheriff, nothing personal"—and then kicked him in the face. Blood flowed from his nose.

By the urinal, a balding middle-aged man wearing a sport coat with a juror badge clipped to the breast pocket stared at Burton. Burton glowered back. The juror averted his eyes and backed up silently. Burton ordered firmly, "Get in that stall." The man with the juror badge obeyed. The sheriff was down but had a gun still holstered. Burton walked briskly out of the restroom and, amid the bustle of the noisy courthouse lobby, exited calmly through the front door. Deputies and guards were yelling and running to the restroom as Burton headed down the courthouse steps to the sidewalk in the heart of downtown Charleston, crowded with tourists and locals on that bright early summer morning.

SECURITY POLICE CAPTAIN Lyle Dawkins sharply rapped his nightstick on the long conference table as the assembled administrators buzzed and chatted. Captain Dawkins had the feel and look of the stereotypical southern law man, early fifties, tall, big gut with muscular neck and shoulders, a full head of crew-cut graying hair, and the requisite reflective sunglasses.

BASH was supposedly a hospital, and that it was. Legislators and social activists, as well as some of the hospital's own employees, believed that criminals who happened to be mentally ill were maybe not as dangerous as your ordinary run of the mill thug and deserved treatment, not punishment. And then there was the law, which declared such to be the case. Lyle Dawkins didn't necessarily believe that, but he was a good soldier, and his job was to keep some semblance of order on the grounds of BASH without cracking skulls or breaking bones, without tasers, tear gas, or bullets, rubber ones or otherwise.

He had the attention of Elliot Desjardins, the hospital administrator, Cookie Blaylock, MD, the medical director, Augie Papadopoulos, the clinical director, and Bob Binder, the assistant clinical director. Binder was young—maybe thirty—slender, and pale, with a modified "faux hawk" hairstyle. The upper managers, middle managers, and a variety of other administrators whose actual functions were not completely clear, crowded the conference room.

Captain Dawkins paused for a moment of dramatic silence and then gazed around the room. "As y'already know, one of our residents managed to hightail it out of the courthouse up in Charleston. We shoulda known something was brewing. I kept tellin' y'all that we need to send one of our own to the court hearings. But no, all I hear about is money and staff cuts. I tell you that wouldn't a happened if I'd a sent one of my boys up there. How much money we gonna save now?"

Cookie Blaylock interjected, "Captain, with all due respect, this kind of sarcasm isn't helpful."

"That's right," added the administrator. "What we have here is an opportunity for improvement. We need to strengthen our security measures."

Bob Binder looked up from his laptop, "Yep, we're already on it. All off grounds activities are cancelled, the wards are locked down, and we're working on a new policy and procedure plan. We're having a meeting of the Quality Improvement Committee tomorrow morning from nine till noon. In the meantime, I want feedback from all the departments on how we can improve."

"Well, I been tellin' y'all to git yer act together here and get your business in one sock," Lyle said, getting somewhat red in the face.

"More police presence is something we've been asking for since the violence has been increasing," Dr.Blaylock noted. "We've asked a dozen times."

Hiram Singh, the assistant director of the Department of Behavioral Health Services, made the trip from the state capitol in Columbia early that morning to make the official pronouncement from the mountaintop. "This is not about more police," he said intently, tapping the point of his index finger on the table. "This is about treatment. Until the State of South Carolina declares this institution a prison, we are going to be a *hospital*—we are going to provide *treatment*. We need to improve the treatment plans, I want Mr. Peals' treatment team writing an addendum to his treatment plan for when he returns. If he does anything stupid out there, we're all on the hook. We must have accountability. The surveyors are going to be furious . . . and we better let Mr. Peals' county community transition team know."

"That's right, he'll never get out now," Bob Binder added without a hint of irony.

Elliot Desjardins looked over his reading glasses, eyebrows raised. "Okay, I need a full interdisciplinary report by Friday. We need input from nursing, from medicine, and psychiatry, psychology, and social work. Also we need to have an analysis from the rehab therapy department. They'll probably be the ones most affected by this. Also, we need to have all the department chairs attend the hospital wide Incident Review Committee."

Bob eagerly chimed in, "We have a plan to have the security police patrol the grounds more thoroughly."

Captain Dawkins asked, "So we're going to increase my budget?"

Desjardins responded, "No, we can't increase budgets—you know that—and there's a hiring freeze with the state right now."

"So how the hell are we going to increase patrols?"

"We're going to better utilize internal resources," Desjardins shot back with a canned response.

"We're already stretched to the limit." Dawkins face was getting redder. "And besides, how is increasing the grounds patrol going to keep people from running away from the courthouse? And why don't we have the patients wear hospital or prison garb when they're off grounds?"

Desjardins just looked down at the table and chuckled. "Lyle, Lyle, Lyle, you know that would be a violation of the patients' rights agreement we have with the feds."

Lyle was convinced that bureaucrats are cowards whose main mission in life is to cover their collective asses. He knew that, but he was part of the system. Some people get so compromised, they lose their skills and motivation to break free and go forth. Lyle saw that happening to him. At least he saw it coming; at least it bothered him. They couldn't fire him unless he really messed up. That felt nice and safe. With five years in the military, which counted toward state retirement, and another sixteen with the corrections department and the last six with the Department of Behavioral Health Services, he could do all right on the family farm right outside of Walterboro. Lyle, boy, just may be best to keep your mouth shut.

"What does the policy manual say about our response to this type of episode?" asked Dr. Blaylock.

Bailey Simpson, PsyD, chief psychologist, was thumbing through volume one, licking his thumb and forefinger before every page turn, leaving quite a collection of saliva on the manual. "Hmmm, can't seem to find anything specific to this. Wait"—he licked his thumb again—"yes, here's something about security risks." He paused. "No . . . that's not it. No . . . that doesn't apply either."

"Well," said the administrator with authority, "we need to have something in place by next week, at least before the surveyors show up. Augie, I'll look for a report and recommendation from you."

Lyle Dawkins, a smart but not all that well-educated man, figured for damn sure he could have written a decent policy on the back of an envelope during lunch. But the way he saw it, the good State of South Carolina was committed to giving work to scores of highly educated folks living and working here in the coastal backwaters of the low country.

CHAPTER 3

Run, you son of a bitch, run like a scared dog. That was the thought going through the mind of Burton Peals as he ran west along Broad Street, then cut over to a side street, and ran toward the tidal pond in a small park known as Colonial Lake. It was quieter there than the downtown area, mostly neighborhood residents strolling with baby carriages or jogging on the sidewalk around the half-mile perimeter of the lagoon and an occasional fisherman, hoping to pull in something for the dinner table.

He had studied the maps of Charleston; but in the heat of excitement, he ran the wrong direction. He should have turned east toward downtown and lost himself in the market place. The neighborhood around Colonial Lake was a mixture of old mansions, apartment buildings, dilapidated clapboard houses, and housing projects. Standing on Rutledge Avenue by the lake, he was in the wide open, visible from many directions. He headed down a narrow side street of tightly packed wooden houses and bumper to bumper parked cars. A wailing police car, lights flashing, sped by on Rutledge Avenue. He zigzagged through the projects. As a tall, light-skinned black man, Burton did not stand out. Maybe it was just as well that he went west instead of north into the market area bustling with white Yankee tourists.

He was wearing a tan polo shirt and charcoal slacks, a description transmitted on the police all points bulletin. He had planned to purchase a change of clothes quickly, but he was not in a shopping area right now and it would be hard to duck into a store downtown. The plan was to catch a bus along Meeting Street to North Charleston, where the interstate bus terminal was located.

Two teens were passing by. Burton made eye contact and said, "Wazzup?"

"Wazzup?" one of them responded.

Burton addressed the taller of the two, "Hey, bro, I'll give you twenty bucks for your shirt," which was a plain gray T-shirt.

The tall boy wrinkled his nose and said incredulously, "Twenty bucks? You be some kinda whack or what? For this?" pulling at his own well-worn shirt. "You gonna give me yours?"

"That's the deal."

"You runnin' from the Man?"

"Twenty bucks for each of you, but we gotta do it now."

The exchange of shirts took place right there on the street. The gray T-shirt was a little snug and smelled of cigarette smoke and sweat. He looked at the other teen. "Thirty bucks for your shades."

"Sheeeit, forty and you got a deal." Burton peeled off two twenties and handed them to the young man. A hat would be good, maybe later.

"Hey, it's been a pleasure, my man," the shorter teen quipped. "I'll catch you later."

"No, you won't," Burton said as they continued in opposite directions.

Burton planned to give a wide berth to the area from which he had escaped and walked the side streets. He passed a corner grocery store with peeling gray clapboard siding and a neon sign in the window with only about half the letters illuminated. The counter was tended by an elderly black man slowly drawing on a cigarette. Burton decided to buy some for himself, along with cookies and fruit. The police would not likely be focusing attention on a man walking with a bagful of groceries.

He circled back to Meeting Street, a mile north of Broad, and waited impatiently for the first bus to come along, any bus. It arrived after about five minutes. As the bus headed north, he saw several state police cars, sirens piercing, heading south. Still carrying the groceries, he was able to transfer to a North Charleston bound bus.

He was not going to hop the interstate bus tonight; the idea was to lay low, get some rest, and then head out in the morning. Nearby was a motel for forty-five dollars in the rough Navy town of North Charleston, not far from where he committed his offense a decade ago. He paid cash and signed in as Jim Thompson. No questions asked. The motel was often used for prostitution liaisons, but there would be none of that tonight.

Burton checked out the room, dimly lit, smelling of stale cigarette smoke, with shag carpet and faded drapes, but there was a working color TV with cable and a porno channel. He was going to sleep in a room by himself for the first time in ten years. He took a fresh apple from the bag and munched it as he flipped on the TV. It was likewise the first time in years he could pick whatever channel he wanted without permission. Maybe he would be featured on the local news. There was more compelling business first. The stinky T-shirt had to go.

A strip mall was located less than a mile from the motel. He bought a duffel bag, underwear, a Carolina Gamecocks ball cap, a fresh pair of jeans

MIKE BARTOS

and shorts, toiletries, and some candy bars, all for under seventy bucks. Burton found a pizza place, ordered a large with pepperoni, and carried it back to the room to enjoy the solitude, just the TV, the pizza, and himself.

He showered, disposed of the old clothes, changed into fresh clean underwear, sat on the bed, and watched TV. Buckingham palace couldn't have been better. He checked the free internet in the lobby. The next bus for Asheville was at 11:00 a.m. Perfect. He could sleep in a little.

He was out during the six o'clock news, but the ten o'clock news made mention of the Great Escape. The sheriff was shaken up but not seriously injured, just a mild concussion and a broken nose. Burton's picture appeared on the screen, but it was a picture of him from ten years ago when he had been admitted to the hospital, with a goatee no less. He was now ten years older and clean shaven. The inefficiency of the system was working in his favor today.

This would be the first night in many years he would go to sleep without medication. He had been taking an old-school antipsychotic drug known as haloperidol, which was supposed to treat hallucinations, delusions, paranoia, and the like. Burton remained on a modest dose in light of the seriousness of his crime. He was sure he didn't need it anymore since he swore off crank and alcohol, except for an occasional slug of a sickening homemade concoction that some roommates made out of fermenting apple and prune juice, known as "pruno."

The bed was reasonably firm and comfortable, and the sheets were clean. The bathroom was all his, and the floor was washed. In the dark and dilapidated bowels of North Charleston, Burton Peals spent his first night of freedom drifting off into a drug-free sleep.

CHAPTER 4

Ashley Roper was lost in the swirling darkness and tumbling in the sand. Flashes of light illuminated the desert, and the noisy bursts of artillery fire shot through his skull to the core of his brain. He could hear men yelling. Were they his men, or were they Saddam's Republican guard or just rag tag conscripts dying under the massive weight of the tank treads? He shouted out and flailed his arms. He opened his eyes only to see the dimly lit ceiling fan rotating slowly above him and hear the soft mechanical purr of the air-conditioning unit.

His wife, who had been snuggled comfortably next to him under the blanket, startled awake. She reached over to touch her husband, slick with sweat and breathing heavily. "Ash? You okay?" It hadn't happened for a while. They both hoped the nightmares would go away for good, but they still hung around, waiting, hiding in the recesses of his mind. Just when it seemed like the demons were buried forever, "Surprise, we're heeere."

Ash sat up, stared straight ahead, and then buried his face in his hands. His long dark hair was matted, sticking to the back of his neck. He took a few deep breaths and then turned to face her. He was calm. "Yeah, I think so. That sucked."

Sally J sat up, her eyes met his. "You want to talk about it?"

Ash sighed, "Not too much to talk about," his usual answer. "It's all kind of a blur now." He told the truth. The details of the nightmares dissipated quickly, like early morning fog.

Hundreds of Iraqi soldiers were buried alive in sandy trenches as American and allied tanks moved forward, 1991, over twenty years ago. Ash was there. He had talked about it before, but it had been years since he attended the therapy groups at the VA Hospital.

"Why don't you clean up? I'll change the sheets," Sally J offered. As Ash took a cool shower and washed his hair, Sally J poured some orange juice. Things were better than the old days, years ago, when he would have taken more than a few hits of vodka. Sally J threw out the liquor bottles when she found them, but they kept appearing under the bed, in the back of the closet, and in the underwear drawer. She knew how that worked. Her daddy up in

Cheraw used to do the same. The difference was her husband quit; Daddy didn't quit until the day he died when she was fourteen.

Nine years ago, Ash ended up in the detox ward of the VA, exhaling the noxious fumes of metabolized alcohol and getting shot up with medication to avoid withdrawal seizures. Sally J made it clear that it was either her or the alcohol. Wisely, Ash chose Sally J, and he kept his promise. He had a wife who made the difference. She stayed with him, although he knew she had dreams and fantasies that didn't always include him.

It was after two a.m. They sat at the round polished cherrywood kitchen table in their carriage house on Cumberland Street in the heart of the old city. The orange juice was refreshing and helped Ash clear his head. Sally J fixed herself some decaf. She warmed her hands on the coffee mug and looked at Ash. Her wide blue eyes were moist and expressive. "Ash, do you think you need to get back into therapy?"

"No, baby, I don't need to go running to a shrink every time I have a bad dream. And as sure as hell don't need any damn pills that leave my dick in the dirt. I'm just a little preoccupied with the paper." She wasn't worried about his masculinity or virility. At forty-three, he was strong and good-looking, muscular, and maybe a little overweight. When he was drinking a decade ago, he was heavier. Nowadays he liked to keep physically active. Working out at the gym, a little boxing, running—all these things he did since he was at the Citadel and in the army helped clear his mind, letting him sleep better. Now he was forcing himself to write, but the stories didn't come and the articles seemed dull and mundane. He was crankier, eating more, and exercising less. He said he would never drink again, and she believed him.

Sally J was still worried. "Hon, you're getting a little worked up. It's going on three. You need your rest. We both do. We have a lot of stuff to do in the morning. How about a foot massage? That'll get you back to sleep."

"Sally J, you're tired too. Thanks for being up with me. I'll take a rain check on the massage." They lay together on the bed. He wore just boxer shorts and stretched out on top of the blanket. She was at his side and curled up against him. He smelled nice after his shower. He turned and faced her in the darkened room and saw the dim light reflected in her eyes, watering ever so slightly. She hoped he would not see any stray tears track down her cheek.

THE SUN ROSE dull red over Charleston, through the mist hovering just above the calm surface of the Cooper River. It was almost eight as the morning

MIKE BARTOS

light radiated through the translucent curtains in the bedroom. The window looked out on a wild garden between the carriage house and brick wall of the main house. Bougainvillea and ivy covered the far wall of the garden, and begonias flourished in the shaded area under a pergola. Sally J arose first and put on the espresso, which they both sorely needed. The hissing of the nozzle foaming up the milk for the cappuccino awoke Ash. He had slept well the rest of the night. Sally J had finally nodded off herself but wasn't completely rested. She asked, "Mind if I crank open the windows, hon?"

"Do it," Ash agreed. It seemed a great idea to let in some fresh air, even if it was heavy and thick with humidity. The fragrance from the jasmine in the garden was worth the effort. They could hear the sound of a sudden gentle shower outside, freshening the flowers. The sheer curtains billowed in the soft breeze.

Sally J heated some scones and enjoyed the morning with no conversation, at least for the moment. Ash started, "Thanks, baby, you really helped me pull it together. Sorry, I woke you." She said nothing, but just leaned over and kissed him gently on the lips.

After a few moments, Sally J decided to bring up the topic of business, the paper, *Charley Town*. Ash didn't want to hear it, not again. "Ash, the ad revenue is down, this is the fourth week in a row our expenses are more than we're taking in." Sally J was the business manager of their weekly tabloid, among a variety of other positions at the paper, including assistant editor. She worried about the money, the bills, the electric, the phone, and the printing contractor. Ash worried about the writing, his writing in particular, or the lack of it lately. Sally J sensed the danger. Early in the marriage, when he got lost in his writing was also the time when he drank the most.

Ash, distracted, gazed out the open kitchen window, watching a hummingbird hover over the jasmine and then pirouette out of view. "Don't remind me. Yeah, we gotta do something. The online edition will take a little time. I think it'll be okay. As soon as I get my *big story*, as soon as I get it going, we'll be back in the black."

The big story. It was the big story that got *Charley Town* rolling in 2002. Ash had lost his job as a reporter for the *Charleston Times*. He had been recognized as a promising writer, but he was missing deadlines and, all too often, missing work altogether. His career was in the toilet; his marriage was suffering; and certainly, the baby idea was off the table, mainly because Sally J put it on hold.

During his sober spells, Ash pounded out his story as a second lieutenant in Kuwait. The events of September 11 renewed the public's interest in Iraq. If he wasn't drowning in vodka, he immersed himself in writing. He would close the door to the second bedroom, shutting out Sally J, tapping away at his keyboard, sometimes through the night. Some mornings he would emerge, tired, holding a dozen pages of raw manuscript, asking Sally J to review them. Other mornings she would find him sprawled on the couch, an empty bottle lying on the floor.

It wasn't until after detox at the VA and another thirty days at a recovery center in the countryside that he was able to finish "The Heart of Kuwait," a dramatic first-person account of the Gulf War, his struggle with post traumatic stress disorder, and recovery from alcoholism.

"The Heart of Kuwait" was rejected by nineteen publishers and six agents. Some publishers praised his writing, but in the end, *Thank you for your submission. We regret to inform you that your manuscript does not meet our current needs. However, we wish you the best in your search for a suitable publisher.*

In early 2002, Ash had no job, little money, a blue chip from AA, a young but troubled marriage, and a good manuscript he couldn't sell. That led to the birth of *Charley Town*. The weekly tabloid took its name for the truckers' CB radio nickname for Charleston. If he couldn't sell his story, he was going to put it out there himself, along with the restaurant reviews and personal ads. His dad, retired army colonel Jeff Roper, loaned Ash ten thousand dollars for the startup. The town and gown paper, like so many others, was given away at supermarkets, gyms, restaurants, hotels, and clubs.

Readers found the story compelling. The book was serialized and appeared in the first eleven issues. As interest in the story developed around Charleston, small crowds of readers waited at various delivery points each Friday to snatch up *Charley Town* and read the next episode. Demand for the paper exploded. Ash paid his dad back with interest within six months.

Sally J rolled up her sleeves, quit her retail job, and put her own writing on hold so she could work along with Ash to produce articles, sell ads, and load heavy bales of papers into their van. She drove around Charleston, North Charleston, and Mount Pleasant, delivering the papers. She was twenty-six years old, strong, and full of energy and hope. She could reach into the back of the van, lift a forty-five-pound stack of papers, spin around, carry it to the doorway of the restaurant or club and pull the door open with her foot, and drop the stack on the floor, slice the twine with a box cutter, and then go back to the van and off to the next destination. She repeated the process twenty times in a day.

The lone agent who believed in Ash was able to sell "The Heart of Kuwait" to a midsize publishing company, with an advance of thirty thousand dollars. Four months later, his book debuted at the number ten spot on the New York Times bestseller list. One prominent reviewer wrote, "Ashley Roper's first-person account of his tour in Kuwait during the Gulf War is compelling, disturbing, and exhilarating." It moved up to the number nine spot for two weeks and then disappeared from the list. Nine years later, "The Heart of Kuwait" still sold several hundred copies per year with enough in royalties per quarter to pay for a nice dinner out.

THE COUPLE WALKED up Meeting Street, past the open marketplace, and cut over to King Street. It was warm and damp even though the sun was bright after the morning shower. Ash was comfortable in shorts, sandals, and a T-shirt with the official *Charley Town* logo. Sally J never even broke a sweat as Southern ladies, it is said, never sweat but merely perspire.

In other climes, an early morning rain might cool the day; but in Charleston, there would be light steam rising from the asphalt as innkeepers set their tables and chairs on the sidewalks. Large-framed black ladies, wearing aprons and head scarves, prepared their stalls in the open market, selling handwoven sweetgrass baskets and fragrant clusters of flowers. During the day, they would sit in rocking chairs, weaving complex patterns with dried wild grasses from the marshes, a craft handed down from African ancestors, practiced through the centuries of slavery in the new world, and preserved today as tourists from Michigan snapped photos.

They made the walk together most days, even on weekends. *Charley Town* was their baby, so they often joked. That was their only baby to date. She wanted a child when they first married, but their problems had been too intense. Ash had been drinking and writing. Once he disappeared for two days and showed up woozy and unshaven at the front door. She never knew to where he disappeared that weekend ten years ago, and neither did he. It was unlikely he was with another woman as disheveled and smelly as he was.

Then there was, as Ash put it, "that lawyer," the one she had lunch with, the one whom she knew since childhood, the one who almost got Ash conserved because of his drinking. Her desire to be a mom was more intense as her biological clock was tick, tick, ticking away. She was willing to take the risk now. If she pushed, Ash, six years older, could be talked into it. Right now, the wheels in his head were turning, grinding, spinning, and struggling to create. She grew to trust him again and was devoted to him. Ash was trusting her more too. "The lawyer" was in the background, faded away into his own quest for money and women. Ash said many times, "Sally J, I'm a one-woman man, and you know damn well Roswell isn't."

Ash was right; she knew that, but still . . .

THE OFFICE WAS in an old brick building on King Street, just above Calhoun, the unofficial dividing line between the charming old city and just the old city, the part of town that was more ramshackle than restored. It was a good solid workplace with a loft, three desks with computers, and two drafting tables for layout and artwork. With 1,600 square feet of workspace, it was larger than their home, which they rented. They actually owned this space and figured they could always live here if they had to. There was a small bathroom with a shower, and a counter with a microwave and mini fridge underneath. The espresso machine was one of the more important pieces of equipment that could be found in the office. In past years, when the Spoleto Arts Festival came to town, they would be so busy with designing ads and writing promo pieces that the two of them would sleep on the double mattress on the floor up in the loft. The espresso kept brewing, the paper was fat, and the money was good. Ash thought of those days as the golden days, a bubble that lasted for a half-dozen years.

The office door was unlocked as Annie McDermott was munching on a gluten-free croissant at a drafting table, which doubled as a kitchen table and conference table. Annie was an artist who could sketch drawings for ads and more lately was the developing skill at using computer graphics for promotions, ads, headings, and announcements. She originally designed the *Charley Town* logo, a water color of the slightly tilted steeple of St. Phillips Church, with a seagull flying by and a tall palmetto tree in the foreground. It appeared on the mast head of *Charley Town* as well as various T-shirts and coffee mugs that could be ordered online from the paper's web site. At age forty-five, Annie looked youthful with brown permed hair, freckles, sparkly gray eyes, and very overly thin. She claimed she had food allergies and worked out a lot.

The air-conditioning was cranking, set at 68 degrees; but as Annie was a Yankee (yes, they still use that term), Ash and Sally J thought that the little extra on the electric bill would be worth it so as not to impair any of her creativity. Artists are supposed to suffer but not when they work for *Charley Town*. That magnanimous thought came from Annie herself.

Earlier that morning, while Ash and Sally J were just waking up, Annie was working on developing the web edition for the weekend. The ads had to be designed and attached to the appropriate stories. Personals were getting to be more of a factor. They used to fill maybe a page in the print version. Now, if anything in publishing was showing some life, it was personal ads. Annie greeted them and sighed, "Hell, between men wanting to meet women, women wanting to meet men, men wanting to meet men, married couples wanting to meet someone gay, I'm going a little nuts. And we can't do free personals anymore—that's where the money is."

"Great," Ash said, "now *Charley Town* can become an internet hookup service. How about ads for escort services and massage?"

Sally J interjected, "What's wrong with massage?"

"Happy ending type, not what I had in mind."

Annie was annoyed with the conversation. "What do you think I've been doing the past couple of weeks? I'm trying to streamline our baby. We're catching up already."

Annie was there from the beginning, when Ash first conceived *Charley Town* and was looking for an art director. They all had magnificent chemistry in creating a work of art. *Charley Town* wasn't just a weekly rag, but it was a thing of beauty, each issue with a snappy color cover and stylistic artwork in the columns and ads. The articles had meaning. It wasn't just fluff. "The Heart of Kuwait" set the tone. Anybody and everybody who wanted to be in the know picked up a copy at the gym, the laundromat, or outside the Piggly Wiggly. Annie wrote horoscopes and capsule movie reviews, and Sally J interviewed locally performing artists or jazz musicians. They collaborated on picking the unsolicited poems and letters to the editor and even selected some syndicated political cartoons. Ash did interviews with local shakers and movers, real-estate developers, and politicians.

"Anything cooking?" Ash asked Annie as he looked over her shoulder at the twenty-one-inch monitor screen.

"Let's see. We have an opera at the auditorium tomorrow night, and the Living Toilet is playing over at Pier Eleven all weekend. The Daughters of the Confederacy is having its annual buffet."

"Is that all we got? What year is this? Please remind me. I thought the Living Toilet broke up in 1987 and the Civil War ended in 1865." Ash slapped the table, grunted, and rolled his eyes.

Annie ignored Ash's mini tantrum and continued, "I saw something online about the mental hospital down toward Bayside. Some jury decided to let this guy who cracked some teenage kid's skull some years ago go even though he's supposedly still batty as a loon. Then just yesterday, one of their patients—remember that guy who strangled a hooker some years ago?—anyhow, he clocked a cop who was supposed to be watching him in the bathroom at the courthouse and took off, right here in Charleston. They haven't found him yet."

Ash snapped, "Think we should lock our doors?"

Sally J tried to lighten the atmosphere. "Maybe he'll stop in here for a copy of the paper, anything to improve circulation."

Annie ignored the foolishness. "Interesting place. Sounds like Bedlam. I heard a lot of nurses get beat up there, and I think a psychologist was killed there a few years ago."

"Some kinda hospital, huh? Sounds worse than the VA." Ash stroked his beard. "I wonder if we could do a story on that place. It might be more interesting than the Low Country Cotillion."

"That's the old place they converted from a military base back in the fifties, isn't it?" Sally J asked. She thought for a moment and asked what the address might be. The state government web site gave a post office box. The paper had about 150 mail subscriptions, two of them going to PO Box 4067, Bayside, South Carolina. Whether it was patients or staff or doctors wasn't clear. The twenty-four-dollar mail subscription covered postage, and the names didn't specify whether or not they were patients. "Looks like we have a couple of fans at the nuthouse," Sally J quipped.

Annie added that the name of the newly freed offender was a Mr. Tyler Goode of McMurtree in Bay County. The news story on the internet version of the Charleston Times said he would be returning to the hospital for thirty days and then would be released to his family (which as of this date would not include his momma.) The escaped killer was Mr. Burton Peals.

Something clicked in Ash's head. "Well, this could be a change of pace. Maybe someone could get an interview with Mr. Goode. How about we talk to our subscribers down there while we're at it?"

He looked at Annie and then Sally J. "I've been to some pretty scary crazy places. In any event, it's a pretty drive—should only take a little over an hour. Annie, you want to come and photograph? I'll buy you lunch at this place along the way. It'll be deductible."

Annie responded, "Maybe. I think an interview with Mr. Peals would be more interesting, but I guess he isn't available. I'll skip the lunch (which she often did), but it might be very interesting and entertaining."

"I'll bet I'll track down Mr. Peals one of these days. Anyhow, Sally J, why don't we check it out?" Ash suggested.

Sally J sighed, "Ash, if you want to go on a little field trip, take Annie and go. We're hittin' the streets today, and ah have to start layin' out next week's edition." Sally J's upstate drawl often intensified when she became frustrated or anxious. "Go ahead and go have a good time. Somebody's gotta stay heah and run the store."

Ash tried to be reassuring. "Hey, darlin', we won't be gone long. You know about opportunity knockin'. You sure you don't wanna come? You might get an eyeful."

Sally J sighed and walked away. "Just don't take all day."

CHAPTER 5

Old Highway 41 runs south from Charleston, winding through the marshes, over narrow bridges, and across numerous creeks and inlets. Ash was at the wheel of his trusty 2002 Honda CRV while Annie gazed out the passenger window at the Spanish moss-covered oaks and stout-based cypress trees, their broad foundations holding them upright in the boggy marshes. She studied a ghostly bare loblolly pine with a hawk atop, surveying the flat coastal plain known in these parts as the Low Country. As a native New Yorker, she still marveled at the lyrical quality of the landscape.

The Bay Area State Hospital was fifty miles South of Charleston, this side of the picturesque coastal towns of Beaufort and Port Royal. Farther down the coast is the resort island Hilton Head, outside of Long Island, the largest island on the US east coast. An inland waterway, constructed by the Army Corps of Engineers and always busy with barges and tugboats, runs from Virginia to South Florida, through the Low Country by way of man-made- and natural channels. At times, from the highway, it seemed like a fishing boat would glide through the forest in the distance. At several locations, the road crosses the waterway on old concrete viaducts or creaky cantilever draw bridges, tended by sleepy operators.

Annie and Ash left Charleston around noon. Traffic was slowed down by tractors and meandering pickup trucks. It was getting close to one, and Ash was hungry. The countryside was dotted with ramshackle cottages, sturdier brick buildings, farm machinery, old cars, and an occasional general store with a faded chewing tobacco ad painted on the entire side of the building. "Tobacco Road lives, Annie," Ash reminded her. "Get a good shot. Let your buddies up north get a gander at our high-living lifestyle here in Dixie."

They stopped at the Ginny's Sea Island Café, an old brick and wood restaurant on cinderblock pilings by the marsh. It was high enough that there were a couple of parking spaces under the structure. It was one of several small restaurants owned and operated by black families along the old road. Ash had been there several times before and always ate more than he really needed to, but the barbecue and liver hash plate were hard to resist. They were greeted by Ginny Smalls, the owner and chef, who remembered Ash's big appetite. She was a tall slender black woman, late forties, wearing bifocals, with a gracious smile accented by a shiny gold front tooth. "Back again? Well, we're glad to see y'all."

"I am glad to be back, and I'm ready." Ash didn't drink, but there was no law against food. Ash made a mental note that he had to do a profile of Miss Ginny and her restaurant in an upcoming issue. Maybe he'd run a free ad because he liked the place so much.

"What you doin' down this way with you lady friend?"

"We're here because I love you and your restaurant. Remember I told you about that paper I do in Charleston?"

"Yeah, now I remember. You writin' about somethin'?"

"Always. Say, you got the fried okra today?"

"Sure, honey, and we got good iced tea. So what you writin' about today?"

Ash remembered his manners and introduced Annie as his photographer. "We're going down to see that psychiatric hospital at the old military base. I think we're only about six or seven miles away."

Ginny's eyes popped wide open. "Oooh wee! I don't want nothin' to do with that place. I hear all kinds of crazy stories. But one good thing, they a lot of people be workin' there and they come up here for lunch sometime. Then one time, they brung five of those people here with some workers or orderlies or whatever, and they took up three tables over there," Ginny said, pointing to the tables along the wall. "I guessed where they from cuz the bus say 'Bay Area State Hospital' right on the side. Well, they was polite enough, and the people who brung 'em paid and all but didn't leave no tip. But that was okay cuz we 'preciate the business. Let me tell you, those folks sure could eat."

"Well, so can I"—Ash laughed—"but don't lock me up because of that."

"Well, I think I know what you havin'. How about you, young lady?"

Annie answered, "How about some of your iced tea and a salad?"

As Ginny walked away with the order, she chuckled to herself. "She need some meat on her bones. Never gonna find a man lookin' like that."

A beer probably would have been wonderful on such a warm afternoon, but Ash had promises to keep and stayed with the iced tea.

"Hey, Annie," Ash said as he was finishing his red beans and rice. "How about getting some shots of this place?"

Annie took a photo of Ash with his arm around Miss Ginny, who flashed a big smile, gold tooth and all. Good times. Maybe Ginny would like to advertise. This wasn't the time to sell advertising but time to get moving. He

MIKE BARTOS

didn't want to leave Sally J at the office too long. He knew she was impatient with his quest for another big first person story. But he needed to prove to his wife that he still had it in him—that he can be as successful as any Broad Street attorney, and maybe prove it to himself as well.

They drove a mile or two, crossed a marsh creek, made a left turn, and then followed a direction sign indicating Bay Area State Hospital. It was a narrow two-lane road, running four miles through the swamps and crossing several small bridges. The final approach to the hospital was recently paved and featured annoying speed bumps. There were further direction signs for the parking lots, one for employees, one marked for visitors, and one marked admissions. There was no sign for discharges. Deliveries, as always, were in the rear.

His first impression of the hospital grounds was that the place appeared quaint and charming. Outside the fenced area was a long row of elegant, somewhat dilapidated mansions and gardens with jasmine, magnolias, and tall crooked palmetto trees. A towering oak stood outside the perimeter fence, with branches trimmed so that they would not extend over the fence into the confined area. The plantation-style mansions were formerly officers' quarters built during the Second World War. There was also a newer, somewhat nondescript military-style two-story office building, which apparently was the home of upper administration. Nearby was a tennis court, unkempt and unused, with a cracked surface, and overgrown with weeds. A fourteen-foot chain-link fence topped with spirals of razor wire enclosed the confined fifty-acre patient area. The guard posts were not manned.

Ash pulled the Honda into the visitors' lot. With the car idling and the air-conditioning blowing, they agreed that the task at hand was to get basic information, just keep it simple for now.

They exited the car and stood on the crumbling macadam. No security staff came to meet them. There was the scent of freshly mowed grass as inmates from the local jail in Beaufort manicured the grounds under scrutiny of several overweight and armed corrections officers. Ash needed a few moments to get his bearings. It didn't seem likely that anyone was going to offer them a tour. Since they were visitors, Ash and Annie decided to go into hospital security headquarters and see if they could at least get an interview with a few hospital cops.

The headquarters was housed in one of the old mansions, named Gifford Cottage after some long-ago military big fish in this formerly small pond of a military base. The interior was arranged into one large office area with a reception counter, several smaller offices, and a conference room off to the side. No one was tending the counter but a young female uniformed desk officer, who looked up from her monitor and asked pleasantly, "May I help you?"

Ash asked for whoever was in charge. "Well that would be the desk sergeant, but I think he's still out to lunch." After pausing for a moment she added, "But I believe Captain Dawkins might be around. Can you hang on for a minute?"

They took a seat on a polished wooden bench against the wall. "Looks like we're going to see the boss," Annie said optimistically. An unbalanced ceiling fan wobbled overhead, squeaking rhythmically. Phones rang, a fax machine hummed, a few uniformed officers chatted, and an old window air-conditioning unit rattled and clanked.

After about ten minutes, Lyle Dawkins appeared through a door leading to his private office. "What can I do for you folks?"

Ash did the talking. "Thank you, Captain, for seeing us. I'm Ashley Roper, and this is Annie McDermott of the *Charley Town* weekly in Charleston, and we wanted to do a story on your facility."

The captain appeared impatient. "Well, first of all, it ain't my facility. It belongs to the people of South Carolina. And second, I ain't even the one in charge around here. And third, I don't know how I can help you."

"Captain, I thought maybe you could get us on a tour inside the fenced area. I'd like to meet some staff or maybe even some patients and get their take on things. Annie here would like to get some pictures too. Anyhow, I've heard stories—"

Lyle interrupted impatiently. "I bet you have. Everybody has."

"Well, I'd like to find out if they're true."

"It depends on the stories. Probably some are, and most aren't. I don't see—"

This time Ash interrupted. "Captain (he actually said 'Cap'n'), you have all the keys here. You know who's who and what's what. You know who and what goes in and out. You know who gets beat up. You know who's doing their job."

Lyle was getting mildly red-faced, and beginning to break out in small beads of perspiration. He took a hankie out of his back pocket and blotted his forehead. "Let's talk in my office. It's coola in there. Caroline, would ya hold my calls for about ten minutes?"

Lyle's private office was about ten by twelve, had numerous bookshelves overflowing with papers and files, a few trophies, and assorted plaques with badges for honors received a decade or more ago. Lyle sat down in an old naugahyde desk chair, leaned back, and folded his hands across his ample gut. Annie and Ash sat across the cluttered desk in the two wooden chairs provided. The window air-conditioning unit was on high, blowing mildewed chilly air into the small room. There was an empty ashtray on the desk, and the smell of stale cigarette smoke.

"Listen good 'cause I'm only gonna say this once. We don't need no stories on this place right now. I'm up to my ass in alligators. There was an escape—you know about that. The courts are cuttin' loose the wackos that don't escape—that was in the news. We know about a drug problem because some of our employees are yappin' about that to the press and online, and I'm tryin' to deal with that. Some Yankee lawyers in Washington are giving us a ration of shit. Something about we're not giving enough rights to the cutthroat lunatics in here, so we have to jump through all these hoops, none of which make any sense. Then the courts are sending around these folks with clipboards to make sure we do all the nitpicky bullshit that some way overpaid consultant said we hafta do. We don't need any more trouble or bad publicity 'cause frankly, that's all we get."

Ash was assiduously scribbling notes. "Can I quote you on that?"

Lyle got redder and sat up. "Son, I don't need no smart aleckey talk today. We're done."

"Can I get your photo?" Annie held up her thirty-five-millimeter digital camera.

Lyle leaned forward across the desk. "You don't hear too good, Little Lady. I'm tellin' ya to get your skinny ass outta here and take your boyfriend with you." His sweaty face was red as a traffic light.

"He's not my boyfr—"

"Now!"

Ash rose and said, "Cap'n, it's been a pleasure. Maybe another time. My card."

"Maybe you can stick your card where the sun—"

Ash tossed his card on the desk and was out the door with Annie before the captain was finished. They walked through the reception area, through the swinging waist-high double doors by the front counter, through the entrance hallway, and out into the bright hot sunshine. The day was getting stickier, but at least it didn't smell like mildew outside, Annie thought. "He's quite rude," she complained to Ash.

"To say the least," Ash agreed. "Screw 'im. We'll get what we need. I smell a good story here."

Before heading back up the road to Charleston, the twosome decided to walk around a little, maybe see what they could through the fence. Outside the confined perimeter were the administrative buildings and "cottages," pleasant lawns, and gardens. Curiously, there was no canteen or snack bar, so everyone either had to bring lunch or drive to a nearby town for good Southern cooking. A plateful of chicken and waffles did not usually precede a productive afternoon.

Ash and Annie strolled along the fence, not seeing anything definitive through the chain links. Although the buildings outside the fenced perimeter had some dilapidated charm and character, the buildings in the confined area appeared soulless and utilitarian, like the old converted barracks they were. In contrast, there was a small cute chapel with a cross over the front door, and an ivy covered building which Ash guessed was a library or recreation facility. There were extensive areas of manicured grass and a few well tended flower gardens.

Patients, actually "residents," wandered about aimlessly on the grounds. They observed about twenty or thirty of them dressed in their "blues"—blue work shirts, blue T-shirts, blue shorts, and blue jeans. The shirts all bore the small insignia "South Carolina DBHS" which stands for Department of Behavioral Health Services. Most residents appeared to be male, about half black and half white, with a few scattered Hispanics and Asians. Some of them walked slowly and aimlessly. A few were sitting at a picnic table under the shade of a large live oak dripping with Spanish moss, several of them openly enjoying a smoke.

Nobody looked particularly dangerous. Most of them looked like poor slobs beaten down by a system that was supposed to help them. Help them do what in particular wasn't all that clear. Help them restore sanity? Help them get out? Help them feel well? Maybe help them get a cigarette?

The afternoon was heating up, and Annie was ready to hop back in the Honda and get the AC cranked up. To the west, there was the distinct low vibrating rumble of thunder, although the sky above was clear. "Hey, Ash, let's hit the road."

Ash was studying the perimeter, just wondering how anyone could get out if he had to go over a fourteen-foot chain-link fence covered with fine screen mesh and topped with spirals of razor wire, or get in for that matter. "Just a sec," Ash replied as he scanned the confined area. There was the smell

MIKE BARTOS

of the nearby marsh, rich with brine and decaying weeds and grass, carried by the afternoon sea breeze that was picking up. The thunder grew a little louder. The leaves of the old live oak about fifteen feet beyond the perimeter were softly rustling in the fresh wind. Satisfied for the moment, he declared, "We're good to go."

Ash steered the car down the curving blacktop out to the old marsh road back across the marsh. He turned right and headed north.

CHAPTER 6

Ernie Joe Plumm was restlessly pacing the hallway of ward K3 on a quiet Sunday morning. He had slept through the breakfast, as hospital residents were allowed to do on the weekend. Now it was 10:00 a.m., and he was hungry. He approached the locked nursing station and pounded on the window, trying to get the attention of Corky Williams, RN, the charge nurse for the day shift. Corky was tired and edgy himself. He had worked two overtime shifts this past week, hadn't been getting enough sleep, hadn't been able to spend much time with his kids, and sure as heck didn't want to be working Sunday. Nursing staff was decimated by stress leave and injuries. Fighting with unruly, uncontrolled residents was part of the job. Sometimes it just seemed like the whole job. Maybe a little stress leave wouldn't be a bad idea. Corky, at age thirty-four, was a strong athletic man, but his lower back ached from one too many wrestling matches on the Lysol-scented tile floors of the Bay Area State Hospital, part of the job they don't teach in nursing school.

Ernie Joe pounded on the Plexiglas window again. Rap rap rap . . . rap rap rap. Annoying as hell. Corky slid open the small window. "Ernie Joe, how many times do I have to tell you to not bang on the windows?"

Ignoring Corky's comment, Ernie Joe bent over to get his mouth at the level of the opening. "Hey, I didn't get any breakfast. Whadya got to eat?"

Corky looked up from the nursing plan he was writing, unsuccessfully trying to hide his annoyance. "Ernie Joe, you slept in—that was your choice. Lunch is in two hours. You may have to wait."

Ernie Joe was a big man, young but very heavy. He had a pale, pasty complexion and short, cropped light-brown hair. He didn't look like the kind of guy who missed too many meals. "Hey, man, I need something or I'm gonna go off." Corky realized that when Ernie Joe had a tantrum, it required a dozen staff to restrain him until the emergency medication calmed him down. Good protocol puts the staff in charge, not the patient, but good protocol also puts adequate nursing staff on the ward, and that certainly wasn't the case today. Corky turned to Teresa Gonsales, a psychiatric technician who was writing shift notes. "Teresa, could you be kind enough to get Ernie Joe a sandwich if you can find one in the fridge?"

Psychiatric technicians have some training in nursing as well as hospital psychiatry. Although not full-fledged nurses, they are the frontline staff in interacting with patients, including physical confrontations. They suffer the highest rate of injury of any type of health-care worker.

Teresa seemed a little unsure. "Corky, do you want Ernie Joe manipulating you like that?" Corky found her response a little insolent but also annoying because she was confronting the truth of the issue. Sometimes, he thought, you have to choose your battles. Down one staff member this shift, the easiest thing was to give in. He figured, *We don't need to do a takedown right now. Give him the damn sandwich.* "Teresa, see if there's a PBJ in the storage refrigerator. I think Martha refused her snack last night."

Corky looked back at Ernie Joe. "Teresa is going to get you something." Ernie Joe sulked away without any further comment. After Teresa came out of the canteen room and offered him the sandwich, he grabbed it, pulled off the plastic wrap, wadded it into a small ball, and tossed it toward the wastebasket but missed. Teresa looked at Ernie Joe and said, "Hey, pick that up. I'm not your maid." As he was bending over, she was almost certain she heard him say "bitch" under his breath. Then he squatted on the floor of the narrow hallway, back against the wall, legs in front of him, obstructing traffic. Corky was watching from the nursing station, thinking, *Pain in the ass.*

Corky picked up the microphone for the overhead speaker system. "Ernie Joe Plumm, report to the nursing station, Ernie Joe."

The big man lumbered down the hallway, having finished the sandwich in two gulps, and lowered his face to the port, which Corky slid open. "Listen, man, why don't you take your grounds card and go for a walk?" Good news for Ernie Joe. "Sure."

It was a hot morning. A lot of the residents preferred to stay on the ward this time of year, but Ernie Joe liked to go out, like a cat that was locked up in the garage all night. Corky was thinking maybe now he'd get some work done. Teresa put in her two cents, "You know, I think he just called me bitch. You want to reward him with his grounds card the way he's been acting?"

No, he didn't, but he needed some peace and quiet. Maybe Ernie Joe would calm down if he got some fresh air. "Be back by lunch," Corky admonished Ernie Joe.

"Uh huh" was the best response Corky would get as he escorted him down the hallway to unlock the back door.

Ernie Joe wandered out into the very warm late morning sunshine. There were very few residents on the grounds. Although the wards were cramped and unpleasant, the hospital grounds were park like, with expansive green lawns, a ball field, mature trees, and flowering gardens tended by the patients themselves. Sprinklers were shooting intermittent jets of water across the grassy areas. Picnic tables were placed under the spreading oaks and magnolias. The buildings included a variety of institutional-looking hospital wards, a library, medical clinic, canteen, and a chapel. This confined patient area occupied forty-seven acres surrounded by a fourteen-foot chain-link fence topped with spiraling razor wire. The only way in and out was through a portal of three successive gates locked and unlocked by the security police behind a glass-enclosed guard station. Vehicles had to negotiate through two successive sliding gates.

Ernie Joe headed down a black asphalt roadway between two of the hospital units. Behind the J wards, there was a garden near the fence with a bed of lilies, recently tended by a crew of closely supervised patients. The flowers bobbed aimlessly in the gentle breeze. The soil was loose and rich. Two lines of pebbles in the shape of a cross were near the edge of the bed. Ernie Joe scraped the pebbles away and then dug in the warm soft earth with his bare fingers.

Doug Riley, one of the rehabilitation therapists working a weekend shift, was on his way back to the ward after escorting a patient to the Protestant chapel. From the asphalt road, he spotted the resident near the fence, digging with his hands in the garden.

Ernie Joe felt the edge of the plastic bag he was searching for. He was able to pinch the corner enough to extricate the clear bag from the soil. The lovely light-yellow powder was visible inside, just as promised.

"You're out of bounds." Doug startled Ernie Joe. "Which ward are you from?"

Ernie Joe turned to the staff member who sneaked up on him. He palmed the stash and attempted to conceal it by holding it behind him. Perhaps he might be able to unobtrusively slip it down his pants. No such luck.

Ernie Joe answered politely, "K3, sir."

Doug wrinkled his brow. "You know you're not allowed to be back here without staff escort. What do you have behind you?"

"Nuthin'. I ain't got nuthin."

Doug was having none of this and held out his hand to Ernie Joe, who stepped backward. The grounds card ID badge was clipped to Ernie Joe's blue cotton hospital shirt. "Mr. Plumm, I suggest you let me see what you have there."

He stepped back again as Doug took a step toward him. Ernie Joe's heel hit something; it was the handle of a shovel that was carelessly left behind the day before by the gardening crew. Ernie Joe lost his balance, fell backwards, and hit the ground, his butt squashing a cluster of orange day lilies. The plastic bag filled with methamphetamine lay by his side. "What in the world?" Doug said out loud. "Where did you get that?"

It occurred to Doug that it wasn't his job to make drug busts and maybe it would be in his best interest to leave and report the incident to security. As Doug turned to walk away, Ernie Joe panicked. He was busted.

Doug felt a splitting pain on the back of his head. He spun around to see Ernie Joe swinging the shovel like a baseball bat as the flat part of the blade caught him on the side of his face. Doug went down like a wet sack of flour. He landed flat on his back, eyes rolled up and groaning. Picking up the shovel with both hands, Ernie Joe aimed the sharp part of the blade at the semiconscious victim's throat and thrust it down like a pile driver through the neck. Blood squirted into the soil, onto Ernie Joe's pants and shirt, and even onto his face. The victim twitched, his eyes rolled up. Blood bubbled up from the neck wound.

Ernie Joe used his sleeve to wipe the blood from his eyes. He had to think. Now what? Ernie Joe was a long-term hospitalized mental patient, standing over a murder victim, holding a murder weapon. That wouldn't look good. But they were in a garden with loose earth with marshy ground underneath. Ernie Joe pulled the shovel from the gash in the victim's neck and dropped it on the ground, next to the plastic bag. After a sniff of the drug from his fingertip, his mind popped and the plan became clear. Ernie Joe started digging. It was 89 degrees, and the humidity was about the same. He shoveled loose dirt on top of the body, obscuring it from view. Passersby returning from the chapel who bothered to glance down to the end of the asphalt road, about a hundred yards yonder, toward the fence, would see a resident digging in the garden, nothing out of the ordinary other than the fact he was unescorted and handling a tool that could only be used under supervision.

It was sweaty work, but he wanted to be done by lunch. He took another toot, which got his motor running. He dug for about thirty minutes. The excavation was four feet by four feet and about two feet deep. When the last of the groups wandered by, he rolled the body into the shallow grave and quickly covered it with earth and patted it down. The garden looked uneven and lumpy, and half the flowers were now squashed or missing. Someone on the gardening crew was going to be unhappy.

Satisfied with his work, he took the shovel and swung it around like he

MIKE BARTOS

was about to do the Olympic hammer throw and aimed it toward the top of the fence. After about three rapid revolutions, he released the shovel, which arced into the air and came down with the blade stuck in the spikey razor wire at the top of the fence where it hung upside down, the wooden handle swinging in the breeze, striking the fence like a clapper striking a bell.

Ernie Joe, covered in perspiration and an inconvenient amount of dried blood, gazed at the shovel, thought *Oh fuck*, reached into his pocket, took another hit, and turned to head back to the ward. "So what if they see the shovel? No way I put it there."

Ernie Joe realized he had a couple of problems:

1. He was late for lunch.
2. His clothing was covered with sweat and blood.
3. Corky was going to be pissed and then some.

The sprinklers were spurting staccato bursts across the lawn. He stood in front of one of the streams, letting the water hit his face and hands and stained clothing. He removed his blue cotton slipover top and rubbed it vigorously against the bloodstains on the pants. He was out on the grounds, bare-chested, an absolute no-no, and standing by a sprinkler, looking like he was doing his laundry. He slipped back into the soaked shirt and rolled on the grassy lawn, attempting to obscure what remained of the bloodstains with muddy water and grass stains. One of the psych techs, Pete Sandoval, who was on the grounds with two other residents, caught the end of Ernie Joe's act. "Dude, what's up?"

Ernie Joe tried to look nonchalant. "Hey, it's hot. I was just coolin' off."

"You need to get back to your ward now." Pete tried to take a look at Ernie Joe's photo ID, which was now smeared and unreadable. "If I see you out here in one minute, I'm calling security." Pete was already obligated to call hospital security. He corralled his two residents to continue their escorted journey, forgetting the incident and the excessive paperwork that would be involved.

Ernie Joe hit the buzzer outside the ward. Corky clicked on the intercom. "It's just me." Ernie Joe was indeed a bit mellowed out by the drug and not too worried about anything.

Corky had already reported Ernie Joe to security since he was AWOL from the ward. He was lucky to get back before they found him.

Corky walked to the back door to unlock it. "What the hell happened to you?"

"It was hot. I fell asleep under the sprinkler—felt good."

It was time for a pat down with latex gloves. Corky didn't catch the plastic baggie stuffed in his ass crack, a rather routine hiding place "where the sun don't shine." He did see blood stains on his blue twill pants, though. Rather a lot of it actually. "Where the hell did this come from?"

"Cut my leg."

"Where?"

"Nunna yer dam business."

"Wanna bet? You better come back to the quiet room."

"I ain't goin' nowhere, Dawg." Corky triggered the alarm device on his belt. Two psych techs and a nursing assistant came running down the hallway. Formerly called a "show of force," it was now officially known as a "show of concern," by decree of the federal surveyors.

Ernie Joe stood in a fighting stance, back against the wall while the staff gathered in a semicircle in front of him. Nowhere to go but to come out swinging. "Let's just talk this over, Ernie Joe. I just need you to cooperate." Corky attempted to defuse the situation.

The loud chiming alarm continued to blast down the hallway. Ernie Joe took a clumsy swing at one of the nurses, flailing wide of the mark. "Let's go on the count of three. One, two, . . ." Corky counted off. By this time, three other staff from a neighboring ward showed up. Wildly outgunned, Ernie Joe, fueled and fired up, wasn't backing down. The staff moved in quickly and, according to written protocol, grabbed both of his arms and forced him down the hallway into a small room with a steel-framed cot. Ernie Joe struggled and fought off his would-be restrainers as they tried to force him onto the cot. He kicked out full force, driving his heel into Carmelita's chest, the smallest staff member present, sending her flying against the wall, striking her crown with a dull thud. Her eyes rolled up as her knees buckled and her back slid down the wall, and then she fell forward into a heap on the floor.

Grady Wilmoth, a nursing assistant from nearby ward K2, felt Carmelita's body slump against the back of his legs and quickly turned around, thinking *Oh shit* but yelling, "Someone get her the hell out of here. Did anyone call hospital security?"

"They're on their way. They said they'd be here soon," a female voice from the melee called out.

"When did they say that?" Grady asked.

"Right after the alarm went off." Someone was supposed to be timing all this.

MIKE BARTOS

Carmelita was still on the floor, looking dazed. Her head hurt, the room was spinning. She got up and slowly walked out of the ironically designated quiet room. She felt faint and squatted back down on the floor in the hallway, still trying to clear her head and remember where she was.

So far, Ernie Joe had one wrist and one ankle in restraints. The other arm was flailing, attempting to punch or scratch whoever got near enough. Two staff dropped their bodies across the free leg. Unlike everyone else in the room, Ernie Joe wasn't getting tired. As far as he was concerned, he could take them all on. The leather restraint was finally affixed to the free ankle and looped through the slot in the iron bed frame. One wrist to go; now everyone could focus on that. Ernie Joe started spitting at anyone nearby. A terrycloth towel was gently dropped across his face, neutralizing that threat for now. There was some worry because Ernie Joe had hepatitis C, a forever-infected liver, a souvenir from years of intravenous drug use. It's not supposed to spread from spit, but it's unpleasant and worrisome in any event.

Ernie Joe yelled through the towel, "Muthafuckas, I'm gonna sue your ass. I ain't doin' nothin'. I'm callin' patient's rights." Both wrists were finally restrained as was the waist, now totaling all five points.

Finally, the doctor on call, referred to as the "On Duty," or OD, appeared. Dr. Rajinder Kapoor, a young, slender Indian doctor with neatly combed shiny black hair, wearing a long starched white lab jacket over his button-down blue dress shirt and red necktie, volunteered often for weekend call. Corky spoke. "Hey, Dr. K, this guy needs a prn. Make it good, would ya? And we need an order for these restraints." Prn is the Latin abbreviation for medication given as needed or for an emergency,

Dr. Kapoor looked around at the assembled staff and the yelling resident restrained on the cot, with the terrycloth towel across his face, and said with an accent more educated British than Indian, "Perhaps you should tell me exactly what is going on here."

Corky explained, "Well, Dr. K, we got a guy who was wandering the grounds, comes back all kinds of bloody, a half hour late for lunch, has nothing to say, then starts swinging on staff and threatening everybody. Cops should be on the way."

"Oh, I see, so I first must talk to him," the cultured doctor said.

"Well, Dr. Kapoor, I don't think he particularly wants to talk to you."

"Has he had anything yet?"

"I think he probably snorted or tooted something out on the grounds. I don't know what."

"So you must understand that I am required to proceed with the utmost caution, as this resident may have ingested an unknown substance and we don't want to cause any adverse reactions."

"Kiss my ass, you Indian cocksucker" was the loud but muffled insult through the terrycloth towel over Ernie Joe's face.

"Hmmm, so I see. Yes, we shall proceed."

Corky suggested, "How about a good slug of haloperidol to cool his jets?"

"Oh heavens, no, sir, we must not be hasty or punitive. I believe perhaps two milligrams lorazepam will be adequate right now."

Corky thought that two milligrams would be suitable for a desperate housewife after a bad day. Or maybe for himself once he gets home.

Dr. Kapoor finally got around to ordering the tranquilizer. "Let's give it intramuscular now."

Corky helpfully added, "Not if he's willing to take it by mouth."

"Is that correct?" Dr. Kapoor queried.

"That's Special Order 402 from the Department in Columbia."

"Hmm, so I see. Very well then, administer as you must."

Corky further updated Dr. Kapoor on the requirements. "It has to be crushed and liquefied."

"Really?"

" The surveyors demand it be done that way."

Patients sometimes "cheek" their medication so they don't have to swallow it or perhaps sell it or swap it for a cigarette or two. Mild tranquilizers can fetch several bucks even if they were in someone else's mouth for a while. Lorazepam can dissolve fast. No matter, what's left over still has market value.

"And mix it with applesauce." Dr. Kapoor added, trying to be compliant.

Ernie Joe was pulling against the restraints and howling. Corky yelled, "Can someone get the freakin' medicine?"

One of the nursing assistants shouted back, "Carmelita is the med nurse. She's on her way to the infirmary." Lucky Carmelita. She probably wouldn't even remember the incident.

"Teresa," Corky barked, "can you get his med and give it to him?"

"Where's the applesauce?" She wanted to know. "And how can he take it if he's tied up with a towel over his face?"

Dr. Kapoor had had quite enough as he watched the young man struggling against the restraints and yelling through the terrycloth towel. "Give this resident some haloperidol IM ten milligrams now!" IM means intramuscular injection.

Grady Wilmoth looked at the doctor and challenged him. "With all due respect, Dr. Kapoor, don't you think five would be enough?"

"No, I do not. He is agitated and dangerous and has already injured one of our staff."

Grady disagreed. "I think five will calm him down. The special state orders mandate that we medicate with the lowest effective dose. Ten could oversedate him.

Kapoor pointed his finger at Wilmoth. "I am the doctor here. This is my order." Corky seemed to agree. He went to the med room and started to prepare the syringe for the injection. "Just write up the order, Dr. Kapoor, and we'll be good to go."

Dr. Kapoor turned his attention to the computer and started typing his note and orders on the approved templates. Corky reentered the so-called quiet room and handed some sealed alcohol wipes to Teresa, who pulled on the elastic waistband of Ernie Joe's soiled pants, exposing the fleshy part of his hip. Wearing latex gloves, she cleaned off a small area of skin while Corky looked for a drop of the liquid medication from the needle, making sure there were no air bubbles. Ernie Joe's eyes were uncovered, and he could see Corky with the syringe and yelled, "You can't inject me with that shit, you black asshole. Get the hell away from me." The needle went into the hip, and then Corky pulled back the plunger, making sure there was no blood, then pushed it firmly and steadily. Ernie Joe yelled again, "I'm going to sue every one of you cocksuckers. You're all goin' down." They've all heard this before and roundly ignored his pretentious threats.

The last step of the process was to cover the injection location with a sterile bandage to protect against contact from the mud and blood-stained pants. The pants were considered biohazardous waste. The cleanup of the room, the bed, and the resident, and the disposal of the clothing were going to be a mess. There was a thick manual with all the details of how to deal with this, but nobody knew exactly where it was. For now, it could all wait a few minutes before he called housekeeping and the nursing supervisor.

Two uniformed hospital security officers arrived just as the situation was quieting down. Sergeant Dooley asked Corky, who was still in charge, "What can we do for you?" Corky was thinking the security cops were a dollar short and a day late.

"Well, we got the seclusion and restraint going. We couldn't wait for you guys. The other thing is that our resident here in the quiet room came back with what looks like a significant amount of blood stain on his clothes, which are still wet. It looks like he tried to wash them off."

The sergeant was astonished. "Any idea whose blood this is and how he got it?"

"Not a clue, guys. He's not talking. Any injured parties on the grounds?"

"Not to our knowledge," Dooley answered.

They looked inside the quiet room to see Ernie Joe in restraints on his back, snoring loudly. "Oh crap, it does look like blood, and it's our buddy, Mr. Plumm." Dooley smacked his head with his palm.

Corky was thinking that this once hopefully quiet Sunday was turning into a nightmare for everyone on duty. A special investigator was going to have to be called in right away. All this blood—what the hell? Then there was the hazardous cleanup and the incident reporting, and no one knew where the blood came from.

Out on the grounds, nursing assistant Penny Ardigeaux was taking a smoke break. She had wandered off the main road between some of the ward buildings. She often favored the area toward the back fence where she could look out at the marsh. It was early afternoon, hot and still. The cicadas buzzed in a midday chorus. Crows were gathered on a mound of earth in the patient garden area, cackling and flapping their wings. Some seagulls were sitting on the oak branches above the garden. As she approached the area, the crows took off in unison and landed on a patch of weeds about twenty yards away.

It appeared someone may have left a work glove in the garden. It might be nice to retrieve it and drop it off at the lost and found. She took a puff from her cigarette, dropped it onto the grass, and then bent over to pick up the muddy glove. As she grabbed it, she realized it was not a glove at all but a stiff lifeless hand, still warm, attached to a lifeless arm under the soil. Vomit rose in her throat, and she was unable to scream. The security police found her pale, faint, and hysterically crying. Penny never returned to work at BASH.

CHAPTER 7

Captain Lyle Dawkins was enjoying another cold beer from a pop-top can on the front porch swing of his old family farmhouse on this very warm summer Sunday. He wore no shirt, and his stout body was slightly glistening from the heat of midday and partly from the extra seventy or eighty pounds he carried on his frame. His plump body was not a sight that he would particularly want to share; but since he lived alone on his acreage, it was no matter. He had a frosty brew, at midday not his first and not to be his last. The Braves pre-game show was on the portable radio. At this time of year, the noonday sun was already directly overhead, but the shade of the porch and expansive oaks and the magnolias that Granddaddy Dawkins planted seventy years ago provided a glorious canopy; and with the gentle breeze off the marsh, it felt almost, if not quite, tolerable. He would probably have to move inside by the third or fourth inning.

Two wives and two daughters come and gone, it was time to get on with life, with no explaining to do. These moments, if not the result of a life well lived, were at the least the reward for surviving life, no matter how lived.

The announcer on the radio advised to stay tuned for the first pitch when Lyle's pager went off. It was inside on the entrance hall table, beeping, vibrating, and restlessly lurching across the smooth mahogany surface. *Probably, someone calling in sick for the p.m. shift,* he thought.

As captain of security, he was on call 24/7. The statewide pager alert system reached almost everywhere. That was all going to stop by the end of this year, he decided. He spent many hours calculating in his head exactly how much retirement he was going to receive. The pager displayed the usual four digit extension, which he dialed.

The desk sergeant answered as Lyle quaffed about half a can of beer in one big gulp. "Captain, Officer Stedman here. Sir, are you sitting down?"

Now, what the hell? Lyle thought as he sighed and said, "Okay, what?" not wanting to miss the first pitch.

"Well, sir, we had an episode here. Okay, I'll try to be brief. We had a murder here on grounds, about an hour ago. It seems a resident took out a staff, a rehab therapist by the name of Doug Riley. The coroner's already been here, and they're loading up the body as we speak. The sheriff and the State Police are here. The staties handed it off to the Bay County Sheriff, so they got him over in McMurtree now."

"Him who?"

"Oh yeah, sorry, sir. You know Ernie Joe Plumm?"

Oh yeah, the doofus who bit my arm last year during a restraint session that made me get eight stitches and antibiotics enough to make me crap out my liver and randomly put seven different nursing staff on workman's comp in eighteen months and two staff to the emergency room—yeah, that Ernie Joe Plumm? "Yes, Officer, I believe I'm familiar with him."

"Riley got a shovel to the back of the head while he wasn't looking; got his throat split open, quite a mess."

Good police work, Lyle thought. *Of course he wasn't looking if it was the back of his head.* "So why the hell didn't you guys call me sooner?" *Like four beers ago?*

"I apologize, Captain, but you know we're short staffed. And on top of that, we had some injuries—a nurse who got popped during the takedown, and the one who discovered the body is carrying on quite a bit and had to get a tranquilizer before the sheriff took her over to McMurtree to make a recorded statement. The administrator on call is trying to hustle up some emergency nursing coverage, and they're going to have to mandate some people to work an extra shift. You get the picture, sir?"

"I'm afraid I do. I'll be there by three or three thirty." Time enough to clean up, get some coffee, drive the forty-five minutes to BASH, and listen to the game on the way in.

The department, licensing, and the surveyors, —yes, the circus will be coming to town. At least Ernie Joe will be wreaking his havoc somewhere else. *Tomorrow is Monday morning. This will be a great way to start the week. It won't be boring, except for the paperwork part.*

Some black coffee, a ham sandwich, and a quick shower and shave, and the captain was on his way. He had a state-issued patrol car, complete with the state seal of South Carolina, palmetto tree under the crescent moon, on each of the two front doors. He used it officially to drive around the hospital grounds, inside and outside of the confined perimeter. Since he was always on call, he at least had the perk of driving it home. Chevy Caprice, four years old, with a light bar on the roof. The flashing light was helpful in clearing the road ahead when rushing into BASH or getting the ice cream home from the Piggly Wiggly before it melted on a hot summer day.

MIKE BARTOS

The baseball game was crackling in from a radio station in Savannah, but he wasn't paying much attention. There were more important things to worry about, like who wasn't going to be happy.

In mental health, it is generally the case that a death is a catastrophic event, especially in a mental hospital. Notices go out expressing various condolences and when grief counseling will be available. Then there are the somber meetings with relatives in the conference room. The real worry is not the supposed therapeutic failure nor the abrupt personal loss, but the lawyers, surveyors, and licensing boards all ready to descend on the staff, the doctor, the hospital police, and the administration for endless investigations, review meetings, reports, and lawsuits. Actually, the lawyers are not unhappy. It's just "bidness," as they say in the low country.

This was not a suicide—this was a murder. And it wasn't a resident who was victimized, but a staff member. Of course, the alleged murderer was a patient, or according to the new politically correct nomenclature, a "resident." Obviously, there was money to be had somewhere by somebody. The boys up on Broad Street would figure it out. There's a widow; she might not even know she was a widow yet. Then there's the victim's two kids ready for college—what about them? The investigators, licensing surveyors, and administrators would be spending a lot of time sifting through files, records, and paperwork, looking for what is not there and, in the lawyers case, hoping they don't find it either. The legal principle here is "If it isn't documented, it didn't happen." The family? An afterthought to be sure. That will fall to the director of public relations.

The entire industry of looking at where somebody else screwed up was ready to mobilize into full swing. Lyle suspected a target on his back. After all, where was security? Of course, another prime target was the treating doctor, something to do with accountability.

The wheels were set in motion. Cops, e-mails, investigators, surveyors, licensing agencies, administrators, and lawyers were ready to gear up like a freight train about to leave the terminal. And like a freight train, when the system gets going, it's hard to stop.

CHAPTER 8

The five hour ride to Asheville was pleasant and air-conditioned. During the twenty minute stop in Columbia, Burton bought two hot dogs in the terminal and devoured them on the bus. Dinner on the Orient Express couldn't have tasted better.

Asheville, North Carolina was not a random destination. Although Burton had never been there and didn't know anyone in the area, it was a college town with students and summer tourists. It was large enough that he would not stand out, especially as an escaped psychotic killer. But it was small enough to be manageable. There was a mental health center in Asheville if he really needed help, but he wouldn't. If he stayed away from drugs and alcohol, maybe he would never be crazy again. It had been years since he was able take an unaccompanied stroll.

He hadn't taken medication the night before. It wasn't the end of the world. Everything was fine although it had crossed his mind that he might really need it. So far, so good.

The bus arrived in Asheville after 4:00 p.m. It appeared to be a bustling but friendly town, surrounded by the gentle green mountains of the southern Appalachians. From the terminal, it was a pleasant walk over to the local campus of the University of North Carolina. Summer in the mountains was warm but not oppressive. The sky was clear blue, with puffy white clouds, not the milky hazy humid sky of the coastal area.

He needed a place to live for now. There were rooming houses and cheap apartments near the campus; but for the second night in a row, he would need to find a motel and get his bearings. There was a reasonably priced motel about three blocks from the campus. After dropping off his groceries and the duffel bag in the small but clean room, he cruised around the campus, marveling at the greenery, the stone and brick class buildings, happy students sitting on the lawn strumming guitars, and the faint smell of marijuana smoke. It was summer term, a more laid back time at the college.

He found a bulletin board in the student union with notices of rooms for rent in private homes. This would be the cheapest and most convenient route for housing. He wrote down several numbers.

The next day, he found a room in a house near the campus, with a microwave and mini fridge. He would share a bathroom with two other renters, both young men. He had spent the past eleven years sharing a stinky bathroom with wild men and demented old farts who couldn't or wouldn't aim into the toilet and who sometimes slept in the shower stalls. The problem wasn't the bathroom but the people who used them. He wouldn't have a problem in the old converted Victorian house near the campus. His fellow roomers sometimes actually cleaned up after themselves.

It was time to find a job before the money ran out. He figured he could manage a few weeks on his cash, so he had a little cushion.

He found an internet café and e-mailed his mother. He told her he was fine, doing well, and maybe someday he could visit, but not now. Perhaps they could have video conversations online; but for financial and other reasons, that would have to be down the road. He did not tell her where he was. He did not want her to have any knowledge that police could pry out. of her. In the meantime, he was in this pleasant town, and it seemed like home, or at least could be home. Burton Peals could make it here.

After mulling over a variety of names on the bus to Ashville, Burton Peals decided to stay with Jim Thompson. Lots of Thompsons; lots of Jims. He didn't want to stand out. He fabricated a social security number and a life history and was ready to go to work. He'd be willing to do work requiring a pee test; he was clean. Fingerprints though? Not so much.

Jim Thompson, thirty-one years old; birthplace, Atlanta, Georgia; registered for continuing education classes at the college. So now he was a "student," quite plausible. Now he needed work. What could he do? He claimed to have a degree in liberal arts from South Carolina State in Orangeburg, at least that's what he said. Maybe they'll check, maybe they won't.

Fast-food work, for a start, would barely pay the rent if he went half time. After several days of looking at the local weekly classifieds and knocking on doors, he visited Great Mountain Auto Parts on the edge of town. Billy Uibel, the general manager, took a liking to this good looking, pleasant, and articulate young man.

"So you have any experience in the auto parts business?"

"Some. I worked one summer in Columbia at an auto parts store. I had some counter experience—did a little inventory. We did it by hand in those days."

"I see. Well, we can teach you our system."

"I'd be delighted to learn."

"We'll start you at $9.50 per hour. That should go up after your provisional period, which is three months. Any arrests or criminal history?"

"I got two speeding tickets, one in '05 and the other—"

Billy interrupted. "No that's okay. Why don't you fill out the application, and if everything checks out, we'll get right back in touch."

"Jim" filled out the application on the clipboard and gave an e-mail address but no phone for now. After he finished, he handed the application back to Billy and added, "I'll drop in after the weekend to see that the application went okay."

Burton left the parts store feeling inexplicably anxious. Everything seemed to go well. Maybe too well. Why was that guy Billy so friendly? Who is he really working for? Do they know who he really is?

The young man at the mobile phone store with his starched white shirt, thin black necktie, and red name tag was friendly enough. But he disappeared into the back room twice. Wasn't once enough? What was he doing back there? Burton had the idea that they knew who he was, tall black man, escapee. He thought he possibly heard his real name being spoken in muffled tones and faint laughter from the stockroom. Perhaps they were bugging his new phone. He shook off the idea but then after thinking about it for a while, realized that people can spy on you through your cell phone. He read about it in the paper all the time. He left the store without the phone, satisfied that he probably didn't need it anyhow.

It was getting close to 5:00 p.m., and he hadn't had anything to eat since 11:30. Five p.m., not frickin' seventeen hundred like at the hospital. Real time for real people, and he could eat whatever he wanted, whenever he wanted.

He strolled down to a local fast-food barbecue joint. One thing he wanted and hadn't had for years was big fat, juicy greasy fried onion rings dipped in barbecue sauce. He had asked about them at the hospital and was told by the dietician that she would "look into it." She came back with the answer that the state dietary committee had not approved this item.

No nanny dietician worrying about his cholesterol now. Worry about your own cholesterol, bitch.

CHAPTER 9

The workday at BASH officially begins at eight; but like most doctors and staff, I get there around eight thirty, in time for morning report. Although that seems a bit late, I am often the first one in the meeting room. Monday morning report is the most important as the charge nurse will report to ward staff what transpired over the weekend. I wandered in with my cup of coffee and chocolate doughnut I picked up at Binky Dee's Drive Inn along old Route 41. If there were a Starbucks anywhere along the way, I'd gladly pick up a mocha cappuccino and a bran muffin. There's one in downtown Bayside, but I don't drive through there. My cottage is out in the backwater, by the marsh, but I can't complain too much; I'm here for the backwater. My home is a very cool one and a half-story cottage on stilts. When the tide comes in, the water sometimes rolls under the house.

My job at BASH takes my energy. The marsh heals my mind and gives me energy. There are needy people on staff and needy people incarcerated here. Sometimes I'm needy, isn't everybody? Being a psychiatrist doesn't mean I'm immune from the vagaries of life. Hell, if that were the case, you could take up medicine, psychiatry, and be like Gandhi. Well, it doesn't work that way unfortunately, or should I say fortunately?

So on the day in question, Monday morning, June 27, 8:40 a.m., I was waiting for the usual slaggards to show up. I was thinking where the hell is everybody? Rosaria Laguitan, the charge nurse, arrived and started with "So, Dr. Kerrigan, I guess you've heard by now." No, I haven't heard.

Rosaria ran through the story of the demise of Doug Riley and the travails of Ernie Joe. I'm losing my appetite for my doughnut, and the coffee with half-and-half and two packs of sugar doesn't seem so inviting either. The story goes on, and all I can think now is *Oh shit, oh shit.*

And then there's the resident, Mr. Plumm. No judgment here. Compassion all around, stupid antisocial bastard. His ass belongs in a state prison, like the one at Broad River, not some squishy hospital with patients' rights advocates running about, inquiring about why so and so resident was getting bologna and not getting tuna fish sandwiches at snack time, or perhaps the other way around. Oh, I'm sorry, am I sounding bitter? Things were going downhill, and it wasn't even 9:00 a.m. yet. Well, you have to admit that finding out your patient murdered a rehab therapist the day before and nobody called you to give a heads up would ruin the day early for anybody.

The team had gathered in the conference room. One of the nursing assistants was shedding a tear; and Cleo Oliphant, the social worker, was looking absolutely shell shocked. Psychologist Holden Enright was staring out the window.

Okay, I was the team leader. The psychologists like to debate that point like they should be allowed to be team leader, not just the psychiatrists. They're pissed off. They make less than RNs. Turf battle. Of course, when the Titanic is sinking, sure, Doc, you're the leader, the captain—aye, aye, sir!

Rosaria started the festivities for the day, reminding everyone that we would be meeting with the Administrative Quality Review Panel (AQRP) at ten and the special investigator at eleven. So much for getting any real work done that morning.

The special investigator was not just investigating a murder, but he was also investigating us, specifically me. Like what did I do or what didn't I do or what should I have done. Then he reports to the AQRP and then to the DRIPS on the Death Review Panel.

This brings us to sentinel events. A sentinel event is basically an event that results in a death or near death of a patient. Technically speaking, the death of a staff member is not in that category. I'm not sure what that says about the life of a patient compared to the life of a staff member. Still, the reviewers would be here for sure with pointed questions, peering over the top of their wire-rimmed glasses, looking all concerned, writing on clipboards, and ultimately demanding some kind of plan to address how we're going to prevent crazy people from doing crazy things in the future. And we will come up with a plan, probably one that no one will follow; but it will be in place, so the next time somebody kills somebody or hangs himself or burns the place down, we'll be covered.

At the morning conference, Rosaria and Cleo discussed how we would need to have a meeting with all the patients on the ward to talk about the death of Doug and to offer support and allow them to express their feelings. That was scheduled for the afternoon. "And we all need to be there for our residents." Rosaria was emphatic.

Doug was based on another ward but worked a lot with my patients. He was the "go to" guy, a good man, a casualty. Cleo started to cry. Rosaria offered a hug. Cleo continued to sob on Rosaria's shoulder. Holden was looking more angry than sad. He was thinking something is wrong and someone is going to pay. How do I know what he was thinking? Maybe it's because I'm paranoid or maybe because I know how things work around here. I should be paranoid.

MIKE BARTOS

It was eleven years since Burton had been with a woman with the exception of two or three very quick and unsatisfactory trysts on the hospital grounds with some quite heavy and not very clean female residents behind scratchy bushes. Nothing with other men. Nothing. In the early years of his incarceration, he was approached by men a few times, with unhappy consequences for anyone who put his hands on him.

It was Monday, midsummer, and fairly quiet on the campus. Burton had spent several days of freedom, getting things in order—going to the job interview, setting up his room, and doing a little shopping. Most of all, he enjoyed walking about the town and campus, breathing the fresh mountain air, despite the campus proximity to the interstate. There were preparations for the upcoming music festival. The bars and pubs near campus were not particularly crowded. He wanted to try the bar scene. He wasn't going to drink, just meet some chicks. He'd like to meet a slender, pleasant smelling young woman, one who could talk, had some culture, knows something, and doesn't curse all the time. Perhaps she would have long silky hair that shines, like on the TV commercials. He would treat her like a princess. During the past few years, Burton had spent some time sketching. He had a modest talent for drawing faces and had perfected a portrait, a portrait of no one in particular but of someone he was seeking, someone he was sure he was going to meet. He called her Serena. Her face was perfect, with long, full, flowing light-brown hair over her shoulders, slightly pouty lips, and sky blue eyes. She was out there, and he was going to find her. Maybe tonight.

Burton went back to his room for an afternoon snooze. He was excited, happy, but a little nervous. Who was looking for him? Did they know he was here? Who were all these people. Did that guy Billy really work there or was it a trick?

No smoking in the house. He stepped outside into the shaded backyard, lit an unfiltered cigarette, blew a couple of smoke rings into the breeze, and watched them dissipate.

The place to be was the Pisgah Lookout Bar, where the Dharma Kings were playing at nine. Monday night special. Rock and roll, beer, dancing, smoke, and ladies. Stay away from the alcohol, though. Burton, a.k.a. Jim, hadn't had a drink at a bar in eleven or twelve years. He made his way to the club and got there a little early. The band was setting up. It was a small club, more focused on the music than comfort. There was a large floor in front of a stage with just a few tables around the periphery. The music fans would stand and shout and cheer and maybe dance during the performances. There were actually three bands playing that night. The Dharma Kings was the headliner out of Atlanta, playing second.

At age thirty-one, Burton noticed he was older than most of the patrons getting their IDs checked and hands stamped with iridescent ink at the door. White kids, early twenties—maybe some were younger—sneaking in with fake ID's. These college kids aren't racists, are they?

The first band started around 9:15. It was noisy, thumping, and a bit cheesy in his opinion. The fans crowded in front of the stage, some of them jumping up and down to the beat. He didn't like the music. They called it indie rock, independent rock bands, alternative rock—whatever. It wasn't soul; it wasn't heavy metal. There was little food. The club had a kitchen, which was closed. Tonight there were just pretzels and chips, but there was a full bar with mirrors, bottles, and decanters with colorful liqueurs, and a bartender shaking icy mixed drinks and pouring them through a strainer. Burton noticed his mouth watering, but for what? Wouldn't a rum and cola be just tasty? It's mostly soda, no harm done? Right? And he's not a patient, not anymore, not a mental case, not a goddamn resident. Rum? House brands okay?

He swirled the elixir in the glass and sniffed at it. The carbonation bubbles tickled his nose. He could smell the sweet soft drink and the heady aroma of the rum, his first alcohol in eleven years, except for a few sickening cups of "pruno."

This was a tasty, real world indulgence. He told himself that he would have just one more. Hardly any buzz at all. Seven bucks—how prices have changed. The second one went down quickly, warm and sweet. He was relaxed. Now he could approach one of the young women on the floor and strike up a conversation. He knew how to handle women. He knew what they liked. Serena was out there somewhere. *Look out, ladies, there's a real man on board. What's the deal with these peach fuzz-faced college boys in skinny jeans? You've got to be kidding me.*

Burton surveyed the floor during a break between the bands. The headliner was coming up. He saw a slender young woman standing alone, maybe twenty-one or twenty-two. He walked up to her and stood casually

MIKE BARTOS

at her side. She held a peach colored drink as she was eating a cherry off a toothpick.

He glanced over. "Hey, so what do you think of this band?"

She glanced at him sideways, not turning to face him. "Which one?"

"The Dharma Bums."

"They're not the Dharma Bums. That was a book by Jack Kerouac. These are the Dharma Kings. I came up from Greenville to see them."

"You must really like them. By the way, I'm Jim."

"Look, I'm sorry, you seem very nice, but I'm here with my boyfriend."

He didn't believe her. Liar. "So where is he?"

"Really? I don't know you. I'm going to meet some friends. Excuse me."

The young woman walked away and melted into a crowd of other young women. Burton needed another drink; he was feeling angry and irritable. Who the hell did she think she was? Straight-up tequila might do the trick. Eleven bucks? "What the hell," he said sternly to the bartender, "you charging me extra because I'm black?"

"No, sir, that's the price."

Burton slapped down a ten and a one on the bar. "No tip for you, asshole."

The bartender was wary of this guy who he'd never seen before. He signaled the unarmed plain clothes security man who was working the door and looked the part of a "bouncer." They agreed no more drinks for this guy; and if he farts backward, out he goes. The bouncer would keep an eye on him.

Burton was not calming with the alcohol. He was getting more restless. He walked over to another young woman who was standing with a small mixed group of males and females. He thought to himself, *Keep cool. I'm just out of practice.*

"Hey, mama, where you from?"

The woman turned toward him. "Are you talking to me?"

"I don't see any other gorgeous foxy ladies here."

"Are you hitting on me?"

"I'm just trying to have a nice conversation, but if you're going to be rude—"

"You're the one who's being a rude asshole. Why don't you just leave?"

Burton knew that young women needed to be tamed; they're looking for a real man to take charge, and this bitch was no exception. He grabbed her arm.

"Let go of my arm, you pig."

A young man with a light blue Tar Heels sweatshirt tried to pull Burton's arm away.

Burton swung his fist and connected with the would-be rescuer's jaw and sent him reeling into the crowd. The bouncer dove onto Burton, taking him to the floor. The band stopped. Several onlookers grabbed Burton's legs and sat on them while the bouncer pushed his face onto the floor. Burton sputtered a muffled "You need to stop her. She's possessed!"

The patrons sat on Burton while the security/bouncer held him in an armlock. The local police arrived within minutes and assisted. Burton continued struggling, this time with the cops who tased him twice, which finally slowed him down so they could slap on the cuffs. The kid who was assaulted told one of the police that he intended to press charges, as did the young lady.

After Burton staggered out, escorted in cuffs, the band announced from the stage that everything was cool and it was time to "par-tay."

ELEVEN THIRTY P.M. "What do we got?" the desk sergeant wanted to know.

"Drunk and disorderly, two counts of assault, resisting arrest, assaulting an officer, no ID, six hundred dollars cash."

"Who does he say he is?"

"Depends when you ask. He's either Burton or Jim, or alpha or omega. Looks like a nutcase. A nutcase with money. He's convinced that some gal at the bar was the Devil."

"Run some prints. See who we got. Put him in isolation so he doesn't kill someone or himself. Maybe when the alcohol wears off, we'll get some better answers."

"Some kids from the Pisgah want to press charges."

The desk sergeant smiled. "Looks like you got some paperwork to do. Best you get on it."

CHAPTER 11

I got the message to meet in the executive conference room at 1:00 p.m. The e-mail listed the time as 1300 hours, typical hospital time notation. We don't usually have meetings right at one. Nobody is ever back from lunch on time. There are a couple of road cafés nearby, and it's about four miles into Bayside if you like to lunch on overpriced fish imported from somewhere else, accompanied by snowbird tourists wearing Bermuda shorts and rumpled fishing hats. In late June with July Fourth weekend approaching, even though it's hot, it's the height of the season. The condos and hotels are full, and the restaurants are bustling. None of that on this day—no getting back at one thirty or quarter to two. Dr. Clark Rheingold, one of the chief surveyors from the the state capital, was going to meet with some administrators, managers, team members, and assorted suckers in "leadership" positions, and of course, yours truly, Patrick Michael Kerrigan, MD, board-certified staff psychiatrist, attending physician for Ernest Joseph Plumm.

We get paid well with civil service step raises and board certification, about $175,000 per year. Not bad for coastal South Carolina. Then there are twelve holidays a year, health insurance, pension plan, and the like. With that level of pay comes a certain degree of risk and hassle. What the bureaucrats and surveyors like to call "accountability," I call vulnerability. When things go way wrong, the lawyers and the administrators don't ask who the nurse is or who the psychologist or social worker is, but "Who is the doctor?" I'm not trying to whine or complain—it's the deal I signed up for, but it hangs over my head like the Sword of Damocles. Maybe I could make a living talking to worried well matrons from South of Broad in Charleston, or not. Sometimes it really seems worth a try. I figured half my pay was for worrying and the other half was for showing up.

Dr. Rheingold was there early, sorting through documents. Also in the room was Elliot Desjardins, Cookie Blaylock, and a few other bigwigs. Then there was Lyle Dawkins, the corpulent red-faced chief of security. He looked somewhat impatient and distracted. Hiram Singh, of the Department of Behavioral Health Services, who made the two-and-a-half-hour drive from

Columbia that morning was ready to weigh in. Dr. Rajinder Kapoor, the OD from that fateful day was summoned to be present for the ritual blame fest.

Dr. Rheingold was an earnest appearing man, heavyset with thinning red hair, sporting horn-rim glasses, and a bow tie. He was busily making notes on a clipboard, although nobody said anything yet. He wore an ID badge, which was more formidable than the usual badge worn at BASH, planned that way I'm sure.

The administrator began, "I'm sure we have all been saddened and shocked by the events of this past week. Dr Rheingold and Dr. Singh are here to look into what happened and to make a report. They are here to help us and make recommendations so we can use this tragedy as a teachable moment and utilize this as an opportunity for improvement. We will open our doors and records to them, and we will fully cooperate. We would like to thank them for making an inconvenient trip here to offer their insights."

I thought this is like thanking the IRS for auditing you.

Dr. Rheingold looked very serious, scanning his notes, scowling, turning his head to one side. He then took a breath and looked about the group assembled at the conference table. "I'm just curious," he began, "why is this place getting so much press lately? I just want to know."

He then stared right into my eyes. Then into Cookie Blaylock's eyes, then back into mine, and then into Captain Dawkins's eyes. He spoke softly but directly. "I'm not here to get you"—he said, pointing at me—"or you," gazing at Cookie Blaylock—"or you," staring at Captain Dawkins." This affirmed my presumption that he was here to get us. "I just want to know what's going on around here. Why the high profile? People are hearing about the Bay Area State Hospital all over the country."

Captain Dawkins began by announcing that the escapee, Burton Peals, was in custody in North Carolina. Nobody was seriously injured; but apparently, he decompensated since he wasn't taking his medication. Nothing really serious, mind you, if one ignores the fact that a college student had a fractured mandible as a result and the lawyers were already talking about suing the hospital, the department, the state, and maybe the doctor—anyone with deep pockets or maybe just pockets. They, perhaps, were hoping the state would cough up a settlement, much easier and cheaper than defending even a frivolous suit, and who needs the publicity? Burton would be back on a neighboring ward, or wherever there was a bed available within the week, but since he was in another state, it would give our state lawyers something to do for several days.

"Who had the brilliant idea of letting your violent patients wander around the community in civilian clothes?" Dr. Rheingold wanted to know.

Elliot jumped in. "Well, sir, it's part of the court-ordered plan to assist our patients in reintegrating into the community. Also there was a consent decree that our residents have the right to appear in court in street clothes without shackles. There is even a special order from the state mandating we have a full reintegration plan in place, Special Order 301."

Dawkins, who was sitting immediately to my left, whispered in my ear, "Maybe I should refer them to special order number one," as he extended his middle finger below the edge of the conference table so only I could see it. Rheingold raised one eyebrow quite seriously and glared at me. "Something amusing, Doctor?"

Rheingold isn't my boss, but he is the medical director's and chief administrator's boss. If he doesn't like me, screw him. "No, sir. I just had a little cough, but I do have some things I would like to discuss."

I had plenty of issues to discuss including poor oversight and bureaucratic bungling to name a few. If we're going down, I might as well have my say. I spoke up. "Dr. Rheingold, I can give you a lot of information about what goes on around here if you have the time—"

Dr. Blaylock broke in abruptly. "Before we go on, I believe we have the chief of psychology out in the hallway, who would like to join us. Could someone go get him?"

Dr. Simpson was escorted in and found a seat at the table. Dr. Blaylock continued, "Dr. Simpson has done a thorough report on the treatment perspectives and review of practices and procedures, which he would like to share with you."

Dr. Rheingold directed his attention to the psychologist, who turned on the projector already on the table. An image of a graph was projected onto a large white area on the wall, which was used as a screen. Dr. Rheingold seemed interested. There were dotted and dashed red and purple lines intersecting and diverging. Bailey Simpson was prepared. "Here we see the number of reported triggers of incidents over the past twelve months, divided into categories . . ."

I suppose showing this type of mesmerizing presentation to bureaucrats is akin to rubbing the belly of an alligator before it bites your head off. No one spoke to me for the rest of the meeting, other than Dr. Rheingold shaking my hand and telling me what a pleasure it was to meet me. I was then summarily but politely scooted out of the administration building and back to my ward. He never said another word to the captain either, nor asked his opinion.

It wasn't until the next day that I ran into Freddy Wildemere, the assistant medical director, who informed me of the final outcome. The hospital was going to be fined somewhere in the range of $38,000 for not providing adequate protection for the staff. "And who is going to pay it?" I inquired.

Apparently it will be paid for by the Department of Behavioral Health Services. And where will it go? To the State Treasury Department.

"So the state will fine itself and pay itself, right?"

Freddy chuckled and shrugged his shoulders. "I guess. That's the way it's done around here."

Well, that should teach us a lesson.

THE WARD ITSELF was quiet. The staff was having its requisite meeting with the patients. Everyone was gathered in a large dayroom. The heavy plastic-enclosed TV was switched off, and most of the residents were reasonably attentive. Typically, I don't have to be present, but this day was different. The consensus was that the patients missed Doug if not so much Ernie Joe. Some of the residents were tearful.

"Doug was really good to me. He always had something planned, and we played music a lot and had a good time," remarked Martha, a fifty-five-year-old woman who killed both her children twenty-five years ago in response to the voices that told her to do that. Now, there was more senseless death. How could she heal in a place where violence occurred so routinely? She would remain in treatment until the day she dies. That's the way the department likes it, and that's the way juries like it. Sometimes, even the patients like it. After killing your kids and living twenty-five years in an institution for the criminally insane, there's really no place to go, despite her regular protestations about how much "I hate this place. I hate it, I hate it, I hate it." Still, Martha would be going to community reentry group and living skills group, if for no other reason than to fill time and look good.

One time, Elliot Desjardins, reminded me that "the state legislature *demands* we provide twenty hours of scheduled treatment per week, tailored to each resident's needs." It worked out that this therapeutic community meeting and any time I spend talking to the patients do not count as treatment, not officially anyhow. It only counts as treatment if there's a logbook, roster, syllabus, and treatment coordinator's signature. Hope, dignity, self-esteem— that's all fine, but it's off the books or under the table. I hope one day a state legislator actually visits us.

Martha wanted to offer a prayer for Doug. She asked everyone to be quiet or join along with her. She closed her eyes, folded her hands, and spoke softly. "Lord, I ask you humbly to take Doug into your kingdom. He was a good guy. He didn't deserve to die that way. We thank you for allowing us to share time on this earth with him. I also pray for the soul of Ernie Joe—may he find forgiveness and redemption."

Not so crazy. It was better than I could have done. I always said that no matter how impaired a patient may be, you can always learn something from just about anybody—you just need to keep your eyes and ears and your heart open. I made a mental note to say a prayer for Doug at mass next Sunday if I went, or even if I didn't. I'm not sure I'm ready to be so magnanimous about Ernie Joe, not yet anyhow. He's made victims out of all of us.

Larry P. was pacing rapidly in the hallway outside the dayroom, looking through the wire-reinforced, large shatterproof window. He stared at the proceedings for about thirty seconds, then quickly turned and briskly paced the hallway again, and then repeated the process. He entered the room and sat down for about thirty seconds and then suddenly stood up and walked out to continue his hallway pacing. This is a process he repeated most days. When asked why he did this or what was going on, his usual reply would be, "What's it to you? The constitution gives me the right to go where I want. I need to see what you're doing. The Supreme Court will sue you if you try to stop me."

Today, during his thirty-second sit-down, I asked him if he would like to say anything. "I got nothin' to say without my lawyer, who's an idiot."

"Any words of remembrance about Doug?"

"No, I think he knew too much—that's what happened. I better not say anything." He sprang out of his chair and returned to his rounds in the hallway.

Others joined in with their final good-byes, some making sense and some not.

There was also the issue of the empty bed, the one vacated by Ernie Joe. There was some palpable relief by residents and staff alike that it was empty and Ernie Joe wasn't creating an atmosphere of fear anymore. The bed would remain empty until administration saw fit to fill it, which mercifully they decided to put off for a little while, at least until things calmed down. There were legally insane inmates in county jails all over the state, just waiting to be shipped to BASH.

Things were quiet on the ward; Dr. Rheingold didn't want to talk to me, and administration apparently didn't want me talking to him. But that didn't mean my problems were over. No, it just meant there was a lull in the storm.

I thought it would be in my best interest to go look over Ernie Joe's chart and see what was in it and what was missing.

After a short but sweaty walk to the portal, getting buzzed through, it's still a hundred yards to Health Information, which is actually the most modern structure at BASH and nicely air-conditioned. Constant temperature helps keep the records preserved, like bottles of fine and rare wine. Danica was there, cute and chipper, always pleasantly energetic, my go-to gal at HI. "How ya doin', Doc?" she greeted me enthusiastically. I wondered how old she was. Mid thirties I guessed, with no wedding ring.

"Danica, could you find the Plumm chart for me?"

"Oh yeah, Doc, I have to go down to the vault for that one. Couldja wait here? It'll take a few minutes." They lock up charts after any kind of serious event like it's national security. We have to keep it unadulterated for the lawyers.

I grabbed a seat at a library table by a wall of charts and checked my personal e-mail on my phone. They have Wi-Fi in here too. Probably a decent place to work. Danica returned pulling a shopping cart with six volumes of records. "You know, Doc, you have to look at them here."

Here's a guy who's been in this hospital for about four years, and his charts are somewhere between one and a half to two feet high. Much of this documentation consists of medication flow sheets, vital sign graphs, and doctor order sheets. The real meat is in the doctor and nursing notes. In the past few years, the STAR plan, required by the courts make up a big hunk of space.

STAR stands for Strategic Treatment and Rehabilitation. This is basically the template for the treatment plan. It includes about twenty pages repeated every month with hundreds of required bullet points. It was all good, except for the patients who continued to be random aggressors or victims. The documentation, however, was vastly improved, or at least more voluminous.

After a survey last year, Elliot Desjardins sent out a joyous e-mail thanking the staff for embracing the STAR plan. I think the only thing we embraced was our ankles.

What I was looking for in the chart was evidence of any major screw-ups, mine or, with some luck, someone else's. He was on proper doses of meds, check. He was assigned to proper group treatments: substance abuse, check; coping skills, check; and anger management, check. He missed a lot of groups, sleeping in, goofing off, or just being plain oppositional.

"Group refusal" was a documented problem on the STAR plan. Intervention was listed as the "patient teaching" about the importance of groups, with the patient documented as being "partially receptive." To be compliant with court ordered improvement, the receptiveness had to be quantifiable and measurable. "Resident will list three benefits of attending group." If I recall correctly, he listed two, one of which was "You'll get off my ass." That last statement was not part of the documentation.

I couldn't really find any glaring omissions or errors on my part. Believe me, I was looking for them because this is the kind of thing the lawyers look for. I decided I could sleep a little better.

On the day of the murder, Sunday June 26, there was a note from Corky Williams, RN: *"Resident returned late from grounds. He has been irritable. Resident returned 1215 hrs unaccompanied with stained wet clothing. Resident uncooperative and combative. Security assisted with restraint. One staff injured. OD notified. Removed from unit by law enforcement. Incident report completed as per protocol."*

I was still the doctor of record, and I was sure I would be answering questions for quite some time. So far, not a lot of major problems on the chart from my perspective, although nursing staff, especially Corky Williams, RN, may be on the hot seat. Too bad, I really like the guy; he watches my back and cares about the residents. Damn good nurse. Then again, since I'm the doctor, the law considers me the "captain of the ship," so all the investigators will get a go round with me.

Upon returning to my office, I saw a little love note stuck under my door, a subpoena to appear in court in McMurtree, signed by Hilton Breuer, Esquire, an assistant DA from Bay County. Nothing I did wrong; he just wanted my "expert opinion" for the current disposition of my patient, Ernie Joe Plumm. So on Tuesday, July 5, at 10:00 a.m., I must "cease and desist all other business" and roll over to the courthouse and maybe have lunch at the Courthouse Café down the street, where they have real bagels. It's not New York, but it'll do for a casual lunch. I like to take a pain-in-the-ass chore like going to court and turn it into something that might be enjoyable in the end. It was time to forget about blowhard bureaucrats.

My main concern was that it was my night to visit the family bar in Charleston, the original Kerrigan's Bar and Grille, started by my daddy and still run by brother Brad. I planned to reacquaint myself with the old Yamaha upright; show off a few runs of blues scales and a few other new licks I've been working on; and of course, have a couple shots of good Irish whiskey. Now that's what I call an intervention.

CHAPTER 12

Bayside,

A popular rehabilitation therapist at the Bay Area State Hospital was found dead on the facility grounds Sunday morning after suffering an apparent head and throat injury. The staff member, Douglas Riley, 44, was last seen escorting two patients to church services. The suspect, Ernest Joseph Plumm, 31, was arrested and booked into the Bay County Jail. Assistant District Attorney Hilton Breuer said the suspect will be charged with second-degree murder. Ms. Leticia Andover Gibbs has been appointed as the public defender for this case and at this time has no comment for the press. Chief of Hospital Security, Captain Lyle Dawkins commented, "We here at the Bay Area State Hospital would like to express our sympathy to the family of the victim and will assist in any way we can to bring the perpetrator to justice. Safety for our staff and patients is our number one concern."

The prime suspect in the case, Mr. Plumm, was known for temperamental outbursts and had previous convictions for assault with a deadly weapon and aggravated rape. He was found not guilty by reason of insanity for assaulting a policeman four years ago. His treating psychiatrist, Dr. Patrick Kerrigan, said he could not comment on the case due to federal and state confidentiality laws.

Hospital Administrator Elliot Desjardins promised a "full and thorough investigation." Several nursing staff commented with the condition of anonymity that the Bay Area State Hospital is a dangerous place to work, that there have been many injuries, and that security has been lax. Many patients have recently tested positive for cocaine and methamphetamine, which is believed to be related to increasing violence and staff injuries.

The Bay Area State Hospital is a facility for people found by a court of law to have committed a violent crime but also found to be insane and thus treated at a long-term hospital instead of

*being punished in prison. The hospital is located in the South
Carolina Bay Area near the coastal resort town of Bayside and
is owned and managed by the South Carolina Department of
Behavioral Health Services.*

The byline on the *Charleston Times* Web site was credited to Carlton
Gaskins.

Ash remembered Carlton from the *Times* when he worked there over
a decade ago. He wasn't a guy long on ambition but currently had a more
lucrative gig going in journalism than Ash had, that is, a steady salary without
overhead.

"Annie," Ash called out from across the room, "we need to pay another
visit to our friend Captain Dawkins."

Annie suggested calling ahead since cold calling probably wouldn't be all
that well received. "What do you have in mind?" Annie asked.

Ash showed her the online article, which she skimmed.

"Okay, so what's your angle going to be?"

Ash was feeling a caffeinated tingle in his fingertips and toes. "There's a
helluva story here. Didn't you feel that when we went down there a couple of
weeks ago?"

"Well, maybe, but your buddy Dawkins wasn't having any of it."

"Look, I could tell Dawkins was pissed and frustrated. We just walked in
on him at the wrong time. I think we should take another crack. If he's not
playing, we can find some other workers there. I'm tellin you, Annie, we got
something here."

Annie sighed, "Yeah, but he's got the keys and the security gates. So you're
thinking of becoming a gossip tabloid?"

"No, Annie, this is hard news, a little sensational but hard news. We
need something a little more than photos of the tall ships in the harbor this
weekend. I can feel this story here."

"Why don't you ask Sally J?"

"Hmm . . . So far she doesn't seem to be thrilled with the idea, but I think
I can talk her into it. She listens to me once in a while. Listen, here we have
this place, practically in our backyard with all this drama, paid for with our tax
dollars. Someone really needs to get into this place. That article in the *Times*
raised more questions than it answered."

"And you're going to answer them?"

"That's what a newspaper man does. I'm calling."

"Okay, Mr. Newspaper Man, do what you gotta do."

The captain's card was in his wallet, where he stuck it two weeks before. It was plainly printed over a background of the seal of the State of South Carolina. There was a phone and a fax number. Ash dialed and was surprised that Dawkins answered the phone himself. "Cap'n Dawkins."

"Oh, hi, Captain. This is Ashley Roper. We met a couple of weeks ago at your off—"

Dawkins interrupted. "Yeah, I remember, that *Charley Town* fella. Listen, I guess you know the grits hit the fan around here, not a good time to talk. But listen, I was gonna call you. I just found your card under the desk."

"Call me?"

"Yeah, like I said, this ain't a good time to talk. You call me later, okay?" *Click*.

Ash called out to Annie who was busy sketching an ad at the drawing table across the room. "Yo, Annie, he said he wants to talk to me."

"Curious."

"I suppose he wouldn't be talking to me at all if he didn't want to. I'm supposed to call back later. He didn't say how much later."

Annie suggested, "Maybe things will quiet down for him right before five. It is a state facility you know."

"Meaning?"

"Not too many people stick around after five."

"It's about two now. Too late for lunch and too early for dinner . . . or not."

"Ash, we got work and a deadline and you're putting on weight."

"Stow it, Annie. You're like a second wife."

"Sorry, we're just falling behind here."

THE DEADLINE WAS 5:00 p.m. Wednesday. Everything carried or e-mailed to the printer Thursday and then distributed Friday morning. Ash got caught up in some layout issues and forgot about the time until about ten after five. *Crap*, he thought and slapped his brow. He punched in the captain's number. It rang a few times, but Dawkins picked it up before it kicked over to the main hospital switchboard.

"Cap'n Dawkins."

"Ashley Roper again."

"Oh, yeah. Thanks for callin' back."

"So, sir, you wanted to talk to me?"

"Oh, that's right. Well, I remember you wanted a story about the hospital. Sorry, last time we met I was a little rough, but I wasn't in the mood and we're not supposed to talk to the press, at least not during work time. Now I've had it up to here, and I think it's high time somebody figure out what's goin' on around here cuz I sure can't. I been in over my head the past two days, and it doesn't look like it's going to get any better."

"So what do you want from me?"

"Well, I'd like to meet you somewhere we can talk in private, if'n you don't mind."

Ash was caught off guard. "Why me?"

"So far, you're the only one who's asked. You can help me, I can help you."

"Sure, we can do that. You name the time and place."

"Okay, there's this place up the road, Ginny Small's place, best she-crab soup on the coast—they make it themselves. Best cornbread hushpuppies you ever ate."

"I know the place real well. I think she closes up around eight, though."

"Well, meet me there tomorrow at 6:00 p.m. I can get away." Ash was thinking an hour after deadline. Sure, he can handle it.

Dawkins added, "I'd like this to be off the record as you news folks like to say."

"Yeah, I can work with that."

Later that evening after pulled-pork sandwiches and a slice of peach pie, Ash reviewed the plans for the next evening with Sally J. They sat in the living room, facing each other in their leather reclining lounge chairs. Sally J decided to go for a tequila shot or two instead of her usual Chardonnay. She put her feet up and tried to relax. The tequila would help. Ash was the alcoholic but no reason not to let other people, especially his wife, enjoy an occasional drink, especially when he was trying to get her to go along with his latest project.

Ash was explaining where he wanted to go with Dawkins. Sally J wanted to be supportive, but the business side of the paper was going to hell. "So what's the deal with that sheriff?"

"He's not a sheriff. He's the chief of security at the hospital there. He's got something in mind. And for some reason, he comes to me. He wants me to keep it quiet, for at least now."

Sally J looked a little perplexed. "Well, hon, if he wants to keep it quiet, maybe he shouldn't be talking to a guy who runs a weekly newspaper." She poured herself another shot.

"My guess is that he doesn't want it quiet, but he doesn't want it to come from him. I'm sure he's got a lot of hassle—wants me to blow the whistle for him. He literally threw me out two weeks ago."

"Yeah, but that was before the murder. Did you consider talking to the other people down there? There's a whole bunch of administrators and doctors and the like."

Ash seemed a little embarrassed. "I thought about it, but I haven't done it yet. I really want to do that, as many people as possible. I need to get started. This could be the start of a big story."

Sally J heard that before but wanted to be supportive. "Sure, we've done a lot of fluff. Maybe this will help you find what you're looking for."

"To tell you the truth, I'm getting kinda nervous about it, but it's exciting. How about another slice?"

"How about not? You've been gaining weight."

"You and Annie are both getting on me. Jesus, is it that bad?"

"Ash, forget peach pie. I got somethin' better."

It had been a couple of weeks since they made love. Maybe that would get Ash's mind off his writing, and she wanted to get her mind off the floundering business side of things. Sally J led her husband to their bedroom. They both started undressing, standing next to the four-poster bed. He reached for her, but she stepped back. "What's the matter?" he asked.

"I just want to look at you. It's been a while. Just be."

Ash pulled off his pants and tossed them over the back of the chair.

"Keep going, you're not done yet." She admired her husband. Despite the fact that he had gotten a little more stout in the past year, his arms, shoulders, and chest were muscular. On his left upper arm was a tattoo of an American Eagle, something he acquired his first year in the army at age twenty-one. His dark-brown hair had a few streaks of gray and was pulled back into a small ponytail. When he let it down, it didn't quite reach his shoulders. His body was military even though his hair was not. When he held her, she could feel his strength and feel safe. He was a soldier who still had his battles but a man who kept his word. He would never drink again, she knew that; he would never hurt her, not in any way. "Your turn, babe."

He smiled and gazed as she teased him, slowly unsnapping her bra, and wiggling out of her panties, standing pale and naked before him, like Venus. In eleven years of marriage, he had never tired of her. She knew what he liked and knew herself as well. Her long hair was also pulled back in a ponytail. She reached back and removed her burette and shook her head quickly to let her long reddish blond hair fall over her shoulders. Her body was full and curved and soft but, like him, was surprisingly strong. At times, Ash thought her paleness almost seemed to make her glow in the dark.

He buried his face in her long fragrant hair and moved his hands along the contours of her smooth body. They spoke no words as they lay down on the comforter. She moaned softly and breathed deeply as he caressed and touched her. He kissed her neck and shoulders with increasing intensity as he moved inside her, feeling her warmth and smoothness and then her spasms as she groaned then yelled out. He continued to move inside her until her moaning subsided. They were both breathless and moist with a fine patina of perspiration.

They smiled, nose to nose, and then both chuckled. Ash looked into her eyes and spoke softly, "You're always here for me, and I want to be here for you. I won't forget."

Sally laughed out loud. "Don't worry, I won't let you."

"By the way, that was better than the peach pie, and that's sayin' something."

Sally J stroked the back of his neck as Ash fell asleep, his head parked on her bosom. He snored softly as she sighed and turned her head and gazed out the window into the dark peaceful garden.

CHAPTER 13

It had been two weeks since his previous lunch at the Ginny's Sea Island Café. Ash left early from Charleston but still got caught up in the rush-hour traffic. Only two tables were occupied. It looked like the captain was going to be late. Ash decided to pass the time checking up on his e-mail on the phone, but cell service was spotty and weak and he kept dropping the service. "Hey, Ginny, how about getting some Wi-Fi in here?"

"Well, we ain't gettin' no Wi-Fi in here any time soon, but we got some plenty cold beer. Settle for that?"

"Love to." Ginny brought Ash a twenty-ounce icy mug foaming over the top and placed it in front of him. It was quarter past six, and Ash was thinking Dawkins wasn't going to show. It was a steamy late afternoon. Ginny had a small screened deck behind the restaurant, overlooking the marsh creek. Her son, Jermaine, would pull shrimp out of the creek or harvest muddy mounds of oysters squirting tiny bursts of water into the air.

It was about 88 degrees but very damp, or "gummy" as the locals would like to say. Still, Ash thought, it might be nice to sit out on the covered deck and watch the egrets or maybe a gator cruise by. Ash exited a creaky swinging door out to the wooden deck on stilts about six feet above the edge of the water. It was close to high tide. Low tide would be about midnight, and the water would drop about two feet. Tied to a dilapidated pier was a small jon boat rocking over the occasional ripples reflecting off the bank. He had the deck to himself. Ash stepped through the screen door to the stairs leading down from the deck to the marsh. He turned over the mug, spilling the beer onto the ground watching the foaming rivulets inch toward the water line.

The late afternoon sea breeze rustled the oaks and bowed the saw palmetto. The rich odor of the muddy marsh, spiced with the smell of salty brine, crawdads, and decaying vegetation, was strong but not altogether unpleasant. Ash was thinking he would enjoy the milieu of this lazy late low-country afternoon and order some sweet iced tea. About twenty after, Lyle arrived. He ordered a draft from Ginny, who pointed to the deck. He asked her to bring it outside to the table where he and Ash would be parked.

Ash greeted the big man with "Thanks for coming. Is out here okay with you?"

"Sure, I like sitting outside even when it's warmer than this. I'll let you know if it's a problem." There was a hum of an air conditioning wall unit around the side of the restaurant, not loud enough to be intrusive. A glowing fluorescent blue bug light was suspended from the eaves. Lyle was out of uniform, wearing somewhat rumpled cotton slacks and a loud Hawaiian shirt, the kind often favored by stout men.

Lyle started, "I'm sorry I'm a little late. There's all these people from the department,the state, not to mention our own committees are lookin' into everything; notes, charts, procedures. They're all lookin' real serious and all, but I think they're enjoyin' it, like it gets their juices flowin'. Makes 'em feel life is good. I have to entertain the lot of 'em, tell 'em how we are really on our toes, what our policies and procedures are, and the like. Anyhow, they had enough for one day, and so have I. The ones from Columbia are staying at the fancy condos in Bayside, at taxpayers' expense. Maybe I can get me one of those gigs after I retire from this place."

Lyle took a long draw on his draft, wiped the foam from his mouth on his sleeve, and exhaled with a satisfied "Ahhh." He continued without eliciting anything from Ash. "So I was thinkin', you seemed to be the kind of fella that wants to know what's goin' on. I think you can help me and the citizens of South Carolina. Maybe you can find out how those drugs are gettin' in. They cause a lot of problems."

Jermaine interrupted to take their orders. The captain ordered shrimp and grits, and another beer. Ash decided to go easy and just keep it to a crab salad. Ash finally asked the obvious, "So how can I help? I was just wanting to get some inside scoop from you."

"Well, hell, I don't know a lot more than anyone else. I'd like to, but I don't." the captain admitted

"Have you thought about an undercover agent or informer, maybe a staff on the inside?"

Lyle explained, "This may be a hospital, but it's like a prison too. A lot of our residents spent a lot of time in prison or county jails. They get arrested for crimes and sit in jail for a long time until they are finally tried and then found insane. Some of them have long arrest records and did time for a variety of crimes before the one they were found insane for. Anyhow, there's a lot of prison culture here, especially when it comes to snitches. Talkin' too much can get you killed, or at least get the shit kicked out of you. We suspect, actually we know, staff brings a lot of dope in. Relatives or friends will pay them on the outside. We found one case where the staff, one of the nursing assistants, was bringing in meth, getting cash transfers directly into his account. For some reason, the charges were dropped. He was fired, but he sued the state and was reinstated with back pay. Now we're not supposed to harass him. He's still workin' here. We keep an eye on him, but not so he notices. Know what I mean?"

"Sure, sounds pretty outrageous actually."

Dawkins continued, "What's really outrageous is the amount of violence. Patients are attacking each other and attacking staff. I guess you know about the murder on grounds. That was drug related. The higher-ups are givin' me a pile of crap. I'm supposed to figure it out. In the meantime, they're cuttin' my staff. Between the unions and the feds, not too much we can do. Thought maybe you could help me out."

"How would I do that?"

"Hell, you're the newsman. You came to me in the first place. I guess you dig around, talk to people."

"Anyway, I can get in?"

"I think that's what you wanted last time you showed up. Sure, we can always clear visitors, and I can take you on a tour so you can get an idea how the place is set up. I suppose you want to know about this murder too and the escape."

"Yeah, there's some good stories there. I think a lot of people would find it interesting. I mean what led up to it—how could something like that happen?"

"Mebbe the question is why it doesn't happen more often. We got a lotta folks in there who aren't just criminals, they're crazy too. Then they get their hands on some drugs. Then you're lookin' at some employee with his throat slit, buried under the petunias. You think at the state prison we'd be sending the inmates off to court with no hospital staff as escort? Hell no! But whoever made up the laws decided that's a good idea cuz after all, they're poor sick people. And if they don't get better, then somebody's not doin' sumpin' right. Then you get stuff like this happenin', and you got the jackals and wolves descending on this place.

"So you think I could get in there for a day. Maybe I could blend in if I dressed like one of the patients."

Dawkins looked at Ash in disbelief. "You think you know how to handle yourself?"

Ash answered, "You know, I'm a Citadel grad, and I served in Gulf War One. I was a platoon commander, not much hand-to-hand combat mind you, but I was trained. I know basic martial arts. I can take care of myself."

"Well, good on you, boy. That was over twenty years ago. Besides you couldn't walk around inside the confined perimeter wearing blues, randomly kicking ass."

"Just taking care of myself. Besides, it would just be for a day."

"Hah! Just for a day. What do you think you'll learn in a day? You think people will confide in you. They won't even know who you are."

"Well, that's exactly the point," Ash replied. "I hope they don't know who I am. I got an idea that maybe I could wear the hospital blue outfit and really blend in, like a fly on the wall."

"And get swatted? I really couldn't let you do that. It could be dangerous. It's also against the rules."

"Yes, it could be dangerous, but don't you have a lot of people there who really need and want help, and they live there every day? I saw some oldsters and small guys behind the fence. If they can handle it, I can for at least a day."

Jermaine arrived with the welcome dinner plates. Lyle ate hungrily as the conversation continued. The shrimp and creamy grits were invitingly fragrant. Ash wished he had ordered some. It looked very rich. He figured he was really better off with the crab salad, which was quite tasty. Traffic on the road out front was tapering off. Listening carefully, he could hear rippling water in the marsh, where birds were landing and fish snapped at mosquitoes. The air conditioner hummed. The bug light sizzled and popped.

Ash tried again. "Isn't there a way you could let me have the patient outfit for the day? Nobody would have to know, and I bet I could find out a heckuva lot. Maybe I could go in as a nurse or the new rehab therapist."

"Yeah, I understand we just had a sudden opening," Lyle said drolly. "I bet you could. But no, I can't see how this half-cocked plan of yours could work. I'll try to figure out some way to get you in, though. Maybe your undercover plan could work using one of my boys, though," Lyle said as he shoveled in another mouthful. "But let's keep in touch. You want a story. I'll help ya get your story cuz that just might help me too. But like I said, you're a civilian. Don't know how we can use you. I don't mean like 'use' you. Well, you know what I mean."

They finished their meal quietly. Ginny came outside and asked, "You

MIKE BARTOS

boys want anything else? I got some good sweet potato pie, homemade." They both thought about it but declined. Ash took the check.

"Lyle, anytime, it'll be on me."

"Thank you, Mr. Roper," Lyle said, wiping his mouth. "That would be my pleasure."

It was still daylight as Ash headed back to Charleston. He thought that Sally J would really like this place.

CHAPTER 14

The next afternoon, Captain Dawkins received a phone call from Desjardins requesting he come immediately to his private conference room. It was about 2:00 p.m. "Damn," Dawkins said to himself. He wasn't so much concerned with a third degree from some bureaucrat, but this was going to disrupt his power nap.

Mr. Desjardins' conference room was nicer than most places in the hospital, as it had been fully renovated. The walls were paneled, and a fancy oriental rug adorned the floor. Several handsome bookcases lined the walls, with no real books other than regulatory and training manuals in large three-ring binders. There was a large glittering trophy on a top shelf with a brassy statuette of a golfer about to take a swing. It was cool too. Lyle thought the big boss should always be comfortable.

Seated around the small institutional-looking conference table, other than Lyle and Desjardins, were several department heads, including medical/psychiatry, psychology, and nursing, and Dr. Hiram Singh, once again visiting from the Department of Behavioral Health Services.

Dr. Singh started, "I came here to meet with your staff and discuss your safety concerns. Who would like to start?"

Dr. Whiteside, the medical chief of staff, who represented the medical and psychiatric physicians spoke first. "I asked all the doctors to feed back to me some of their concerns. I made a list and sent it off to Columbia but haven't heard anything back yet. I also gave the list to Mr. Desjardins here, and he said he wanted to hear from you first."

Elliot spoke up. "That's true, we don't have the funds, so there's not really much we can do. We have a budget, but we're pretty limited in our resources."

Dr. Whiteside continued, "We're interested in an improved alarm system and some type of video surveillance system that's monitored. Banks and convenience stores have them, and we probably need them more than they do."

Wilma Severnaque, the director of nursing chimed in, "The nurses are usually on the frontline, taking the hits. It would be good if we can get security personnel on the wards, or at least near the wards, so we don't have to wrestle with the residents."

Dr. Singh leaned forward, clasping his hands on the table. "You have to understand that most of these things will not happen. I want you to know I discussed your requests very carefully with department administration. First of all, the video cameras are a violation of patient privacy, which new federal laws say is a patient's right. Our own attorneys have interpreted the law to preclude any such surveillance."

Lyle spoke up. "Wait a minute, they have these cameras in prisons for people who are no less dangerous—"

Dr. Singh interrupted. "Keep in mind that this is a hospital. And until the state declares otherwise, we are not a prison. We provide treatment, not punishment. If somebody is acting aggressively, then it should be addressed appropriately in the treatment conference and you should provide appropriate behavioral interventions."

Lyle continued, "We do that and people are still getting hurt and killed. I need more officers."

Dr. Singh responded, "I'm very sympathetic to the challenges you all face working here. I am working hard with your medical director, Dr. Blaylock, and Elliot here to help make our hospital a safe facility providing state-of-the-art treatment. Captain, you are a vital part of our mission."

"How's that?" Lyle wanted to know.

Dr. Singh leaned back and chuckled as if the answer were patently obvious. "You are the head of security, sir, and I'd like you to work with your administrators here in coming up with a more efficient and effective deployment of your personnel."

"I'm not sure I know what you're looking for. We're already stretched thin."

"Well, good news, captain, I have put in a budgetary request for three additional full time officers for your department."

Lyle was getting a bit frosted. "Let's see, that's one officer for each of three shifts, five days a week. You see Dr. Singh, we run 24/7 around here, weekends, holidays—"

"I'm sure this will be helpful. You are getting more than a lot of other departments. And then with the new fiscal year, we can request more."

"Okay, so you're requesting new positions, like we don't really have them yet?"

"Well, this is very true, but I'm sure we will have no problem getting this through the legislative budget committee."

"So how long will this take?"

Singh was getting impatient. "I don't have a crystal ball, but I hope we can start interviewing candidates the beginning of August."

"So how does that help now?"

"Captain, please, please, I am not here to debate and argue with you. We need to move on."

"What about the drugs getting into the facility? That's getting out of control. We need some help here."

"Captain, as I said, we are doing everything we can to help you. Everyone who works here is responsible for safety, but you are the official in charge. As I've told you, we are increasing your resources. Now really, sir, we must move along."

Lyle got up abruptly to leave the room. Desjardins said, "Captain, we're not done yet. We would appreciate it if you could stay. Your input is important."

Lyle sighed, rolled his eyes ever so slightly, and said, "I've got to tend to some urgent bidness. Please excuse me. Mr. Desjardins, Dr. Singh, Miss Blaylock, ladies, gentlemen," and turned and left the room.

The application for state retirement was sputtering out of the printer in Lyle's office. He wasn't sure if he was going to fill it out and submit it right away; but there it was, like a life boat. He was not the type of man to have a financial advisor. He thought that if money managers knew so much about money, what did they need him for? They could just get rich on their own. The state had all his retirement funds. He did have the thirty-acre family homestead by the river, all paid for, with just a little fixing-up needed. Really, who needs all this crap? He would be fifty-five in November. That could work. But some answers were in order. Why the increased violence? Why did a good man get killed? Who was turning the other way? Or was it just plain carelessness, bureaucrats too busy covering their asses to pay attention?

There was a bed open on ward K3, at least for the moment. That was Ernie Joe's bed in a three-man room on a coed ward. That could be at the heart of the matter. That Roper fella from Charleston might just figure out something for a day. He could say he was just transferred in, snoop around undercover for a few hours. Nobody would be the wiser. Lyle could send notice to the ward of the new admission. He could say his records have been delayed from some upstate county and then walk him out through the portal around 6:00 p.m. and say there was a new minute order from a judge ordering him back to his county for another hearing. Lyle thought he might even treat him to dinner that evening. There was the not so small matter of informing administration about this plan. They would absolutely never go for it, too dangerous and probably not legal. What the hell does that say about this place—that it's even too dangerous for a supposed patient?

Lyle had asked for undercover cops to go in several times in the past year to find out about drugs and other contraband. The response from administration usually was along the lines of doing more drug screens and better substance recovery groups for the residents.

This might be risky for his own career; but if he could get some good information, bust up whatever drug ring was going on, he might have a leg up on starting his own private investigating business after retirement. Now that would be fun and profitable.

TEN THIRTY THE next morning, as Ash was staring at his word processor, he received a call at the office of *Charley Town*. He was surprised but pleased to hear it was the captain.

"How you doin'?" The captain's gruff manner was not evident, replaced by a calmer, more friendly demeanor. After an exchange of pleasantries, Dawkins continued, "Well, I worked it out so you can spend the day down here. You'll be able to move around, blend in, wear the blue outfit. You'll have lunch with the residents in the chow hall. Maybe play a game of softball if it's not too hot. I think you'll get a whole new perspective. Plan to spend the day. I'll get you in and out. We even got a name for you."

Ash was amazed and had to interrupt. "Do I hear you right? You're going to sneak me into BASH? I thought you didn't like the idea."

"I thought it over, and you just might be the right man for the job. You seem like an eager sorta fella. You wanna go nosin' around. You just might find out sumpin', at least more than I'm gettin', and I can use all the help I can get."

Ash thought about it for a moment and then asked, "Can't we get in trouble for this? I mean false pretenses and all?"

The captain replied, "I always say it's easier to ask for forgiveness than asking for permission. Remember too, I'm the chief of security 'round here." Then he chuckled and added softly, "This'll be our little secret for now."

"So how is this going to work?"

There's an inmate at the jail up in Colleton County, white fella, 'bout your age, who passed away last week. You're gonna be him for a day. Don't worry 'bout it, though, most of the residents say the food ain't too bad and the wards are air-conditioned," Lyle added, trying to be reassuring. "He wasn't no child molester or anything like that, so you don't have to worry about bein' a target. His name is, or was, Garrison Bridgeman. Get it in your head."

"When can I do this?"

"Well, we gotta hustle and get goin' tomorra. We got the Fourth of July holiday comin' up, so you can get in and out before the long weekend. If we wait, that might blow the whole deal."

Ash took a deep breath and let it out slowly. "That's kind of short notice. I'll have to check with the wife, but I think I can swing it. Anything else?"

"Well, now that you mention it, you'll probably be takin' the place of that boy who did that awful murder last weekend. Still in?"

During the conversation, Ash was typing on the blank document, "BASH: The Life and Times of the Bay Area State Hospital." He figured the only way to make the rest of the story happen was to get in. "Oh, I'm way in, Captain."

"Okay, be here around six thirty tomorrow morning. I'd like you here before the staff checks in for the day. Go to where it says admissions." The captain abruptly hung up.

"YOU'RE GOING TO do *what?*" Sally J was astonished and nervous.

"I'm going to check into the nuthouse. It's not like I haven't ever done it before." Ash was referring to a long-ago stint on the detox ward at the VA.

"Well, there's a bit of a difference between an alcohol ward and a hospital for the criminally insane. I mean people get killed there."

"Listen, baby, this is a story with my name on it, and it'll only be a day. It's a hospital, not a war zone."

"Not from what I've been reading. How do you know you'll be safe?"

Ash was getting a little impatient, but he wanted to soothe his wife's worries. "Like I said, it's a hospital with doctors and nurses and security. Anyhow, you know I can handle myself."

Sally J sighed. It seemed like an overall bad idea, but she didn't want to squelch what Ash seemed to think was his big chance. "You sure you can handle this? How am I going to keep in touch with you? How am I going to know if you're going to be all right?"

"The best I have to offer is maybe a call from the pay phone. But I should be leaving there by six p.m., and I'll call you then. I should be home by tomorrow evening by this time. I'll take you out to the Holy City Café for dinner after I get home. Make a reservation for eight thirty."

Ash continued, "We'll be out of touch for the day. I don't think they'll allow me to have my phone in there. I can try it, though, but don't expect a lot in the way of texts. The cell service isn't too good down there. Once I get on the highway, it should be better."

"I don't like this. It's really scary." Sally J frowned.

"Yeah, it is, but this will be in the grand tradition of investigative journalism, the way it used to be," Ash replied. "So here's to the old school." He held up a half-full mug of diet root beer. He repeated what he told others and himself in an attempt to reassure his wife. "Besides, I know how to take care of myself."

"So you're not worried?" she asked.

"I'd be a liar to say I didn't have some anxiety here, but it's manageable. I have to think about how I'm going to take notes or maybe just keep them in my head. I'm thinking more about how this is going to be a great opportunity for me, for you, for the paper."

"Ash, I just don't know."

He put his arm around her shoulder. "I need you there for me, baby. This isn't just for me. This is for us. You're my muse, you know."

She knew he had a point. If he could get the spark to motivate his writing again, things might just warm up between the two of them. Maybe some money coming in wouldn't hurt either. "Ash, if this is what you gotta do, honey, then I'll give you my blessing and an extra prayer or two."

FIFTY MILES AWAY, Lyle was in his old oak rocking chair, on his screened back porch, listening to the river ease by. He was enjoying the cacophony of crickets and bullfrogs, loons, and bass jumping out of the water. The temperature was down a little, but the humidity was high enough that the stars were barely visible on a clear night, and there was a halo around the light down by the dock. He was somewhat uncomfortable since the meal at the roadhouse. It sat like a lump in his stomach. It wasn't like Lyle to skip his evening beers, but tonight he felt it would be better to just let things digest. "If only I could let out one good belch," but the belch didn't come.

He had second thoughts about letting this dumb-ass newspaper guy walk into a domain he knew nothing about. If something bad happens—well, nothing that much can happen in a day, can it? He started to perspire, which wasn't unusual when sitting outside on a sultry summer evening, something Lyle had done throughout his life. They didn't have air-conditioning when he was a boy, living on this humble plantation. The air tonight was stagnant, closer, maybe even oppressive. He went inside and flipped the air-conditioning on high and went to bed.

CHAPTER 15

Friday, July 1. It was a quiet, bright morning as Ash parked his mini SUV in the employees' parking lot, which was only about a third occupied. He thought it appeared very quiet, maybe even a little spooky. The night shift was gone, and the day shift was getting underway on the many patient wards at Bay Area State Hospital. Some workers scheduled vacation time to get an early start for the long holiday weekend.

The non-nursing treatment staff, including psychiatrists, psychologists, and social workers, due in at 8:00 a.m. would start to trickle in around 8:20. The morning was warm and misty, the sun getting an early start heating up the dew-laden lawn. Through the fence, Ash could see virtually no one on the grounds. It was a peaceful, still, summer morning.

He walked around that building to an old gray Victorian mansion, which was labeled Admissions/Discharges. Dawkins told him that all patients entering the hospital come through admissions, usually in a police van and handcuffed. He entered through the front door, which was unlocked. He saw and heard nobody. The old mansion, although partially renovated in recent years, had the musty smell of a house in a humid environment that had been closed up too long. There was a sign over one of the hallway rooms marked "Initial Processing."

Captain Dawkins, looking tired, emerged from the room and began, "You made it. Good. Come with me." They shook hands briefly and then entered the processing area. "Okay," the captain added, "I got your papers here. For today, you are Garrison Bridgeman. Got it?"

"Got it, Garrison Bridgeman." Ash understood.

Ward K3 is expecting you soon." The captain sized up Ash. A little stocky perhaps, but looked in good shape for his age. Dawkins gave up worrying about his own weight years before, after he and his second wife split up.

Ash asked, "So tell me about this Garrison Bridgeman and what did he do?

Dawkins shuffled through the files. "Normally that's protected information, even if he is dead. But I guess since you're him, you got a right to know." Dawkins handed Ash a thick sheaf of Bridgeman's mental health records from Colleton County. "Let's see. It looks like he assaulted his girlfriend with a knife, cut her up pretty bad. He was doing meth at the time and was pretty messed up. When he was arrested, he was talkin' outta his head. He got some smart Charleston lawyer to have him plead "not guilty by reason of insanity" and got away with it. Now he died last week from complications of years of alcohol and drug abuse, hepatitis C, and cirrhosis. He actually died at the local hospital after being pretty sick for a while at the jail. They was goin' to send him down here, but the judge up there ruled he would have to be treated medically and he would have to be stable before they moved him here. That didn't work out very well, so you're here, 'Garrison.' Got it?"

Ash nodded as he thumbed through the paperwork. There was a police report including photos of the victim, a young female with tussled blond hair and bruises around both eyes, and separate photos of gruesome slashes on her shoulders, back, and abdomen. A sudden vision of wounded soldiers flashed through his head. Ash took a deep breath and turned back to focus on the captain.

Dawkins went on. "He wasn't on medication right before he died, at least psychiatric medication as far as I can tell. For a while, up at the jail, he was on olanzapine, which quiets voices someone might hear, but it makes you fat too. His hallucination voices stopped because the meth wore out of his system after a few months, so they stopped his psych meds. You should know that they can't force you to take medication without a court order unless it's an emergency."

Ash wanted nothing to do with medication. He had been on antidepressants years ago from the VA. They just jacked him up and reduced his sex drive, "took a little lead out of the pencil" as they used to say. "That's good to know," Ash responded.

"Okay, then, change into these duds right here." Dawkins handed him neatly folded blue jeans with an elastic waistband, a blue work shirt, a white undershirt, underwear, and shoes with Velcro straps instead of laces.

"I figure you to be about five ten and one ninety, so I got you a large outfit. If they don't fit right, bring 'em back tonight and I'll give you your money back." Lyle chuckled a bit. "You can keep your cell phone, try to anyhow. Coverage is spotty, and keep it out of sight. If the ward staff confiscates it, I'll get it back to you before you leave. I'm gonna drive you through the portal down to ward K3, where they'll take care of you. I have to cuff you. It's regulation. Don't worry about it, I'll get 'em off you as soon we get through the portal. Once you're in the confined perimeter, we can't even use cuffs. It's against patient's rights unless they're under arrest or being transported."

Ash was changing into his new outfit behind a privacy screen as the captain spoke. The clothes fit fairly well; the shoes were a little large.

"You'll be under the care of Doc Kerrigan. People seem to like him. Actually, you won't really be under his care since you aren't really a patient. I'll let him know about you not being a patient so he doesn't shove all kinds of medication down your throat. I'll tell him this is a special research project, which I guess it is."

Ash returned to perusing the Bridgeman file. There was a mug shot of the man whom he was supposed to be, a white man who although was several years younger than Ash, looked several years older, unshaven, with disheveled hair and a trailer park mustache that was like a bushy extension of long sideburns.

"By the way, you'll supposedly be taking the place of the guy they hauled off for killing that staff member. You'll be assigned to his bed. Don't worry, they changed the sheets just in case you need a little nap. I have a grounds card you can pin to your shirt. Let me snap a photo for the records and your ID badge before you go. If you get in trouble, call me from the pay phone on your ward or your cell phone if you still have it. I'll be around. Otherwise, I'll be in to get you before six." The captain was perspiring and seemed a little short of breath.

"You okay, Captain?" Ash asked.

"I've been havin' some indigestion since we had that supper over at the café the other evening. Sumpin' disagreein' with me. I have a little Maalox in the office."

Ash was changed and ready to go. The captain snapped on the handcuffs loosely, which were then attached to a chain around his belt line. The cuffs were cold and heavier than he expected. The shackles were a new experience, like the real deal, frightening, with the sense of losing control of his body.

"We're ridin' in the police car today. Ya ever do that? Might be fun. You'll be sittin' in the back. We'll be goin' through the vehicle portal. You're with me, so they'll wave us through. Don't say anything."

Ash sat shackled in the back of the police car. It was just a hundred yards or so to the portal where the officer at the gate signaled the car to wait. The cyclone-style gate slid open slowly. The police car eased past the open gate and then stopped in front of a second gate. The first gate slid closed, leaving the car trapped in a no man's land. Lyle got out of the car and swiped an ID card through a transponder. There were two loud beeps, and the second gate started to slide open. Lyle returned to the car and waved at the guards behind the window. He drove into the main hospital treatment area, a campus like setting with scattered buildings looking like old converted barracks. The grounds were quiet as the patients were in their respective dining rooms or chow halls, leftover military jargon. They passed a softball field, a chapel with a simple cross over the door, and an ivy-covered building designated as the library. Lawn sprinklers were shooting intermittent streams of water into the air, making a hissing sound. There were several magnolia trees with baseball mitt–sized white blossoms and scattered long-limbed oaks and tall crooked palmettos reflecting the bright morning sun off their fronds. Ash thought, *So far, doesn't look so bad.*

"Okay, Mr. Garrison Bridgeman, you're about to be on your own. Gee-zus, but it's sticky today. The air is really dense. Haven't seen it like this for a while." Even with the AC on in the police car, Lyle was breaking a sweat on his brow.

Ash asked, "By the way, don't forget to e-mail that doctor about me or call him."

"I'm on it like white on rice," Lyle answered.

The car stopped in front of a one-story institutional-looking barracks or dormitory with a lawn sign that said, "Long-term units, K1–K6."

Lyle stopped the car. "Okay, out ya go." Ash swung his legs around; Lyle grasped him under the arms and helped him stand up. He unlocked and removed the cuffs and waist chain. Ash rubbed his wrists, although Lyle had not applied the cuffs tightly. The captain escorted Ash through the front door. "I hope you realize you're getting VIP treatment. Not just anybody gets escorted in by the captain."

At the entrance to the ward, Lyle took out a long skeleton key and unlocked the door with an echoing thud. Ash looked down a long hallway, only about six feet wide, with doorways on either side, which he figured were patient rooms. The floor was tiled and shiny. At the end of the hallway was an office with transparent fracture-resistant windows. They walked together down the hallway to the locked nurse's station. An athletic-looking black man, midthirties, with short cropped hair, emerged from the office carrying a clipboard. Charge nurse Corky Williams greeted them. "This must be Mr. Bridgeman. How do you do, Mr. Bridgeman?" Corky extended his hand, and Ash shook it firmly.

So far so good. Ash was on his own now. The door at the end of the hall where he had entered, slammed shut without the captain saying good-bye.

Ash thought about it and figured he wasn't being dropped off at summer camp, so he shouldn't really expect a good-bye kiss.

The residents were returning from breakfast. Apparently some had not gone to the chow hall since they were hanging around the hallway. The door at the end of the opposite hallway opened as the majority of the ward "residents" returned from breakfast. There were about thirty men and fifteen women. Some of the men were clean cut and nicely groomed, some wore disheveled hair and beards, with egg stains splattered on their light blue sweatshirts. It was likewise with the women. Some wore makeup, some were totally unkempt, some conversed, and others gazed nowhere in particular. Almost all of the residents were overweight. Some of the women showed some noticeable facial hair.

Ash was having second and third thoughts about pursuing this adventure, but here he was. *No turning back now. Let's get this show on the road.*

Corky addressed Ash more directly. Ash was impressed at how open and friendly this staff member seemed. "Can I call you Garrison or Gary?" Ash didn't know. Garrison would work. Corky continued, "I have to talk to you for a while. We have to get to know you."

Ash had no clue how to answer the questions but he figured that as Garrison Bridgeman, he would answer as honestly as possible. He was going to play the meth-addicted trailer park guy. How would he answer? Corky had a copy of the initial workup from the Colleton County Jail as well as a lengthy rap sheet and copies of previous admissions to drug treatment centers. Corky started with "So tell me about how you ended up here?" Fair enough. What could he remember about this dude? Okay, "I had a drug problem, and I did some stupid stuff while I was high. I hurt somebody I cared about."

This would be scored as a very good answer, taking responsibility, not in denial, acknowledging his addiction problems. He might be ready to be discharged in just a year or two.

"Do you have any medical problems we need to work on?"

"No, I'm pretty healthy, a little overweight. Sometimes my blood pressure is a little high."

Wrong answer. Maybe that was the right answer for Ash Roper but not for Garrison Bridgeman.

"Well, I see here you have hepatitis C and cirrhosis of the liver."

Ash recovered, "Oh yeah, those aren't causing me problems now, so I forgot to mention that." *Those problems actually killed the person you think I am.*

"All right, let's look at your psych meds. It says here you aren't on any."

"Right, I don't need them. I needed them last year after my offense, but I got better."

"Did you have any treatment in the jail?"

"Just some pills which made me gain thirty pounds. But after the voices went away, I just refused to take it anymore. Then they stopped it. I don't think I'm going to need anything. I'm fine."

Corky thought about how many times has he heard this before. "Well, let's leave that up to Dr. Kerrigan and the treatment team. Anyhow, you'll be meeting with your team probably next week. It's a holiday weekend, and a lot of people took off a day early. Dr. Kerrigan said he'd be in sometime today."

"The cop who brought me in said I can go out on the grounds today. He gave me this card," Ash said, pointing to the picture ID tag clipped to his shirt.

"Yeah, I gotta let you know the hospital police don't make that call. It's up to your doctor and the team," Corky responded. "They usually like to observe you for a week or two before you can go out unescorted."

Ash sighed. He had been misinformed. According to what he just heard, he wasn't going to be able to go out on the grounds and snoop around. He was hoping his doctor would get here soon. The doctor would be privy to his secret and let him out with a grounds pass. Corky continued, "So you know your legal status?"

"Yeah, I'm here because I'm not guilty by reason of insanity."

"Right, but what's your status? Your length of commitment, your community support?"

Ash was feeling a little panicky; he wasn't prepared to answer these questions. He was going to sound like a dope, maybe like a real mental patient.

"I don't remember right now."

"Oh, okay, we have a Legal Status Group we'll get you into next week. Knowing these things is part of your treatment. You get into any fights in the jail?"

Ash didn't know the answer. He didn't remember how long he was supposed to have been there. What do people say when they're really mentally ill? "Nothing serious I guess. It's jail you know."

Corky continued perusing the records. "Says here you were in solitary twice, once for attacking a guard and once for starting a brawl in the dining room. That was less than six months ago."

"Right, I was sick then. I'm doing better now."

"What did TransCom have to say about that?"

"TransCom?"

"Yeah, the Transition Community Reentry Agency. Didn't they ever visit you in the jail?"

"They may have. I don't remember."

"You know they like to see patients assault free for a year before taking them out to a halfway house."

"I didn't know that."

"Well, that will be a big focus of your treatment, making sure you stay assault free."

"Shouldn't be a problem, Corky."

"You know about the guy whose bed you're taking?"

"I heard something about him. Sorry about the guy who got killed. I guess you worked with him." Ash had no intention of spending a night in that bed.

"Yeah, it's pretty sad. The rules are getting more strict since that happened." Corky informed his new patient.

"How so?"

"It's harder to get out on the grounds, and they're getting tougher on assaults. There's more groups for the residents on violence prevention. Doug led a lot of groups that the residents liked. There's nobody to replace him at the moment. We're trying to figure something out. Sorry about that. We're doing what we can." Corky appeared frustrated but sincere.

"So how will I be spending my time?"

"You'll still have groups and activities. There will be more free time, though, with Doug gone, and we're down to just a half time psychologist now."

Ash decided to be a little challenging and do a little interviewing himself. After all, he was a journalist. "So you say they're cracking down and getting more strict, but at the same time we're getting less treatment?"

"Garrison, we're having unusual circumstances, and everyone has to be patient."

"Like patient for however many years it takes?" Ash wasn't scoring points. "What do I do with my free time?" Ash was hoping to track down Burton Peals and Tyler Goode, and talk to the people who knew Ernie Joe. That might not be too hard since his new roommates were Ernie Joe's roommates.

"We have games and books in the dayroom and TV. We're doing karaoke tonight. We'll have smoke break in the courtyard in a little while. You can shoot hoops. It's the start of a holiday weekend. Things might be a little slow for a few days. Right now, you gotta make up your bed area. I'll have someone get you some clean linen. There's a men's bathroom in your hallway. You can get a clean towel and state issue soap and shampoo, or you can buy your own at the canteen. We go to lunch at noon."

"How about phone calls?"

"There's two pay phones in the hallway. I think one of them is out of order, as usual. The social worker will let you make phone calls from his office during phone group, but you better sign up soon."

"Phone group?"

"That's what they call it. You just sign up for your time to use the phone."

"How about the weekend?"

"On the weekend, you have to use the pay phone."

"What if I have no money?"

"Then people have to call you. That's free."

"How about cell phones?"

"Ha, that's big-time contraband. Security issues, just not allowed."

Ash felt his phone in his pocket. His doctor would let him use it.

"When do I get to see the doctor?" Ash was getting more anxious. He wasn't able to control the situation as much as he would have liked. *Maybe the captain didn't think this through too well. Maybe I didn't think this through either*, Ash thought.

"He said he'd be here this afternoon after lunch. I'm sure he'll catch you then. Otherwise, the doctor on call will see you."

Ash figured that wouldn't help. He needed to see the real doctor.

The first alarm of the morning sounded, a repeating gong, like at the firehouse but much louder. *Ding . . . ding . . . ding . . . ding*, once a second through the loudspeakers. Corky said, "We're about done. Gotta go," and dashed into the hallway.

Standing in the narrow hallway in his underwear was a male patient with a gray bushy beard and scruffy hair. He was irritable, angry and disorganized. He was red-faced, yelling and waving his arms. In one hand was a telescoping radio antenna, fully extended. He was whipping it around and poking it like a sword at an unseen enemy. "Keep him the hell away from me," he yelled, pointing at another patient. He keeps coming into my room. What the hell are you doing in my room, you bastard?" he asked, taking a step closer to the supposed offender.

MIKE BARTOS

One of the psychiatric technicians ordered loudly, "Everyone into the dayroom or you own room. Clear the hallways."

A few patients complied; most of the others took a step or two backward. Corky moved forward and calmly asked, "What's the trouble, Ronnie? What can we do to help you calm down?"

"Keep him the fuck outta my room. He comes in there when I'm sleeping, trying to steal my stuff." The alleged offender, Jake, stood nearby.

Jake responded, "I didn't do anything. I was in there trying to get my CD back that I loaned him, and he says he doesn't have it."

Jake was a reasonably trustworthy patient; staff would believe him. Corky remained calm and skillfully talked Ronnie into relinquishing the antenna and was led back to his room. No punches thrown, no takedown—a good outcome. Staff from another unit was just showing up as the confrontation ended.

An incident report under the category of "threatening behavior" was required to be entered into the computerized module, detailing the behavior of each of the residents involved, probable causes, interventions, and solutions. After the holiday, there would be a weekly meeting with a dozen or so middle managers to detail all the recent incidents with recommendations to the treating doctor and team who would then incorporate that into the treatment plan with specific interventions and measurable results. But not in this case since Corky, as shift lead, decided to ignore the episode. Recently, at a monthly administrative conference, the question was raised as to why staff were not complying with incident reporting requirements. Nobody seemed to have an answer.

Ash went to room 154 as assigned. Although it was midmorning, the room was quite dark with the shades drawn and lights out; one of his new roommates was in bed, covers drawn up over his head. He wanted to be compliant and make his bed, but it was difficult with the lack of light. He flipped the switch for the overhead fluorescent light, which sputtered on over his bed. The somnolent roommate didn't budge. The mattress was a simple plastic-covered institutional type. Ash checked it out as if he were testing a bed at a hotel. Not too bad, not too good. The roommate didn't look like he would be talking much about Ernie Joe this morning.

IT WAS GOING on 11:00 a.m., and he really hadn't talked to anybody besides Corky. He wandered over to the dayroom. There were patients playing dominoes. One was writing on a notepad. The TV, behind a thick protective plastic shield, was excessively loud. A game show was playing, and no one was paying attention. Two middle-aged residents, one male and one female, sitting in adjacent chairs, were holding hands. Ash went to the nurses' station and requested some paper and a pencil and returned to the dayroom and started writing observations and thoughts about the day so far. Even if he didn't find out about any shenanigans, the observations so far were worth writing down.

The dayroom was furnished with large, plastic upholstered chairs, too big and awkward to pick up and with a low center of gravity so they couldn't be tipped over either. One of the male residents on the ward pushed one of these heavy chairs across the tile floor, which screeched in protest, and parked it next to Ash's chair. The resident was younger, overweight, white, maybe midthirties. He plopped himself in the chair and turned to Ash, presenting his right fist, not as a threat but for a fist bump. Fist bump greetings were called "dap."

"Yo, you're the new guy, the guy replacing Ernie Joe. I hope you're not like him."

"No, I wouldn't worry about that too much. I heard about him," Ash answered calmly.

"I'm El Caballero."

"That's like a cowboy, right? What's your real name?"

"El Caballero is all you need to know. What about you?"

"Garrison."

"Like an army unit, huh?"

"I never thought of it that way. So what's it like living here?"

"It sort of sucks. They're lookin' at you every which way you turn. They know what you say and what you're thinking. So watch what you say, or don't say anything at all."

"Are they listening now?"

"Maybe, but if we sit close and whisper, they probably can't. It all goes back to the Gray Ghost in the command center."

"Did you know Ernie Joe?" Ash figured now was a good a time as any to start getting information.

El Caballero responded, apparently not too worried about the Gray Ghost, "Yeah, everybody on the ward knows about Ernie Joe."

"So what was he like?" Ash wanted to know.

"Well, he was a big asshole and a bully. Anyhow, he ain't here no more. They dragged his ass outta here," El Caballero responded.

"Did you ever talk to him?"

"Yeah, I talked to him."

"So what did you say?" Ash really wanted to know.

"I called him an asshole."

Ash was thinking this interview was like pulling teeth. "So what did he say?"

"He said, 'Fuck you.'"

Nothing much for a story so far.

"See that guy over there?" He's an asshole. His name is Julio. He thinks he's hot shit because he used to be some kind of gang banger low rider. So he's telling me how great low riders are and how he and his buddies could ride rings around a cowboy, and I tell him I could ride a horse and jump over their cars and through the woods, and they could never catch me. He gets mad, and I tell him, 'The truth hurts, doesn't it?' Then he calls me a punk so I have to smack him cuz I don't put up with that kind of shit. Then he belts me and then the staff sets off the alarm and they write me up but not him."

"Why not?" Ash was making mental notes about the absurd confrontation.

"It's obvious I know too much, and they're trying to show me who's in charge. But they're wrong."

"So who's in charge?"

"I'm not telling you. You'll probably find out."

"Do I want to know?" Ash asked.

"It doesn't matter what you want. They'll tell you what they want you to know whether you like it or not. You're best off just mindin' your own business."

An accented female voice shouted over the PA system. "Smoke break in the courtyard." Virtually everyone in the dayroom got up slowly and filed down the hallway to the courtyard exit. Eleanor unlocked the door with a loud clank. Everyone including Ash filed out to the large fenced courtyard. The midday sun was overhead, and the air was thick and moist. The residents placed some scattered plastic chairs in the shade of a large lone oak tree dripping with Spanish moss. Six pelicans flew low over the courtyard in a lopsided V formation. One of the nursing staff wheeled out a cart with packs of cigarettes in plastic drawers labeled with patients' names to be distributed. They lined up quietly for their smokes and walked over to a metal box mounted on the wall near the entrance. It was about five feet off the ground. A patient would place the cigarette between his lips and stick the other end in a hole in the box. Pushing a button would ignite a spark that lit the cigarette. Most of them would find an isolated spot, preferably in the shade, and smoke quietly without talking, just focusing on the Zen of the tobacco, closing their eyes, taking a slow deep draw; and blowing out a long stream of smoke aimed at the clouds.

Ash quit smoking years ago, about the time he stopped drinking, but saw this as a good opportunity to mingle. He had read recently that the vast majority of diagnosed psychiatric patients are smokers, and about half of heavy smokers are psychiatric patients. Raise taxes on cigarettes; these are the poor slobs who pay.

He watched as one old bearded guy smoked the cigarette down to the nub, making every precious puff count as the blue gray smoke curled skyward. His fingertips were stained yellow from years of pinching the butts. Head bowed, he dropped the depleted remnant to the ground and crushed out the remaining tiny spark with his shoe.

A few of the younger residents, mostly black, took basketball shots at a crooked rim. The ball bounced wildly away in random directions. One of the young females, beaded strands woven into her braids, joined the males in the unorganized game, laughing loudly at the men, punctuating each missed shot with a playful smart aleckey comment, much as was the custom in her old neighborhood.

One of the young men tossed Ash the ball. "Hey, new guy, let's see what you got." Ash paused for a moment and then dribbled and eyed the hoop. He moved to his left, spun around on his heels, and drove toward the basket, laying the ball up on the backboard. It bounced, in and through hoop, rattling the chain-link net.

"Well, all right, you got game, my brutha." The young man introduced himself as DeShawn. He was slender and tall, his hair woven into corn rows. "Dap for you." He offered a fist bump.

"Thanks," Ash replied. "Maybe we can get a game going later." In reality, Ash suspected he would not be able to keep up with DeShawn and company.

Corky came out to the courtyard with his clipboard. "Ladies and gentlemen, let's go in and get cleaned up for lunch."

The bathroom looked like hell. A rank odor was evident as he waded through crumpled paper towels, leaving muddy footprints on the wet tiles. Toilets were not flushed, shimmering puddles of urine dribbled slowly along the grout between the floor tiles to a drain in the middle of the room. The soap dispenser hung halfway off the wall. Bring your own soap was the rule.

This diverse crew of mental patients was ready for the main event that structured the day, that being the midday meal. Ash, a.k.a. Garrison, was to remain behind until he could be seen by the doctor. The kitchen prepared a low-fat meal, which would be part of his default diet plan until the doctor could see him and write an order.

LYLE DAWKINS RETURNED to his office outside the Confined Perimeter and plopped into his patched and well-worn reclining desk chair. He sorely needed to rest after all the confusion of the morning. It crossed his mind that maybe sneaking a local writer into the hospital as a patient was not such a good idea after all. The available bed was that of a murder suspect recently dragged off to the county jail. There was an escape and a murder, and now he's tossing this sucker into the vortex. He'll probably be all right. He seems like a bright enough fella who should be able to take care of himself. Anyhow, it was his idea, wasn't it?

The murder was drug-related, or so it seemed. *It's all been about the drugs,* he thought, *anything to help solve the problem. Once it gets solved,* he thought, *it should be a feather in my cap, a pat on the back, a grand "attaboy."* He had it all planned. "Dawkins Investigations," that could be his business, on his own terms. Screw the bureaucrats. The customers, the businesses, the police, and the banks would come to him and say, "Aren't you the cop who cleaned up the state hospital? Yeah, well, we would like to hire your company to help us find out . . . find out whatever."

It was so damn hot, even with the musty chilly flow of air from the wall unit blowing right on him, he found it hard to catch his breath to cool off. The pressure started just below his sternum; it felt like someone sitting on his chest, and then a heavy dull pain spread to his back and shoulders. A tingling and then an ache flowed down his left arm to his hand. He opened and closed his fist, trying to get the circulation going. Perspiration increased and soaked through his uniform shirt. The feeling of being hot turned to chill and shivers as his skin went cold and the pressure tightened on his chest so that he couldn't breathe at all. He tried to yell out, but he could produce nothing but a muffled grunt. He reached for his phone and pushed the emergency number, which would go to the dispatcher twenty feet outside his door. The dispatcher answered as Lyle's face hit the desk pad, and his eyes rolled up.

"Hello, dispatch, what's your emergency? Hello? Hello." No answer was forthcoming. Captain Lyle Dawkins was found a few minutes later, unresponsive, clutching the telephone handset.

CHAPTER 16

The residents lined up in the narrow hallway as I entered the ward through the main door and tried to make my way toward the nurses' station to check up on the new admission. Everyone seemed to need me at the same time. Maybe they didn't really need me; but my presence, I've always suspected, triggers a longing to be taken care of, to get attention.

"Hey, Doc, can you change my meds?"

"Dr. Kerrigan, I need to talk to you right away."

"You need to call my lawyer."

"When am I going to see TransCom?"

"Can you change my conference time?"

"Kerrigan, you dipshit, I need a tranquilizer or I'm going to go off."

"I'm gettin' the shakes. Can you do something about it?"

"Johnny grabbed my ass this morning. I want to file a complaint."

It's like Mother Theresa walking the streets of Calcutta, except she probably was not called dipshit. I've always wondered, is this sense of being needed one of the benefits or liabilities of this job? The real problem is I can't meet all these needs. Maybe one at a time, or maybe a few a day. Whatever I can do.

I needed to see the new resident. He was already chatting it up and making friends. That's good. Somebody not too complicated to round things out before the July Fourth weekend.

Before the crew headed out the door, I wished them, "Guys, have a good lunch. I'll catch you this afternoon."

The new resident approached me. "Dr. Kerrigan, I really need to talk to you. It's important." He asked if I could see him right away. His name on the chart was listed as Garrison Bridgeman. We agreed it could wait until after lunch.

"Are you okay? Do we have an emergency? Can it wait until after lunch?"

"Sure, if I have to, but I'd like to see you now."

"You'll be first on my list, promise." He was the new kid on the block, and I had to get him squared away before the three day weekend.

The assembled group made its way through the door and filed down the hallway. Thank heavens it was quiet. I had about forty minutes to get stuff done before the horde would return from lunch.

It was Friday before the July Fourth weekend; and like most every other employee at the state hospital and the whole state of South Carolina for that matter, I was looking to sneak away a little early. The beaches were crowded, the ocean was warm, the bluegrass festivals were in full swing, and the flounder was frying along with the okra and hushpuppies. It was hot as hell, but the tourists crowded into every hotel room, time-share, and condo rental in Bayside. Forget trying to get a seat in a restaurant unless you don't mind sitting out on the screened porch or at the bar. I don't mind the last choice.

I must admit that I can succumb to this civil service fever, wanting to keep it light and get off the ward early. But business is business and I am a doctor and I have to clear up stuff before I vacate for three days away from this stink hole. Because of the details of taking care of loose ends, it was more likely I would end up leaving late instead of early. All those things the residents ask me when I walk through the ward do need to be addressed. I wasn't going to call anybody's lawyer; they're usually public defenders and civil servants themselves. Anyhow, that's not my job, and I don't have a lot to say that's going to help their case anyhow.

I didn't know much about the new guy, other than there were some incomplete records and Captain Dawkins himself brought him in that morning. Corky, the charge nurse, was telling me that he seemed okay, a little bit of attitude, and in denial of some of his past offenses. Also, he didn't seem to be actively psychotic, probably more of a drug addict with antisocial personality issues.

It was already after one thirty, and I still had a ton of chores. This was not the best day to be seeing a new resident. I figured I might as well get started.

Garrison was sitting in the dayroom, playing cards with a few other patients, chatting it up, so apparently he was not an isolative sort of fellow. The chart said he was in his late thirties, although he looked to be a little over forty. Considering the history of drug and alcohol abuse, I'm surprised he didn't look even older. He was a little husky but otherwise healthy. He had dark brown hair, fairly long, covering his neck in the back and a full beard, short and neatly trimmed. His attitude, posture, body language, and expression told me a great deal about his mental state even before we spoke a word. He seemed fairly confident and at ease.

I poked my head into the dayroom. Mr. Bridgeman remembered me from before lunch, a seemingly trivial but valuable piece of information. I knew

MIKE BARTOS

without asking him a single question that he had at least some short term memory intact, he could socialize, and he was alert enough that he could focus on a card game with his peers, that is, other residents, long enough not to get kicked out of the room. Believe me, this isn't a very tolerant group.

He came with me willingly—noted for the record. There was a small conference room with a reinforced window on the door; so if I hollered, someone could see in and give me a hand if needed. It's not the best idea in the world to go alone into a locked room with a patient who committed a violent crime and found not guilty by reason of insanity. These people are called "criminally insane" in books and movies. It's not a term we use in psychiatry. We don't even use the term *insane*—that's for the lawyers and judges. There was a sense that I would be okay talking to this guy, and I wouldn't need one of the big nursing aids sitting in there with me.

We sat down facing each other across the chipped formica conference table. Just as a precaution, those extra few feet between us made a nice buffer, particularly since I didn't know this guy.

I started. "Greetings, I'm Dr. Kerrigan. I'll be your doctor here. I want to find out more about why you're here and what we can do for you."

He leaned in eagerly. "Did you get a phone call or e-mail from Captain Dawkins about me?"

"Not that I can recall. I haven't been down to my office for the past hour or two. So I don't know. Why would the captain be calling me?"

The new patient sighed, "Well, he brought me in here—"

"I know he brought you in here. They told me—"

"Let me finish, please." Corky warned me he had attitude. "I'm not Garrison Bridgeman. Garrison Bridgeman died last week in Colleton County. He was at the jail up there. My name is Ashley Roper. I'm the publisher of the *Charley Town* weekly. I'm doing an undercover story investigating drugs, violence, and whatever irregularities I can find here. I'm not a patient. I don't belong here."

I was thinking, *I don't belong here*. Now if I had a quarter for every time a patient told me that, I could park all day at the parking meter in front of the city hall. I've been a psychiatrist for fourteen years, and I drew from all my skills and experiences to figure out what to say next. "Tell me more."

"I know this sounds ridiculous (and I must admit it did) but the Captain said he would let you know and he would pull me out of here around six this evening."

"So why are you not just touring the grounds? Why are you on this ward?"

I was waiting for the telltale disorganization of speech and paranoia to spring forth. Under the heading of "Chief Complaint," I wrote down, "I'm not a patient. I don't belong here." He gets to have his say, though.

"So, Doc, could you call the captain or check your e-mail or something?"

Most psychiatrists wouldn't bother, and I was pretty close to not bothering either. There was a computer and hospital phone right there in the conference room.

"Okay, Mr. Bridgeman, or Mr. Roper, I'll check." There were several e-mails for me, none from the captain. I called hospital security. They told me that sometime this morning, the captain had some kind of episode in his office and an ambulance and paramedics showed up. I relayed the message to the patient.

"They say the captain has taken ill and left for the day."

"Shit, so how am I going to get out of here?"

"Well, we have a program here, and you follow it—"

"Doc, please listen up. The captain would have told you if he hadn't gotten ill. One more thing. Check the *Charley Town* Web site. It's Charleytown.com. My picture, me—it's there."

Okay, he's sending me on a wild-goose chase. As they say, I was being "manipulated" by the resident. That's supposedly a crime in the mental health world. I booted up the desktop, logged on to the internet, and entered the web address. What came up was "*This site is blocked; listed as entertainment and recreation.*" I guess we can't have that. We were at the end of the road. Except the patient handed me his cell phone. That's not blocked. On there was the site for this weekly paper. The signal drops. He asked me to go over to the window; the signal was a little better there.

"You're not supposed to have a cell phone," I reminded him.

"The captain said I should have it. Let's try the web site again."

Okay, we gave it a shot, holding the phone by the window. The site was typed in, and we got "loading . . . loading . . . loading . . . loading." Finally, the site appeared. I know *Charley Town*. I pick it up when I'm in Charleston for the weekend. I let this guy scroll through a little.

Finally, a picture of the editor and publisher showed up; and holy Mary mother of Jesus, it was him. The internet connection froze out again, but there was his picture, along with some other staffers at the paper. He adds, "I'm on Facebook too if you don't believe me."

I looked the patient over carefully. It sure looked like him. "Mr. Roper, we have—"

"Call me Ash."

"Ash, we have a situation here, don't we?"

"How's that?"

"First of all, I don't think you're here legally, and the man who brought you in isn't here to take you out. Then we have a liability issue and a confidentiality issue and probably a big HIPAA violation. Oh, and there's your safety too."

HIPAA is the Health Insurance Portability and Accountability Act; it's federal law. Without the patient's permission, nobody can tell anybody anything about a medical record. I call it the Medical Records Criminalization Act. But that's just me.

Ash stroked his beard. "Can't you just take me out? Discharge me?"

"I'd love to take you out, but I don't discharge people from this joint any more than a prison doctor can let someone out of prison. I can't just walk you to the portal and tell the guards that 'This guy doesn't really belong here. Would you kindly open the gate and just let him out please?' They'd lock me up in a skinny minute. People leave here only when they get an order from the judge." They call it a minute order, despite that it takes sometimes months to get.

"How hard would that be under the circumstances?"

There went any plan I may have had of getting the hell out of here early. I had to calculate in my head how I was going to proceed. I rummaged through the chart I had in front of me. I was looking for the legal section. Strangely enough, there was a court order dated two weeks prior from Judge Max Colman of Colleton County ordering Mr. Garrison Bridgeman to Bay Area State Hospital. But this isn't Garrison Bridgeman. Or is it? The man sitting in front of me had a picture ID badge with his picture labeled as meth-tooting, girlfriend-stabbing Garrison Bridgeman.

I admitted to the gentleman seated before me, "It shouldn't be hard. That doesn't mean it will be easy either."

"Would it help if you called my wife? Call the office of *Charley Town* and ask for my wife. She knows I'm here. Don't take my word for the number. Look it up. I told her to stick around the office during the day. Her name is Sally J. Look up the number yourself if you don't believe me."

So I found the Charleston directory mixed in with the other South Carolina directories and dialed the *Charley Town* office. A woman answered the phone somewhat excitedly. I asked for Sally J. "This is she."

"My name is Dr. Kerrigan at the Bay Area State Hospital, and I'm here with a man who claims to be your husband and publisher of your newspaper."

"Ash is there? Can I speak to him? I've been worried sick."

I handed the phone to Ash. It was safe enough to assume that was his identity.

I heard him saying that there's been a bit of a problem, that the captain is ill and had to leave and that he might have a bit of delay getting out of the hospital. He handed the phone back to me. I continued to speak with the wife.

"I'll work on it. I'll get our legal office involved, and I'll call administration. This is kind of a mess. As I explained to your husband, I can't just escort people through the exit. Security will either need an okay from the captain or a court order or we will be in contempt."

"Can't the captain just call in?"

So I had to say this so both Ash and his wife could hear, "Captain Dawkins apparently is ill and isn't around."

"What did you say? You're tellin' me my husband is stuck in there?" this Sally J character asked.

"Look, Mrs. Roper—"

"And my name isn't Mrs. Roper. I'm Sally J Gaffney, okay?"

"You're his wife, though, right?"

"Everybody doesn't change their name when they get married. Get over it. Yes, Ash is my husband. Yes, Ash got sneaked in there by Captain Dawkins. It seemed like a good idea at the time, at least Ash thought it was. Guess it wasn't. I'm sorry I'm so upset. It's not your fault (thank you), but I want this fixed now!"

"Look, Ms. Gaffney, if we have any hope of getting this solved, I gotta get on this."

We swapped numbers; I gave her my personal cell number, which made her feel a little better. I then told her when visiting hours occur, and she rocketed back, "You mean he might still be there tomorra? He needs to come home tonight, you hear me? I had enough of this monstrosity. What's wrong with you people?"

I didn't create this mess; apparently these people did, but here it was in my lap. "Trust me, I'm going to work on this. I'll do my best. Let me get back with your husband."

She nervously replied, "Call me as soon as you cay-an. Ah'll be waiting." Her drawl was thickening as we spoke.

Ash was pacing back and forth in my small office. "So now what?"

"Okay, here's what. Since we're a forensic hospital, I need to talk to our legal coordinator so we can get the door open. I can't have you tagging around with me. I'm going outside the portal. At least I can get you a grounds card going. I wouldn't broadcast to everyone that you're not a patient. That could put you in danger. Just be cool. Go out. Go to some groups. You might learn something. Remember that when you write anything, you have to respect patient's confidentiality—that's the law—so change names and identifying characteristics. We can get sued. You can get sued. I'll try to get you somewhere safe as long as you're here."

It was time to start sorting through this messy adventure, and I was sure there was no written policy for this. I went back to the nurses' station to write the order for the grounds card. Corky read the order and protested. "Doc, he's brand new. You can't just let him out on the grounds. We have to do the normal assessment. Don't you think this can wait until after the weekend?"

"Corky, I know you're sensitive to people not paying attention to your opinions, but trust me, this guy is fine to go out on the grounds."

Corky complained, "C'mon, Doc, he had assaults at the jail in the past six months, and he's in total denial of his offenses."

"He hasn't caused any problems lately. Corky, trust me. I'll explain it to you. It's for the best. Just let it go for now."

"Sure, you're the doctor. I guess you know what you're doing," Corky sighed and walked away, throwing his hands in the air.

I told him I'd be back and he was to page me if there was any problem. I left the ward and headed to my office. It was two thirty in the afternoon; and when I got to the office wing, it was spookily quiet other than my steps echoing down the deserted hallway. People were bailing early for the holiday weekend. Good, maybe nobody would bother me while I straighten this out. I had all the things I needed in my little office: my easy chair, a phone, a computer, and a little fridge set on high with icy cold cans of diet cola. I spend more time here than with the patients. There's paperwork, documentation, charting, ordering and reordering meds, and a host of required programs and formats I still didn't understand. The surveyors don't say how these things help, just get them done or else.

First call was to my colleague and not so much friend over in the psych/legal liaison office. All I got was a recording, "*You have reached the voice mail of Dr. Gunther Wardell. Please leave a message. If this is urgent, please call extension 9643.*"

I left a message. "Gunther, this is Doc Kerrigan. It's urgent. Give me a call." Then I tried the main number for the department, 9643.

"Hello, you have reached the psychiatric forensic department at the Bay Area State Hospital. Our normal hours are 8:00 a.m. to 5:00 p.m., Monday through Friday. Please listen carefully because our menu options have changed. If you know your party's extension . . ." After another minute of this nonsense, I punched zero. That usually works.

"Just a moment, you will be connected with that extension." Good.

It was ringing. It answered, "Hello, you have reached the psychiatric forensic department at the Bay Area State Hospital . . ." No, I hadn't. I might have to go over there in person. That left the administrator. Oh boy, good luck with him. That's the next place to go. I dialed his extension, and a live person answered. "Administration, where may I direct your call?"

"This is Dr. Kerrigan. I need to speak with Mr. Desjardins. It's quite urgent."

"Let me see if he's available," she said with a thick upstate drawl. After a moment, she came back with "He's in a meeting right now. May I have your extension where he can reach you?"

"Look, this is really an emergency. Can you please tell him?"

"Just a moment, sir." After about a minute, she came back. "He says he promises he'll call you back in just a few minutes, or would you rather hold?"

"I'll hold."

There was some vague soft music interspersed with "Thank you for holding. Your call is very important. Please stay on the line and your call will be answered in the order it was received." How the hell many calls does he get? Who else is waiting? This was like ordering the Chop-O-Matic from an infomercial.

Eleven minutes came and went. My call was still important, so they told me. Then the line went silent and then a rapid busy signal. Good grief, I called back. The soft, sweet drawling voice answered again.

"This is Dr. Kerrigan again. What happened to Mr. Desjardins?"

"I'm sorry, he left for the day. He said he had to take care of some business before the weekend."

"Didn't you tell him this was urgent, and didn't he say he would call me back?"

The unnamed receptionist seemed to be getting flustered and defensive. "Well, I told him you were holding, and he said he'd take care of it. He had a lot of other calls, and then he ran out the door and said give you his apologies."

"Okay, so who's in charge right now?"

The young lady responded, "It looks like the administrator on call for the weekend is Bailey Simpson, Chief of Psychology."

"Can you put me in touch with him?"

"He comes on call at five, but I can page him now if you want."

It was 3:45 p.m. "Okay, give it a shot."

Nothing, nothing till 5:15 p.m. I was hoping to be on my way to Charleston for the weekend. Big date planned for Saturday night.

My extension rang. It was Dr. Simpson.

"Listen, Bailey, I have a situation here. I have a patient who is stuck here who's not really a patient. He's a newspaper guy that Captain Dawkins brought in undercover this morning, and Dawkins is gone and I can't get him out."

"Hey, Doc, you're shittin' me, aren't you?"

Right, I was hanging around the hospital at the start of a holiday weekend cracking jokes. "No, Bailey, I'm quite serious. I have him ID'd. I have his wife. I have his Facebook page. He came in as somebody else who's apparently dead."

"Well," says Simpson, "this is a bit of a cluster fuck because unfortunately Captain Dawkins died on his way to the hospital this morning."

"Died?"

"Yeah, he was found slumped over his desk, looking kinda purple, around ten forty-five this morning. The paramedics got here from the Bayside ambulance company and did some CPR and intubated him, but he didn't even make it to the hospital."

"So is that why Desjardins wasn't returning my call?"

"I guess. All hell broke loose when we got word of his death. The captain died on duty on the premises."

I was curious. "Does that make it worse?"

"Hell, yeah, that makes it worse." I'm sure the hospital and the state are going to have some manner of liability. We know there's two ex-wives and two daughters who'll be showing up in court sooner or later."

"People die of heart attacks. It's not necessarily anybody's fault."

"You're a psychiatrist. I'm a psychologist. We know all about job stress. I shouldn't tell you this but Dawkins was getting counseling for stress, and he was pretty pissed off about everything. He was getting ready to take stress leave. One of my psychologists was treating him."

"So sneaking in a reporter was a way of getting even?" My curiosity was really tweaked at this point.

"Probably, but you better save that for the judge on Monday, or Tuesday I guess since Monday is the Fourth."

"He can't stay here until the fourth or fifth. He's not even a real patient. We need to get him out," I insisted.

Simpson continued. "So he has an ID badge with a picture—his picture—a name to go with that picture, and a court order that matches the name and the picture, right?"

"Right, but it's not really him."

"Maybe so, but I can't order him released any more than you can. Maybe this guy isn't who he says he is." Simpson was sounding impatient.

"I saw his Facebook page."

"Sure, and there are fifty-year-old men who pass themselves off as thirteen-year-old girls."

"So who's in charge of security now with Dawkins gone?"

"I believe that would be Lieutenant Evelyn Garner. She's on the pager now. You might want to talk to her or try walking your boy out the portal and sweet talking the guards that he's with you. By the way, you never heard that from me. If you say anything about what I just said, I'll deny it."

"Thanks for the moral support," I said.

"I know this is a mess, but it doesn't sound like a real emergency. I don't think we're liable for anything since all the documentation is in place." The most important issue, of course.

"Well, this is documentation for someone else, not for this guy," I reminded Simpson.

"Right, that's what he says."

"I'm satisfied that he's right."

Simpson rebutted, "Sounds plausible, but I'm not thoroughly convinced. You know, the story of the captain's death was circulating around before it was general knowledge. Your patient may have picked up on something and decided to use it to his advantage. Do you know what kind of mess we would have on our hands if we just opened the door and let a dangerous psychotic criminal walk out without a court order? I suggest you exhaust whatever administrative and legal channels we have at our disposal before you stick your neck out."

"Can you help?"

"I can't spend the whole three-day weekend on this. We're not going to find a judge Friday at 6:00 p.m. I'm the administrator on call. We're short staffed, nurses calling in sick, a dead security chief, air-conditioning on the blink over in the admission units. We can't take anyone in right now until we get that fixed. A couple of county jails are howling that we need to take some of their newly adjudicated inmates off their hands *now*. And then we have this. So look, I'm around. I've had my pager go off three times since we've started this discourse. I gotta go. If you need anything, please hesitate to call." He hung up.

I looked at my cell phone. Three messages from *Charley Town*, and one text message from S. J Gaffney. The text said, "Haven't heard from u, on my way down." I punched in her number. "This is Sally J."

"Hi, Ms. Gaffney. Dr. Kerrigan here."

"I've been trying to get hold of you all afternoon!"

"Sorry, really. I've been trying to work this out without a lot of luck. Your husband is safe. Looks like the captain who brought him in had a heart attack and died later this morning. That's the main hang-up."

"Say what? You serious?"

"Quite serious, I'm afraid."

"I can't believe that. No way!" Her voice was sounding stressed. I was detecting the drawl intensifying again.

"Where are you now?"

"Just going past the Kiawah exit, about thirty minutes away."

"Look, it's against my better judgment, but I'm going to try to get him out the gate to the parking lot as soon as I can. You wait there until we can get there. Any chance you brought some clean clothes for him?"

"Ah thought of that, some shoes too, and some ID." She sounded quite anxious, not to say I could blame her. I did my best to reassure her.

"Look, Sally J—may I call you Sally J? Anyhow I'll do what I can do to help straighten this mess out, really, if I have to stay here all night." Heaven forbid.

She sounded a little shaky—maybe tearful—thanked me, and hung up.

I headed back to the ward. It was after six. Ash, or Garrison, whatever the case may be, was in the dining room with the other patients. They were almost done with the evening meal. I asked Sandy, the p.m. charge nurse if she could call over and have him brought back.

"They'll be back in five minutes. They're just finishing up. There's no one free to bring him back."

I waited somewhat impatiently; but soon enough, the ward door unlocked with a clank. The patients dressed in various shades of blue started making their way back down the hallway. Ash was chatting with an older female patient who seemed to be enjoying the conversation. I made a mental note that I should talk to the patients more often. I intercepted Ash. "Okay, we need to go for a walk."

Ash responded, "I've been waiting for you all afternoon. What's going on?" I suggested we wait until we get off the ward to continue. I told Sandy that I need to chat with Mr. Bridgeman and finish my evaluation and that we would do that outside. Fortunately, she gave me no argument. Ash/Garrison could be classified "low profile," not causing any trouble, staying under the radar. In any event, he was a positive replacement for Ernie Joe. BASH would hate to lose him so soon.

We left the ward, headed down a long hallway until we reached an oversized metal door that led to another hallway in which there was a long row of identical doors, like something out of *The Matrix*. My office was behind one of the doors. To ease the confusion, I put a Carolina Panthers bumper sticker smack in the middle of it. We entered my office. There was room for my desk, easy chair, and another plain chair, state issue. "Ash, I got a call from your wife, who is coming to pick you up, or at least try to pick you up. You need to know Captain Dawkins had a massive heart attack and died only a few hours after he brought you here, so obviously he's not taking you out, so I'm going to give it a try. No promises."

Ash turned pale and contemplated the situation for a moment. "Dawkins dead? Holy shit! So what now?"

"I'd like to get you out the portal, pass you off as a visitor with me going out. There's a good shot this can work. Your wife brought a change of clothes. You stay here. I'll go get them."

"Dawkins is dead?" Ash repeated. "Ohhhh fuck!" he exclaimed and buried his face in his hands. He mumbled, "Sally J was right."

I had to slip into psychiatrist mode. "Ash, listen up, take a deep breath. I need you here with me." He seemed to pull something from inside of himself. He became focused and attentive.

"Just stay here and be cool, okay? I'll be back in about thirty minutes or less."

"I'm fine. I can deal with this. I appreciate your help. Really." Ash pulled it together pretty quick.

I HAD TO act fast. The patient was signed off the ward, supposedly with me, and I would be walking the grounds by myself while the "patient" was sitting unattended in my office with a computer and a telephone, scissors, stapler, and letter opener. How many rules can I break at one time?

I moved easily through the three-gate pedestrian passage, getting "buzzed through," the first gate, showing my ID, and then getting buzzed through the next two gates. It was quiet at the portal this time of day, especially late Friday before a three-day weekend.

I meandered out to the parking lot, to see a pleasant-looking woman, midthirties, with reddish blond hair pulled into Heidi braids. She was wearing an ankle-length flower-print skirt and holding a shopping bag. If I weren't expecting her, I would have thought she was lost and looking for Woodstock. I greeted her. "You must be Sally J."

"And you are Dr. Kerrigan?" She appeared calm and in control, but her jaw was clenched, and she gripped the shopping bag tightly.

"Yes, nice to meet you. I wish it could be under less stressful circumstances. Ash is safe because he's in my office right now, but he's unaccounted for. I signed him off the ward. But sooner rather than later, they'll be looking for him." We sat at a picnic table in a grassy area at the far end of the parking lot.

She showed me the shopping bag. Inside were neatly folded khaki jeans and a polo shirt. I noted that's good. The patients wear blue jeans or blue sweat pants; employees and visitors are not permitted to wear them on grounds. There was also a pair of skateboarding shoes, which Sally J told me were his favorite.

"I need to take these back to my office for Ash. Then I'll need to bring him back out looking good as new. You can wait right here." I went to my Mustang and opened the trunk, which had several six-packs of diet soda in plastic bottles. The soda felt hot from sitting in the car all day. Good thing they didn't explode. I put two of the six-packs on top of the clothes and walked back through the portal.

I passed through the first compartment where I showed my ID badge and then through the second chain link gate to where security can inspect packages and backpacks. I stood there for a moment until Sergeant Bradley emerged from the air-conditioned room behind the glass to take a look at my belongings. I placed the bag on the folding table. He smiled briefly. "You workin' late tonight, Doc?" He eyeballed the bag and felt the soda with rubber gloved hands.

I distracted him with a comment. "Really sad about Captain Dawkins, huh?"

"Yeah, it's quite a shocker." He pushed the bag back to me. I took it nonchalantly. The sergeant sighed, "He will be missed, he will be missed."

"I guess you guys are all scrambling now."

"We're a little disorganized now. Dawkins had his finger on everything. It'll be hard to fill his shoes. Lieutenant Garner will probably be here all weekend to do her best to fill in the gaps."

"Well, good luck with that."

The sergeant sighed, and I caught a hint of an eye roll. "Thanks, we'll need it." He motioned to the officer behind the glass. There was a buzz and a click as the last gate unlatched and eased open a few inches.

I hurried back to the office hallway. I knocked on my door; Ash let me in.

"I have some clothes here for you"—Ash reached into the bag—"and I'll leave you to change."

Ash said, "No matter," as he dropped his trousers and slipped into his starched khakis. He pulled off what looked like a light blue scrub top and donned his red polo shirt. He folded his "blues" and put them in the bag. I put one of the six-packs in my mini fridge.

"Ready?" I say.

"Let's do this thing." He seemed a lot more confident.

We walked out into the warm evening sunshine and took the walkways across the expansive manicured green lawns. It was 7:30 p.m. but still bright enough to need sunglasses. I asked Ash, "Do you ever get over to Kerrigan's Bar and Grille?"

"Sure, they get some good bands over there."

"My family owns it. My brother runs it."

"No kiddin'? We've run some ads for you and done some reviews. I think your yam fries are awesome." I was pleased. Those yam fries are from my recipe.

"When this is all over, let's all get together over there. Your wife seems very nice."

"Thanks, and she loves the blues."

Approaching the portal, I signaled him to stay back and be quiet. "I'll handle this."

The first gate buzzed open. We weren't carrying anything, so we got buzzed through the second gate as well. The sergeant was manning the gate. I showed my ID and said loudly through the little round grated port in the glass. "This is a visitor. He's been with me all day. He's with me."

The sergeant pushed the intercom button. "He has to sign out. What time did he sign in?" Sergeant Bradley picked up a clipboard and looked at it with a frown and wrinkled brow.

Ash blurted out, "I don't think they made me sign in."

The sergeant asked, "Okay, do you have your visitor's badge?"

"I don't think they gave me one of those either."

Ash could see Sally J at the far end of the parking lot. She was walking toward us. "Well then, your driver's license would be a good start."

The driver's license and wallet were locked up with the rest of his clothes and shoes in admissions. Dawkins locked it up himself. No way of finding that now.

"I don't have my wallet."

"Just a minute." We were locked between the middle and outer gates. Through the tinted glass, we could see the sergeant talking on the phone. The intercom was off, so we couldn't hear what he was saying. We stood in the evening heat silently. The cicadas were buzzing loudly; there was the hoot of an owl and the sound of a basketball ricocheting off a distant metal backboard. I felt the perspiration starting to seep through my shirt.

The middle gate clicked open again. Through the intercom, the sergeant said, "Can you step back through the other gate, please?" We go back a few steps. "Not you, Doc." The middle gate closed. Ash is back in the first section.

"Lieutenant Garner is on her way over to help straighten this out. It shouldn't take long." We continued to wait; I continued to sweat. There were a couple of folding chairs. I remained standing.

A thin, nervous, and somewhat tired-looking woman with permed brown hair in her early forties entered the chamber from the hospital side. She was wearing a blue police uniform with officer's insignia. She addressed me. We've met on a variety of occasions related to hospital security.

"Doctor, can you tell me what is going on?"

"Lieutenant, this is Mr. Ashley Roper from the *Charley Town* weekly newspaper in Charleston. Captain Dawkins brought him in this morning undercover. He had him take over the identity of a patient from Colleton County who unfortunately passed away last week, but the court order was already down here before his transfer. The captain decided to let Mr. Roper assume the identity. Since the captain is not with us anymore, I'm trying to get him out of here. His wife is right here."

Sally J was looking through the first chain-link gate and yelled across the first secured compartment and into the second. "Can I pleeeease talk to you, Officer?"

The Lieutenant agreed to talk to Sally J and include me in the conversation.

Ash remained stuck between the second and third gates. The lieutenant and I got buzzed through the first gate and out to the parking lot. Sally J was frantic. She produced a passport from her purse and waved it in the lieutenant's face. "This is my husband's passport, okay? It's him. He's a free citizen."

Garner looked at the passport, saw Ash's picture, glanced at Ash through the fences, and looked back at the picture. "Well, it sure looks like him," she conceded, "but not exactly," as she flipped the passport closed. "Problem is we also have a picture of him as someone else who is a dangerous and mentally ill offender. Now I'll look into this. I'm not sure about this passport either. I know people who can get these made up for two hundred bucks. I'll keep this as evidence and have it checked for authenticity."

"You can't keep that. It's not yours!" Sally J screamed. She quickly snatched the passport back from Garner and grasped it firmly. The lieutenant tried to grab it back, but Sally J turned quickly and started running back to her car. Garner knocked on the observation window and said loudly, "Yo, I can use a little help out here." Sergeant Bradley emerged. Garner pointed to the woman charging away from them, braided pigtails jiggling. "She is interfering with process here and has evidence which she took from me. We need to intercept."

They both ran toward Sally J, leaving me alone for the moment. Sally J was in her car, but her pursuers reached her before she could slam the door closed. Bradley pulled the door open and grabbed Sally J by the arm and tried to yank her out of the car. As she did not have her seat belt fastened, she fell out easily onto the hot blacktop, scraping her knee. Ash yelled helplessly from inside the locked portal. I rushed over to the scene where Sally J was pushing the chest of the large officer and punched him on the fleshy part of his arm. I tried to intervene. "Will you leave this woman alone? She is just trying to get her husband out of here. And give her the passport back for crissake." Sally J stood there with the officer's hand grabbing her arm. Her pretty flowered skirt was torn, her lower lip trembling, and tears ran down her pale freckled face.

Garner said, "Ma'am, you're under arrest for assaulting an officer. I'm a witness. And as far as you're concerned, Doctor, you were trying to aid and abet a lawfully committed patient to leave the confined perimeter without authority. So now I'm going to suspend you. Even if he is who you say he is, you can't move people across the fence."

Sally screamed again, "Are you out of your fucking mind? This is false imprisonment, you rent-a-cop moron."

I added, "You don't have the authority to suspend me, and you don't

MIKE BARTOS

have the right to confiscate passports. And yeah, I agree, you are a fucking moron."

Garner straightened her posture and took a deep breath. "Neither of you are helping yourselves. Doctor, I'm the acting chief of security right now, and I do have the right to confiscate your ID badge, so you can hand it over. And keep in mind, we are sworn officers of the law, not rent-a-cops." I presumed Sally J hit a nerve. Being a state hospital cop is not a job with a lot of prestige; but then again, neither is being a state hospital doctor.

"Am I under arrest?" I asked.

"Not now, no. But you're in trouble."

"Well, then, you can kiss my Irish ass," which in retrospect I meant. "I'm keeping my badge."

"And you Mrs. J, or whatever your name is, we're taking you over to McMurtree and pressing charges. Sergeant, do you have that fake passport?"

Sally J grumbled, "It's down my panties, if you perverts want to get it." There were several onlookers in the parking lot. Garner thought better of that strategy.

"Let me talk to her a few minutes before you haul her off." I put my arm around her, and we walked away from the two police. I whispered to her that I'll do what I can and everything will be all right. She seemed comforted. I gave her a hankie to wipe her eyes. She knew what to do as she handed me back the hankie with the passport wrapped up inside.

Garner made a call on her radio, and an official Bay Area State Hospital Police car pulled up within a few minutes. Garner told Sally J to put her hands behind her and slapped on the cuffs. The lieutenant pushed down Sally J's head as Garner guided her into the backseat of the police car. In the meantime, nobody was getting in or out of the secured area, and it seemed that it was quite a show for the line that was forming on both sides of the portal. Ash was yelling from between the gates inside the portal.

Garner said she would drive into McMurtree and told the officer whom she replaced, "See that guy in the portal. Get him the proper outfit and get him back to his ward and recommend that he be put on special observation. Escape risk."

Garner drove down the shaded lane leading away from the hospital and slowly over the speed bumps with Sally J in the backseat. It was the same car that Ash had arrived in that morning.

CHAPTER 17

I followed the police cruiser out of the hospital over to the county seat in McMurtree. Lieutenant Garner led the somewhat disheveled Sally J Gaffney into the station. The desk sergeant and most of the cops in the town were familiar with, if not buddies with, the state hospital cops. Not exactly buddies because the BASH cops were always dropping off their problems here. Last Sunday, it was the murderous Ernie Joe. Then there were thugs who slugged their fellow patients, and those who attempted rape, especially on staff nurses. Why couldn't these hot shot security police handle it themselves? Could it be because the hospital isn't a jail?

The DA made quite clear that unless there was blood or broken bones, he wasn't going to entertain charges from the hospital, which had some type of assault on almost a daily basis. Patient assaulting patient—didn't want to hear about it. Patient assaulting nursing assistant—not so much. Patient hitting doctor—express route to the jail. There were a few cases of doctors hitting doctors—not his problem. Now there was the issue of a visitor hitting a cop.

The lieutenant then told the desk sergeant, Mac Dolino, "She took evidence from an investigation and assaulted an officer."

The sergeant was writing and asked without looking up, "What evidence?"

"A passport."

"Whose passport?"

"Her husband's, or she said it was her husband's."

"Where did you get it?"

"From her. I confiscated it, but she snatched it back."

"Was she a suspect in anything when this all happened?"

"Not really."

Dolino continued, "Whom did she allegedly assault?"

"Sergeant Bradley."

"Where's Sergeant Bradley?"

"He's at the hospital."

"Is he going to press charges?"

"He didn't say."

"I don't know, Lieutenant, not much to go on. We're going to have to ask the magistrate. He won't be so hot about coming in on a holiday weekend. Do you really want to pursue these charges? I don't think Judge Sandifer will be all that happy."

It was after eight thirty. Garner looked at her watch and sighed. She wasn't as anxious or as angry as she had been. She looked at the woman still in handcuffs. This probably was going nowhere. This was her first day as chief, acting chief really, and less than a full day at that. Garner decided not to play this note. She had plans for the evening. BASH was crazy enough without adding this mess to the in-basket. Besides, she made her point; she's the chief and people need to listen to her. That's all. People saw that in the parking lot. Just because she's new and a woman doesn't mean she should be taken lightly. She would be magnanimous and drop the charges. Besides, this situation might get out of hand.

Garner removed the cuffs from Sally J, who pulled away quickly and glowered at Garner, eyes tearing with rage. "What about my husband?"

"We'll work that out. We will follow the law. If he is really your husband, he'll be out. If he is who he says he is, he broke the law and took unnecessary risks. He'll be out, but it's not happening tonight."

"Who do you think you are?"

"I'm just doing my job, ma'am."

Sally J held up her reddened wrists and then pointed to her torn dress with spots of blood. "This is your job? You do one fucked-up job. How about getting my husband out?"

"We're not going there again. I can't do that, not right now."

"Yes, you can."

I finally decided to interject. "Lieutenant, I think this is more about watching your butt than doing what's right."

The desk sergeant asked, "Is this her lawyer?"

"He's one of our doctors."

"Psychiatrist?" asked Dolino.

Garner shifted her taser belt slightly. "Right, listen, I'm done and out of here. We can forget this unpleasant incident. Dr. Kerrigan, you're still suspended."

Sally J shot back, "No, no one is forgetting this incident."

Garner asked Sally J, "You need a ride back?"

"Go to hell."

Garner turned and left without any further comment.

Dolino took his report, ripped off the sheet on which he was writing, and fed it to a whirring shredder. If it's not documented, it didn't happen. He wasn't sure exactly what did happen.

I walked with Sally J out the door onto the quiet streets of McMurtree.

"Looks like you need a ride, a Band-Aid, maybe a drink. Anything I can do to help?"

"Thanks for your effort, really. I need to get back to my car and get back to Charleston. There's a lot I have to do," Sally J said, holding back angry tears.

"Okay, I can drive you back to the hospital. You need something to eat at least before you drive back. I could use some food too." She declined the dinner invitation but accepted the ride, obviously being preoccupied.

It was about a twenty-minute drive back to the hospital. She asked to borrow my phone and tried to make a call en route, but service was too spotty. No luck.

Sally J's car was in the lot, door still partially open, and purse still on the front seat. It was in view of the security kiosk, which probably contributed to the car and purse being undisturbed. Her phone was in her purse. Cell service is better at the hospital because it's only five miles out of Bayside.

She slid into the front seat of the car, fumbled through her purse, and pulled out her phone. She pressed a number on her contact list. Friday night, holiday weekend—it was going to be difficult. She left a message: "Hello, Rozzie, this is Sally J. Listen, I have a real emergency. I know it's a holiday weekend, but please get back to me."

She called another number. This time she got an answer. "Annie, Ash is in trouble. We need your help. That undercover idea of his is freaking out of control. He's stuck in there. Seven at the office tomorrow morning. I swear I'll pay you double. Get whoever you can in there."

She looked over at me. "I think I got it from here. Thanks a lot for your concern. Take care of Ash until we can bust him out. Keep in touch." She closed the car door and headed the car back to Charleston.

I wasn't sure what she meant by "bust him out." I wanted to help out, but now I was going to have a time getting back on the ward. At least it was worth a try. I walked over to the portal entry and got buzzed through the first gate. A different officer was behind the window. He looked at me, then at a blown-up file photo originally taken for my ID badge four years ago, and then at me again. The officer pressed his intercom button and said, "Sorry, Doc, I can't let you through. Orders from the chief. She said I gotta get your

ID badge if you try to get through, so I need you to pass it to me before I let you go back out."

Okay, they got me. I unclipped the badge from my lapel and slipped it into the small tray beneath the window. The officer looked at it and fastened it to a bulletin board and said through the intercom, "I'll take good care of it. Good luck, Doc." The outer gate buzzed and eased open a couple of inches as the electronic lock disengaged. I pushed it open the rest of the way and closed it gently behind me as the electromagnetic lock engaged with a hum and a click. It was too late to head up to the pub in Charleston. Nothing to do now but go home. It was after ten; I was tired and hungry. Grover hadn't had his supper yet either. It wasn't going to be as a relaxing weekend as I had planned.

CHAPTER 18

Sally J was almost back to Charleston when she got the return call. It was Roswell Chamblee, Broad Street attorney. "Hey, sweetie, just got your message. What's up?"

"Rozzie, I'm in a panic here. Ash got this birdbrained idea to get himself locked up at BASH down in Bayside, kind of an undercover story. I'm afraid I went along with it. Anyhow, to make a long story short, he was supposed to be there just for today. Now he can't get out."

"What the hell?"

"The chief of security was his man on the inside and sneaked him in. As it turned out, this chief had a heart attack later in the day and died on his way to the hospital before he could spring Ash."

Sally J was almost breathless with anxiety; her voice started to break. Then through tears, she said, "Oh, Rozzie, ah'm so scared. He's locked up in there with all those crazy violent people. You got to help him. Help me." She was too distracted to drive and pulled into a gas station.

"Jesus H. Christ!" Roswell had a lot of questions, but he could hear her panic and fear. This was not the time for a cross examination.

"Is he safe? Maybe I can talk to the doctor or the administration or somebody."

"Rozzie, this is such a mess," she said, reverting to her childhood upstate drawl, "may-ess."

"Look, I'll give you time to settle down. Do you want me to come over?"

"I would. I'll be home in fifteen minutes, but I'm so tired. I'm 'bout to give out. I was arrested today and—"

"You were what?"

Sally J sighed, "It's a long story. I'm okay now."

Roswell Chamblee, Esquire, of Givens, Levin, Pratt and Chamblee, was angry. He was a true Southern gentleman until he got pissed off, which he was now. "Listen up. Compose yourself, go home, freshen up, have a drink or two, sweetie, and I'll be over in an hour or so."

"Thanks, I'm gonna owe you one."

SALLY J GAFFNEY and Roswell Chamblee grew up together in Cheraw, South Carolina, a small upstate town, best known for being a stronghold of the Confederacy and later as the hometown of Dizzy Gillespie. They went to high school together, and Sally J was Roswell's date for the senior prom. Roswell came from an old respected family that fell on hard times. His family lived in a once elegant but now somewhat dilapidated plantation house. His daddy, Roswell Chamblee, Jr., was a lawyer who drank a little too much and took on a few too many pro bono cases.

Roswell was a good looking athletic teenager, six feet two, with dark brown hair and piercing blue eyes. He dated the cheerleaders and prom queens. But he was inexplicably drawn to the freckle-faced girl with braids and a middle initial but no middle name who wrote poetry and didn't have a lot of time for the old Southern ways. She was going to go to New York and be a writer when she had the chance and leave Cheraw in her rearview mirror once and for all.

That summer before college, they would take long walks by the tobacco farms and watch the field hands hang the large fragrant leaves in the open sheds. They would tell each other stories, and she would read him her dreamy poetry. He started to write some poetry and short stories, and she would critique them. He wrote all his poetry in rhyme, while she in free verse.

The spring and summer of their high school graduation year, 1991, was one of young infatuation. It was that summer, at age seventeen, that Sally J Gaffney gave to Roswell Chamblee the love she thought she would save for marriage. She had brought a blanket so together they could lie out under the stars and count the constellations. The gnats and no-see-'ems were impossible, though, so they fled to the screened deck behind the old Chamblee mansion, near the tobacco fields. It was late. Roswell's mom and dad had long gone to sleep. A quick thunderstorm had doused the countryside minutes after they found themselves on the blanket covering the wooden deck, listening to the rain pelt the tar paper roof above them. They laughed about how lucky they were. The rain dissipated, the clouds rolled away, and bright moonbeams shined down on the fields outside Cheraw, gently illuminating her soft pale skin. A chorus of frogs, grateful for the rain, covered the fields and trees with so much racket that Sally J and Roswell didn't need to worry about being heard. They could hardly hear each other whispering, although their faces were inches apart. But Roswell could feel her warm sweet breath on his cheek. He was her first love. No matter what happens in life, your first love remains your first love.

MIKE BARTOS

As fall approached, he was off to the University of Georgia in Athens, and she was going to Clemson. They met for occasional weekends, but he pursued career and fraternity life, while Sally J became more involved in her writing. Roswell's poetry diminished, but he wrote letters, sometimes mentioning the sorority girl he met and their future plans. Her sadness provided the fertile soil for more passionate poems. Eventually their correspondence stopped.

Roswell was out of her life until the summer of her twenty-sixth year. There was an announcement in the *Charleston Times* about the hiring of a new associate in the Broad Street law firm of Givens, Levin, and Pratt, one Roswell Chamblee III. She was engaged to the soldier/poet she had met, the man she called her "Warrior of the Heart." Still, it would be good to see Rozzie, maybe just for old times' sake.

She dropped in unannounced several times, but he was in court or in conference. She did not know if Roswell was married or divorced, or just happily or unhappily single. Late one Thursday afternoon, the receptionist told Sally J she would check with Mr. Chamblee to see if he was available. She pushed the button on the intercom. "Mr. Chamblee, there's a Ms. Sally J Gaffney here to see you. Are you available?" Moments later, Roswell bounded into the reception area; Sally J rose to greet him. He was as handsome as when she last saw him when they were eighteen. Instead of a polo shirt and jeans, he was wearing a three-piece pin-stripe suit, looking nattier than he did at the senior prom. "Oh my god, Sally J." He hugged her, almost squeezing the breath out of her. "Let's go back to my office."

Roswell never married that sorority girl; it hadn't been all that serious. Sally J figured that Roswell needed an excuse to avoid a deeper commitment. He wasn't ready as a youngster at nineteen or twenty. Who would be? He stayed single and unattached, a ladies' man to be sure but never really getting connected. She asked him why not, and the best answer he had was "Because, just because." He asked about her life.

She glowed when talking about the army lieutenant who left the military because that wasn't the life for him. "He's a writer now," she explained. "He writes for the *Times*, and he's working on some freelance articles, and he does a little poetry." He was a brave and strong man. He had been awarded the Combat Infantry Badge and the Bronze Star. But he was sensitive and creative. They were to be wed the next spring.

Roswell rocked back in his leather desk chair and looked at the woman who was not the first woman he had ever made love to, but the first woman he had loved. Her face was a little softer, her lips were fuller than he remembered, and her eyes were deeper blue. Her hair was not in braids that day but long and full, with a slight wave, streaks of blond accenting the red, draping over her shoulders. She met his gaze with her moist wide eyes. She tilted her head slightly when she looked at him. They were both silent for a moment.

"So, Sally J, you and Ashley are getting married. Congratulations."

"Yeah, it's going to be small. We're planning just a few guests, or witnesses. Maybe you'd like to come?" It would be okay, they were just friends now.

"I'd like to meet your Ashley," and honestly he did. He wanted her to be happy, perhaps more than he wanted her to want him. Of course, being a normal man, Roswell wanted to size up the competition he lost out to.

That next April, when the azaleas were in full bloom, Ashley Roper and Sally J Gaffney were wed in the park across from the Charleston County Courthouse, next to the statue of General Beauregard. Roswell was one of the few guests and witnesses. He sighed as he signed the marriage license but kept the unspoken covenant of friendship with her intact over the years since. Sally J truly loved Ash, but Roswell always wondered if her heart was filled or perhaps there was a little space left for him. He remained single, no easy feat for a young successful Charleston attorney from a fine background, now a partner in the firm.

SALLY J WAS sitting in her small living room with exposed brick walls. The air-conditioning hummed away, blocking all outside noise. She had just one lamp on in the cool quiet room, keeping sensory stimulation to a minimum. She was on her second glass of chardonnay when Roswell knocked on the polished wood door. She let him in, and they hugged quietly for a moment. She offered him a wine glass, which he took and promptly filled,. He sat across the footstool from her in a plush, winged easy chair. He was wearing a polo shirt and jeans. He started the conversation. "I'm sorry you have to deal with all this, but let me assure you you're not going to have to do this alone." When Sally J called Roswell, she was quite sure that he would be there. She had not spoken with him for over a year prior to the call. He was still on her telephone address book, though.

"So what's going on?"

Sally J gave a recap of the past day up to and including the arrest just several hours ago.

Roswell looked at her in disbelief. "You mean they know he's not a patient and they won't let him out?"

"Well, I don't know if they know it or not. Apparently they have official records, or at least official looking, with Ash's picture but someone else's name and history, and the guy who set it up is dead."

"So who arrested you and why?"

"That was some lady cop who took over for the late Captain Dawkins. I just don't think she knows what she's doing. She cuffed me and dragged me all the way into McMurtree, then decided to drop the charges. Then she split."

"But why?"

"I took Ash's passport down there for ID, and they must have thought it was fake or something. They snatched it away from me, and I snatched it back and ran away. When the big fat cop grabbed me, I pushed him. I mighta hit him on the shoulder."

"Do you still have the passport?"

"Oh crap, I think that Dr. Kerrigan has it. I slipped it to him before they put me in the police car."

Chamblee thought for a few seconds. "I think I can get an emergency court order and get him out. There should be a judge on call. It'll have to wait until at least the morning. When all is said and done, we can celebrate, and then I'll make you guys rich, trust me."

Sally J responded, "I just want my Ashley back safe and sound. This isn't about money." Roswell assumed she would eventually change her mind about a lawsuit. Great case.

"In the meantime, I'm going to see what I can do to arouse the slumbering bureaucrats."

"Me too," said Sally J. "First thing in the morning, we're going to have a meeting at the office. We're going to blow the lid off this thing."

"What do you mean?"

"We're going to put out a special edition of *Charley Town* so that everyone from Hilton Head to Myrtle Beach is going to know what's happening."

"Okay, but Sally J, that will blow Ash's cover."

Sally J pursed her lips for a moment and responded, "I think the word is out anyhow, and that lady cop said she wanted Ash under secure observation. His time is up there. He needs to be out. I think this will help. The bigwigs at the hospital and in Columbia have only one goal in mind, and that's to cover their asses, individually and collectively."

"And the threat of a lawsuit and big publicity might move them along. I see where you're coming from," Roswell added. "Look, sweetie, as your friend and attorney, I think you need to be really careful here. Let's try the legal route. Embarrassing the state government may backfire. Ash may have broken some laws. I'll research that a little bit, but if you want to start writing something, maybe you can use it later."

"Maybe you're right, Rozzie. I just don't know. I'm just so upset."

Roswell stood up and stretched. "I'm heading home. I'll see if I can find a judge in the morning. I'll let you know what's going on. I'm around all weekend."

"Thanks, I hope I didn't tear up your plans.

"Not too bad. I was going to go sailing in the bay tomorrow with a few guys. I think it's going to be pretty crowded in the harbor. Nothing is more important than helping you and Ash." He didn't mention his hot date for Saturday night, another younger woman.

They hugged, perhaps a moment longer than either one of them expected.

CHAPTER 19

Alyse Hazelwood came to Charleston by way of Athens, Georgia. It was time to leave the college town behind and find her career. She was twenty three, five feet eight inches tall, honey blonde, with sparkling white teeth and diamond blue eyes, and slender as a willow branch. She spoke with a lilting drawl, somewhat attenuated by four years at the University of Georgia in Athens, where she majored in broadcast journalism. While in school, she worked night shifts in town at the FM station, more for experience than the minimum wage she got paid. She could run her own board, cue up the music, segue through the ads, read the transmitter dials, and patter over the music intros. She started interviewing some of the local rock bands on the air and developing her own Twitter following. A local promoter hired her to emcee some rock concerts on campus. But that was Athens. There was only so far to go in a college town, and Alyse was not going to be enticing to the college crowd for long, despite the rather significant male attention that came her way. "A beautiful woman like me needs to be on TV" was her mantra.

A résumé consultant put together a nice little package with airbrushed color studio portraits, along with some audition videos showing her reading the news. Turns out there were a lot of pretty women who can read the news or interview the police chief, more than she counted on. There was some interest in Topeka and Bangor, but she got feedback that although she was "quite charming" she would have to lose the regional accent. There was some interest from a non-network station in Charleston for the *Live on Eleven* evening weather reports. Being a weather babe wasn't what she had in mind, hell, but it could get her in front of a TV audience, even if it was in a market barely in the top one hundred, on a station whose newscasts ranked last in the local ratings.

At her interview, the accent was actually a plus, something the Low Country audience might appreciate. When the program and news directors at WCHA channel 11 interviewed her, they had a premonition that this gal may bring some needed viewers to the struggling evening news at six and ten. News director Tony Most was especially entranced by this lithe and vivacious young woman. His heart went a flutter and his pate perspired beneath his toupee as he agreed to hire her. He thought she would be great on the weather, maybe even the sports, although she knew very little about either.

Two years out of college, Alyse had still been hanging around Athens because she needed her measly jobs. Now she finally had a real job, a job that would pay for food and an apartment. Her daddy was happy too now that she would be self-supporting but still only a few hours away. He thought, sometimes hoped, a rich guy would hook up with her, and so did she, but not a lot of wealthy eligible bachelors were hanging around Athens. More likely, there were nerdy professors who were too old and football jocks who were now getting to be too young for her.

It was a clear, azalea-filled spring day when Alyse arrived in Charleston in her eleven-year-old Toyota Camry. *That's going to have to go as soon as I can work it out*, she thought. It runs but it doesn't have the class she thought she might need. There were some college friends to stay with, for a few nights anyhow. She stood at the tip of the Battery, by the sea wall, looking out toward Fort Sumter and then turning and surveying the lush park with its central gazebo and Civil War cannons on display. She spoke softly, to no one in particular. "Are y'all ready, Charleston?"

WCHA-TV, channel 11, was located in a red brick building on a clearing surrounded by oak and pine forest on John's Island, the blue-collar neighborhood across the Ashley River from downtown Charleston. Behind the studio and business building was a six-hundred-foot transmitter tower or "stick" with flashing red lights all the way up to the top. The signal reached almost to Columbia, 110 miles up the road. The engineers always thought the location, right near the coast, was sort of a waste in that a lot of signal went out to sea and therefore half the potential audience was fish.

Alyse was born and raised on the southeast Georgia coast, in Brunswick, so she knew something about the climate she was now charged with informing an apathetic and diffuse audience stretching south to Hilton Head and north to Myrtle Beach. As an independent station, the news came on an hour earlier than the network-affiliated rivals. *The Ten O'clock News* continued to struggle against the local competition and numerous cable channels.

Now she was going to be "*Stay tuned for Alyse Hazelwood with the weather right after these messages*," although she didn't know much about forecasting weather. Also the station was low budget so the weather had to come from the National Weather Service, which prepares reports available to the public. The other stations paid for private weather services, and one of the competitors had its own professional meteorologist, the well-respected Gloria Considine.

MIKE BARTOS

She had to practice speaking in front of a blank green screen, looking off camera to monitors that showed her standing in front of a full weather map with arrows circling around high pressure areas and raindrops or lightning emanating from low-pressure areas. There were numbers for the highs and lows for tomorrow or five days from now. Part of her new job was to program the computer and prepare these graphics properly so the production crew could get it right when she was on the air, which would be less than three minutes.

It was early April. Her first night felt like she was stepping onto the Broadway stage. Bob Osterwalt, the silver-haired anchor, introduced her. "And tonight we'd like to introduce you to our new meteorologist, Alyse Hazelwood, who comes to us from . . ."

"Athens, Geowgia, Bob, Bulldog Country." Alyse picked up the rehearsed cue. "But we love the Tigers and Gamecocks too. It's been a gawgeous spring day heah in the low country, blue skies, low humidity, and more of the same for tomorra, but keep those umbrellas ready for the week-ayand. The National Weather service is calling for showas to move in from the northeast coolin' us down into the sixties by Friday, but ah hope it'll cleah up and wahm up by Sunday. Good chance for that. Back to the uppa seventies. Tomorra we can look for about seventy five degrees along the barria ahlands and eighty inland." She had to pause and look at the monitors off to the side of the stage to see exactly where to point on the blank screen. "Low tonaht in the sixties."

Bob, the anchor, chuckled. "Okay, thanks, Alyse. Looks like another nice spring day on tap for tomorrow. Ryan coming up with sports right after this."

Alyse didn't realize how much she was perspiring. "Note to self, more antiperspirant tomorrow." Maybe a little too much accent? That can be worked out. Tony Most was watching from his office. He was perspiring too but for a different reason. He thought to himself, *We definitely got to expand her segment.*

Over the next two months, ratings for WCHA news crept up. By June, Alyse's picture appeared on a billboard on the crosstown highway: *"What's Hot in Charleston?" Find out on the Ten O'Clock News and Weather Live on Eleven."*

The male demographic for the news continued to increase, and so did the advertising rates. There was Alyse, drawing attention, and her segment led into sports with Ryan Philmore. Her slice of time on the news increased to almost four minutes, with a two-and-a-half-minute ad window before and after. Her weather forecasts were peppered with human interest stories and weather preparedness.

The sponsors for beer and tires and other male-oriented products were lining up. Ryan had to pick up the pace as well. He started replacing interviews with the local high school soccer coaches with stories of NBA bad boys and segments of "The Best Plays of the Day," forty-five seconds of mindless entertainment. Alyse led the way of WCHA-TV morphing from local news into total infotainment. Bob Osterwalt, old-school broadcast journalist as he was, didn't like it, but that's the attitude that led to his getting kicked out of Detroit. In the twilight of his career, he thought he might as well go with the flow. After all, business is business.

AS SPRING HEATED up to summer, Alyse sharpened her on-air persona. Ratings were up eight points, and July Fourth weekend was coming up. The early part of the weekend looked promising, a three-H weather pattern was in place: hazy, hot, and humid. "A hah pressure ridge over Bermuda is pumping moist tropical air to the southeast coast. So if y'all are out playin' ball or golf or barbecuin', make sure to drink plenty of watah. It's gonna be a hot one out theyah, fer sure."

Facing right and moving her left hand deftly lower against the blank green screen, the viewers at home saw her point to a spiraling mass of clouds on a satellite photo somewhere south and east of Florida. "Now if y'all look heah, you can see tropical storm Cleo movin' to the north and east at about fifteen miles per owa, and she is expected to turn into a hurricane overnaht tonaht. The National Weather Service is calling for a turn to the north but possibly could affect our weatha by the Fourth, so stay tuned. There will be strong currents and high surf at the beaches by Sunday and July Fourth Monday, so be careful out theyah." Her hand swept over the satellite image of the storm and, with the back of her hand, gracefully traced a path along the Atlantic right to the South Carolina coast. She was so intent on passing along the message that she almost forgot to enhance her drawl.

That was the end of the hurricane story. "So let's see how the town of Summerville is preparin' for the community carnival this weekend." The next scene was parents and wholesome looking kids painting an American flag on a huge poster and putting up a dunking booth where citizens could line a tennis ball at a target, which if hit would have various community leaders drop off a stool into a tank of tepid water, a Fourth of July tradition.

She closed the segment. "That's for y'all who couldn't get your parking ticket fixed or worried about the potholes up theyah in Summaville. Back to you, Bob."

"Thanks, Alyse. Braves in a close one tonight. Ryan will be back to tell you how it turned out right after these messages."

CHAPTER 20

Elliot Desjardins was enjoying a glass of fine imported Scotch over cracked ice, taking in the view from the sixth floor balcony of his beachfront condo along the strip in the town of Bayside. The air was thick and heavy with dampness, like a soft warm cocoon. He wore a terry bathrobe, hairy legs comfortably crossed at the ankles as he stretched out on the cushioned deck chair. Sitting next to him on an equally comfortable deck chair and wearing only a bathrobe was Evelyn Garner, the acting chief of security. It was after midnight. The beach was dimly lit. Despite the warmth of the night, some intrepid young partiers down below were laughing, hooting, and drinking cans of Low Country Beer in front of a crackling bonfire on the beach. July Fourth weekend was getting off to a lively start. He could see sparks pop out of the wood fire on occasion. Soft flashes of thunderless lightning reflected from beyond the horizon. There was a dull rhythmic thud of bass and drums from a rock band at Captain Jody's, down by the pier, about a quarter mile away. He was glad he didn't live closer.

Evie swirled her own glass of scotch, preferring cubed ice, listening to it clink against the crystal. She put the glass down on the table between the two deck chairs and picked up a neatly wrapped joint and lit it with a small lighter. She squinted as she drew hard, trying to keep it burning. The end glowed brighter. She tilted her head back and blew a narrow column of the herb scented smoke out to sea. She offered it to her partner for the evening. He waved it away saying, "I'm fine with the drink here."

"Good stuff, you ought to try it," she suggested.

"I'm not really into it. I'm old school, if you know what I mean. Where did this stuff come from?"

"The usual." They both chuckled.

After dropping off the hippie bitch at the McMurtree police station, she figured she had enough for one week and certainly one day, the day she ascended to become acting chief of security. She would have to be busy at the hospital all weekend. New job, longer hours, still same old pay. With any luck, she could be appointed to the chief job, get promoted to captain, an extra grand a month. Evelyn Garner was proud of her performance today, stepping onto the big shoes of the big man, cracking down, and bringing law and order to this rowdy hellhole of a hospital.

The good will of the administrator wouldn't hurt either. She lived in a rented condo in Bayside but couldn't afford beachfront luxury like Elliot. After a quick detour home to lose the uniform and badge, she called and dropped by; Elliot was usually around Friday evening. They ordered pizza. He would eat five big slices, so they ordered two large pizzas. She was hungry too. He insisted on anchovies, at least on one. After a toke or two, she wouldn't notice the smell.

The weed and the alcohol made her a little dizzy. She was tired but amorous now. A little touching wouldn't be a bad idea. The pale, corpulent, balding man next to her could fill the bill, or whatever needed filling. She loosened the belt on her robe and opened it, revealing a taut, lean tan body, much in contrast to his. She liked the warm air caressing her skin. Elliot was holding his empty glass on his rotund belly, eyes closed, but woke himself after he issued a sharp guttural snort.

Tonight might not be the night, maybe just drift off to sleep. "Hey, Elliott," she nudged her reluctant paramour.

"Yeah, I'm with you. It's been a long week. How about we get frisky tomorrow?"

She was disappointed but not totally. It was after midnight, and sleep would be welcome, but spending two nights in a row here, maybe not so welcome. They returned inside to the cool bedroom. Evie had decided tonight would be a good night to kill two birds with one stone, please the boss, and please herself. It didn't look like it was going to happen. At least the sheets were crisp and clean. She disrobed and slipped naked into bed. Elliot did the same. She liked the warmth of his hairy body, and the lights were out, so at least she didn't have to look at him. Although she often thought him to be an asshole, he had his sweet moments. He was probably twice her weight, but she held the scotch better than he did. His alcohol-enhanced snoring didn't bother her. She thought of him as a big tomcat purring. "Shit," she said to herself, "this isn't working."

She was sleepy but still tense, as was often the case. She gave him a couple of pushes on the shoulder. He awoke. She kissed his neck and stroked him. That aroused him further. She needed it now. He breathed deeply and groaned. He wasn't all that talented of a lover, but he was big enough, and that would work. "C'mon, Mama's waiting. Mama doesn't like to be disappointed, does she?" She thought, *Do I have to do all the work around here?* She slapped

MIKE BARTOS

his face; that awoke him. His eyes popped open. She growled, "What the hell are you doing, you son of a bitch?"

He grabbed her and tossed her to the other side of the bed. She was wiry but thin and light. She smacked him again, on the other side of the face, and then smacked his bulbous butt, leaving a palm print.

He rolled on top of her. She grunted, "El-li-ot . . . can't . . . breathe." She pushed at him until he rolled to one side. Being flattened like a pancake wasn't in her personal Kama Sutra, so Evelyn took charge and rolled him on his back and sat up on top of him. Now he was almost ready. She smacked him one more time, more than playfully hard. He yelled, "Shit, Evie, you trying to kill me?"

"Just trying to get your attention, you bastard."

She straddled him. She was so wet and ready, and he was hard out of his mind. He pushed and she groaned. He pushed again, and she shrieked and panted. They came quickly and together. She slumped over on top of him.

He whispered, "Who's your daddy?"

She returned the question with a question. "Who's your mama, big boy?" She was still on top of him when Elliot started to snore loudly.

That was done with. Now she could definitely sleep. No way in hell was she coming back here tomorrow night.

CHAPTER 21

The last Ash saw of his wife, she was being pushed into a police car, and he was helpless to intervene. Ash was now on specialized observation, generally known as one-to-one. That is, a nursing staff member was assigned to be with him, and only with him, around the clock. No doctor had ordered it.

I was ordered off grounds and couldn't get in to write orders, but I was still a licensed MD and had privileges at the hospital. I could log in orders if I could find a hospital computer outside the confined perimeter. A security cop can't remove those privileges.

I didn't have a key to the administration building or library, which had hospital computers but were locked up securely for the weekend. The last bit of control I could imagine was to get hold of the OD, who was covering for the night. Tonight it was Morty Frizell, one of the regular psychiatrists moonlighting on night duty. Our basic salary was good; but for many doctors, it wasn't enough. Morty had an ex-wife and two young kids who ate up a lot of dough, so he worked one night a week pulling down sixteen hours of extra pay until 8:00 a.m.

It was after 11:00 p.m. when I dialed the hospital operator and asked her to page Dr. Frizell to my cell phone. Ten minutes later, he returned the call.

"Hey, Doc, Morty here. What's going on at this hour?"

"Listen, Morty, I've got a situation here. I have a new patient on K3, name of Garrison Bridgeman. Apparently he's on a one-to-one. Just to let you know, he's actually a reporter and his real name is Ashley Roper. I have an ID, passport, Web site, his wife, whatever. Problem is that Dawkins brought him in under a fake ID, bad plan especially since Dawkins died today. Now we can't get him out."

Morty answered, "I think I know this guy, I mean not personally, but he's the *Charley Town* guy, right? I subscribe to his paper, comes every week, great singles ads. You oughta check 'em out, Patrick. They're wild, man."

"Maybe another time. I'm calling you because I'm locked out of the grounds and somebody needs to check in on him and make sure he's doing okay. Don't force-feed him meds. He doesn't need them. As far as—"

"How'd you get locked out?"

"Long story. Lieutenant Garner filling in for Dawkins can't figure out squat. I tried to walk this guy out, and she busts me and takes my ID badge. I guess she figures she's in charge and no one is going to second guess her. In the meantime, we have a citizen locked up on a chronic ward."

"What are you gonna do?"

"I'm working on it, believe me. Pass the word along to the weekend ODs, would you?"

"Sure enough, Doc."

"I was starting to say maybe he doesn't need to be on a one-to-one. What do you think?"

"Well, he's not dangerous or suicidal, right? Do you think a ninety-eight-pound nursing assistant will protect him? Sounds like a waste of resources since you asked. Who ordered it anyhow?"

"It wasn't me, and I know police can't give orders. Maybe one of the other ward MDs did."

"Okay, I'll check it out. Go home and go to sleep." Morty advised.

I headed to my trusty Mustang. Home is only about fifteen minutes from the hospital, along a marsh creek. It's a fine wooden house eight feet above the ground on reinforced timbers to protect against floods. It's not very big, two bedrooms, more than enough for me and Grover, my faithful golden retriever, and an occasional female guest.

I'VE BEEN MARRIED and divorced twice, but I do have a true love, my Baldwin baby grand piano, which dominates the living room. I've played blues all my life. I've never become master of the keyboard, never really had great chops; but with the right tune and a bass and drums behind me, I can perform a number or two.

The blues have a rhythm, form, and structure that allow the musician to play with just about anyone else who knows blues. This is music from the heart and for the heart. Playing the blues is almost better than whiskey or a Valium or even a little weed. Maybe in my next life I could be a blues or jazz pianist. A little voice inside my head sometimes says, "What about this life?" Maybe with three hours of practice a day, I could get there.

Grover was in the yard, panting and jumping like a kid on a trampoline. It was late; he was hungry. I squatted down and rubbed the dog's neck and face vigorously. What could be better than this? "C'mon, boy, I got you something good. Yeah, boy." The dog attacked a full can of Alpo and then jogged over to me, wagging his tail.

What to cook at midnight? Fortunately, there was a bowl of leftover spaghetti with the sauce I concocted a couple of nights ago. Nothing that a little Chianti mixed in with and heated couldn't help. I ate the whole damn thing. Grover and me, two hungry bachelors chowing down. I promised myself to start losing weight after this whole mess blows over.

I thought I'd wrap it up with a good shot of Irish whiskey. I sank into the leather couch, flipped on the TV, and gazed at a program showing cop car chases. Mindless enough. Grover rested his head on his front paws, let out a big sigh, and slept on the floor by the couch. That's the last I remember about that Friday night.

CHAPTER 22

A sh was relegated to a small room with just a cot. The door was unlocked and open, and a young male nursing aid was assigned to watch him. This meant that he had to keep him in view throughout the shift. Ash was able to get a hold of a three day old *Atlanta Journal Constitution* to pass the time, which he read while sitting on the side of the bed. Rudy, the psychiatric technician, sat in a wooden chair in the hallway outside the door with a clipboard on his lap. The chair was tilted backward, resting against the wall in the hallway. Rudy rested his head against the wall, intermittently dozing. Whenever patients tried to pass, they had to tap the chair, which would awaken Rudy, who had his feet propped against the opposite wall, totally blocking the hallway. Armando Ruiz, the shift lead for the evening, had to counsel Rudy several times about this saying, "Rudy, put your chair down. You are not looking professional."

"Sorry, boss," he said as he got into a more attentive position for the next ten minutes. In Rudy's defense, one might say that watching an otherwise healthy patient read the newspaper could be quite tedious and soporific. Rudy's job wasn't to wrestle with or constrain an unruly patient but just to "observe and report" and most of all to document.

Documentation was the key to meeting state and federal requirements. Every fifteen minutes (or in medical jargon "q 15 minutes"), Rudy had to make a notation. At 10:15 p.m., he wrote "quiet, reading paper." This was identical to the previous eight notations.

Ash was worried about Sally J. His cell phone was confiscated when he was brought back to the ward, and a notation was made on his chart for possessing contraband. The chart note read. *"Resident brought back to ward by hospital security. Searched for contraband, cell phone confiscated and sent to patient locker. Teaching provided to resident about rules concerning contraband."*

The teaching in this case was a quick lecture from Armando, which consisted of "We don't allow no cell phones in here, bro."

Sally J finally got through to the ward via the hospital operator. The conversation was not helpful. She had called while waiting for Roswell to show up. She had asked for "whoever is in charge." After about five minutes of listening to background conversation and random noise, Armando picked up.

"This is Sally J Gaffney calling. My husband Ash Roper is a new patient there. Is he all right?"

Armando knew the rules. First of all, there was no official listing for any Ashley Roper on the ward. Second, he had to follow federal guidelines as mandated by HIPAA, which basically says you can't tell anybody anything about any patient without written authorization.

"Sorry, ma'am, we can't give out any information over the phone about patients here."

"I forgot, he is going by some other name—"

"As I told you, we can't give any information about who is or who is not here."

Sally J was getting quite flustered as her drawl leaked out again, "Well, how in the hay-ill am ah supposed to know how he's doin'?"

"I'll give you the patient pay phone number, ma'am. It's late and it's after phone hours. You'll need to call back in the morning." He gave her the phone number and hung up. Likewise, Ash didn't know how Sally J was doing, and he couldn't make a call. He asked for a pencil and some paper. Rudy told him fine, but the mail probably won't be going out until Tuesday. Well, maybe someone will take it out; hopefully, he'd be out well before then anyhow. Ash obtained a legal pad and a pen cartridge in place of a full ballpoint pen. A ballpoint pen could be used as a weapon.

Ash started writing a summary of what transpired so far that day. For the next observation report, Rudy documented that his patient was engaged in "letter-writing behavior." While Ash was writing and Rudy was dozing, two patients, one an oversized country boy and a smaller compact Hispanic man, poked their heads inside the door. The Hispanic guy asked, "Hey, man, what you in for? You got papers?"

The big boy laughed. "I hope you ain't no child molester. Really, you better not be."

Rudy snapped awake and looked at them. "Jesse, Harold, you guys beat it. This isn't your hallway. You need to be in bed. It's late."

As the two patients walked away, he heard Jesse, the smaller man say, "Yeah, I heard he's a pervert—fucked his daughter or something like that."

Ash had done a little homework before this fiasco and knew that patients in the state mental hospitals don't have "papers" but prison inmates do. These are documents listing the charges, conviction, and sentence. In prison, inmates are often coerced into showing their "papers." Child molesters are not treated well by fellow inmates. Fortunately, Bridgeman didn't have any history of that nature; but still, making trouble is a popular pastime in this otherwise dreadfully boring place. Ash was hoping he wouldn't have to deal with these mutants, but he was immersed in this alternate reality. He had a staff member watching him. Maybe that was a good thing after all.

It was after eleven, time for shift change. Rudy went to report and was replaced by ninety-five-pound Sylvia Concepcion. Armando complained during shift report to the night supervisor that there wasn't enough nursing staff to assign extra people to sit with a clipboard all night long, watching one person. It was a holiday weekend, everyone wanted time off. There were about eight nursing staff crowded into the nursing station, some coming on for the night or NOC shift, and some going off. The night nursing supervisor was there at Armando's request. "Look, we got this new guy who's doing nothing. He doesn't need to be on one-to-one."

The supervisor asked, "Who's been watching him?"

Rudy responded, "I have. He's just been sleeping, reading the paper, writing—nothing much. Jesse and Harold were messing with him, but he didn't do anything. I think he's okay."

"Who ordered it?"

Armando looked embarrassed. "The cop who brought him in said he was an escape risk and we should put him on a one-to-one."

"Did you get a doctor's order?"

Micky, the night supervisor, looked on the computer and, after a few clicks and flashes, said, "Nope, nobody ordered it."

"So should we just DC it?" DC is verbal shorthand for "discontinue."

Micky answered, "Let's get the night OD to do that. Who is it?"

"I think it's Dr. Frizell. I'll give him a call," said Patty Candler, the RN charge nurse coming on for the NOC shift.

"Okay, if you wait an hour before you call and Dr. Frizell stops the one-to-one, you'll have an extra staff for the night. I'd love to stay, but there's hell breaking loose over on the L units. I'd better get over there."

About half past midnight, Dr. Morton Frizell showed up on ward K3. He had been distracted by numerous pages, crises, and the normal business of a mental hospital with 517 patients at night. He had forgotten to look in on Ash, and he was glad he was reminded. Tonight he sported a knee-length white lab coat with red stitching over the breast pocket: "Morton Frizell MD" in stylized cursive writing. He asked to see the new patient.

Ash was asleep on the cot in the unlocked seclusion room. Petite Sylvia Concepcion was now sitting in the hallway outside the room, intently focused on a paperback Sudoku book. Frizell looked at Sylvia and said, "Take five. I'll watch him."

He entered the small bare room. "Hi, I'm Dr. Frizell. Your nursing staff, and Dr. Kerrigan asked me to look in on you. Dr. Kerrigan told me who you are."

Ash woke up a little disoriented. He took a moment to find his bearings. "I'm glad you're here. Who did he tell you I am?"

"You're Ashley Roper of *Charley Town*. I know who you are. I read your paper every week. I get it here at the hospital. It's a good way to pass the time. I'm a fan. So what's the deal? You doing some kind of a story?"

"Dr. Frizell, I'd love to chat, but I'm stuck here and I can't get any word in or out. I don't know how my wife is. She doesn't know how I am. Could you call her and give her some word?"

"Oh, sure. You know I would love to write some kind of psychiatry advice column. You think you could take a look at some ideas I have?"

"We can talk about that later. In the meantime, I'm sort of frantic here. I really need your help."

"Uh-huh."

"Okay, if you can help me out here, I'll get you a column in the print and online edition."

"You have an online edition?"

"Just started up a few weeks ago."

"What's your wife's number?"

After Ash gave him the number, Frizell added, "Then there's this business of you being on this close observation. I'm getting pressure to take you off. It's not like you're going to escape through three locked doors then over an electrified fence. I guess you'll be out soon enough anyhow."

"I know, but I'm getting harassed by some of the other patients about them thinking I'm a child molester."

"So you're peers are threatening you?"

"Uhmm, I don't think you should refer to those assholes as my peers."

"Right, anyhow, we don't have enough nurses on a holiday weekend."

"Tell me, Doctor, what would you want if you were in my shoes?"

"These guys talk and talk. I think you'll be just fine. Just tell staff if there's any problem. I gotta take you off."

"I don't know."

"Hey, if something happens to you, I don't get my column, do I? And if you're looking for a better story, you won't get it with some little nurse's aide, sitting outside your door."

"Point well taken. Just call my wife, would you?"

Frizell got up to leave. "I love you, man."

About fifteen minutes later, Nurse Patty roused Ash. "Mr. Bridgeman, you can go back to your room." Ash hadn't spent any time in his shared room since he put sheets on his bed shortly after his arrival. It was quite late. Despite his lack of physical activity all evening, he was exhausted. The day began so long ago, almost in another dimension, with the now deceased Captain Dawkins escorting him into this hellhole. It was after 1:00 a.m. His room was dark, with two other beds with unconscious forms under blankets. Both men were snoring loudly. Ash suspected it was the result of the endemic overweight and heavy medication administered to keep the internal demons at bay. He drifted back to his infantry days in the Gulf War, sleeping with one eye open.

CHAPTER 23

About the time that Ash was getting to bed in his assigned room, Sally J got a phone call from Dr. Frizell. She was sleeping heavily with the aid of most of a bottle of Cabernet. The sound of the ringing phone slowly plowed through her mental haze until her eyes popped open. Her head was pounding from the wine. She was still in the easy chair in the living room, and the portable phone was within easy reach. She grabbed it and pushed the answer button and excitedly said hello. The phone was upside down as she heard a muffled voice. She righted the phone and heard "You hear me?"

"Yes, yes, go ahead."

"Is this Sally J? This is Dr. Frizell at Bay Area State Hospital. Your husband and Dr. Kerrigan asked me to give you a call."

"Thank heaven. Is he all right?"

"Yes, he's fine. I saw him just a half hour ago. He was comfortable, reading, staying out of trouble."

Sally J asked, "Can you tell him I'm okay too. I'm home and safe."

"I will when I get the chance."

"And can you tell him we're doing a full-court press to get him out of there and that our friend Roswell is on it."

"Sure, and just to let you know, I'm a big fan of your paper—read it every week," Frizell volunteered.

"Fine. I think I can probably get a hold of him on the pay phone in the morning and check on visiting hours. "

"Good, I'll check with Dr. Kerrigan too." Dr. Frizell sounded reassuring.

"I don't know how much good that will do. Dr. Kerrigan is banned from the hospital grounds for now." Sally J vaguely remembered something about the lieutenant bringing up the suspension. "I still think I'll keep in touch with him. I think he can help. Can you make sure he stays safe? I mean he's in there with all those criminal inmates."

"We call them residents. Anyhow, give him a call in the morning. I think phone hours begin around nine. I've already told the nurses to take it easy on him. I won't be here after eight. That's when my night shift ends. I'll give you my cell number."

"Thanks. I might need it. I can use all the help I can get."

"Good luck with the paper. I'm going to check your web site."

"Would you check on Ash again before you check the web site?"

"Sure, I just checked on him, but I can check on him again."

She wrote down his number and thanked him. Right after he hung up, Frizell called unit K3. He reached Patty Candler and said, "Hey, Nurse Patty, would you do me a favor and tell Mr. Ro . . . I mean Mr. Bridgeman that his wife is all right."

"Sure will, Doc."

"And have a great Fourth."

"That too, you too. Buh bye."

When she finished auditing a nursing note from the day shift, she walked over to Ash's room and saw he was sound asleep. *I'll tell him when he wakes up*, she thought to herself.

SALLY J WAS wide awake now, head throbbing and nerves twitching. Damndest thing about red wine, she thought, puts her to sleep and then keeps her awake. Nothing a couple of ibuprofens and a cup of brewed coffee can't fix. She perked a pot of French roast that filled the kitchen with its aroma. She foamed some milk and made a cappuccino. It was hot and very satisfying and, along with the medication, neutralized the headache. She felt tired but almost normal. She had a meeting, a very important one, with her friends and coworkers in just four hours. She sat back down in the easy chair with a second foam-topped cup and thought about the strategies that lie ahead. It was going to be a busy day. Since she was an around-the-clock caffeine aficionado, she was able to drift back to sleep in the chair for a couple more hours.

"Our friend Roswell." Sally J was in a state of semi-sleep. Roswell wasn't really "our friend." He was her friend. She and Ash had used him as their attorney. He never charged them. Eventually Ash told Sally J he would be happier using another attorney. Her mind drifted through a fog of memories. She relived the evening of her first love with Roswell twenty years ago. Ash knew they "dated" in high school, but it seemed there was more to it than that. There was the way she looked at him when he was helping them with their incorporation and the way he smiled at her when he handled the real estate closing on the office.

She hazily relived another evening, years later, the night that she and

Roswell had drinks at the Holy City Café two months before her wedding. Ash was employed at the *Times*, working on a late deadline. Sally J still stayed at her downtown apartment most nights. He knew she was going to "meet with the lawyer to go over a few things."

It was a mild February evening; they laughed and drank. She had two cosmopolitans and was buzzed but not drunk. Roswell put his hand on hers, and she put her other hand on top of his. Sally J felt her insides tingle and melt. "I need some air," she told him.

They walked hand in hand in the cool misty February air, down Meeting Street, toward the Battery Park. It started to rain lightly. Roswell's house on Tradd Street was nearby. Neither had an umbrella, so they detoured to the yellow wood-frame house to wait out the shower. The rain came down more heavily, and by the time they reached Roswell's house, they were both quite wet. Sally J shed her coat as Roswell lit the gas fireplace. She had goose bumps on her smooth soft arms. Roswell rubbed her flesh with his warm hands. She took his face in her hands and kissed him gently on the lips.

Roswell was surprised, pleased but surprised. He wanted her. He whispered her name and then returned the kiss. "Roswell, I need you now," she gasped.

"You're an engaged woman."

"I'm not married yet," she whispered.

He led her to his bedroom. She was wearing a sleeveless cotton dress that revealed her lovely shoulders. Roswell tugged the top of her dress, tearing it.

"Easy, Cowboy, let me help." She pulled the dress up and over her head, tossing it on the bed, and stood before him in her bra and panties. Roswell reached around her and unsnapped her bra, which fell to the floor, and then without a word, tore at her underwear. He pulled off his clothing quickly. They embraced naked and warm and then fell to the bed, still embracing. She was ready for him. Sally J gasped and shuddered, and then groaned as they moved together. Roswell lay next to her, heart pounding as if he had run a marathon.

They both caught their breath and relaxed, but the years of pent up desire welled up within them, and after a few minutes, they were again locked in physical passion. This time it was slow and tempered, deliberate and methodical, rhythmic and pulsating. She let out with a shout that tapered to a groan and then slow deep, satisfied breaths. Roswell yelled out as well as the second time around; the climax was gradual in building and more intense than the first.

They spoke no words; their bodies had done the talking. Sally J fell asleep in the dark quiet, nestled against Roswell's chest.

Sally J was embarrassed to admit that sometimes over the years since the marriage, she would arouse herself during sex with Ash by recalling that encounter. The memories would often come during troubled restless nights, like this one, and sometimes helped her forget her anxieties and calm her mind.

Roswell and Sally J never spoke of their sexual reunion again. In an ironic way, her tryst with Roswell allowed her to move ahead with the wedding. Sally J thought of it not as the renewal of a relationship but as a release of desire, the closing of unfinished business. It was the secret in her heart that she would never share with Ash.

As for Roswell, he wanted her, but he was still not about to settle down. Ash would be there for her. Ash was her rock, her soldier,

IT WAS ABOUT 5:30 a.m. when the predawn light in the garden filtered through the living room window. It was chilly in the house. The air-conditioning had been blowing the whole night. Sally J rose and reheated the coffee, grabbed a bagel, took a quick shower, and changed into clean clothes. She wondered what her husband was doing. She had the ward pay phone number and would call later.

She set out the front door to the cobblestoned Cumberland Street and along the sidewalk to Meeting Street, up to Marion Square, then over to King Street. When she arrived at the storefront office space of *Charley Town*, she could look through the window and see no one was there yet. She let herself in and started brewing more coffee. She wasn't going to have any more right now, but Annie and some of the part-timers would probably want some on an early Saturday morning. Morning thunder was rumbling east across the harbor. It was quite humid in the office. Jets of condensing vapor were visibly streaming from the air conditioner.

At ten after seven, Annie pushed through the door, as a brief downpour had caught her a block away. Sally greeted Annie, "I'm glad you came in, especially in this weather."

Annie seemed intense. "If Ash is in trouble, I'm here. You don't even have to pay me. I called all our contractors, including the printer. Sam and Ada are coming. The printer is going to call me back. They're business as usual today. Our Fourth of July edition already hit the streets."

"Okay." Sally J was measuring her words. "We're going to put out a special

MIKE BARTOS

edition. It's going to be just four pages, front and back cover and the inner two pages, one sheet total. We can add to it if we need to later on."

Sam came in quickly, hair wet, followed by Ada Santos. Sam Bixby, a student at the College of Charleston, was doing a summer journalism internship with *Charley Town* for a grand total $120 per week, Something way less than minimum wage, but he was learning everything from writing and editing to layout and working the coffee machine. Ada worked part-time as a feature writer. She was looking for full-time work. Her husband was a student at the Medical University. Ada and her husband were from New York, bringing perspective and attitude and a connection with Annie. Sally J was surrounded by New Yorkers, wishing at times she could be one too.

Sally continued, "Guys, you heard Ash is in trouble. That's why we're here. I think I told you how Ash was going to do an undercover story at BASH. Well, because of some screwup, they're keeping him locked up in there. They think he's a real patient."

Sam and Ada looked at each other, stunned and silent, and then looked at Sally J intently. "Some people there know he's not a patient, not supposed to be there, but that doesn't matter because the bureaucratic assholes don't believe them and are covering their backsides. They even kicked out his doctor for trying to help him and me."

Sam said, "That's a story, don't you think?"

"What we're doing is blowing the lid off this crock of bullshit. We're going to be all over town with this. I need you guys to help make this happen. You want to be journalists, writers, molders of public opinion? Now is the time."

Sam was excited. "I'm in."

Ada dug in her purse for her cell phone and hit the button for home. Her handsome doctor-to-be husband's picture appeared on the screen while the phone rang. "Honey, I got something big going on here at the paper. I need to get on it . . . Yeah, today would be a great day for you to pick up some pizza . . . it's hard to explain . . . sure, if you want to drop by, I'll show you . . . I don't know. Maybe we can meet for lunch . . . Okay . . . okay . . . right . . . okay . . . love you. Bye. Okay, guys, I'm in."

Annie had some photos of the hospital parking lot and some buildings through the fence. One photo seemed to have some particular artistic merit. It simply depicted the chain-link fence topped with barbed wire in the background and a large oak tree dripping with Spanish moss in the foreground. Annie had taken that photo from the parking lot on the day of their visit. She wanted to superimpose Ash's picture over that. Sally J didn't want Ash's picture on the cover as she figured that might compromise his security. She also kept mum about the name Ash had assumed.

Sally J wrote her version of what happened and named names. She had particular vitriol aimed at Lieutenant Garner. Sam got busy with layout and did computerized cutting and pasting, fitting the photos and stories together. No ads, no personals, and no reviews. There was just one story today. Annie added details about Captain Dawkins from what she knew. Ada was researching details about the hospital and its history, from its inception in Columbia seventy-five years ago to the move to the coastal Bay Area forty years ago.

It was after nine. Sally J dialed the number of the ward pay phone number. It was busy. She tried every ten minutes for the next hour. It remained busy.

On ward K3, Belinda Jackson was talking to her sister on the phone. Time limit was ten minutes. Nobody paid too much attention to time limits. Ash was pacing, needing to use the phone. He asked Belinda if she was going to be long. Her reply, "Shut yo ass up."

Jesse nearby heard the interaction. He added, "The lady says shut your mouth, pervo. Don't be botherin' her again." Belinda and Jesse were somewhat of an item.

Ash realized he didn't have any quarters. He knocked on the locked nursing station door. There were three staff in the locked chamber. Peter Jackson, no relation to Belinda, one of the nursing assistants, waved Ash away. He yelled through the reinforced glass, "Go around to the window." There was a small sliding glass window on the other side of the nursing station through which the residents could make requests. It resembled the type of window one might see at a Dairy Queen. Ash went around and tapped on the reinforced glass. Peter opened it. "What do you need?"

"I need to make a call. Can I get some quarters?"

"Do you have any money?"

"It's with my stuff."

"That's in patient property. We don't have a spare staff to send over there with you to get it right now. Maybe after lunch."

"Could you lend me some change?"

"Can't do that—against the rules." There were indeed rules about lending the resident's money.

Ash angrily moved away from the window. A patient he hadn't met yet, a paunchy middle-aged balding white male patient with bags under his eyes walked over to Ash and handed him four quarters. "Here ya go, buddy. Pay me back when you get the chance."

"Hey, thanks. What's your name?"

"Levi, and you?"

Ash thought about it for a moment and decided he was tired of being called a name he is not. "Call me Ash." They shook hands in the traditional way.

Belinda was no longer on the phone, but the handset was dangling by its flexible metallic cord. Ash picked it up. Jesse walked over and scowled at Ash. "Hey, I'm usin' that phone."

Ash held the phone up to his ear. "I don't hear anyone on the line."

The heavyset Harold walked up and stood next to Jesse, dwarfing him. He crossed his arms over a stained T-shirt. Stained with what Ash was afraid to conjecture.

"Look, guys, I don't mean to be rude. I have to make a quick call, and I'll be right off."

Harold said, "I don't want of your perv germs on our phone."

"I washed my hands, okay?"

Ash put two quarters in the phone and began to dial. Fifty cents would cover four minutes to Charleston. He knew enough to not turn his back on his two fellow residents. Jesse's ears were turning red. He wouldn't be disrespected by a new guy, a child molester no less. He charged at Ash. Ash outweighed this guy by at least forty pounds, but the smaller man was fast and landed a punch on the side of Ash's face, splitting his lip. Jesse charged again. Ash brought his knee up into the groin of his attacker, who doubled over. A repeating chime, the alarm, was set off in the office.

Big Harold ran at Ash, pushing him against the wall. The bulky man outweighed Ash by at least a hundred pounds. Ash dropped to the floor. Harold stood over him, yelling. Ash rolled to his left side and curled up his right leg in what seemed to be a defensive posture. As Harold lifted his right foot to stomp Ash, Ash extended his leg and swept the left leg out from under Harold, whose oversized frame came flailing forward toward the floor. Harold landed on his knee and then collapsed onto Ash, all 310 pounds. Ash was now squashed under a sea of flesh. His breath was being squeezed out of him. He could smell the huge man's sour sweaty odor. He couldn't push Harold away.

Staff from several neighboring units arrived and were attempting to pull Harold off. He was on the floor now, swinging wildly at staff members, connecting with one female nurse who held her jaw and backed away. Ash slid away from the melee and stood up with blood streaming from his lip. The loud alarm gong continued, adding more noise. Jesse was sitting on the floor nearby, trying to catch his breath.

Harold was losing steam. It took about eight staff members to roll Harold on his side while a nurse stuck a syringe into his large butt. She pulled out the cylinder slowly and when she saw there was no blood, slowly pushed the cylinder back in, emptying the contents through the needle.

Several other nursing staff rolled a low gurney down the hallway and parked it next to Harold, who remained flat on the floor. Picking up a 310 pound combative lug with a possibly broken knee is no easy task. Harold kept yelling, "Son of a bitch, my fuckin' knee, son of a bitch."

"One of the nurses said gently but firmly, "Harold, can you please roll on to the gurney so we don't have to pick up your leg?"

He cooperated but was tearful, crying and whining loudly. "Son of a bitch broke my knee. I was just yellin' at him, so he decides to break my knee. I'm pressin' charges. You're goin' down, motherfucker."

At that point, three hospital police officers, two males and one female, appeared on the unit. The alarm was still chiming. Corky, was on duty as shift lead that morning. "Cut the alarm, okay?"

One of the cops asked, "You folks have it under control?"

Corky responded, "We have one split lip, one injured groin, one cracked knee, and one nurse with what looks like a broken jaw. Other than that, we have everything under control."

CHAPTER 24

I woke up Saturday morning before the sun came up, maybe around five, and moved from the couch to my bed. I probably had one too many. Grover was whining a little, so I let him out to the yard. He has a doghouse he rarely uses out there. I figured he'd be all right.

The morning sun filtered through the dense growth of subtropical maritime forest, then through the translucent window shade, and right to my closed eyelids. It was after nine, late for me but no real reason to get up. Saturdays are beautiful days any time of year, and sunny mornings make me happy. There are birds and frogs and crickets in the marsh; but this time of year, the cool central air-conditioning is humming and the windows are closed. Grover had his paws up on the back door when he heard me stir, his tail wagging vigorously. Is it the canned dog food or me? I guess I would do the same if I were a dog.

So now, I had to deal with the mess at the hospital. I wouldn't be able to get in. I had promised to get in touch with Sally J as well. I wasn't sure what I could do for her. I called her, just to check in and let her know I'm still alive, and hoped she was too. As it turns out, she was quite alive and well. She was kicking ass down at their newspaper office, working on a project relative to her husband's incarceration. She wanted me to give her lawyer buddy a call and see if I can be of assistance in some way. Actually, I hope he can assist me. I've heard of the firm. They're on Broad Street; I think that adds an extra fifty bucks an hour to the fee. He might be worth it. I can't sue the hospital or the state at this point, I presume, because despite the fact that I'm quasi suspended, I still get paid full salary. That's the way it works; it's happened before to people I know. I still had a subpoena to be in court on the following Tuesday relative to Ernie Joe's arraignment.

In the meantime, I had planned shopping, doing my laundry, a cleanup, and an hour or so at the gym over in Bayside. Bachelor stuff. I wanted to get up to Charleston by five and check in with brother Brad. I had a date planned for seven with my new love, Cassandra.

I have a small apartment above the bar in the building we own, sort of my pied-à-terre in Charleston. It's right on the Market, prime location. A little small for Grover, but there's a modest courtyard behind the building, and he seems to enjoy that. I planned to stay over through the weekend and then head down to McMurtree for the hearing early Tuesday.

First things first. I had to get a hold of Bailey Simpson and let him know what's going on. I called the hospital operator and ask him to page Simpson.

Twenty minutes later the phone rang.

"Hi, Bailey."

"Hey, Doc, so fill me in on what's going on."

"Well, Bailey, tell me what you know so far."

"Sure, first of all, I know you're on administrative reassignment—"

"You mean suspended."

"No, Patrick, you're on administrative reassignment. You're not suspended. We don't have to make a report to the medical board."

"That's nice. Where am I reassigned to?"

"The staff library."

"What will I do there?"

"Wait for an assignment."

"To where or what?"

"Wherever we need you."

"Don't you need me treating patients?"

"Not right now."

"Then where do you need me?"

"In the library." It appears we have officially chased our tail and caught it.

"So I can't see patients?"

"No, not right now"

"Then that means I'm suspended."

"No, you're just reassigned."

"Why don't I just stay home?"

"You do want to get paid, don't you?"

I think Sally J's lawyer, Mr. Chamblee, could probably kick this guy's butt from here to Atlanta and back. Simpson's right, though, at least I'm getting paid.

I asked what he knew about the Ashley Roper issue.

"Your boy (my boy?) is maybe who he says he is and maybe not. In the meantime, we're stuck with him and he's stuck with us. That's the word from Lieutenant Garner. I haven't been able to get a hold of Elliot Desjardins. He's off this weekend. I don't have a whole lot to go on right now. The lieutenant hasn't shown up. I guess she's mega stressed out, having to take over suddenly. She called. She'll be in later."

Grover was on his hind legs, his nose pressed against the kitchen door window, giving me a sorrowful look. "Keep in mind, I'm supposed to be this man's doctor. And if he is a real patient, he'll need treatment. And if not, he needs to go. Also he has a pissed-off wife, and they run this weekly newspaper together. We need to get this resolved soon, or it'll be all over the coast."

"Hmm, yes, I see the problem here. Okay, just keep in touch. I don't have anything else to tell you." Simpson seemed in a hurry to go.

Next, I dialed the number of Mr. Chamblee. He answered the phone. I introduced myself.

Chamblee said, "Oh yeah, Sally J and I had a long talk last night. Thanks for helping her out."

"I'm afraid my help will be limited, as they kicked me out of the hospital for trying to help Ashley."

"Yes, very unfortunate, I heard."

"Hey, can I hire you to help me kick some ass down there?"

"Chamblee chuckled. "Oh, don't worry about that. I love to sue people, but one thing at a time. Let's help get my friend and your not actual patient out."

"If I can be of help, call me. I have to be in court in McMurtree, different case on Tuesday."

Chamblee said, "We'll talk. I guarantee we can help each other. Sally J isn't able to get through to Ash. Maybe you can find something out. I may have to go down there myself later. I got your number. You going to be around this weekend?"

I told him that as a matter of fact I was going to be in Charleston for the weekend starting tonight.

"I'll catch you, Dr. Kerrigan. We can talk in person."

"Call me Doc. Come on over to Kerrigan's Bar and Grille if you have time tonight. It's our family place. There's going to be some Memphis blues tonight. I'll be there all evening. Dinner'll be on me."

"Oh, that's your place? Maybe I will. I need to meet with you. By the way, I have a friend."

"Me too. Be there seven thirty."

CHAPTER 25

Officer Naomi Weiss took the radio mike that was velcroed to her shoulder and called in to dispatch that no further backup was needed. Dr. Kapoor, the daytime OD for this fine Saturday, came by to look at the swelling and tender knee of the fallen big boy. He was greeted with a now cheery "Hey, Doc, you think I could have a shot of Demerol?"

"No, sir, I don't believe that is necessary at this time. Perhaps you will feel better with a hydrocodone tablet." Harold would have to settle for that for the moment. An ambulance was on its way to transport him to Beaufort Regional Medical Center, about a half hour away. There he would have an x-ray and further treatment.

Harold yelled to the three officers as they headed off the ward, "Hey, I wanna press charges. Aren't you assholes listening?" Apparently they weren't.

Corky had his hands full. The staff from the other nearby wards were returning to their home units. He had to keep hostile forces apart. Belinda got in on the fracas, taking Jesse's side and cursing at Ash. Corky and a nursing assistant stood out in the hallway between the antagonistic factions. "Why doesn't everybody just settle down?"

Dr. Kapoor was standing halfway down the hallway, out of fist's reach. Corky yelled to him, "Hey, Doc, we need some prn's and a seclusion order, and you have to help with the incident reports."

The doctor walked cautiously toward the battlefield. "It looks like you have satisfactorily controlled the situation."

At that point, Jesse was quietly approaching Ash from the rear as he was leaning against the wall near the pay phone. He reached up and from behind put a chokehold on Ash, who couldn't get enough air out to yell. A big hard ham of a fist rocketed into the back of Jesse's head. Jesse loosened his grip and whirled around to face his attacker. Wham! A fist thrust went right to the Adam's apple. Jesse dropped to his knees for the second time in fifteen minutes. Levi shook out his sore right hand. "Fuck you, Jesse."

The alarm sounded again. Belinda took a swipe at Levi, rapping him in the ear. "I saw you hit him from behind, you old punk." One of the nursing aids shouted through the PA system in the nurses' station, "Everybody back in your rooms, *now*!"

Most patients complied. Martha stood in the hallway, trembling and crying, "I hate this place. I hate it, I hate it. I hate it." Another older female patient took Martha by the hand and guided her back to her room. At least Harold wasn't participating at this point, lying on a stretcher, mellowing out on prescribed narcotic.

Corky looked at Dr. Kapoor. "Doc, we need to separate people now. Teresa, roll Harold down toward the end of the hall by the exit. Garrison, go to the quiet room and chill out."

"I am chilled out," Ash said, rubbing his neck.

"Listen, just go there for your own safety right now, wouldja?"

"I need some ice for my hand, Corky," Levi said, looking at his swelling knuckles.

"Not good timing. What's with Jesse? Oh shit!"

Jesse was lying motionless on the floor. His leg twitched momentarily and then stopped. The protocol for an unresponsive patient starts with setting off the alarm. The alarm, however, was already going for several minutes. Since a variety of staff from other wards came and went and were being called back again, they were slow to return. Corky took command. "Dr. Kapoor, we got a man down. Get on it."

Corky quickly dropped to his knees and felt for a pulse while asking, "Jesse, you okay?" No pulse, no response. Corky started rapidly leaning on the chest, hands interlocked, applying rhythmic compressions. Ash, with his military training was familiar with cardiopulmonary resuscitation. He volunteered, "I know CPR. I can help."

Corky was in stress mode. "Get the hell away. You've caused enough trouble already. Someone get him to the quiet room. Someone get the goddamn crash cart and call 911."

Ash decided his best bet was to retreat to the quiet room, out of the way.

Dr. Kapoor stood dumbstruck nearby. He had his mandatory CPR training a few months ago. He didn't remember much, but the doctors always pass the course. Corky was pumping the chest. Dr. Kapoor wasn't about to seal his lips around this guy's mouth, especially since he noted a little blood on the lips. Dr. Kapoor shouted to a nurse's aide. "Please get an ambu bag quickly." The ambu bag is a football-sized rubber air bladder or bulb with a mask that goes over the face to provide air or oxygen when the rubber bulb is squeezed.

The red metallic crash cart was wheeled up next to where Jesse lay. The doctor was handed the ambu bag wrapped in a clear plastic, which he couldn't quite open. He finally got it onto Jesse's face and started rhythmically squeezing the bag. The chest was not rising. Blood was seeping from the corners of Jesse's mouth. Corky paused to feel for a pulse; there was none.

The same three police officers, seemingly annoyed, walked briskly down the hallway and cleared through the crowd of patients and staff. Corky said forcefully but calmly, "You guys need to take over the CPR. I gotta shock him." He took the plastic briefcase out of the crash cart. "Dr. Kapoor, help me get these pads on the chest."

Dr. Kapoor fumbled with the electrode pads, looking at the directions pasted on the inside of the lid. Corky grabbed them away and applied them to Jesse's chest. He heard the automated electronic voice say, "Analyzing rhythm." After a pause, the electronic voice continued, "Apply shock." Corky pushed the red button. Jesse twitched. After a pause, the electronic voice said, "Continue CPR."

Three paramedics came running down the hallway, one of them carrying a large case by the handle and another pushing a gurney. "We'll take it from here." Everyone stepped back. They donned rubber gloves and masks and then expertly started an IV drip and hung the fluid bag on a telescoping pole. They attached electrodes to the chest, which were hooked up to an electric EKG monitor. The blood was extruding more quickly from the mouth.

"Should we intubate?" One of the paramedics asked the other two.

"We'd better suction first."

"He'll drown if we don't."

The suction machine was in the treatment room. Teresa rolled it out. The plug didn't reach, and there was no socket in the hallway.

One of the paramedics attempted to get a tracheal tube down Jesse's airway. After thirty seconds of manipulating the instrument, he said, "I think I got it." The ambu bag was attached directly to the airway tube.

"Hurry, give this guy some air."

One of them squeezed the large bladder. The chest stayed still; the stomach rose.

"Shit, you got it in the esophagus, not the airway."

"Let's just get him the hell out of here."

They slid a fiberglass board shaped like a coffin under the wounded Jesse on the floor. They lifted him up and slid him on the board onto the stretcher.

An electronic alarm sounded from the monitor. The cardiac rhythm was a series of crowded ragged ripples. One of the paramedics exclaimed, "Ventricular fibrillation, shock him again."

The paramedics had a better defibrillator. One of the paramedics squeezed some jellylike goo onto the metal paddles and rubbed them together to spread it evenly and then applied the paddles to the chest. "Okay, everybody stand back. Clear." Then a zap; the body jerked. The abnormal rhythm continued.

"One more time . . . clear." The cardiac monitor did not show definitive beats, just a squiggly line. One of them pounded the center of the chest to provide rhythm to the cardiac muscle; the heart wasn't doing on its own.

"We're losing him."

They pushed the stretcher down the hallway toward the exit and kept the chest compressions going. "Someone get that tube out of his throat." The police unlocked the rear door, and the gurney and its attendants flew by, followed by the heavy slamming of the door. Through the locked doors, Ash heard the wail of a siren as the ambulance with police escort headed down the road toward Beaufort.

For a moment, the ward became eerily quiet. Breaking the silence from the other end of the hallway, Harold called from his stretcher, "Hey, what about me?"

CHAPTER 26

The coffee was brewing inside; and outside, the steamy morning rain had dissipated. Sunbeams slanted through the front window, casting shadows of the gold lettering on the front window so that *Charley Town est. 2002"* was spelled out on the floor and across the desks inside. Tourists and shoppers passed by on the sidewalk, paying little attention to the goings on inside the storefront office. There were no antiques, hip fashions, or handcrafted jewelry to view, just four very busy people.

Sally J was not able to completely focus on the task at hand. She received a call on her cell from Ash around ten. She pressed the button on her earpiece.

"Ash!"

"Yeah, baby, I'm all right. Are you all right?"

"Yeah, I got a ride back to the hospital with that nice Dr. Kerrigan. That cop dropped her fake charges."

"Thank goodness. You wouldn't believe what goes on in here."

"Where are you?"

"I'm still on ward K3. It's like bedlam in here. Some tough guy came after me, and I got rid of him once. Then he came at me again, and guess what? Another patient took him out, I mean really took him out, like in an ambulance. Some frumpy middle-aged white guy. Turned out he used to be a middleweight boxer—caught him in the throat. He's the one who loaned me the quarters to call you. I don't think the other guy will be back anytime soon, if at all. He was some kind of a drug dealer and bully. By the way, I haven't heard from Kerrigan."

Sally J told him, "Kerrigan got suspended for trying to help you. Rozzie said he's going to try to get a court order. We talked last night. I haven't heard from him yet today. If I don't hear from him, I'll call him in an hour. Hon, it sounds like you're in danger."

"You got Roswell in on this?" Ash asked, mildly annoyed.

"He's our friend Ash. He cares what happens to you. You got someone better in mind? Didn't you get my message last night?"

"'Fraid not."

"Trust him, Ash. He's a good man to have on your side. He's on our side. He didn't hesitate for a second when I asked him to help us."

"Okay, baby, I'll owe him if he can get my ass outta here. Whatever it takes."

A female voice interrupted. "Please . . . deposit . . . thirty-five cents."

"Listen, baby, I'll be okay, but I can't stay here forever. The food is actually not bad. The cops are here. I gotta talk to them."

"Please . . . deposit . . . thirty-five cents."

"Hey, baby, I love you. Try to call me ba—"

"Thank you for using Low Country Telecommunications. Good-bye." *Click.*

Sally J had the number of the pay phone. She dialed back quickly. There was a rapid busy signal. She tried again, same result.

The next call was to Roswell Chamblee. His voice mail answered immediately. She tried his home number, no answer.

UNDER THE GRUFF *exterior and behind the badge of Captain Lyle Dawkins, there was a heart and a conscience. The heart stopped beating just yesterday, exhausted from a life of worries and the stresses of an institution he vowed to keep safe and whole. But the death of a staff member at the hands of a patient, the escape of another, and the influx of illicit drugs beyond what was supposed to be a secure perimeter, vexed Captain Dawkins to the point where he was ready to try something radical. He would never win approval for a unique strategy to garner information, information he would never live to see . . .*

Annie was pleased with her article, which would be the lead for the special edition of *Charley Town*. Annie and the two kids were putting together the brief special edition. They had to have it to the printer by 4:00 p.m. Drug dealers, fights, and a dysfunctional environment with a good doctor sent away. She was ready to put it all down and set it out there. Halfway into writing the story, it occurred that if the issue around drug dealers and obnoxious cops hit the street, she would further imperil Ash's safety behind the fence. She saved what she had written so far and decided she might have to simplify it.

Sally J decided to call a meeting. They gathered around the old conference table. There were two hours to get to the printer. "Gang, we have to rethink this. Ash is at risk if we blow the whistle on this deal while he's still locked in there. There's trouble there. Maybe we should put this project on hold. We might get him killed instead of out."

Young Sam made a suggestion. "Maybe we can run the issue and make no mention of Ash. You know, just murder and mayhem."

Annie seemed to agree. "We can wait until he gets out, then we can pull the trigger, so to speak."

"We won't have anything ready in the next few hours," Sally J said.

Sally J heard a beep in her earpiece. It was Roswell.

"Sally J, I wanted to patch together some details before I called. I've been trying to track down Judge Silberman. We play golf sometimes. I think he'd help us. Problem is he's playing in some kind of tournament on Isle of Palms this weekend. I don't know if he's staying out there or not. I don't have his cell number. I left him a message at his chambers. Maybe he'll check this weekend. Otherwise, we'll have to go into court first thing Tuesday."

Sally J was alarmed. "It sounds like he's in the middle of some trouble there already. He got in a fight, and there's drug dealers. This is supposed to be a hospital?"

"Okay, I'll call whoever is in charge at the hospital—pay them a visit. I'll serve them notice. I'll do what I can."

"We should go visit. I can give Ash some quarters at least."

"Maybe we can get down there today. I checked and visiting hours are one to three thirty."

It was almost noon; it would take over to an hour to get there. Sally J thought about it. She agreed. Roswell would pick her up and scoot down there in his Beamer. She was tired and a little too distracted to drive.

She announced to her crew. "We're going to put the issue on hold. This is getting complicated. We can't put Ash in further danger. Keep everything you've done. We're going to use it but not right this minute."

"What can we do to help?"

"You're doing it. We have a story here. But if we slash and burn right now, it may backfire. We're going to have to move in another direction. I'm going down to visit now. I'm going with our lawyer. Save all your work. We're going to use it. You guys are great for coming in. I won't forget it. Ash won't either. Go home, get on with your weekend, but don't disappear . . . and clean up a little before you go, okay?"

About fifteen minutes later, Roswell pulled up in front of the office and honked. Sally J waved and thanked everybody again and jumped in the car, and they headed out of Charleston across the Ashley River Bridge and south along the coast.

The traffic was light on this holiday weekend. The small sports car was warm even with the air-conditioning. Roswell explained that doctors work weekends and take calls. Nurses and cops work weekends. Judges and lawyers don't unless they can charge more than their usual four hundred dollars an hour. Most lawyers don't even have an answering service or voice mail after hours. If they are working, it's somewhere deep in the bowels of a law library.

Sally J gave details of the inappropriate arrest she endured while Roswell made mental notes. He felt quite sorry for what Sally J had gone through but looked forward to the skewering of the hospital that would take place once it was all resolved.

The roadside stands selling seashells, woven baskets, and homemade peach pies along the coastal highway were doing a brisk business with the vacationers and tourists. The small car turned smoothly onto the exit for Bay Area State Hospital. A variety of moths and dragonflies splattered onto the windshield as they cruised the marsh road toward the hospital. Roswell down-shifted into second gear to take the speed bumps along the driveway as they entered the grounds. Waves of heat radiated off the blacktop. He parked in the visitors' lot, and the two of them walked over to the security station by the fence. Roswell spoke to an officer through a small circular vent in the side window in the portal kiosk. "I'm here to see . . ." He turned to Sally J and asked, "What's his name here?"

She answered him and the officer at the same time, "Garrison Bridgeman."

" I'm his attorney." He handed the officer his driver's license and business card.

The officer checked a clipboard and then tapped some keys on the keyboard and paused. Then he picked up the phone and turned sideways, facing away from Roswell and Sally J. They saw him nod and say, "Uh-huh . . . hmm . . . Uh-huh . . . yes . . . yes . . . I see . . . uh-huh."

Okay." He held the phone and said, "I'm afraid there's a bit of a delay."

Roswell lowered his face and put his mouth up to the vent. "Perhaps you didn't hear me. I'm his attorney. According to South Carolina state law and federal law, he has a right to see me. Which part of the law don't you understand?"

"You see, Mr. Bridgeman is tied up right now."

"Well, tell your boss, or whoever is running the show, that if you don't want to get slapped with civil rights violations and criminal charges, get him over here to the visitors' center post haste. That means now, Officer."

"Let me call Lieutenant Garner. She's in charge." The lieutenant had wandered in around noon. The joys of being in charge, she was finding out, aren't so joyous after all. The officer called the lieutenant and spoke quietly

MIKE BARTOS

for less than a minute. He nodded to Roswell and said, "Okay, we'll sign you both in." They were given visitor's badges and entered through a gate different from the one into the main grounds. They stopped in an area between two sliding gates; as one closed, the other one opened.

Roswell said, "They can do their interrogation with me here, so I don't want any further delays." The visitation area was partly inside and partly outdoors with picnic tables and a colorful flower garden of roses and gardenias, cared for by the patients themselves. Like the rest of the hospital grounds, it was set off from the outside world by a fourteen-foot cyclone fence topped with razor wire.

Lieutenant Garner thought it best to be present during the interrogation. Sally J cringed when she saw the lieutenant, who said, "Good afternoon, Ms. J. I hope you don't have a lot of hard feelings about last evening."

"Not as many as you're going to have, Ms. Garner." Roswell was glad to see Sally J was spoiling for a fight. Garner wasn't too worried. She was a state employee immune from personal liability, and anyhow, she was quite sure she did everything by the book. Quite sure.

Ash appeared through a door from the visitors' center into the courtyard. The left side of his face was swollen and discolored with four stitches along his lower lip. Sally J gasped and ran to Ash. She gently touched the wounded face. Ash winced. "Easy, baby. It's okay. It's not as bad as it looks."

Roswell gasped and then gritted his teeth seeing Ash's bruised face. "It's been awhile. Good to see you Ash, maybe not under these circumstances. How you feeling?"

Ash shook Roswell's hand. "I appreciate your helping me out. I'm okay."

"I'll do whatever it takes to straighten out this mess." Roswell meant it.

There were a number of visitors, but they preferred the air-conditioned indoor visiting room. Ash and Sally J were sitting at a picnic table under a big oak tree. It wasn't particularly uncomfortable despite the 91 humid degrees, just as long as they stayed out of the sun.

Accompanying Ash was a clean cut, muscular young man dressed in civilian clothes, except for a badge hanging from his belt. He was actually fairly upbeat and pleasant, Roswell thought. Lieutenant Garner introduced him as Drayton Smith, Special Investigator.

Roswell addressed both the lieutenant and the investigator. "What kind of hellhole are you people running?"

Smith responded, "I'm sorry that this happened, sir. Your client is not involved in the homicide other than as a witness."

Roswell was incensed. "My client is here one day, and in that short period of time, he is assaulted and then the perpetrator is murdered?"

Garner broke in. "These things happen, but—"

Roswell interrupted. "Yeah, but this isn't supposed to be a riot zone."

"Yes, sir, it's unfortunate. This was a rare and unlikely occurrence," Garner conceded.

Sally J looked at Ash. "How are you, hon?"

"About as well as anybody could be after being locked in this joint. The company's not too great, the mattress is thin, not much to do on the weekend, food's not bad. I miss being home. The face looks worse than it is, nothing broken, just a bruise."

Smith started, "This resident, first of all, is insisting he's somebody other than who he we think he is."

"Okay, let me interrupt," Roswell responded, "and this is for you ears too, Lieutenant." I have known this man for ten years as a friend. He is an innocent man, as sane as you or I. This man is Ashley Roper. I am a licensed attorney in the State of South Carolina. I will sign an affidavit to that effect."

"And he's been my husband for nine years, I can attest to that too." Sally J added.

Smith asked, "So who is Garrison Bridgeman?"

Ash was happy to answer, "He's a real patient, or rather he was, up in Colleton County, who died a week or two ago. His file was sent here for transfer, then he got sick, so his transfer was delayed. Captain Dawkins, for whatever reason, thought it would be a good idea to allow me to go undercover for a day using that identity. He fingerprinted me, took my picture, and used that file to get me in here."

"Under false pretenses," added Garner. She turned to Roswell. "If what your client says is true, he committed a felony. This is causing us a lot of problems too."

Ash was feeling defensive. "I suppose, but it was only supposed to be for a day. Then Dawkins died that very day. He was going to get me out around six. Nobody was supposed to know."

"Sounds like a mess," Smith added not so helpfully. "I'll put all this in my report. But I need to find out more about this homicide."

Roswell asked, "What is my client's role here?"

"He and the decedent were in an altercation less than a half hour before the death. There was a second altercation in which a third party, a resident

MIKE BARTOS

by the name of Levi Cort, intervened and supposedly struck two blows, the second one fatal."

Roswell asked, "So who's being charged with what?"

"Mr. Cort was transferred to the county jail in McMurtree. I can't tell you what the DA will charge him with yet, but at least assault with a deadly weapon and probably voluntary manslaughter. There might be a hate-crime enhancement since Mr. Cort was known to make frequent racist comments and the victim was Hispanic."

"And my client?"

"From what we can see so far, he was being assaulted and did not retaliate. A little earlier, he kicked Mr. Villacruz in the groin, which was either a retaliatory or defensive move. That's also under investigation."

Ash added, "This is just my first day too."

Roswell asked, "So what happened, Ash?"

"This guy Jesse was harassing me while I was under observation. When I got off observation, I tried to use the phone, and he just charged me, swinging. I gave him a knee as he was coming back to hit me again." Ash pointed to his lip. "A few minutes later, he tried choking me from behind when Levi intervened. For all I know, he might have saved my life."

Smith was busily writing on a clipboard. "So you are basically a writer who found himself locked in here and in the middle of a conflict?"

Garner added, "He didn't just find himself in here. He went out of his way to get in here."

Roswell asked Garner. "Have you verified my client's fingerprints?"

"I thought we had them."

"Well, you do. Did you compare them to the prints in Colleton County?"

"Not yet."

"Lieutenant, you're a moron." He regretted his outburst as it passed his lips. At least they weren't in court. "Do you know what false imprisonment is?"

"I didn't bring him here, he brought himself here, don't go popping off at me."

"Fine, but you're keeping him here. Are you proceeding with due diligence?"

Smith continued to write.

"You know, Lieutenant, this isn't just a civil matter, but a criminal one as well. I want to walk out of here with my client now."

"We just can't let people walk out of here with their lawyers. We need a court order." Everyone at the table was glistening with a patina of perspiration, except for Lieutenant Garner, who was sweating through her uniform with large dark stains becoming more noticeable under her armpits.

"No, Lieutenant, you can't just let committed patients walk out, but you can't keep visitors."

Beyond the fence, Ash could see a crane lift off from the marsh, long graceful limbs trailing behind as the bird ascended. *Freedom*, he thought.

"Okay," Garner sighed. "Let me check on a few things. If you'd like to wait in the air-conditioned room, you might be more comfortable."

Smith was okay with that. "I'm getting the picture here. I've got just a few more questions."

Garner went into the air-conditioned guard station. She was tempted to hold her armpits over the air-conditioning vents, but that wouldn't look like leadership. She called the sheriff's office in Colleton County and asked for Bridgeman's prints to be faxed over immediately. She made it clear it was an emergency.

Now she needed privacy. She made her way through the heat back to her office outside the secured area. Bailey Simpson was the administrator on call, but she knew she could bypass that clown. She called Elliot.

He was at the clubhouse of the Bay Inlet Golf Club. He quit his round after nine holes. Too damn hot. Shot a fifty-four on the front nine. Screw it. He was watching a golf tournament on the flat screen TV over the bar. Golf, as far as Elliot Desjardins was concerned, was all about the rehydration. The rest of his foursome continued without him. *They won't make the full eighteen*, he thought. The phone vibrated in his pocket. He fumbled for it and saw Evelyn's name. Personal or official business? He thought he better take it.

"Yup."

"Hey, Elliot, I got a problem here."

He sighed and rolled his eyes. "Yes, Evie, what's up?"

"That guy who came in yesterday morning is here with his Charleston lawyer and hippie wife. It's looking like he isn't really a patient, went undercover to investigate the murder, escape, and whatever else. I'm running his prints with the feds and checking them against the ones in Colleton. I'm guessing he'll clear. I'll have to let him go."

"Without a court order?"

"We're not releasing an offender. We're releasing someone who isn't really a patient. Besides, do you want a reporter snooping around on the inside of the hospital? You know we had another homicide this morning. This reporter was being attacked, and another resident took out the guy who was choking him. Now he's a witness. I don't know if we have to keep him here until we get a court order or what."

"For crissake, Evie, can't I take a weekend off without another shit storm?"

"I'll take care of it, Elliot."

"Make sure you do. I'm turning off my phone. If you need anything, call Simpson, anything hospital related that is. And don't do anything that'll get us into trouble. Get a court order before you do anything." End of conversation.

She checked her fax machine. An official document from the sheriff's office with Garrison Bridgeman's mug shot and prints came through. Whoever was in the photo was not the man sitting with his lawyer in the visitors' center. Stamped across the top of the form was "DECEASED." It was going to be apparent that the prints would not match unless the guy in the visitors' center was dead. The prints clearly did not match. She had seen Ash's passport too, albeit briefly, before it disappeared. She was going to have to wait twelve to twenty four hours for the prints to come back from the Department of Defense. He was military. They'll be in tomorrow, or Monday or Tuesday.

Garner returned to the visitors' center. Smith had disappeared. "Mr. Chamblee, it looks like there is some sort of misunderstanding here. We have a court order for this man who presented himself as Garrison Bridgeman to be here. Well, it turns out he is apparently not Garrison Bridgeman since Mr. Bridgeman is deceased."

"So you're holding a dead man here, or someone who is not who you think he is," Roswell added.

"Or someone who is here illegally. I know this is a sticky situation, but he is booked in here. And as acting chief of security, I just can't let him walk out of here. That will take a court order." Garner was feeling a little more confident in herself, figuring the truth is the best way to go.

Roswell was getting irritable and frustrated. Sally J's pale complexion was reddening. Roswell spoke. "We're going to get a court order as soon as humanly possible, and I'm serving notice on you, ma'am. I'm holding you personally responsible for my client's well-being. And furthermore, you and your minions are not to question Ash any further without my presence. Got that, Lieutenant?"

"Perfectly clear, Counselor. We'll make Mr. Bridgeman's safety our first priority."

"And another thing, you can stop calling him Mr. Bridgeman. Mr. Bridgeman is dead."

"Mr. Chamblee, unfortunately, we have to hold him here, but I see your point. We'll do our best to see he is safe and comfortable. I believe our special investigators are done with your client for now. However, I do see that there may be a problem here with your client's assumption of someone else's identity. We're not going to worry about that here."

"Yes, Lieutenant, that is not your problem, but you don't have to lock him down, and you need to keep him away from the dangerous patients."

"Counselor, we can't keep anyone away from dangerous patients all the time. We can let him out on the grounds. We don't let the dangerous patients out on the grounds."

"That's not what I've been reading in the papers."

"Bad things still happen. We'll just do our best to keep an eye on your man. We'll try to get him moved to the honor unit until we can get this mess straightened out."

The honor unit was kept unlocked during the daylight hours. Patients were required to sign out for groups or activities on the grounds or for leisure time on the grounds if not assigned to other activities. This ward was populated by patients who were within a year or two of discharge. There were also a handful of patients who were very chronically mentally ill, with little hope of discharge, but were calm and compliant enough to be placed on the honor unit if there was room for what was termed "quality of life" issues.

Sally J raised her voice. "You can't just keep him here if you know he's not supposed to be here."

Ash turned to the lieutenant and asked if he could be alone with his visitors for a few minutes, even though visiting hours were over. Rain started pounding on the tin roof of the visitors' center. The lieutenant was happy to excuse herself and did so.

Ash put his arm around Sally J and seemed relatively calm, given the circumstances. "Okay, this isn't turning out quite the way I planned. I'm finding out a lot more than I would have found out in eight or nine hours. I may as well make the best of it. Roswell, how long will it take to get a court order?"

"It's taking longer than I thought. There aren't any judges around on a Saturday of a holiday weekend. I'm working on it, but you might be stuck here a few more days. I'll be checking in on you. Are you feeling safe?"

"Well, this is a combat zone, but since I was in a big fight and came out ahead, the patients here respect that and are even watching my back. I should be okay. If I can take the lieutenant at her word, they'll get me in a better environment."

"Yeah, I think she got the point."

Sally J was not so reassured. "Honey, I'm so scared for you." She touched her forehead to his shoulder and started to cry. He held her close. He wanted to be strong for her.

"Sally J," Roswell declared, "if I can't get a court order by the end of the weekend, Tuesday at the latest, I'll be down here with the goddamn National Guard. Trust me." Ash noticed Roswell gently touched her hand.

"No one said going undercover is a walk in the park," Ash added. "Sally J, it's hard to get to the phone. People tie it up and guard it. I don't want to get into another fight over that."

"Ash," Sally J added, "we were going to put out a special edition to blow the whistle on this place. You on the front cover and everything. We thought we should probably hold off. What do you think?"

"Maybe put a lid on it for now. Looks like I'm stuck here for the weekend. We'll roll with it as soon as I get out. I'll be able to contribute. I've been taking notes."

"Okay, I think we can get the regular issue out next week. We have the annual pizza review issue."

Ash just sighed. "Sally J, you don't have to come running down here tomorrow. I'll get in touch when I can. If you don't hear from me, it doesn't mean anything, okay?"

"Sure, hon. I brought some quarters, though, so you don't have to borrow any from the Boston Strangler."

"Right, I can have up to five bucks of quarters with me. They figure any more than that is a weapon."

One of the uniformed security officers entered the conference room. "It's after four folks. The lieutenant said you could have a little extra time, but it's time to go. We have to get your husband back to the ward."

Sally J gave Ash a long hug. Roswell clasped Ash's hand with two hands. "Buddy, I got you covered." Ash didn't know if he could completely trust Roswell; but for now, he didn't have a choice. He asked Roswell, "Watch Sally J, would you? I'll owe you."

"I'll settle for some of your fancy paella."

"Deal."

Roswell put his arm around Sally's shoulder as they left through the series of three gates and out to the parking lot.

CHAPTER 27

It was after seven, and I was entertaining myself and a few customers at the bar with my version of "'Round Midnight." Six flats, played mostly on the black keys It's a rich, moody, melancholy number, Thelonius Monk's signature tune. My goal was to play it in front of a small crowd with no one paying particular attention and not flubbing what was little more than the basic fake book version with only minor embellishment. Monk's harmonies pushed the envelope in his time; and if I made a little slip, I hoped no one would notice. It seemed to go well enough; two people applauded. I had a tip jar, and I got fourteen dollars for the set, which I donated to the bartender tip jar. The idea that someone thought my playing was worth even a buck was thrilling enough.

I was waiting for Cassandra, who appeared at seven fifteen, sauntered over to the baby grand on the bandstand where I was seated alone, put her lovely sleek arm around my shoulder, and gave me a hello kiss on the cheek. Her silky brunette hair made her green eyes stand out like the hills of Killarney on a sunny day. That was enough to get me to leave the keyboard and move to a quiet table with my hopefully new found romance. For a weekend that started pretty crummy, things were looking up.

Paul, the bartender shouted, "What are you guys having, Doc?"

"A cosmopolitan for the lady and the usual for me."

I turned to Cassandra. "I got that right I hope."

"You did," she whispered. "You listen."

"Well, I'm a shrink. I'm supposed to listen."

Paul said loudly, "Houlihan's?"

"Is there any time you see me drinking any other?"

She tilted her head slightly and touched my hand for a brief moment as she smiled.

"Cassandra, we're having some acquaintances joining us tonight."

"So who would that be?"

"A lawyer, Roswell Chamblee, and his date. Actually I just talked with him on the phone. It's an odd situation." I went on to tell her the story as it unfolded so far and how I got into trouble for no particularly good reason. Her eyes opened wide, and she listened intently. I don't think I was violating any confidentiality, as Ash wasn't a real patient. And sooner or later, it would be public knowledge whether it would be Ash or someone else telling the story. Our drinks arrived.

"So this Mr. Chamblee is going to help this guy and you?"

"I certainly hope so, and I'm worried more about Ash than I am about myself. Frankly, I'm in a lot better company tonight than he is."

"You're so sweet. Maybe I should buy you dinner?"

"It's okay. The state is still paying me, and after all, this is my joint."

Mr. Chamblee arrived with a lovely sylphlike woman on his arm. She wore a chic slinky black dress with a slit up the side revealing a long graceful leg. He had no trouble being directed to us, table for four in the bar. The two big TVs over the bar were each flashing a different sports channel. The TV sound would be muted when the actual band starts. God, I love this place.

I stood and introduced Cassandra and myself. Roswell's companion was named Kimberly. He ordered a Low Country beer and Kimberly had a sparkling water.

Roswell took a long thirsty draw from the bottle. "I'm sorry I'm a little late. I had a helluva day down there at BASH. I can't seem to get Ash out of there with a tow truck. Sally J was with me. She's exhausted. She's been up since dawn trying a number of different strategies. I got her home after five, and I think she went to get a bath and go to bed early. By the way, Doc, you should know there was another homicide on your ward today. Somebody went after Ash, and another patient apparently found an excuse to take that guy out."

I blurt out, "Holy shit! Let me guess. Jesse?"

"Yeah, some guy named Jesse was the victim"

I didn't expect that. Jesse the victim? I honestly have to say I'm not sorry the little prick is gone. "Is Ash okay?"

"Oh, he's quite okay. I've known Ash a long time. Lieutenant in the first Gulf War, Citadel grad. He still keeps in shape. I'm thinking he wanted another combat mission. He took out some huge guy named Harold, put him on the floor anyhow—big guy, not very swift or coordinated."

I chuckle to myself, then think *Bad attitude, Kerrigan. No wonder they suspended your ass.* But I get over it. These were all my patients, but the good news is as I was "reassigned" during this melee. I'm now not the doctor of record. The investigators can harass somebody else. Maybe if they had let Ash out when they found out the story, none of this might have happened. "So who's the perp?"

"Apparently a patient named Levi Cort. They hauled him off to the county jail."

"Levi? I thought he was on his way to the honor ward, so now it's jail instead. I guess Levi was being harassed for money. As long as Ash is okay, I'm okay," and I meant it.

Roswell added, "Ash had a bruise on the side of his face, nothing too serious. The acting security chief said she'd move Ash to the honor unit tomorrow."

"Good, he'll be safer there. What prompted her to do that?"

"They ran his prints. They know he's not the patient they think he is." Roswell took another swig of beer emptying the bottle. "So, I don't know why they just don't cut him loose."

My contribution based on experience was "Nobody knows what to do, so they've gone with Hobson's choice—do nothing." They're pretty good at doing nothing, nothing useful anyhow. I noticed good whiskey in the bottom of my glass, waiting to be refreshed. "I propose a toast to your friend, and I hope soon to be my friend Ash."

"Here, here." Oh that whisky went down good.

I figure Ash's presence on my turf was a wrinkle in this mad universe that may just be the catalyst for something good to happen. I can't say I wish death on anyone, even a punk like Jesse, but with Ernie Joe and now Jesse off the ward, some of the other patients may be able to focus on recovering some semblance of mental health. That's what I'm here for. Right? That's why we have a hospital, not a prison, a place of healing, not a repository for ass-covering civil servants. "Hey, Paul, set us up with another round."

Roswell offered, "Let me get this one."

"Hell, no. If you want to be generous, tip the band."

"Okay, Doc. What's your specialty here?"

"Is everyone down with beef ribs? I know you ladies are all dressed up, but we do have my own patented top secret sauce. We have warm washcloths for after the ribs. Then there's the sweet potato pie. I grew up on this stuff. That's one reason I'm a man of, shall we say, substance. And Roswell, I'm getting you one of our mint juleps. We gotta unwind."

"Sure, I guess we can walk home from here."

Kimberly broke down finally and said, "I'll have one of those mint juleps too if we can get a carriage ride home."

"So is there anything else I can do to help?" I wanted to know.

"Just keep in touch with Sally J and me. You have our numbers. And see if you can get your colleagues on duty this weekend to keep a special eye out for his well being. I can't get a court order till Tuesday at the earliest."

"Sure, we don't need more mayhem. Maybe we should start worrying more about the bad guys. They seem to be leaving feet first lately."

"I know"—Chamblee frowned—"but it sounds like a dangerous place, even for a guy I know who can take care of himself."

"If I could get in to the secured area, I would stand guard myself." I meant it. I wasn't sure who was on duty tonight, but I would have to get in touch. I thought, *We're all standing guard from a distance. It's the best we can do right now.* A basket of biscuits arrived. There was plenty of butter. Cassandra and I were on our second round of drinks. I had a warm buzz going, but there was the worry underneath, concern for the good man I just met yesterday and for the people who apparently love him. If Karma means anything, he'll come out of this okay.

Roswell was turning and talking to young Kimberly. I guessed she was twenty-five, maybe twenty-six. The ladies were not really part of the conversation so far. I turned to Cassandra and moved closer. She smiled as I leaned toward her. She exuded a slight fragrance of French perfume.

I told Cassandra that under the circumstances, I would be more relaxed if I could check the ward and see who was on tonight, so I asked to be excused for just a minute. I nodded to our company. It was getting noisier at the bar, so I stepped out the backdoor into the small garden where Grover, feeling neglected, nudged me with his nose. The hospital operator informed me that Dr. Donna Thibodaux was on duty tonight. She rang one of the wards.

"Dr. Thibodaux here, yes?"

"Hey, Donna, Doc Kerrigan here. Listen, I have a special patient on my ward, the name on the chart is Bridgeman. Long story but he was involved in a melee today."

"Yes, I heard about that. Quite a donnybrook, I understand."

"I understand that my patient who goes by the name Ash is going to be moved to the honor ward tomorrow."

"So how does that happen after a big fight?"

"Well, security cleared him, and it's kind of for his protection. As I mentioned, it's a long story. Lieutenant Garner worked it out. Anyhow, I can't get in."

"Yes, I heard about that too. Sometimes I think the inmates are running the asylum."

"Might be an improvement if they did," I said with not so subdued sarcasm.

"Why did they suspend you? You didn't do anything wrong."

"The usual somebody's investigating something bullcrap."

"Yeah," Donna replied, "happened to me about two years ago. Remember? Something to do with a patient slipping on the wet floor and breaking his wrist. Someone in administration raised the idea of patient abuse or neglect. So they sent me to the library, and I got to study for my boards for a week."

"So would you look in on Ash and make sure he is doing okay and move him somewhere if there's any hint of danger? I'm worrying about this guy."

"Certainly, Patrick."

"I'll owe you one."

"Oh, that's not necessary. I got you covered. Just chill and enjoy the downtime."

"I wish I could, but I'm worried about this guy."

After that, I felt somewhat better. Relaxed enough for maybe one more whiskey. I don't usually do three, but there's a little extra tension in the air, including sexual. By the time I got back to the table, my companions were going at the ribs. My plate was waiting along with a half-empty (or half full?) drink. Both needed attention, not to mention a very beautiful woman who needed and was going to get my fullest attention. I raised my glass and announced to my company that we will meet here again and soon, with Ash and Sally J joining us.

By the time we finished the sweet potato pie, I was perhaps a little too mellow. The music was starting, electric guitar, thumping bass, and funky fatback beat on the drums. Good to listen to, but not so good for conversing over.

I'm gonna love you, baby, you're all I really need
Oh I'm gonna love you baby, you're all I really need
Don't you leave me waitin'
Please don't make me plead

I looked at Cassandra and mouthed the words along with the lead singer. I think she found it sexy or sweet or amusing. The blues are sensual; the rhythm is sexual. The blues make things happen. Roswell and Kimberly listened for a set. I suppose this wasn't their cup of tea. When the music stopped for the break, we shook hands, Cassandra and Kimberly exchanged hugs, and we all agreed to do this again soon. I would keep in touch with Roswell every day. Whatever happened with this sorry episode at Bay Area State Hospital, I would be richer by a couple of new friends.

The second set was starting soon. Cassandra was into it. I turned to the bar. "Paul, a little coffee with sugar and cream for a nightcap, please."

CHAPTER 28

A sh was safely transferred to the honor unit Sunday morning. His record still indicated he was Garrison Bridgeman, but he introduced himself as Ash. He was allowed on the grounds by just signing out. His fellow patients were among the highest functioning in the hospital. The hallways were wide and clean, and everyone overall seemed considerably better behaved. Starting a fight would at least lead to a ticket back to the locked units, and probably hold up any potential discharge for a year or two. He was issued a green ID card, kept at the nurses' station, which would be given to him when he signed out for the grounds. He had two roommates, both reasonably well functioning but still on a fair amount of medication to keep them that way.

The room was peaceful when Ash took a nap after lunch. Maybe this was the way to wellness. You can't heal in a violent environment. Ash thought that maybe some of the sicker patients on other wards could do better if they had an opportunity to be on a ward like this. The catch, of course, is that someone already had to be better to get here.

Ash decided to get out on the grounds and have a look around. He hadn't been unescorted on the grounds since he got here two days before. He had called Roswell and Sally J earlier with some of his quarters and told them he was fine. "Don't bother coming to visit today, just relax."

It was another Sunday afternoon, July 3, peaceful, unlike the lethal Sunday the week before when Ernie Joe was doing his dirty deeds. On these hot days, most patients chose to stay inside. Some were restricted from going outside because certain medications cause bad reactions in hot weather. The dew from the grassy lawns had dissipated. One of the roadways leading to the area behind the wards was blocked off with orange cones and yellow crime-scene tape. Two security officers wearing khaki shorts and pith helmets were chatting by the garden of death.

Ash saw the ball field and a chapel. There was a weedy area near the perimeter fence marked "Out of Bounds." He ignored the sign and wandered back through the tall marsh grass and cattails. He stepped on a tennis ball hidden in the grass and then picked it up. There was a narrow strip of duct tape around the middle. He started to peel off the tape when he heard a voice.

"Dude, you're not supposed to be here. It's off limits." Ash turned around and was surprised to see a middle-aged balding patient with a long droopy mustache. The man held out his hand and said, "I believe that belongs to me." Ash handed it to him without any argument.

"Looks like we're both out of bounds," Ash responded.

"You can lose your grounds card walking around back here. They're cracking down on the residents wandering where they ain't supposed to be."

Ash crossed his arms, and looked at the man with the 1890s mustache. "Really? What about you?"

"I wander back here sometimes, when the coast is clear. You shouldn't be pokin' yer nose where it don't belong. Let's put it this way, there's the cops and the bigwigs don't want you back here, and neither do I."

"I got that. You mind tellin' me who you are?"

"I'm Victor. You're a new guy. I'll cut you some slack. Just put it this way, everyone knows there's lotsa good reasons to not be wandering back behind the buildings. Bad things happen to people who wander back in these parts. Maybe you read the paper."

"I read the paper every day."

"Well, good. I suggest you scoot and get back to the approved areas."

At this point, Ash figured discretion was the better part of valor. "I guess I'll see you around, Vincent."

"That's Victor, and there's two ways you'll see me around. One is if you make an appointment, and two is if you piss me off. I suggest you make an appointment."

"Why do I need to make an appointment?" Ash asked, arms still folded in front of him.

"I really don't have much more to say, buddy. I got things I gotta take care of."

Ash dropped his hands to his side and walked away. The moist air blew through the high grass, bending it over in waves flowing through the narrow field. He turned and saw Victor carrying several of the taped tennis balls, apparently hunting intensively for more, like a kid searching for chocolate Easter eggs on the White House lawn.

A RATHER LEISURELY game was in progress on the softball field. Two recreation therapists, one middle-aged male and another younger female, were in attendance with clipboards in hand, each wearing shorts, T-shirts,

MIKE BARTOS

sunglasses, and sun visors. More would be coming in the next day to help prepare the Fourth of July festivities. The cookouts would be held in the courtyards and fenced-in fields adjacent to the various wards.

The inmates, that is, residents, as Ash was learning, were dressed in their institutional blues, which as a full wardrobe included blue Bermuda-length shorts and darker blue T-shirts. Staff could not wear blue jeans because they too closely resembled patient garb.

Ash peered through the chain-link fence around the ball field. The batter, a massively overweight young black woman named Ophelia, took a swing at the slow moving softball floating in over the plate. She connected and sent the ball skipping along the ground past the pitcher. He watched it bounce toward the second baseman, who scampered toward the ball and reached down and fell over. The ball rolled to a stop a few yards beyond. Another young male player picked it up as Ophelia chugged around first base, sweating, panting, and grunting, and waddled toward second base.

Nicole, a young female therapist pulling some extra pay for weekend duty, acting as coach and umpire, yelled, "Run, Ophelia." The young man who fielded the ball tossed it to the second baseman, who was recovering to his feet. He caught the ball, but Ophelia gasped by and he didn't tag her. He lobbed the ball to third base, where one of the more athletically capable young males was standing in front of the base, held the ball in front of him as Ophelia, now completely out of gas, walked into it. Nicole yelled, "Out!"

Ophelia was sitting beyond the base, legs splayed out in front of her, and simply responded, "Well, sheeeit, I shudda stopped at second." It didn't much matter as no one was keeping score, and the team makeup changed from minute to minute, depending who was interested in playing. There was a friendly large oak providing shade next to the bleachers and a cooler filled with ice water surrounded by paper cups randomly tossed on the grass.

Ron, the other therapist, looked through the fence and saw Ash. "Hey, you wanna play?" Apparently the potential batters were mostly gathered in the shade by the cold water and exhortations of "Who's on deck?" went largely unheeded. Ash looked over his shoulder, saw no one else, and concluded he was the one being addressed.

"Sure, why not?" He walked through the opening in the gate toward home plate. Nicole introduced herself and added, "Hi, I gotta see your badge and get your home unit." The ID still indicated the name of Bridgeman, ward B-1. "Call me Ash."

"Okay, Ash, grab a bat." He picked up one of the two bats lying near the backstop and swung it around a few times. The staff in attendance had to keep an eye on the bats. He hadn't played since his intramural days at the Citadel. On the mound was a tall hefty white boy with a red face and crew-cut brown hair whom the other players had referred to as "Pooter." Ash took a batter's stance and readied himself for the pitch. Pooter lobbed the ball about two feet wide of the plate. "Ball one!" exclaimed Ron. The next pitch traced an arc over the plate at about the speed of a floating Frisbee. Ash swung full force and sent the fat softball high over the rear fence of the softball field. Ash trotted around the bases as some of the lounging residents greeted him at home plate with fist bumps and high fives. Nicole said, "Good work, Ash. We need to sign you up for the team." In the meantime, the only softball was somewhere beyond the left field fence in some weeds. The game was suspended while a search detail was sent out to retrieve it.

One of the residents, known as "Old Wally," shouted, "Here it is!" What he actually found was a tennis ball with duct tape wrapped around the middle. Some of the residents hanging around under the tree looked at each other with astonishment and a few laughed. Pooter was out in the grass and said, "Uh oh! I think I stepped on somthin'." He retrieved a somewhat flattened tennis ball and then tossed it back in the grass with a dismissive "I don't want it."

The softball was returned, but interest was rapidly flagging in resuming the game. Martha had one of the tennis balls and was intently peeling the tape off as the group was lining up at the fence to be escorted back to the ward. "I think I've heard about these things."

Nicole took the ball from Martha and said, "I think I've heard about these as well, Martha. You need to give that to me."

Nicole removed the rest of the tape and opened the ball. She removed a sealed plastic bag containing yellow powder. "Holy crap!" She called over to Old Wally. "Hey, Wally, bring me that tennis ball."

Wally responded, "I ain't got no ball."

"Well, I need to call the hospital police when we get back."

The balls were found seventy-five to a hundred yards from the perimeter fence near where Victor's tennis ball garden was located. These balls clearly didn't belong so close to the softball field.

Watching from a distance with great interest was Victor. The balls got moved by those stupid dogs again. They're not toys dammit. And what about that chick calling the po-po? He was going to have to make some phone calls himself. Those friendly K-9 patrol dogs needed to be trained to leave the friggin' tennis balls alone.

It was almost 5:00 p.m. when Nicole made a call to hospital security. Dispatch said an officer would be right over. All the residents were accounted for on the unit. Nicole reported what happened to the shift charge, Davis Swann, who seemed annoyed. "Nicole, you're supposed to report these things to me first before you start calling campus police."

"Well, you would have called them anyhow, right?"

"Of course, but I have responsibility for what goes on during the shift, and I have to document it. Anyhow, what did you find?"

"The residents found some tennis balls behind the ball field fence in the weeds."

"What were they doing back there?"

"Looking for the softball. The new resident hit a home run."

"That's why we send extra staff along. You can't keep much of an eye on residents traipsing around in the weeds, can you? And you don't know what kind of contraband they can come up with, case in point," he said, holding the small sealed packet of what appeared to be methamphetamine, maybe cocaine. "Anybody could just sneak off with this stuff, and you would never know."

"Which is why I called security," Nicole responded. "They need to do a thorough search of the area, probably bring the dogs in."

"Let me take it from here. I'll file the incident report." That would save Nicole about thirty minutes on the computer.

A few minutes later, the rear door to the back of the ward, facing toward the service road unlocked with a thud that reverberated down the hallway. Officer Pete Tuolumne entered with another frontline officer and a very friendly golden retriever wagging her tail and sniffing at everyone's feet and socks as she walked by. Some of the residents lining the hall bent over and petted her. She licked a few hands.

"What do we have here?" By this time, Swann had possession of the packet and handed it off to the officer.

"One of the residents found this out on the grounds."

"Behind the softball field," Nicole added.

"Yes, I see," Officer Tuolumne noted. He scowled as he examined the packet, held it up to the light, and sniffed at it. He held it low so Candy, the golden Lab, could offer an opinion. She sniffed at the bag and wagged her tail and resumed her happy rounds of checking out socks and sneakers and a few crotches.

"I guess we'll just have to send this out for testing." The cop then placed the packet in a larger plastic evidence bag. "Is that it?"

Davis shrugged his shoulders and raised his hands. "I guess that's it."

The two officers headed back down the hallway with Candy and out the back door, which slammed closed. The staff knew that was the last they would ever hear about the contraband.

CHAPTER 29

The residents were enjoying a midday July Fourth barbecue in the courtyard shared by several surrounding wards. The returned escapee, Burton Peals, was lunching in the secure courtyard at a steel picnic table bolted to the concrete patio.

Ash had been asking about the man who made the news so spectacularly just a few weeks before. Burton was not allowed away from his ward because of his escape, but the courtyard was considered secure.

Ash held a plastic plate with a grilled hot dog, a pickle, and chips as he approached Burton, who was taking a big bite of a grilled hamburger.

"Mind if I have a seat here?" Ash asked.

Burton looked at Ash. "You can sit wherever you want."

"You're Burton, right? I'm Ash."

Burton kept eating and said nothing.

"I wanted to meet you and talk to you," Ash said politely.

Burton responded, "If you're looking for advice on how to escape, you better ask somebody else."

"No, I really want to talk to you."

Burton finished the last of his burger and wiped his mouth. "I think I'll get another."

Ash offered, "Let me get it for you."

"I don't need nobody getting anything for me. I don't know what the hell you'll put in it."

Ash looked at Burton and smiled. "You think I want to poison you? Why the hell would I do that?"

Burton answered, "People do a lot of crazy shit. Go get it if you want to."

Ash went over to the grill, which was being tended by Nicole wearing a chef's hat and apron. A couple of patients were volunteering to help out. When he returned with the fresh hamburger, he noticed his hot dog was almost gone, as Burton was finishing it off.

"Was it tasty?" Ash asked sarcastically.

"Yeah, man, I figured it was safe, just the right amount of relish too."

"Well, I guess I'll have this burger then," Ash replied.

"Be my guest, I'm getting kind of full."

"Listen, Burt—"

"Call me Burton, would ya?"

"Anyhow, Burton, like I said, I'd like to talk to you about your escape and capture."

"Wazzup with that?"

"Okay, I'm a writer, and I own a weekly paper in Charleston and your experience might make for a good story. That's why I'm here."

Burton burst out laughing. "You're a writer—that's good. That's why you're here. Yes, that's a new one. Well played, my friend."

"Okay, it's funny, so you gonna talk to me?"

"You gonna pay me?"

Good idea, Ash thought. "How about fifty bucks?"

"Payable when?"

"When I get it, which I will."

"I'll give you a week, and if I don't get it, I'll kick your ass."

"You'll get it. I'll make it sixty."

"Whatever. Who's going to read this?" Burton asked as he reached for the hamburger on Ash's plate.

"You must be hungry," Ash observed.

"Well, they're loadin' me up with all kinda meds since I got back, and they make me gain weight. I guess the food's okay. I don't see anyone dropping over."

"Ready to start talking?" Ash asked. Burton just nodded. "So how long did you plan this escape?"

"I guess not long enough."

Ash listened; he didn't take notes. He knew how to engage a subject. It was quite hot, but they had cool overly sweet lemonade to take the edge off. "Burton, you have a story to tell. I want to hear it. People want to know. This is your chance."

"Yeah, I saw myself on TV. I guess I'm famous." It took several minutes until Burton spoke freely. "I just needed to get out of this place. I made it up to the Smokies."

The paranoia that ended his freedom in the world a dozen years ago ended his freedom again. "You see, wherever you go, they got these devil women. You can go ahead and laugh, but I see 'em. Somehow I find them, or they find me. You know, I don't like to hurt people, but sometimes I don't have a choice."

"They say you were doing well here with treatment. Didn't you qualify for release? I heard you were a model patient."

"Well, I wasn't really. Anyhow, the County DA would never let me out without a fight. I committed a high profile murder, but I had to take a shot," Burton answered.

"But you qualified for release by law, at least a chance to go into the transitional community program, didn't you?"

"On paper, yes, but if the DA doesn't want you out, he'll talk a jury into keeping you forever. The legal department here isn't too keen on it either. They won't recommend release if your crime was bad enough. If some doctor thinks you're doing better, maybe deserve a chance at supervised community release, the legal department will beat that idea out of him before he gets to court."

"Even if you are doing better, even if your illness is under control?"

"If you think turning into a zombie, thinking what *they* want you to think, then I guess that's what they call doing well. Tell that to your readers. Tell 'em how they fuck up your mind here so you never want to leave. I can't leave, they don't want me to go, and there's no place I can go. I thought I could. It was worth a try." Burton bit his lip, his eyes began to water.

"You know, I guess I'm safe here. I needed a vacation. Everyone needs a vacation. I probably won't be going anywhere for a while." He placed the half-eaten burger back on the paper plate. "You can have the rest."

Ash thought about it, then picked up the half eaten burger, looked Burton in the eye, and took a bite. Ash said to Burton, "If it's good enough for you, it's good enough for me."

Burton laughed. "You're crazy man. You don't know what kinda diseases I have."

Ash said, "I trust you wouldn't let me go ahead if you knew it was harmful."

Burton was surprised. "You trust me? I never thought of people trusting me. I think you're all right, man. I guess we can talk. I'm down with that. I still want my sixty bucks."

"Hey," Ash responded, "we trust each other, right? I want to know about this business about women being possessed."

"That comes and goes. When I'm on my meds, it gets better, like the thought never completely goes away, but if I'm drinkin' or doin' crank or forget my medication—the thoughts get out of hand—then it gets very real. I fucked up out there, didn't take meds, started drinking, so here I am back home."

"Home?"

"Looks that way."

"Do you have any hope?"

Burton sighed and then smiled. "I try not to think about that too much. You know, I got out of here for a week, I got up to the mountains, a lot of excitement, at least until the end. Then it sort of went bad. I think I got it out of my system."

"You're only thirty one, though."

"Yeah, only thirty one." Burton looked down at his plate and was silent.

Ash asked, "Did you learn anything?"

"Yeah." Burton paused. "Drinking is overrated."

CHAPTER 30

Monday, July Fourth. It was supposed to be a holiday. But at the small-budget studios of WCHA, Charleston's channel 11, Alyse Hazelwood was on duty. Sorry, no paid holidays for first year employees, no paid overtime, and one week paid vacation only after one full year on the job. No union here. That was okay with Alyse. It was sweaty hot outside, and at least one thing always working in broadcast studios is the air-conditioning.

She was preparing for the six o'clock news. The longer-term employees and the on-camera "talent'" were off for the day with an inexperienced young weekend anchor, an enthusiastic, slender, young black guy, Lamont Andrews, holding down the news desk. Alyse wanted to try her hand as weekend anchor, but management thought too much gravitas would dilute her sugary image. Alyse knew she was a draw and thought she could negotiate paid major holidays by Labor Day.

In the meantime, she was looking at some printed charts from the NWS, the National Weather Service. Hurricane Cleo, now a category two (or "cat two" as they say in the business), slowed up just a little north of the Bahamas. Although it wasn't spoiling the Independence Day holiday for people enjoying the day in the Low Country, the news wasn't good. Cleo was meandering around in the warm waters, feeding off the Gulf Stream, building strength. The predictions were vague. On some of the other stations, the pricey private weather services where in disagreement as to where the storm would go. She wasn't allowed to use information from other stations. Using information that wasn't paid for could result in a lawsuit. It wouldn't have helped too much today anyway, as no one knew where the storm was headed. The NWS posted hurricane watches from Daytona Beach to Nags Head, North Carolina. Alyse explained that a watch means a possible strike but not clearly evident that the storm would actually hit. Keep your eyes open. A warning is posted once a storm is predicted to hit the area. There were only watches, not warnings posted so far.

Her job was going well; she was getting attention and actually learning about meteorology. It was interesting, but the predicting part was still a challenge. The NWS provided a forecast, and she would add her own little twist. She visited weather chat rooms online and made some knowledgeable friends, especially after she posted her picture.

It's not really difficult to predict the weather for the South Carolina coast in the summer. Just look for hazy, hot, and humid, with a chance for afternoon thundershowers. But now, a six-hundred-pound gorilla of a storm was hanging out over tropical waters to the south and east.

Earlier in the day, she shot some footage of the local Red Cross and hurricane preparedness officials doing their thing. No one was panicking; no rush to the supermarkets for supplies. There was only a small bump in the business at the big box construction supply marts.

She looked at the radar and then the satellite image of the soft-looking white pinwheel of a storm, five hundred miles to the southeast, wobbling, not making a commitment. Didn't Hugo do the same thing back in 1989? Although Alyse grew up along the southern Georgia coast, she had never experienced a real significant hurricane during her lifetime. Now this could be exciting.

Alyse watched the video of the noon forecast from rival channel three. Gloria Considine, an actual certified meteorologist, was off for the holiday. The channel three weekend weatherman utilizing data from SkyTime Weather had the storm turning to the north and grazing the outer banks. There was a similar forecast from the other major rival channel that also had the hurricane tracking to the north.

High pressure was predicted to move over the northeast coast, divert the hurricane, and shear away some of the intensity of the storm. The computer models were in agreement. Alyse studied the graphs some more. Her retired professor chat-room friend had his own ideas. What if? What if the front slows down? Another high-pressure developing system over the Leeward Islands could kick the storm smack into the southeast coast. Or not. That wasn't predicted by the major weather services.

Pete Pollard, the technical director for the weekend news was going over the graphics with Lamont for the local news and sports, as Lamont had to double up and do both. He checked in with Alyse to review the choreography of the newscast and the order of the on air traffic.

"Whadya think of this storm?"

"I don't know what to think, but if I have to guess—"

"That's your job, isn't it?"

"Right, so I'm going to tell the audience to get their asses in gear because Cleo is coming our way."

Pete scratched his head. "Wait a minute, where the hell did you get that from? Everyone else is saying it's blowing to the north."

Alyse assertively stated, "Well, I'm not everyone else."

"Well, then, you're going to get people panicking and evacuating and canceling things."

"Maybe they should."

Hurricanes pass by every summer. I ignore them. I sleep like a log."

"I hope you're a log that can float."

"Y'know, you pull this stuff on the weekend, management will have your ass tomorrow."

Alyse chuckled. "They've wanted my ass since I got here. If they haven't gotten it yet, they're not going to now. Do you want me to explain why I don't agree with the other forecasts?"

"Forget it, just tell me what you got for us. I don't do the programming around here."

"Okay, I want a graphic of this hurricane moving toward us, maybe Charleston, maybe a little south."

"Are you just guessing or just trying to juice up ratings with a little drama?"

Alyse smiled. "Well, either way, people will be watchin', won't they? And that's money. And nobody will say I'm stealing information because I'm the only one right now who's calling for it to hit."

"Okay, when?"

"I'd say Wednesday late, maybe Thursday."

"Are you sure you want to do this? If you flub it, cause a big brouhaha, and nothin' happens, they'll show you the door."

Alyse had some inquiries from other bigger markets, Memphis and Charlotte most recently. *I'm out the door with or without their help,* she thought. *And if I'm right, well, then who knows where the big opportunities lie. And hell, I might just save a few lives.*

Alyse wasn't just guessing, though. She was considering a rather esoteric algorithm for hurricane tracking predictions, which she didn't completely understand but went to an internet weather chat earlier in the day where she had a bit of back and forth with a recent online friend, a retired meteorology professor from Penn State. He was apparently entranced with her photo on the station web site and thought he may as well share his unpublished theories. They exchanged numerous instant messages and e-mails.

She shared her quandary, and the old professor ran some numbers and wrote back, "All the predominant weather services have their heads up their collective asses. They're talking through both sides of their mouths. I've been tracking this beast for a week, and she's not going north. The front over the southeast is going to occlude, and another low pressure ridge is going to develop off shore and kick this thing right into the Carolina or Georgia coast. My calculations don't lie." He proceeded to give her his detailed prediction on how the life of this particular hurricane was going to play out.

She showed her gratitude. "Professor, I'll send you a file with my forecast segment. You are so sweet. I'll owe you one. :-) xoxo, Alyse."

He wrote, "Keep in touch!" She would.

And now for the WCHA Live on Eleven six o'clock news with Lamont Andrews and Alyse Hazelwood.

Lamont looked into the teleprompter and smiled. "Good evening, Charleston and the Low Country. Tonight we start off with a special report from Alyse Hazelwood and some breaking weather news. What do you have for us, Alyse?"

Alyse decided to back off the sugary drawl. This recording was going into her portfolio. "Thanks, Lamont. It appears the South Carolina and Georgia coasts are bracing for what is now a category two, soon to be a category three hurricane. You can see on the satellite photo that Hurricane Cleo is wobbling out here in the central Bahamas. We thought she was going to turn and head north, but my computer model now has Cleo picking up speed later tonight, intensifying and shifting on a more rapid westerly track. You can see a large eye at the center of the storm, but I expect that to tighten up as circulation around the eye wall becomes more intense. Right now the central pressure is at 970 millibars or about 28.70 inches of mercury, and that will be dropping through the night. If you live along the barrier islands or other low-lying areas, it's time to consider boarding up your homes, protecting your property, and moving your family and pets to higher ground. We're looking for landfall about 48 to 60 hours from now."

Gloria Considine had the evening off and was in her kitchen frying hamburgers for the kids. Her husband, Rick, was watching the news when he called Gloria to "get in here quick. You won't believe this." He hit replay on the DVR, and Gloria stared at what she considered to be her younger and prettier but scatterbrained rival going out on some kind of forecasting limb.

"Let me see that again." She squinted and looked up and said, "What the fuck? Where did this bimbo get that idea? That's ridiculous!"

The unattended burgers started to burn. "Mommy, it's smoky."

"Shit," she said as the smoke alarm went off. She ran back to the stove and flipped the burgers into the sink and ran water over the pan. Steam and smoke filled the kitchen; the alarm continued to shriek.

"Mommy, what are we gonna have for dinner?"

Her eyes bulged, and she spoke a very constrained "Not . . . now! Rick, fix the kids something and open the goddamn windows."

Gloria headed into her personal study and reviewed the charts and graphs. She ran through the past six hours of movement and breathed a sigh of relief. "No way, this bimbo is full of crap. I'm going to be embarrassed for her."

Calls started coming in to the station even during the newscast, but the listed numbers go to the office, not the newsroom. One call did come to the newsroom directly, after the newscast ended. Pete answered the phone. It was Tony Most, "I want to talk to her, now!"

Alyse's glow didn't last long, but she was expecting the call. Tony curtly asked, "What are you doing?"

"Forecasting the weather, Tony—that's my job."

"You're telling people to evacuate. You're not the governor. You're not the sheriff."

"I'm trying to save lives."

"Well, I've been watching the other stations and following the web sites, and you are the only person making this bizarre prediction."

"Tony, I think you'll thank me. If I'm wrong, I'll quit."

"We'll all have to quit."

"No, we won't, and you'll be giving me a raise, and Labor Day off. Look, you hired me to predict the weather."

"Not really, we hired you to read the NWS reports and look pretty while doing it."

"Now I'm going to look smart too. You watch my 10:00 p.m. report tonight and watch the other weather reports, and if you don't like it, you can fire me first thing in the morning,"

"I'm planning that anyhow."

"Then who'll do the weather forecast?"

"I don't know—the cleaning lady, anybody who can read and take directions."

"Tell you what, Tony, if I'm right—and baby, I will be—then you apologize, and you can do a weather forecast."

"I might have to tonight for all I know." He hung up.

Alyse stepped outside and took a deep breath of the thick, late afternoon air. Kids were popping off their cherry bombs and getting a head start on the bottle rockets. Maybe nothing like two or three nights from now when the storm moves in. She decided to indulge in a real Southern supper. What could be better on the Fourth of July than some fried chicken and corn on the cob? Not the usual fare for slender Alyse, but she was nervous too.

She got back to the station at eight. The evening lineup consisted of syndicated game and cop shows. After logging onto the NWS Web site to review the progress of Cleo, Alyse said to herself softly, "Cleo, you and I are in this together. Don't let Mama down." The latest reading showed the central pressure had dropped to 962 millibars and movement shifted more westerly. The latest update described a western shift in the path, with sustained winds now at 110 mph. The professor was right on track. Projected impact was now on the outer banks of North Carolina. Given that, she was certainly justified in warning the locals to be on guard, although as of yet, they were not predicted to be in the direct path. She planned to bring the revised NWS forecast into her report.

At 9:30 p.m., Tony Most showed up at the station. People were gathered around Charleston Harbor to watch the big fireworks display. He would have been there sooner, but traffic coming over the bridge was awful. He hoped not too many people were going to be watching the ten o'clock news.

Tony found Alyse. "I don't think I can let you go on the air tonight."

"Say what?"

"We have a responsibility in situations like this to not cause undue drama."

Alyse grabbed Tony by the arm and pulled him over to the computer. "Look, in the past few hours, things are changing with this hurricane. I'm right."

Tony looked at the repeating loop of the storm's progress. It was 9:45 p.m. The NWS was now predicting landfall of a cat three along the North Carolina/South Carolina border. With any further change, Charleston would be in trouble.

"How did you know this?"

"I had a little help from my friends."

"What friends?"

It's a long story, Tony, but my source is impeccable and free. We're going to come out on top in this one."

Tony sat down in one of the soft swivel desk chairs, closed his eyes, rubbed his forehead, and sighed, "Okay, go with it. I hate to root for a hurricane, but I pray you're right."

CHAPTER 31

Plato Ballinger, former member of the local chapter of the Silver Swords motorcycle club and chief cook for the meetings, was cooking up some sticky yellow-white powder in his barn, on the outskirts of Wadsworth. The door was wide open, and the overhead exhaust fan was drawing in the summer night air. Just to be sure, there was a hood with its own exhaust fan to draw off the noxious fumes as he carefully added the platinum oxide to the crushed pseudo-ephedrine. The ingredients were getting harder and harder to obtain. It might be time to retire from this business. Just a few more paydays.

When he wasn't synthesizing meth, he customized bikes. His own club sported signature long, sleek choppers, painted silver with silver accessories. These were the swords. His own bike was "Excalibur."

The meth was something he didn't use anymore; and he helped get his woman, a quiet twenty-six–year-old by the name of Greta, clean and sober. She had been getting painfully thin. Once pretty, she had been getting more like a scarecrow with multiple tats, piercings, and spikey green and blond hair. That was a year ago; since then, she had gained about twenty pounds, which still left her on the slender side of average. She let her gelled hair down, shampooed into a normal feminine look, and let the green grow out. The acne and scabs had cleared up. She actually became younger in body and spirit.

She had been prostituting herself when Plato found her. They tooted together, and she rode with him on Excalibur in the "bitch seat." She told him of her childhood sexual abuse. He wanted to kill the perverted stepfather who perpetrated these atrocities, but he was late. Stepdaddy died years ago from a heroin overdose. He wore the colors of a different club, the Croozers. They were into pimping and prostitution. The Silver Swords were more into drugs.

They stopped together, about a year ago. It was Plato's idea to get Greta to stop, which she always wanted to do anyhow. But she wouldn't stop unless he did as well. One fine night, a year ago, they closed themselves in the farmhouse and smoked the night away until they reached a state of frenzy and then collapsed. That was the last hit, and they never looked back. Still, Plato cooked up a batch every week.

He left the Silver Swords with a no-compete clause. The Swords ran the meth business along the coast. Plato couldn't really quit the club; he still rode the bike, wore the colors, displayed the tats on his beefy arms, and paid dues. But he rode alone, except when he rode with Greta. He still had one secret customer. His old buddies would never find out. Every few weeks, his client would ride over to the farmhouse and give Plato six crisp one hundred dollar bills in return for four plastic sandwich bags filled with the magic crystals, all high quality. He didn't know exactly what his client did with it, although he correctly surmised that he sold it for three or four times what he paid Plato for it.

Greta was morphing into a real woman. He wanted to shut down his lab for a number of reasons. He might get busted, his old buddies might kill him, and maybe Greta, while they were at it. Most of all, he was beginning to love this woman, who was just a little more than half his age. She needed him, right? Or did he need her? Anyhow, it might be good to get rid of the lab before it blows up and gets rid of him. That happens. But there's the matter of the money, a major issue. There was no easy solution at the moment. Get honest work? Who's going to hire a fifty-year-old fat biker? Maybe he could step up the customizing business. Oh yeah, if he had a real job, he would have to pay real taxes. Running his own legit business was probably the best bet.

One good use for the money was paying for Greta's therapy. There was a psychologist in Beaufort who was doing good work with her. He needed money from the meth lab to pay for her substance recovery treatment. Whatever it takes. Greta wanted Plato to come with her to Narcotics Anonymous meetings, but he figured he couldn't get better listening to a lot of other people's problems. He would stay out of trouble working on his bike in the barn and maybe cooking up more methamphetamine, maybe just one more time.

On the night of July Fourth, around eleven, Plato was relaxing on his back porch, pumping beer out of a quarter keg parked in a tub of ice. Greta was in the bedroom of the somewhat shabby farmhouse that had a foundation of random unsecured cinderblocks. She was reading the New Testament, something she had taken up in the past year, although she did it as a child, hoping for refuge from the abuse and violence of her biker stepdad. There was an old TV in the living room hooked up to bent rabbit ears. They didn't watch very much. The bedroom was the only room in the house that had an air conditioner. It hummed and rattled, noisy inside and out. They were used to it. Neither of them heard the doorbell ring or the pounding on the door that followed.

The uniformed police officer walked around the back of the house

MIKE BARTOS

and caught Plato somewhat by surprise. Plato looked at the officer with a quick startle. "Dooley, you scared the shit out of me. Don't you believe in knocking?"

"Hell, I almost took your front door off. Got some extra of that beer?"

"Sure, I got plenty, grab a cup. I'm just gettin' started." There was a stack of red plastic cups on a picnic table.

"Where's that lovely young thing you keep around here?"

"She's up in the bedroom reading the Bible."

"I guess she won't be joining us, then."

"Nah, she's into this clean and sober business. She wants me to go all the way with it. I gave up my ice. I ain't ready to give up my beer—don't think that's ever gonna happen."

"Yeah, I hear you," Sergeant Dooley agreed. "Just as long as she leaves you be."

"I think I met her more than halfway, just as well."

Dooley downed a cup, about half filled with foam. "Looks like you've put on a little weight, my friend." He refilled his cup from the tap.

"Beer is a lot more fattening than meth, doncha know?"

"Listen, I can't stick around all night. The wife is expecting me home. The kids are probably still up, excited from the fireworks and all. I have the money. I hope you don't mind twenties. I had to stop at the ATM machine after hours."

"As long as it's green and it's real, I'm okay." Six hundred dollars in an envelope; Plato didn't count it. They walked to the barn in back of the house. It was equally as dilapidated. Plato handed the cop a brown paper bag with four plastic bags inside, each filled with the promised goods.

"I guess you'll clear twenty-five or thirty bills out of that."

"I wish," Dooley said. "I got expenses, you know."

Plato never asked who Dooley's customers were, despite the South Carolina Department of Behavioral Health Services logo on his uniform and badge. He could guess, but he really didn't want to know. If it was going to patients, it probably didn't matter. He supposed they were all pretty fucked up to begin with.

Dooley walked around to the front of the house and got into a black-and-white police car with "Bay Area State Hospital" on the front door, superimposed over an outline of the State of South Carolina. The car pulled out of the muddy unpaved driveway and turned onto the two-lane blacktop in front of the house.

As he was driving away, Dooley thought to himself, *Damn, I forgot to tell him to watch out for the hurricane. Oh well, he'll probably catch it on the news.*

Waiting and watching from across the road were two men sitting on their long sleek silver choppers. It was eleven thirty. Assorted cherry bombs and M16s were exploding in random backyards of the old rural houses nearby. The two men dismounted their bikes and crossed the road by foot, across the sloppy mud, and around to the back porch. Each carried a sawed-off 20-gauge shotgun, easily concealed as they rode. They rounded toward the back of the house, one man circling from the left and the other from the right. Plato was squeaking back and forth in his old rocker on the loose wooden planks of the back porch. He was lifting a refreshed cup to his lips when he froze, and his eyes bulged. "Beau, what the hell you doin' here?" He knew damn well what his former roadmates were doing here. The shotguns were plainly visible.

Unlike Plato, Beau was skinny, wearing a baggy undershirt. He was balding, with a thin wisp of a goatee. "Plato, I didn't know you were so friendly with the cops."

Plato sputtered, "He's not a real cop, just a state hospital security cop. You know that place over in Bayside."

"We know all about it. And we know business is real slow over there. We were kinda wonderin' why. Now we know."

"This was going to be my last batch, I swear."

"You got that right. And for old times' sake, we're gonna make it real quick. Consider yourself lucky."

"But I—"

"I thought you were like a brother to me until you dropped out. Now this."

A cherry bomb went off at a neighbor's house about fifty yards away. Beau pulled the trigger as an explosive burst of shot tore into Plato's chest. Blood spattered on the porch and on Beau's jeans and undershirt. Plato slumped forward onto the floor. Beau bolted off the porch and started to run—"C'mom, man"—and disappeared around the side of the house. The other man, Reggie, saw an envelope on the picnic table. There was cash sticking out. He grabbed it and stuffed it down his pants, took a quick gulp of beer, then ran around the other side of the house.

The men ran together across the muddy yard, back across the road, and then hopped on their bikes. They separated and roared off in opposite directions.

The explosive shot jarred Greta awake. She looked out the back window

MIKE BARTOS

and saw nothing. She figured some redneck might have gotten carried away and set off a stick of dynamite. It's happened before. Or maybe the boiler exploded (again). She went down to the back porch and saw the horrid mess and stood frozen at the screen door. Plato was face down in a puddle of blood. She shrieked and ran to him and turned him over. The scattered shot had hit his chest and gut, and there were some wounds in the neck. Plato gasped; he was still alive. He looked into Greta's face; and with his last breath in this world, the only thing he could say, with fluid gurgling up into his throat, was "Beau."

CHAPTER 32

The Fourth of July was quiet for Sally J. She stayed away from the hospital at the request of Ash, who was talking and listening to a variety of patients, learning what he could without the distraction of her visit. Ash was not one to play victim. As far as he was concerned, he was on the job gathering information, getting the story that would rejuvenate his writing career. There was more than an article here; there was an exposé, a human story, a story about defeat and victories of the spirit. But he couldn't stay there forever. He should be out this week sometime, probably sooner than later. That's what he had in mind. Roswell Chamblee would make it happen.

On that hot breezy night, while Alyse Hazelwood was outside the TV station admiring a sliver of grinning moon in the hazy velvet sky, Plato Ballinger's bloody body was being cradled by his grief-stricken woman, and Roswell and Sally J were in the living room of the charming brick carriage house on Cumberland Street, discussing plans and strategy for the coming week. Roswell had spent the afternoon drawing up his motion, which he would present to Judge Silberman in the morning, provided, of course, that the Judge was in bright and early. The low rumble of the not too distant fireworks, entertaining a large throng along East Bay Street and the Battery, had ceased along with the Charleston Symphony's rendition of *Stars and Stripes Forever*. Families with kids were heading home, back to John's Island and Mount Pleasant, while the younger, single folks sought out a variety of Charleston pubs and eateries, including Kerrigan's Bar and Grille.

Roswell was prepping Sally J for court. "Sally J, you'll be telling the judge about what happened. You have the passport?"

"Kerrigan has it, but I have a copy of the marriage certificate and his birth certificate."

"That should work. You probably won't need them, though."

"Oh, Rozzie, you think we'll get him out tomorrow?"

"I think so, if we can get the judge to issue a minute order and fax it down to the state hospital. They'll have to let him go within a few hours. I hope we can drive down and pick him up. One of us can drive the Honda home. I guess that would be me. This is a little more complicated than it first seems, though, but I'm confident we can get the order signed."

Sally J poured another glass of Chardonnay for herself and Cabernet for Roswell.

"Maybe he could drive himself home if he can find the key to the Honda."

Neither of them spoke. Sally J was tired; she had been drinking more wine than usual this weekend. She asked, "What do families do when they have a loved one locked in that awful place for real, for years?"

"I guess they just pray a lot. That's what I'd do."

"That's what ah've been doin'."

Roswell savored the full-bodied Napa red; Sally J remembered Cabernet was his favorite. He spoke. "Listen, sweetie, it's late, and I better get home and get some rest. I'll get going. It's about a ten minute walk, but in my current condition, it'll probably take a little longer."

They both rose from their chairs to share a customary good-bye hug and stopped. He gently put his hands on her waist. Sally J was slightly off guard. He looked in her eyes. She returned his gentle gaze, her eyes moving across his face. They said nothing. He hesitated but then moved his lips toward hers. She reached toward him and slid her arms around him until they were in full embrace. Their eyes fixed on each other. Their lips met, softly at first and then passionately. She pulled her face away and fixed her eyes on him once again. She breathed heavily. They kissed deeply, in full embrace, standing in the living room, pressing themselves tightly together, as if to make up for all the space between them over the years.

"Roswell," she whispered his name softly. He caressed her face gently, brushing her reddish blonde hair away from her face and lips. He leaned toward her and again gently touched his lips against hers, planting light kisses along her neck as she tilted her head back, inviting him to kiss her smooth white throat. Without saying a word, she took Roswell's hand, guiding him toward the bedroom.

The bedroom was nearly dark except for the soft glowing light reflecting from the nearby living room. They sat on the bed as Sally J pulled off her sleeveless blouse. The dim light illuminated her pale flesh as he remembered from that moonlit summer night so many years ago. The lavender lotion she used, then and now, enveloped her with an erotic fragrance and made her shoulders soft and smooth to his caress.

The years between then and now collapsed and dissipated, as if the events of half their lives never happened. They were together on the back porch of the plantation house in Cheraw, young and filled with anticipation of an infinite future. They reclined together as Roswell cradled Sally J in his arms. They kissed again as Roswell moved his hands gently over her breasts and back.

Sally J exhaled with a sob and buried her face on his shoulder. She cried with gasping hiccupping spasms. "Rozzie, no, I can't, not now, not in our bed." Her tears wetted his shirt and ran onto the pillow.

"I know, sweetie, I know. I love you. Let's just be, just now." He wanted to hear her say it, just once. That's all he wanted. It would make a difference. He would know; he could live with that.

Roswell felt her sadness and his own as well. He rocked her gently until she calmed and breathed softly and then slept.

After an hour, she stirred and snuggled against the arms around her. "Ash?" She opened her eyes and looked at Roswell. "Oh, Rozzie, oh I'm so sorry. I feel like such a fool."

Roswell answered softly, "You're anything but . . ." He kissed her on the cheek.

"I don't know what I was thinkin'."

They held each other, still and quiet. His chin rested on her head as she curled into him and buried her face in his chest. After a few minutes, he broke the silence. "I wonder if we could have been happy."

Sally J was sleepy but aroused. "Maybe, I don't know. I think about you a lot, I still do."

"I didn't know that."

"Yes, you did."

Sally J lifted her head and looked into Roswell's eyes in the dim light. "I'll always have a place for you in my heart. But I can't live two lives, I just can't."

"I'm not asking you to."

"Ash is a struggle, a pain in the ass sometimes, self-absorbed, exasperating but exhilarating. I'm not always happy, but he's my life." She sat up and smoothed her hair with her hands. As she moved her arms over her head, he looked at her small firm breasts, still pert and perfect after all these years. She leaned forward and kissed him lightly on the cheek. "If I don't get up and get dressed now, I'm not going to."

"Roswell touched her naked shoulder gently. "It's your call."

"I'll be right back." She got out of the opposite side of the bed and slipped back into her tank top. "Let me just splash off, then we can talk."

Roswell stood up. "I probably ought to go now."

"I wish you didn't have to."

"I wish I didn't have to either." She moved toward him, and they embraced once again.

"Listen . . ."

Roswell hugged her, caressed her back, and simply said, "Shhh."

After another moment, they parted. "I'll call you tomorrow when I find out what's going on." He walked out into the living room and squinted in the light. She followed him. He looked at himself in the small mirror over the fireplace, straightened his hair with his hands, licked his fingers, and patted down his cowlick. At thirty-seven, Roswell was more handsome then he was at seventeen, with his lawyerly hair, thick and dark and not so well combed, contrasting with his piercing blue eyes. Rough dark stubble of whiskers were starting to show on his otherwise smooth clean-shaven face. He opened the front door.

"Rozzie, one more thing."

He turned and listened in eager anticipation. "Yes?"

"Thanks for everything."

He smiled as he left and closed the door behind him.

CHAPTER 33

South Carolina State Police Detective Lieutenant "Big Mike" Luskasavitch was awakened from his slumber at about 0300 hours on Tuesday after enjoying a holiday with his family. Being roused in the middle of the night was part of the job—a pain in the ass but the overtime was good, good enough to pay for a mortgage on a new house by the golf course and college up north for his daughter. The call was from the Bay County Sheriff, BD Harmon.

"Hey, Mike, Sheriff Harmon here. Sorry to wake you, but we have a hot crime scene here, and I thought you better take a look at it."

"Okay, give me a minute here." The detective slipped into his sneakers by the bed and padded down to the den so as not to awaken his wife. "Wha'dya got?"

"We have a 10-36, old biker blown away at his residence along county road 219, single shotgun wound to the chest, meth lab on the property, not much product, though. Happened about 2330, common-law wife on the premises. Says she heard the blast, thought it was some cherry bombs at first, went down to investigate, found him still alive. She stayed with him, but he died within a minute or two."

"Did the victim say anything?"

"She isn't sure, something like Bo or Bro. He was choking to death at the time."

"Any physical evidence?"

"No weapon found. Lots of shot in the body of course, some shot in the wall. Widely scattered. We're guessing sawed off 20 gauge. Beer keg on the back porch, several cups, one only half finished, the victim was holding a cup when he was shot, that was found on the deck about six feet from the victim. The half-finished one was undisturbed on the table. Maybe we can get some DNA or lip print off the cup. Looks like a guest may have gotten ungracious and rowdy. There was no cash found. Maybe whoever it was decided to take off with the drugs and money."

"Well done. What else?"

"The front yard is muddy, quite a collection of footprints and tire tracks, so maybe more than one person involved."

"Are they four-wheeler or two-wheeler tracks?"

"Good question. Looks like car tracks. Deep, clear tire tread impressions. We got photos."

"Any molds?"

"We can't get a tech over here right now."

The detective bristled, "I'll make sure someone gets there soon. Give me your exact 10-20, and protect the scene."

"Okay, we're about 4.2 miles south of Wadsworth on 219. The squad cars and emergency vehicles are lighting up the place like a Christmas tree. You won't miss it. It's not supposed to rain today, but a big storm is due in later this week, so I know we need to get moving before the evidence washes away."

"Where's the wife?"

"They let her clean up. She was covered with blood, real shaken up. She's not a suspect. One of the deputies is taking a statement from her. We thought she might need some sedation, but she refused a ride to the ER. Said she can cope without meds."

"Listen up, it sounds like you have the situation under control, thanks. I'm gonna shower up, get some coffee, and make my way over there."

"Okay, I'll stay here. We have the whole property cordoned off with yellow tape. I'll send somebody to pick up some doughnuts and coffee."

LUSKASAVITCH ARRIVED IN the reddish glow of early dawn. The coroner and emergency vehicles had come and gone, but several state and local squad cars remained. The forensic technicians were on the scene, casting footprints and tire prints. Luskasavitch took a gander at some of the raw tire prints in the thick mud. Sheriff Harmon greeted the big detective. "See something?"

"I'm not totally sure, but these tracks look like they're from an eighteen-inch V-rated tire, you know, the kind you'd see on a Caprice."

"You mean like a cop car?"

"Unless you know any drug dealers who ride around in a Caprice."

"I've seen these before, but the Highway Patrol doesn't use this specific model."

"How about local cops?" the sheriff asked.

"I don't know everything. You're the sheriff here. How about doing a little research on that?" said Luskasavitch, slapping away a swarm of mosquitoes. "You got any bug repellant?"

"I got some in the car." He returned a moment later to find Luskasavitch intently looking at the muddy front yard.

MIKE BARTOS

"What I see here is one set of foot prints coming from the car to the house, and a reverse set of the same prints. Looks like boot prints. There's different boot prints around each side of the house, boots with thicker heels. We'll have to check the victim's shoes too. Can someone get a sample of the mud from the yard?"

"Already done, Mike."

"Good, looks like we all have some work to do. I hope to hell we don't have cop involvement here."

"Yeah, but it won't be the first time, probably not the last. Are you getting the Drug Investigation Unit involved?"

"You bet. I'll make the call after 0830. We'll need all the help we can get."

The rising sun cast a golden orange radiance across the tops of the surrounding loblolly pines. There was not even a hint of breeze. Clouds of mosquitoes hummed, looking for breakfast. They would retreat into the shadows for the day as the sun would rise higher. Big Mike needed to return to the Walterboro barracks. This wasn't the only crime on his plate. The drug dealers were wreaking havoc these days, while law enforcement staff was being cut.

CHAPTER 34

Damn! I slept too late after a fine weekend. It was Tuesday, July 5, a little past 6:00 a.m. Despite the early hour, the sun was glowing through the blinds in my apartment. I had to be in McMurtree by ten for a court appearance. I took Grover downstairs and scooted him out to the courtyard behind our pub. The sheets still had Cassandra's perfumed scent from Saturday night and Sunday morning. I made a note to myself to run a load of laundry, but I wasn't planning to be back until the following weekend. I had decided to rest July Fourth night, chill out, not go out. But the July Fourth revelers were in full swing out on Market Street and in the pub too. I guess I'm in the unique position of staying in, taking it easy, yet having a bar with a swinging band underneath my feet. I probably should have gone back to my bungalow on the marsh Monday night but I didn't. No excuses, sir, except, life is short.

It's a small apartment, but there is a glorious skylight in the bathroom that opens with a chain. During the long days of June and July, the sun illuminates the apartment with slanting beams of dusty sunlight in the early morning hours. No alarm necessary. I took a quick shower, as a spiraling column of steam twisted its way up through the skylight and vented out to early morning Charleston.

I shaved quickly in the small sunlit bathroom, with a towel wrapped around my waist while the percolator, ten steps away on the kitchen counter gurgled rhythmically, brewing the dark brown morning nectar, ready to bring my brain up to speed. A bowl of instant grits, sprinkled liberally with cinnamon and sugar, and I was almost ready to go. It was just a little after seven, not bad timing. Grover wolfed down a full can of dog food, did his business in the courtyard, and then scooted into the backseat; and we were off, back home to Bayside. We'd arrive at the house about eight fifteen, driving against the rush-hour traffic, and then I would drop Grover off at the house, and then be at the courthouse a little after nine. What a way to start the week.

Driving down the coastal highway allowed me time to think because I don't do it enough at other times. I hadn't spoken with Sally J since Sunday afternoon. She was anxious, of course, but she and Roswell were preparing to make their move today. Roswell was going to be in the Charleston County

Courthouse this morning, filing for a writ to get her husband out of BASH. I couldn't do too much, being on "administrative reassignment" and not being able to get inside the confined perimeter.

She wanted to interview me on life at the state hospital. I suppose right now, while I'm struggling to keep my job intact, would not be the most propitious time to start pissing people off. It occurred to me that might have been what Dawkins wanted to do, and he ended up in a position where he wasn't going to speak his mind. I dismissed that idea as paranoid.

Once I cleared the West Ashley traffic, I thought about the hearing. I was subpoenaed by the DA; I was going to be his witness as to why Ernie Joe was dangerous and had to remain at the county jail. He was being represented by the public defender, Ms. Andover Gibbs who wanted to move him out of jail and back to the hospital. The lady doesn't let up until the judge brings the gavel down. She has been in contempt a dozen times, but she pays the fines, occasionally spends an afternoon in the slammer, but keeps on shouting down the opposition on cross-examination. On this particular day, that would be me.

Actually, I like the lady outside of the courtroom. I have been her witness on a couple of occasions. We had lunch together a couple of times, and she could be charming, sharing stories about her teenage son and how she was training for a marathon; but generally, she would leave her personal charm outside the courtroom door, except of course, when addressing the jury. I suppose if I were locked up in BASH, I would want her fighting for me. A woman who runs marathons won't quit. I don't like being on the opposite side from her, but at least I know what to expect.

She was just going to love that I was on administrative reassignment. This hearing was a court hearing; that is, the judge decides the matter, not a jury, so at least Leticia wouldn't have to put on that big of a show.

We reached the bungalow, and I closed the gate on Grover in the backyard. I tossed him a hard baked pig's ear to keep him happy for a while. I went inside, put on a nice red tie, which I never wear except for court, checked out the bathroom, and back to the car for the twenty-minute ride over to McMurtree.

It was a fine morning—bright, clear blue sky, no haze, calm, and just enough breeze to rustle the leaves at the very top of the trees. That's why I was surprised to hear on the car radio that the low country was at high risk to get hit by a strong hurricane within the next couple of days. Now that would suck. Those of us who make our home along the South Carolina beaches, marshes, and coastal plains, known as the low country, have to keep hurricanes in the back of our minds. Since Hugo hit Charleston in 1989, everyone is more conscious of safety. My house, which is six years old, is nine feet off the ground on cinderblock pilings, as required by FEMA, the Federal Emergency Management Agency. But a lot of the older houses, especially on the barrier islands and marshes are ripe for getting washed away with a good-sized storm surge. I worry about some of my humble neighbors. I'll have to keep tuned.

On this lovely morning, the town square, courthouse, and fountain were picture postcard perfect. I had to meet with the assistant DA, Hilton Breuer, before the hearing. I've worked with him before, as has everyone. Hilly has been around, some think, since the Civil War. He retired from private practice ten years ago but couldn't enjoy doing nothing. He appeared to be the quintessential southern gentleman, with a flowing mane of silver hair and bushy gray eyebrows. He spoke slowly and in measured tones, taking time to pause in front of a jury for effect. He and Ms. Andover Gibbs provided a good and entertaining matchup. Despite the adversarial relationship in the courtroom, they would be invited to each other's Christmas parties. On this day, however, Christmas was a long way off.

It was about twenty to ten when I was ushered into his office in a small two-story building a half block from the courthouse. He stood to greet me, looked me in the eye, shook my hand with his right hand, and firmly grasped my right elbow with his left. He smiled gently and said, "Doctor, It's always a pleasure to see you, I'm glad you could make it."

Like I had a choice. "It's a pleasure to see you again, Hilton."

"Donut?" gesturing at a pink bakery box of glazed doughnuts.

Not a bad idea to gird up before battle, I always say.

He leaned back in his desk chair and crossed his legs. "So we have your boy, Ernie Joe, and I understand the state's position of wanting to keep him in the jail, away from the other patients. So the purpose of today's hearing is to determine the disposition of your patient, and I know you'll agree with the state."

"Done deal as far as I'm concerned. You need to know something, though. I got myself on administrative transfer on Friday."

"What the hell is that?"

It's like a suspension, but they stick me in the library. I don't see patients, but I get paid."

"What did you do?"

"It's a long story. I don't think I can explain it now, but there's no malpractice or moral issues involved."

"Okay, so you're not officially suspended?"

"True, I'm not suspended."

Breuer added, "I'll shut up Leticia if she tries to make a big deal out of it."

"I'm sure she will."

"I'll just ask you about your credentials as usual, and I'll ask you why you think your patient should stay at the jail. Mrs. Gibbs can make all the fuss she wants. Judge Gaillard is usually on top of these things."

He paused momentarily to answer the phone. After a brief conversation, he said, "The judge will be ready in a half hour. They're bringing Mr. Plumm over from the jail. They had to find a deputy for escort."

"So shall we go?"

"Would you like another doughnut first?"

I wouldn't usually agree to a second doughnut, but this must be nervous eating day.

We walked out into the warm sunshine. There was the sound of a power mower being pushed by a county laborer across the large green lawn in front of the courthouse and the smell of freshly cut grass.

People were relaxing on benches in the shade under the expansive oak tree known as the Governor's Tree. In 1934, then Democratic gubernatorial candidate Olin Dewitt Talmadge Johnson gave a campaign speech under that very tree. He won the democratic primary, which in the Solid South was tantamount to winning the general election, which he did handily as there was no Republican to oppose him. He went on to become a US senator, and the citizens of McMurtree dedicated the tree to his honor.

Out by the fountain on the green stands a pedestal with a bust of the fabled Senator Strom Thurmond. Three flags fly on three poles in front of the courthouse, the American flag, the flag of South Carolina, and the Confederate flag. McMurtree is a town of the Old South, taking its good old time moving into the twenty-first century. It's the county seat of Bay County, the same county that is home to the town of Bayside and the Bay Area State Hospital. McMurtree is twelve miles and a world away from upscale and yuppified Bayside with beachfront and marsh front condos, "award winning" golf courses, and restaurants with their own executive chefs.

Twenty years ago, if someone had told the county council that there would be a restaurant with a sommelier in their county, they would have laughed him out of the state, after they figured out what a sommelier was. Now the county council members were at the bidding of the developers,

MIKE BARTOS

approving every high-rise project on top of the dunes and every sea wall that protected the new hotels from the encroaching surf, holding the sea back in front of the favored developments and sending it around the walls up into the dunes and onto nearby streets at high tide.

"Hell," the county council president once inadvisably told a Charleston reporter, "people in McMurtree wouldn't know a condo from a condom. And those folks in Bayside don't vote here. They got summer homes here and live in Charleston and Atlanta, or they're Yankees from somewhere up north, New York and the like." He was reelected in any event.

Now me, I'm registered to vote in Bayside, as I'm technically living in the municipality even though I'm about four miles from the beachfront strip and the touristy downtown area. They don't fly the Stars and Bars in Charleston anymore, so even Charlestonians are sometimes looked on with suspicion.

Hilton and I had to sit around the courtroom for a half hour longer than anticipated. Judge Gaillard smiled pleasantly and said, "I hope you don't mind, but I have to do some quick arraignments. Thanks for your understanding." That was the second time this morning I was being thanked for something for which I had no choice. Several young males were paraded one at a time into the courtroom in bright-orange jumpsuits and wearing shackles around the waist, accompanied by deputies. There were some whispering, exchanging of documents between the judge and the public defenders, and setting of dates, and out the door, followed by another defendant in the same unfortunate circumstances. This process repeated about five times, and then we were ready to begin.

Ernie Joe entered the courtroom similarly shackled, wearing the bright-orange jumpsuit with stenciled letters spelling out "Bay County Jail" across the back and front of the outfit. Apparently the federal court mandate requiring the removal of shackles, and the wearing of street clothes was being roundly ignored today. He sat at the defendant's table with Ms. Andover Gibbs at his side. The deputy removed the shackles as Ernie Joe sat there calmly.

The judge explained the process to everyone in the courtroom, which included about ten spectators and an equal number of reporters. The purpose today was to determine if Ernie Joe should remain at the county jail pending his trial or, as Ms. Andover Gibbs petitioned, "be transferred forthwith to Bay Area State Hospital, where he may receive proper treatment for his severe mental condition and his special needs be appropriately addressed and managed."

Judge Gaillard began, "Okay, are we on the record? Mr. Breuer, do you have any witnesses?"

Turned out it would be me and only me. I was the state's case.

Mr. Breuer asked for my expert credentials: University of South Carolina undergrad, Tulane Medical School, psychiatry training at the Medical University in Charleston. board certified, and so forth.

The judge looked at Ms. Gibbs. "Any other questions before we start with direct?"

"Just a few Your Honor. *Dr.* Kerrigan, where are you employed?"

"Bay Area State Hospital. Technically I'm employed by the State of South Carolina, Department of Behavioral Health Services."

"Yes. Thank you, *Doctor.* So what duties do you perform?"

"I attend to, take care of, mentally ill patients who are criminal offenders."

Hilton jumped in. "Your Honor, we've been through this many times before. Can't we just stipulate—?

Ms. Gibbs cut in. "I'm just trying to make a point that maybe Dr. Kerrigan here is less than qualified to render an expert opinion."

Judge Gaillard said, "Go on Ms. Gibbs, but get to your point."

"Of course, Your Honor. So, Dr. Kerrigan, you would be taking care of Mr. Plumm should the court see fit to return him to your facility?"

"Not at this time, Counselor." Son of a bitch, she knows.

"Wait a minute, you are his doctor of record, aren't you?"

"That's true."

"Well, could you explain to the court why you wouldn't be taking care of Mr. Plumm."

I had to take a deep breath. As they say, the truth will set you free, or not.

"I've recently been transferred to other duties."

"What other duties?"

Hilton interrupted. "Objection, can we just get on with my examination?"

Judge Gaillard: "Overruled. Doctor, please answer."

"I've been transferred to what administration has called a special assignment." I'm getting my ass kicked before I even have a chance to get started.

"That's bureaucratese for suspended, isn't it, Doctor?"

"Objection."

Judge Gaillard instructed, "Ms. Gibbs, could you perhaps rephrase the question?"

MIKE BARTOS

"Aren't you in actuality under suspension, Doctor?"

"According to the personnel department, no."

"But you are not allowed, at the moment anyhow, to see patients at the hospital where you work?"

"I suppose."

"Yes or no, please, Doctor"

"No . . . but . . ."

"Why are you under suspension?"

"It's hard to explain."

"I have a police report from the security department at Bay Area State Hospital stating you were involved in trying to move a patient through security without court permission, without authorization, am I correct?"

"Not exactly, no, he wasn't, isn't a patient."

"Isn't there a court order saying that he is?"

"Well, no, it's not him, but it's a case of mistaken ident—"

"No further questions. Your Honor, I would like to move that Dr. Kerrigan be disqualified as an expert witness. He is under disciplinary action at this time related to his personal actions defying court orders. He has shown bias in wanting patients out of the hospital despite court rulings and hospital policy."

The judge turned toward Hilton. "Mr. Breuer?"

"Well, Your Honor, these are absurd arguments. The witness has not been charged or convicted of any crimes or even any civil violations. He is a distinguished psychiatrist who has been deemed an expert by this court many times in the past, and I suggest to the court that he remains a viable source of expert opinion."

You tell 'em, Hilly.

Ms. Gibbs stood up at her table. "Your Honor, he is under investigation, and he is not allowed to see patients. Someone who is not allowed to see patients cannot be counted on to give quality testimony."

Hilly came back, "Dr. Kerrigan has no restriction on his license. He could see patients in the community or anywhere else."

Ms. Andover Gibbs countered, "But he is currently representing the state hospital, the very entity that wants no part of him."

"Enough," declared the judge. "I'll make a ruling. We have always respected Dr. Kerrigan's testimony. But Ms. Andover Gibbs has a point. We cannot accept his expert testimony on behalf of the very entity that currently is investigating him based on his judgment. I'm sorry, Dr. Kerrigan, but you will have to step down. Thank you for your time. Mr. Breuer, do you have any other witnesses?"

At that point, I was wishing for another doughnut.

Ernie Joe Plumm was scheduled for transfer back to BASH that very afternoon.

CHAPTER 35

The Tuesday morning news on Charleston TV and radio was leading off with the story of the impending hurricane now starting to turn west off its previous northern course. Hurricane Cleo, which had glanced off Haiti and the Dominican Republic, according to most sources, was going to head north through the Bahamas and graze the outer banks of North Carolina but was now aiming further for a somewhat more southerly target. Vacationers were jamming Myrtle Beach, and this would be a disaster for business during the July Fourth vacation week. So far, only one local weather babe was calling for the storm to threaten a direct hit on the low country. Still, there was enough concern for various elected officials and safety personnel to start issuing alerts and advising viewers to stay tuned for more details.

Roswell lived in a restored wooden house on Tradd Street in the prestigious South of Broad Street historic area. It was just a few minutes' walk to the courthouse or his office. It was convenient, beautiful, but expensive. This is a neighborhood of charm and elegance—manicured gardens behind wrought iron fences, polished brass doorknobs, small parks, fountains in private yards, carriage houses, and rich odors from a mixture of subtropical flowers and the old sewers not too far below the streets and sidewalks. A variety of statues and plaques honor Civil War heroes and signers of the Declaration of Independence. General Beauregard, immortalized in brass in a small park across from the courthouse, has spent the last century watching Charleston evolve into a modern gentrified city.

Roswell had left a message for Judge Silberman right at 8:00 a.m. and hoped the grand old jurist would be in on time. He walked quickly, carrying his leather briefcase with all the documentation he needed, or at least all that he had. Sally J was at home on Cumberland Street and would be available if needed. Roswell figured the judge would not want her in chambers right now. He probably didn't need an anxious lawyer in his chambers first thing after the holiday either.

Court did not usually start until nine or nine thirty, so he had to intercept the judge before he was tied up all day.

There were actually several attorneys waiting outside the judge's chambers that morning, and apparently Roswell was not the first one. Mary-Lynne, the judge's veteran secretary, was talking to one of the attorneys. Roswell recognized him as one of the slick ambulance chasers named Gerson Ryder from another somewhat less prestigious firm in town. Roswell was getting anxious and impatient to get her attention, but the conversation was animated and going back and forth. Mr. Ryder was waving papers, digging in his satchel for more, talking loudly, holding a sheaf of indecipherable documents with one hand, and tapping the pile with the back of his other hand for emphasis. Mary-Lynne was obviously getting agitated with the whole process and was waving her hand at Ryder.

Roswell interrupted. "I hate to be rude, Mary-Lynne, but I really need to get in to see the judge before court today."

"Well, good luck with that, honey. First of all, do you have an appointment?"

Ryder looked at Roswell annoyed. "Excuse me, Mr. Chamblee, but we're having a conversation here. I need to see the judge too."

Playing the card of "but this is really urgent" wasn't going to fly well today. "I called in first this morning and left it on your voice mail."

"The judge is wrapped up with jury selection this morning. I can't get you in until this afternoon. How about four fifteen? Then the judge has to leave for an appointment. He's not seeing anybody right now, not you either, Mr. Ryder."

"Okay, four fifteen then. Are any of the other judges available this morning?"

"Hah, lots of laughs. Do I look like I'm the secretary for five judges? I have a hard enough time with this one. That's off the record, of course. I have your number in the address book. I'll call you if court breaks early. In the meantime, y'all have a nice day. That means you too, Mr. Ryder."

Judge Silberman breezed into the anteroom and picked up a stack of pink memo notes. Roswell thought he'd take a chance. "Your Honor? Could I—?"

"Oh, hi, Roswell. Listen, I'm over my head with crap already and the day has hardly started. Work something out with Mary-Lynne, would you?"

Mary-Lynne gave an ingratiating smile and said, "We already have, judge," as he entered his chambers and slammed the door behind him.

Roswell was reeling from frustration as he mulled over what his next course of action might be. He could return at four fifteen, but he knew damn well what courts and judges schedules were like, never predictable. He could try another judge in Charleston, or he could head down to McMurtree and

MIKE BARTOS

find Judge Gaillard, who was known to be reasonable and fair-minded. One other option was to file a writ of habeas corpus. That forces a hearing, but it takes a day or two. That was something he could do right now while trying to expedite matters in the meantime. He could lean (gently) on the court clerk, flattery, candy—whatever it takes to get on the calendar. He's done it before.

The trouble was the short week because of the holiday and staff, including a couple of judges, were on vacation. He finally landed a writ hearing for Thursday morning, July 7, 10:00 a.m. He filed on behalf of Ashley Roper, a.k.a. Garrison Bridgeman, as Ash was a resident of Charleston County. Still, this was forty eight hours off but not an unreasonable time delay considering. He still might try to short circuit the process by meeting with the judge at the appointed time, but it was likely that the judge would kick the can until Thursday, when Judge Rufus McFarland would be presiding. The state was not likely to call any opposing witnesses since they know they screwed up. The department was most likely wanting a judge to officially pull the trigger on this case and end it.

Of course, Roswell had his own practice to worry about, and he would need to head over to his office to catch up on a bunch of details. He didn't have to be in court this week for any of his clients, thank goodness. Sally J wasn't going to be happy, though. He wasn't as worried about Ash, who seemed to be taking care of himself despite the bruise on the face. He called Sally J while walking to his office and told her about the hearing Thursday morning.

"Say what? You've *got* to be kidding me, Rozzie."

"I wouldn't kid about something like this, sweetie. I'm pissed off too, but half the judges are gone. At least this should be the final chapter."

"Rozzie, he's been in that hellhole for goin' on five days now. Ah am *so* pissed!" she said, slipping back into her stress induced drawl.

"Sally J, could you just visit him or call him today? He should be getting a copy of the writ that I filed today. They can't screw that up."

"I guess. Listen, about last night—"

"Sally J, you don't have to say anything. That's something just between us. Right now, our business is helping your husband. I need you to stay cool."

Sally J was frustrated. "I'm not cool. I'm not cool about a lot of things. I'm confused and I'm sad. I've spent most of the morning just gazing out the bedroom window, just watching the flowers in the courtyard. You know I love Ash. I would never hurt him. I love you too." He finally heard it.

"That's not the important thing now. What's important is your husband's safety," Roswell responded, pretending to be in control.

She sighed and bit her lip. "Rozzie, I'm countin' on you."

"I won't let you down, sweetie. Call me on the way back. Drive carefully, okay? We'll get this all worked out and soon."

"We're going to owe you big time, Rozzie."

"Sally J, you owe me nothing. I just want to help you get your life back, and for you and Ash to be happy."

"I know you do, Rozzie. I'm glad we stopped last—"

"Sweetie, let it go. Let's move on. I've got to get to work now. I'll keep you in the loop every step of the way. Keep your cell close at hand. Things'll be fine, I promise."

Roswell clicked the phone off as he reached the door of his office. He picked up his stack of messages. Damn these three-day weekends. You don't really don't get a break from work. It just condenses a five day workload into four days. He bounded up the stairs, taking two at a time, to his second floor office and dropped his messages next to the phone. Two clients, two lawyers, and one insurance company—all wanted to be called now. Roswell figured everyone has crises. The money in law is good, but everything is a goddamn crisis. Today he had his own crisis.

He clicked on the Charleston News web site. Top news, some biker near Wadsworth with a meth lab in his barn got his head blown off, under investigation. It's not Charleston County, though, but there's been a fair amount of investigation from the state Department of Justice. This should stir things up. The next story drew his attention.

Hurricane May Affect Low Country

"Hurricane Cleo, now approaching category three status has turned west northwest after causing significant damage and flooding in the Bahamas. The storm was originally projected to turn north and at worst, brush the outer banks of North Carolina. The National Weather Service has revised the projected path to possibly impact the Carolina coast between Nags Head, North Carolina, and Myrtle Beach, South Carolina. Tourists and residents in the area are now being advised to prepare to evacuate. There are no mandatory evacuations ordered at this time, but those visiting Myrtle Beach and the Grand Strand area are advised to continue to monitor the situation. Local meteorologists are watching the situation closely as to how the storm might impact Charleston and the Low Country. Alyse Hazelwood of local

television station WCHA, Channel eleven, told a Charleston
Times *reporter that her computer model, based on an algorithm
developed by Dr. Stoddard Caldwell of Penn State, has the storm
being forced farther south than current predictions, bringing the
storm onto shore in the area between Charleston and Beaufort.*

*The storm is moving across open water and crossing the
Gulf Stream, where the water temperature is 86 to 88 degrees
Fahrenheit. According to Ms. Hazelwood, "This is a prime
temperature for enhancing development of a tropical storm
or hurricane. With the lack of wind shear, I'm predicting the
hurricane will develop into a category four storm before making
landfall in the next forty-eight hours."*

*Gloria Considine, a certified meteorologist and member of
the American Weather Society, and is the longtime forecaster
on Charleston's channel three, disagreed and said most reliable
models have the storm striking Myrtle Beach at the southernmost
point and probably turning north and striking the Cape Lookout
area. This is more consistent with the National Weather Service
forecast. Nonetheless, local safety officials concur that the residents
of the Low Country should stay alert and check for updates."*

Roswell assessed what he read and concluded there might be some
problems with the roads later this week. It wasn't clear where the storm would
be centered. Still, it pays to be safe and keep your eyes open.

He called the sheriff's department to find out about transport from
Bayside to Charleston for the hearing. They bring people up for hearings the
night before and house them at the county jail overnight. That wouldn't do.
He spoke to Deputy Sheriff Tisdale, who assured Roswell that it would be
more convenient for everyone to have Ash picked up early Thursday and be
transported before the hearing.

"Will they bring his possessions with him since he'll probably be cut loose
at the hearing?"

"Well, sir, we just do the transportation. Usually we bring them back for
formal discharge and outprocessing if the court orders a release."

"Can't we at least get his wallet?"

"I'll see what I can do. I believe the sheriff will escort your patient himself,
so I won't be involved."

Roswell sighed, "Okay, thanks. Tell the sheriff to be careful."

rnest Joseph Plumm was driven through the portal gate, wrists shackled at his side to a waist chain. He was being driven by the Bay County sheriff's deputy, Garth Tisdale, who was an old hand at pickup and delivery at BASH. He knew the guards on a first name basis and sometimes shared drinks and barbecue sandwiches with them over at the Stars, Bar and Grille outside of McMurtree, where many of them lived.

As he pulled past the first sliding gate and into the contained search area, he was greeted by a loudspeaker through the one-way glass window. "Afternoon, Garth. Ya got a surprise package for us?"

"No surprise here, Cesar. Bringin' back your celebrity patient, which I guess you're expectin'." Ernie Joe was back in the hospital clothes in which he had been arrested ten days prior.

"He behaving himself?"

"Guess he don't have no choice. He's been quiet the whole way. Damn shame about Lyle. Good man. I'm gonna miss him."

"Yeah, that's for sure. Everything is in chaos right now."

The motorized gate slid shut. Two officers were present, one already in the search area between the gates as Cesar emerged from the security station. The men chatted amiably. Cesar hopped into the passenger seat of black-and-white sheriff's car. I'll ride with you over to the ward. You can drop him off, then we'll take over." The second motorized gate drew open. The car headed onto the service road behind the wards. They parked by the concrete ramp that led up to a loading dock, and the backdoor of ward K3. Deputy Tisdale put his hand under the arm of Ernie Joe and helped him out of the car. The deputy pulled out a retractable keychain from his belt and unlocked the shackles and waist restraints. "There you go."

Cesar took Ernie by the arm. "I think we can handle it from here. I'll take him onto the ward and walk back to the gate. Thanks."

"My pleasure. Y'all take care now." Tisdale eased back in the driver's seat and headed back toward the gate.

Cesar turned the large skeleton key, unlocking the back door. Ernie Joe was cooperative. They headed down the back hallway to the locked nursing office. Several of the patients milling the hallways stopped and stared at Ernie Joe, who responded with "What the fuck you lookin' at?" Most of them turned away and retreated to the dayroom or their own rooms.

Cesar knocked on the nursing office door. Corky was the shift lead on duty. Cesar said, "We got a customer for you."

Corky poked his head out the door and saw Ernie Joe and thought but did not say, *Oh, shit*. Oh shit because he wasn't called and advised that Ernie Joe was going to be back so soon. Cesar handed Corky the court order. He thought about calling the clinical administrator and griping, but that would lead nowhere but to a "just do your job" type of admonition. And oh shit because there was no doctor covering the ward right now or the accused murderer whom the court decreed needed "services and treatment."

Doctors cover other doctor's wards routinely for vacations or sick days. This was the first full workday since the events of Friday night, and some of the doctors on nearby wards were not completely up to speed. There was a belated e-mail sent out by administration to the doctors about the lack of coverage on K3. Apparently, a lot of e-mails were unread that morning. Dr. Mandlebaum, on ward K4, got a call from Corky. "Dr. Mandlebaum, I'm sorry to disturb you but are you covering for Dr. Kerrigan?"

"Nobody told me that."

"Well, we have a situation here. Ernie Joe is back."

"You mean the one who killed our rehab therapist? Who the hell's idea was that?"

"I don't know, sir. I just got the court order."

"Why can't Kerrigan handle it?"

"Kerrigan's not here, sir."

"Why not?" Mandlebaum sounded irritated.

"I don't know, sir. You'd have to call the medical staff office. Anyhow we need orders."

"How about his previous orders?"

"We can do that, sir, but they would still need your signature."

Cesar, the hospital security officer had disappeared out the back door. Ernie Joe was making himself comfortable in front of the TV in the dayroom. He shouted, "Hey, what's for lunch?"

"Which reminds me," Corky added, "we'll need dietary orders too."

Mandlebaum sighed, "Okay, I'll be over as soon as I can. I'm taking care of someone we just had to put in restraints."

"Thanks, Dr. Mandlebaum."

MIKE BARTOS

Afternoon report was about to begin. Nurses, rehab workers, social workers, and doctors generally take part. Carmelita, who had the wind knocked out during Ernie Joe's infamous takedown a week and a half ago, saw him in the dayroom and let out an involuntary gasp, put her hands to her face, and went running down the hallway, yanked out her key, unlocked the door, and disappeared without bothering to lock the door behind her. Corky ran down the hallway and pushed the door open. "Carmelita! Carmelita!" She was gone. Corky pulled the door closed and locked it. He walked slowly back to the nurses' station, sighing and shaking his head.

At shift report, the returning nurses were shocked and amazed that Ernie Joe not only had returned, but returned to the ward where he was housed when he committed his murderous offense. Imelda Calderon, one of the older nursing assistants, said, "Why is he here? He is not to be back here. This is outrageous." Most of the nurses and aids said nothing, looking down at the floor.

"He needs to be on a one-to-one. He is a murderer. He needs to be out, out!" Imelda continued.

Nicole, the K3 rehab therapist, young and optimistic, stood up and spoke. "I know this isn't easy, but we have a job to do. This is what we do here. This is our business. I don't like him being back here either, and he probably should have gone to another ward. I don't know what's with the people who run this place, especially since we don't have a doctor right now."

There was a bang on the door. Patients aren't supposed to disturb the staff conference. Another series of bangs. One of the aids cracked the door. Ernie Joe was standing outside. "I'm hungry. I've been here an hour and nobody's given me anything to eat. I'm callin' patient's rights."

Nicole said gently, "We will get you something in a minute," then pulled the door shut.

Corky said, "Sofia, would you get him a sandwich or something before we get a blowup?"

Imelda was riled. "We cannot let him make the rules. We must have structure."

Corky countered, "Maybe you're right, but right now, someone just get him a sandwich."

Another knock on the door. Several people tensed up. There was the turn of a key, and Dr. Mandlebaum entered the room. He was short, stocky, and sixtyish, with a salt and pepper beard, and wearing a knee-length white lab coat and rumpled baggy slacks buckled above navel level. After a brief greeting, the nursing aids all started talking at once, mainly complaining about this administrative insult. "I'm just here to write the orders," was all Mandlebaum was willing to contribute to the discussion.

Corky stood up, and faced the doctor, "Well, someone needs to assess him a little bit. We don't know if he's off or on meds, and the nursing staff wants him on a one-to-one. I don't know if we can do that with staff shortages. I just had one staff run off the ward, so that leaves us one down already."

"Good Christ!" Mandlebaum groused, wishing he had taken a few extra days off as he originally planned. He now had the hot potato; if anything went wrong, another injury, escape, fight—whatever—it would be his ass dragged in front of various and sundry committees. "That's why you get paid the big bucks" was the usual administrative response. Not big enough really.

Mandlebaum had heard about the reassignment and thought it might be related to last week's murder, but it wasn't. In any event, here he was, covering this undesirable and dangerous thug—now not officially a thug, just a patient until the courts decide otherwise.

"Okay," he decided, "you don't have staff for one-to-one. Sorry, you just don't. He's already court ordered for meds. He won't bother anybody. I'll medicate him up the wazoo. I know how to do that. If he wants extra food, that's okay too. I'll tell the dietician."

The nursing staff, for the most part seemed satisfied with that. Ernie Joe got two sandwiches, lots and lots of meds, and slept the rest of the afternoon and evening, breaking only for dinner with double portions, almost unable to keep his sedated head off the table.

CHAPTER 37

Sergeant Dooley of the Bayside State Hospital security police pulled into the parking lot about twenty minutes before his shift was to begin at 1430 hours. He worked the holiday, got time and a half for his whole shift yesterday, and was poised to clear another 1500 or so bucks tax free the coming week. Life was good. The little cash cow was spitting out nice handfuls of dough whenever he felt the urge to do some spending, or just pay the household bills. There was an ATM in the lobby of the administration building. He had just enough time to pick up an extra two hundred cash to fatten up his wallet for the week.

He had six plain white envelopes, each with a hundred-dollar bill, except the envelope intended for Lieutenant Garner, which had two crispy Franklins intended to reward her non service. He would stick them in various boxes in the mailroom after hours, around 10:00 p.m., distributing them like little valentines from secret admirers. No one asked where the gifts came from or whom they were from. But the recipients of this anonymous largesse figured that there was a certain degree of selective inaction that seemed to get rewarded routinely. There were no conspiracies or conversations that might be recorded. Just money. Just keep doing what you're doing, or not doing. Oh! And yes, keep your mouth shut.

Once every week or two, after his shift was over, he drove around the back side of the fence and tossed the balls over into the high grass. It's not that he couldn't carry them through the fence, but this was his choice of distribution method. It certainly wouldn't be fitting to be seen hob knobbing routinely with suspected patient drug dealers, even if buying and cutting tennis balls in half was a pain in the ass. Victor Enale was the main guy, picked from a variety of trustworthy and connected candidates, a man who knew how to protect his interests. Dooley needed someone on the unlocked ward with access to the grounds.

The sergeant locked his precious envelopes in his desk drawer and then clocked in. He needed to get to shift report. Dooley was the lead officer for the evening shift. Sergeant Bobby Creel was reporting for the outgoing morning shift.

"Okay, folks, it's been a busy day and weekend. First of all, we'll be having a memorial service here at the chapel for Chief Dawkins, Friday at 1400. That's around change of shift time so we'd like as many people as possible to be here. The funeral will be at the Southern Cross Funeral Home in Walterboro on Saturday at 10:00 a.m.

"Lieutenant Garner has been on duty most of the weekend, and she really has stepped up to the plate under stressful circumstances, so we need to give her our support."

I'm certainly doing my share, giving her support, thought Dooley.

"Ernie Joe Plumm came back this afternoon for holding until his trial, which will be who the hell knows when." There was a collective groan from the incoming shift. "From what I hear, Dr. Mandlebaum, who is covering for Dr. Kerrigan, has the situation under control and the ward staff on K3 have reported no incidents.

"We received a bulletin this morning about a drug-related killing out near Wadsworth, and the perpetrator or perpetrators are still at large." That woke up Dooley, who suddenly felt his face turn hot and tingly, and a twinge of nausea punched him in the gut. Maybe it wasn't his boy. Maybe it was.

Creel continued, "We're letting you know this because there is some possible connection to some of our residents here who may have had some dealings with this fellow."

Dooley asked, "Got a name?"

"Let's see. Hmm." Sergeant Creel leafed through some papers; Dooley estimated the number of seconds as infinite. "Oh, yes, it looks like Pluto. No, it couldn't be Pluto. Oh, right, Plato Ballinger, age fifty-one, former biker with a drug gang. It says the state and local police are on it, and they might even bring in the feds on this one. Killed with a shotgun they believe. There may be some witnesses. They're trying to locate some."

Dooley got up and started to leave the small conference room. Creel spoke. "I'm almost done here."

"Sorry, I have a little emergency," which involved a dash to the bathroom and kneeling over and retching into the toilet. He was pale, and fine beads of cold sweat covered his brow. After five minutes he recovered some composure and stood at the sink, looking at himself in the mirror. He splashed off his face and dried himself with rough brown institutional paper towels. If nothing else, he was certainly a material witness, and most likely a "person of interest." It was going to be a rough shift.

In the rural outskirts of Wadsworth, the molds of the tire tracks were ready to be transported to the state crime lab in Columbia. The beer was siphoned out of the plastic cup, and then the cup was carefully sealed in a plastic evidence bag, which would be going to Columbia as well, along with various shoe and boot prints. For now, most of the initial investigation was complete.

Greta made some calls and was going to stay with her sister in Anderson. The sheriff reminded Greta not to travel too far and remain available. The house itself was to remain sealed off while further investigation continued.

The meth cooker was transported to the sheriff's department evidence room, where it would take up too much space, but off it went.

By late afternoon, the murder scene was quiet. Dried blood remained spattered on the back deck, and the chalk outline of the body remained. The hazardous waste and crime scene cleanup crew would be by tomorrow.

Dooley made it through an hour and a half of his shift, reported in sick, and went home, driving in the very cruiser whose tracks were found in the mud of the front yard of the house on County Road 219. The first stop, however, was the U Spray fifty-cent car wash on the outskirts of Bayside. He spent at least six dollars getting the car and tires sparkling clean. Law enforcement has to present a clean image, if nothing else.

When he got home, his wife, Lucy, was surprised to see him. "Not feeling too well," he explained.

"Yes, you don't look too well. Maybe you should rest."

Dooley repaired to the bedroom with a Charleston phone directory and started thumbing through the "Attorneys" section.

CHAPTER 38

A sh received a call from Sally J to tell him she would be down to visit later that afternoon. Visiting hours were from one to three, a time when no groups were in progress. He reminded her to bring some quarters and a few one-dollar bills. He was allowed to have up to ten dollars for the phone and canteen. He was writing notes from his interviews with some of the patients, and he wanted to pass those along to her. He had not yet received a faxed copy of the writ hearing coming up, but Roswell assured her it would be first thing Thursday morning. That gave him today and tomorrow to gather up more information about the workings of this crazy place. Although he had been here since the previous Friday, this was going to be the first normal full working day at the hospital. It was Tuesday after a three-day holiday weekend, and it was a big vacation week for a lot of the staff. His new doctor on the honor unit, Dr. Carol Stumbacher, was at the morning staff report. He hadn't met her yet. Patients weren't being allowed out on the grounds this early. Breakfast was over, meds were being passed, and many of the patients were standing idly in the hallways, watching the comings and goings of staff and other patients.

A loud female voice with a thick Filipino accent yelled into an already overly loud PA system, "It's time for morning medications, ladies and gentleman, if you are scheduled for morning medication please line up now." Ash thought the volume was suitable for deaf patients. Why do people have to yell into a microphone? She wasn't done. "Please line up now. Medication is ready."

Ash stayed in the dayroom, watching the morning news on a TV behind a shield of Plexiglas. The sound was indecipherable through a series of small holes drilled in the thick sheet. On the screen was a jovial man pointing to a map of the southeastern United States and a puffy white pinwheel of a storm over the ocean a few hundred miles to the south and east over the open Atlantic. The map included a red path from the storm to the North Carolina/South Carolina border and a wider yellow path that spread out to include the Outer Banks down to Hilton Head Island. Ash recognized a projected path for a hurricane. The most likely path did not include Bayside, but a wider less probable path did.

He wondered what precautions the state and hospital personnel might be making. He had just graduated from the Citadel and was stationed at Fort Bragg when Hugo hit in 1989. He missed the brunt of that one, and wouldn't mind missing this one either. It looked like Bayside would be mostly out of harm's way, but Charleston fifty miles to the north might be a little closer to the hurricane's target. He would have to remind Sally J to take some precautions. The house might need some sandbagging, and Ash wasn't sure he would be there in time to help. The *Charley Town* office was on slightly higher ground, maybe by two feet. That might be enough, still, it would be wise to move as much equipment as possible up to the loft. But according to what he saw on the TV, problems for downtown Charleston weren't likely.

One of the patients, Joe Hammond, wandered into the dayroom after getting his morning lithium. He sat down next to Ash. Joe was about Ash's age but looked considerably older, with a wrinkled weather beaten face. Drugs do that to a man.

He wanted to talk to Joe who seemed mellow enough. Ash struck up the conversation.

"Looks like we might get a storm in here."

"Yeah?"

"That's what I'm seein' on the TV." Ash lapsed into a little more relaxed local dialect.

"Da tee vee."

"Yeah?"

"Supposed to hit up north, but could hit here."

"Ya don't say?"

"Ever been in a hurricane?"

"I been here eleven years. I'm from Spartanburg. We didn't get Hugo"

"Good thing, huh?"

"I guess."

"Eleven years is a long time."

"I guess."

"How come eleven years?"

"They don't let me out."

"Why not?"

"I keep getting dirty urines."

"Doin' drugs? You in here for drugs?"

"Not so much."

Ash was getting more curious. "Then why?"

"Stealin'."

"What did you steal?"

"Anything I could get my hands on."

"For drugs?"

"Oh, yeah. I committed some 300 burglaries."

"Is that a record?"

That got a chuckle, the first hint of emotion from Joe. "Prolly not."

"I'm interested. Could you tell me more?"

"What's to tell? I used to drive around Spartanburg during the day, park the car, go around the back of people's houses, watch a while. I'd knock on the back door. If they was home, I'd say I was from the electric company or fire department or some such bullshit. If not, I'd try the back door."

"Isn't that a bit risky?"

"People leave their back door open more'n you'd believe. So I'd look around a little more, then go in."

"I don't want you to get mad for asking this, but what gives you the right to just go into peoples' homes just because they left the door open?"

"I never said I had the right, oh no. I don't have the right. It's just what I do, and now I'm here."

"Well, why here and not prison?"

"I was in jail a few times and was out on parole the last time I was busted. Cuz I was fucked up out of my mind on drugs, and the lawyer said if I plead insanity, I wouldn't have to go to jail and I'd be out of here in a year."

"But you're still here."

"No shit, Shakespeare."

"So why's that?"

"I keep using drugs. TransCom won't take me out if I have any drugs in my urine in the past year."

"Can't you quit?"

"Maybe, maybe not. I just don't want to quit."

"And stay here?"

"It ain't so bad here. It's easier to get meth here than on the street."

"Can I get me some?"

"Yeah, you know who to talk to. I saw you talking to him."

"How much?"

"Don't ask me. Ask him."

"Maybe I will."

"You're gonna need someone on the outside. No money changes hands inside the CP."

"Hey, thanks. You don't need to say any more. I don't want you getting into any trouble."

"No trouble, I get ten bucks every time I make a referral."

Most of the treatment groups were cancelled on this sunny hot morning as many of the staff were on vacation. The honor patients could sign out for the grounds and enjoy the fresh air before the full heat of the afternoon drove everyone back inside. It was a particularly lazy quiet Tuesday morning. Many of the patients were sleeping off the excitement and barbecue of the day before. Ash caught sight of Victor Enale lounging under a large magnolia tree sprinkled with great white flowers in full summer bloom.

Ash approached but Victor spoke first. "I see you talkin' to my man, Joe."

"Just passin' the time. He was tellin' me how you could help me out."

Victor crossed his arms and gave Ash a stern look. "Right, but you already knew that, right, bud? You wanna do business with me. There's real strict rules."

"I got to thinkin' about ways to pass the time. There's a lotta time I need to pass. No harm in making it go quicker."

"I wish I could help you out, but there's been an interruption in the supply side."

"That's a bummer," Ash responded, pretending to be sympathetic.

"Yeah, a bummer all the way around. No crank for now, maybe a little herb, but that's about it."

"Okay, that's better than nothing I guess," Ash said, sounding like he was willing to be flexible.

"I can get you a couple a three j's but my expenses are up. Sixty bucks."

"That's sorta steep."

"Not so much, not in this place. I'll get you one this afternoon. You can pay later."

Ash thought owing money to this character would not be such a good idea. "I'd rather pay up front."

"Have it your way. Have your person send a check made out to VictorE Supplies. Make sure it doesn't bounce. I'll get you the address."

"I can remember."

Victor gave a post office box in Savannah. Pretty cautious using an out-of-state post office box but not so cagey using his real first name on the checks, Ash thought. Curious.

"You can pay online too. VEpaynow.com."

MIKE BARTOS

"Like with a shopping cart and checkout too?"

"These are modern times, my friend. I do whatever helps to enhance collections. It's all encrypted."

"How much for some crank?"

"I told you, that's not happening for a while."

"Well, when you get some."

"That won't be for a while, and expenses keep goin' up. This isn't like we're on the streets of North Charleston. I have no idea. I'll let you know."

"I guess the current supply is gone?" Ash was probing.

"Over the weekend, the cops were playing with the dogs back here. The dogs were picking up my tennis balls and playing with them and running them around. These are the supposed drug-sniffing dogs. They couldn't tell a bag of crystal from another dog's ass. The cops were walking off with the balls. They're supposed to know better."

"I'll let you know how my finances are and get back to you."

"Like I said," Victor countered, "I can advance you a joint today. I'm sure you'll pay me back."

"Uh, thanks, but today wouldn't be a good day." Ash stopped using drugs years ago, so no day would be good.

Victor turned and walked away. "You know where you can find me."

Ash's thoughts turned to his wife's visit. He sorely missed her.

CHAPTER 39

Sally J and her husband sat on an aluminum bench/picnic table combination in the air-conditioned visitors' center. It was a Tuesday and not very busy. She had to be searched with a metal detector wand before entering, but no pat-down. They feasted on fast-food fried chicken and homemade peach pie she picked up on the way down from Charleston. He polished off more than either of them would have imagined. She stroked the side of his face. She was careful not to touch the still bruised side of his lip.

"How ya doin', baby?"

"Not too bad. I think I'm becoming just one of the guys. They trust me. I'm getting some good stuff. Stitches come out tomorrow. I made notes talking to some of the patients. Can you take them home and put them on my desk? How're you doing?"

"Ash, I think you are probably doing better than I am. I've been like a total wreck. At least I know you're coming up to Charleston one way or another day after tomorra, and Roswell is one hundred percent certain the judge is going to have to let you go."

Ash chuckled. "With the way things are going, maybe he ought to call it 98 or 99 percent."

"Don't talk like that. You're comin' home to me and that's that."

"I think you're right. Are you following the hurricane?"

"Yeah, Rozzie told me all about it. He said it's supposed to maybe go up into North Carolina, but this one weather girl, the one you like to watch so much, she says its kinda headed this way. I hope not, that would hold up your court hearing." Her 'I' was still coming out as 'ah.'

Ash tried to be reassuring. "I'm not too worried. I saw the news here this morning, and the weatherman on the network news looked like he was agreeing with the hurricane heading up north. Still, can you get some sandbags around the house?"

"I hired Sam and some of his college friends to take the pickup and bring back some sandbags for the house and the office. I offered them fifteen bucks an hour to work."

"Did they accept it?"

"Hella yeah, it's good money. Anyhow I insisted. Did you see your new doctor yet?"

"Yes, a Dr. Carol Stumbacher, young gal, I think she just finished her training. This must be her first job. I saw her for ten minutes. She thinks I might need to be on medication. I told her my story. She thinks I might be delusional. Can you have Kerrigan call this lady? Anyhow, in South Carolina, they can't force me to take meds against my will unless it's an emergency. Also, I got my court order and told her when I go to court, I shouldn't be on new meds.

"And?"

"She bought it, but says she'll talk to TransCom about me not wanting to be cooperative with treatment. That's low on my list of worries. Also, that murderer Ernie Joe came back to the hospital a few hours ago. I think he's in the room I was in on K3. I don't think there's any doctor covering that ward right now. Dr. Kerrigan got busted for trying to sneak me out."

"Good Lord. You're not going to see that Ernie Joe are you?"

"Well, he should be on lockdown, not on the grounds. I've heard the staff everywhere bitching about it, some of the patients too. I'm trying to figure a way I could talk to the guy, though."

"You can't reveal confidential stuff about patients, can you?"

"A lot of what's going on with this guy is public record. Anyhow, I'm not a health care practitioner, so screw 'em."

Time was up. Sally J needed to get back to Charleston. A somewhat modified *Charley Town* was going to press, minus any "Ash in BASH" story. " She kissed Ash gently; his lip was still sore, and the cheek was a little puffy, the black and blue bruise fading to yellow. She took his notes.

Sally said, "See you in Charleston on Thursday."

"And Thursday night," Ash added.

Sally J headed toward the one way turnstile and then hesitated before hugging Ash, glancing first at the guard and then at the other patients with their families, not sure of protocol. Ash smiled reassuringly and gestured "come here" with his hands and drew her against him, whispering softly. "It's okay, Baby. There's no crime in holding you close."

MIKE BARTOS

Sergeant Dooley had an emergency appointment with Charleston criminal attorney David Leclare. Leclare was known to be a hard working and skillful attorney, having handled some of the biggest criminal cases in the Low Country over the past two decades. He was among the best known, revered, and expensive members of the Charleston Bar. There were no appointments available; but when he heard that the potential client was a cop, he wasn't going to blow it off.

His office had gotten a panicky call right around eight-thirty that morning. Dooley identified himself as a policeman. Although he worked for the security force at BASH, he, as others working there, were academy-trained sworn officers. "Give him the noon slot," he told his receptionist.

Leclare usually enjoyed a fine lunch a few blocks down the street from the courthouse at one of Charleston's trendy restaurants during noon recess. Just because the jury was deliberating on his client's life, there was no reason not to enjoy the calming influence of a light meal on an outdoor patio while considering other business, billed at the rate of 500 dollars per hour. On other occasions, he might take lunch in his office with a client, a delightful way to do business.

Wednesday lunchtime would be a good time to have a meeting, which he would have in his elegant wood-paneled office on East Bay Street. Lunch would be brought in for his potential client as well as himself. Leclare liked to treat members of the Thin Blue Line with deference, as they often returned the favor. In one polished oak cabinet were some fine bottles of brandy, whiskey, scotch of course, and vodka. Often these were brought out to celebrate a brilliant courtroom victory but sometimes to console the loss, or calm the nerves. There was also a small refrigerator, likewise hidden from view, with ice, and imported beer. If you're going to charge your clients, you may as well treat them right, he always told his colleagues. Perhaps he might foist this case onto an associate for a mere $350 per hour. Cheaper, but then, no first class accommodations.

As a special courtesy, this first consultation appointment would be free, pro bono. He had defended cops before, good cops and bad cops. Sometimes there was good publicity and sometimes bad publicity, although Leclare figured there is no such thing as bad publicity.

Dooley sat in the waiting area, looking through an old copy of the *Charleston Legal Reporter*, checking his watch and jiggling his legs. Eliana, the Brazilian-born receptionist was used to seeing anxious clients. She poked her head through the door and asked, "Can I get you something?"

"What do you got?"

"Soda, water, juice—could you use a beer?"

"Beer? Sure that might be nice."

"How about a nice Heineken?"

"Uhh, yeah, sure."

Eliana added, "Mr. Leclare asked me to order up some pizza for all of us, is that okay?"

He realized he hadn't eaten breakfast. "That would be great."

He drank directly from the very cold green bottle, feeling a little calmer. This was the first beer since the night on Plato's porch. He now remembered that he left his cup there, probably in a plastic evidence bag somewhere. That thought ruined the calm moment.

Eliana's instructions were to serve no more than two beers to a client. He drained the bottle; and without asking, she offered another.

Leclare entered his office through the waiting room and greeted Dooley. "How shall I call you? Sergeant? Mr. Dooley?"

"Joe, just Joe will be fine."

"Okay, Joe, let's get started, shall we?"

They went back to his private office. Leclare had an impressive regal desk and floor-to-ceiling built-in mahogany bookcases. They sat in facing each other in leather wingback chairs. Joe noticed the room was very quiet, except for the soft hum of the central air. *It must be soundproofed*, he thought.

"To get to the point, Mr. Leclare—"

"Dave, please, let's be equal on a first-name basis."

"Sure . . . Dave. As I was saying, I believe my footprints and tire tracks are at a murder scene being investigated."

Leclare scowled and cocked his head slightly to one side, listening intently. "Please go on."

"You may have heard of a murder outside of Wadsworth a couple of nights ago on the fourth, drug dealer. This is all confidential information, isn't it?"

"Absolutely, lawyer-client privilege, even if we choose not to work together."

"Okay, anyhow, I don't know how to say this, but I was the victim's last

MIKE BARTOS

client. I drove my vehicle onto his lawn, bought some meth for six hundred bucks, had a beer and left."

Leclare leaned forward. "Were you using an official state vehicle?"

"I'm afraid so. I'm not officially supposed to have it off grounds, but no one ever complained."

Leclare sighed softly; he didn't want to appear alarmist or judgmental to his client. "Okay . . Joe, what else is going on?"

"I guess I left footprints. I was wearing my uniform boots."

"So you were in uniform?"

"Yeah, I guess so."

"Okay, what about the murder?"

"I swear I had nothing to do with it. It happened right after I left. They must have been waiting."

"Any idea who?"

"My guess, some of his former biker buddies. He wasn't supposed to be in the meth business. It was their turf."

"What about the drugs? Do you still have them?"

"I tossed them in the marsh last night."

"Tossed them?"

"They were in tennis balls."

"Why are they in tennis balls?"

"Okay . . . I sold them at the state hospital. I had a distributor."

Leclare held up his hand to stop the sergeant. "Just so I have this straight, you are a sworn officer who was obtaining illegal drugs from a dealer, using your position to get drugs into a mental hospital setting, and after you make a face-to-face purchase, your dealer is whacked by persons unknown moments after you leave the scene."

"That's about the size of it."

Leclare was intrigued and flummoxed at the same time. "And you're coming to me because the police are going to track you down and suspect you of premeditated murder. Anybody see you?"

"His girlfriend has seen me before, but I didn't see her that night. She was in the bedroom upstairs."

"So we don't know if she saw you. She can recognize you. But if she saw the shooting, she could clear you, right?"

"I suppose. Can you help me?"

"Oh, I can help you. If you didn't commit this murder, I can help get you cleared."

"That's a relief."

"Well, you may not be going down for murder, but you have a lot of problems."

"You mean all the drug distribution?"

"Yes, for a start, then there's the issue of taxes."

"Taxes?"

"I assume you did not pay federal income taxes on your profits."

"Am I supposed to?"

"Yes, sir. You're looking at tax evasion."

"How bad is that?"

"Bad enough, that's what sent Al Capone to Alcatraz. But we may be able to preempt trouble by going to the IRS before they come to you."

"How much is this going to cost me?"

"My retainer for this will be seventy-five thousand up front. My guess is that you have it somewhere or most of it. You do not want a public defender on this one. I have some connections in Bay County. Since you would be coming forward voluntarily, we can probably get you out on reasonable bail, maybe even on your own recognizance. You get me the retainer by tomorrow morning, and I'll walk you to the County courthouse. You'll have charges in Bay County for the drugs. The state will oversee the prosecution."

"Will I go to jail?"

"Probably, unless we get lucky, depends how well you can sing for your supper. You'll need a negotiator, that's me. We will not go to trial. That'll save you a quarter mil."

"Yeah, I don't have that kind of money."

"Don't hold out on me. I demand honesty, complete and thorough. I'll bust my ass for you, and you'll pay me very well, and it'll be worth it. But if you lie to me about anything, I'm gone."

There was a knock on the door. It was Eliana. "I have pizza."

She brought it in and placed the box on the coffee table. She returned a moment later with bone china plates and linen napkins. Leclare asked, "Will you be having pepperoni or Hawaiian?"

"Pepperoni and another beer please."

"Tell you what, Joe, and I don't often do this, but that pizza might go down better with a good shot of scotch, just this one time, okay?"

Leclare helped himself to a shot as well, midday or not. He didn't toast out loud, but he thought, *To one helluva case.*

CHAPTER 41

The Big Man stepped out of the passenger side of the unmarked state police car in front of the Bay Area State Hospital security headquarters. He wore slacks and a white shirt open at the collar and sported a bolo tie with a turquoise clasp. The only part of the official State Police uniform he chose to wear today was his signature state police "Smokey the Bear" tan hat, summer issue. The driver was a uniformed sergeant from the investigation team. They entered the old converted Victorian mansion and stopped at the reception barrier.

Jennifer stopped typing and looked up at the imposing figure. "How can I help you gentlemen today?"

Mike Luskasavitch spoke. "We're here from the State Police to see Lieutenant Garner, who I believe is your acting chief."

"She's out on the grounds, but I'll give her a radio call. Won't you have a seat?"

"That's okay, ma'am. We've been sitting the whole ride over from Walterboro."

Walterboro? Jennifer got up and walked over to a radio console panel, pushed a button, and picked up a microphone attached to a short stand. "Lieutenant, there's a couple of State Police here wanna talk to you." After a muffled crackling response, Jennifer smiled and reported, "She'll be back in just a minute."

It was more like two minutes. Evelyn Garner briskly entered through the front door and saw the two state cops waiting. *Now what the hell?* she thought.

The Big Man extended his hand and introduced himself. "Detective Lieutenant Mike Luskasavitch, out of the Walterboro barracks. This is Sergeant Barry Willis."

"Yes, Lieutenant, I'm acting chief Garner." Maybe a chance to pull a little rank, not that being the biggest fish in this very small pond would impress the detective. "How can I help?"

"Thanks, Chief." She liked the sound of that very much. "We're investigating a murder out our way, a drug deal may be gone bad. We don't really know. Anyhow, we have some tire prints and footprints from the crime scene we're checking out. It appears that perhaps one of your vehicles may have been at or near the scene outside of Wadsworth on the night of July 4, around 11:30 p.m."

"Hmm, why would one of our cars be out in Wadsworth?"

"We were wondering that ourselves. Maybe one of your officers lives out that way. We have the tire make and model and photos of the tread. We'd like to look around."

Garner looked very surprised, as indeed she was quite shocked. "Let me check with personnel about our officers' addresses."

"That would be very kind if you would." Big Mike offered, "We'd like to visit the grounds. Can we get into the confined perimeter?"

"What would you be looking for in there?"

"Well, you have some of the cars patrolling back there."

Garner asked, "It'll be hard to look at tire prints, won't it?"

"Right now we'll just be looking at general level of tread wear. That'll narrow it down," answered the detective.

"I suppose you might be looking for a muddy car or muddy tires?"

"Au Contraire, ma'am, we'll be looking for an unusually clean car and tires. (*And she's the head cop here?* he thought.) If you could check some addresses please. We'll be back."

"Sergeant, would you check your weapon here, before you go behind the fence?"

The sergeant checked with Big Mike, who nodded and motioned for him to hand over his sidearm.

Garner called on the radio for one of her officers to come over and escort her colleagues through the portal and to offer any assistance necessary. After a few minutes' wait, one of her officers, Cesar, appeared, introduced himself, and left with the visitors.

Lieutenant Garner walked over to personnel in the next building to check on home addresses. She knew where to look first. That would be the officer who called in yesterday afternoon saying he needed personal leave, one Sergeant Joe Dooley. No plain white envelope with money in her mailbox this week, one drug dealer down but miles away, one less sergeant on p.m. shift. Her thought now was maybe Dooley had found some unfortunate end, or more likely one found him. Officially, she knew nothing about drug distribution on grounds; there was no paper trail, and now there might be one less witness as to what went on in the underground drug trade at BASH. Sad, though, as he had two young kids, one in pre school.

As far as Garner knew, the late Chief Dawkins suspected a lot but actually knew very little, other than the drugs were there and someone was letting them in. His blood pressure went up enough that his portly face would turn beet red when he complained to administration about the bogus decoy K9 corps pretty much limited in skills to a lick of the hand and the sniff of the crotch. Dawkins knew a little pot was around. Hell, the staff smoked it on breaks at times. That wasn't the end of the world. But speed, that's another story. Speed, amphetamines, crank, ice, whatever they call it, can produce psychosis in normal people, let alone a population of chronically mentally ill violent offenders. It counteracts all the treatment and medication, and treatment planning and intentions of the court. But then Garner would say to herself from time to time, what the hell did Dawkins know?

All this treatment and most of these unfortunate losers who cost the state three to four times what a prison cell cost weren't going anywhere despite the pretense of treatment. The whole of BASH was a paean to a humane approach to the sickest of our citizens, or perhaps to a state jobs program for people like herself. "It's all going to hell." Garner told herself. She was acting chief for less than a week, and as Dawkins used to say, "The grits are hittin' the fan."

She went into her office—formerly Dawkins's office, still full of Dawkins's stuff and stale cigarette smell—and locked the door. Dawkins kept a bottle of gin in the lower desk drawer. She took a swill right out of the bottle and then another. She leaned back in his old naugahyde desk chair, put her feet up on the desk, and dozed off.

CHAPTER 42

Joseph Dooley, Hospital Police Sergeant, pay grade 17, lived in the town of Wadsworth, about a thirty-minute drive from the hospital. The workers of BASH came from a wide geographic area. It was a magnet of secure civil service employment. BASH was a little dangerous, a little dirty, a lemon of a job, but a clever person could find his way around and make lemonade. So it apparently was for Dooley, a job rife with opportunity for extra income.

While Lieutenant Garner was halfway dozing and thinking about what to say about the absent Sergeant Joe Dooley, there was a team of investigators with a search warrant rooting through drawers and closets of the home of the same Joseph A. Dooley, a modest but neat two-story white frame home on the edge of Wadsworth. The tread of the tire on the patrol car parked in front of his home clearly matched the imprints from the muddy Ballinger front yard. His wife, Lucy, stood in the front yard with her two young children, shaken and angry. Joe Dooley had taken the family car for an appointment in Charleston, for what, she did not know. He was not answering his phone.

Dooley had left the attorney's office with a resolve that this was going to be a rough ride, a ride about to get a lot rougher. He was walking off his alcohol buzz. He didn't need a DUI on top of everything else. He checked his messages. There were two texts: "Joe, there are police here with a search warrant. Call now." The second text, eleven minutes later read, "Where the hell are you? What's going on?" The last one was about thirty minutes ago. Holy crap, they were on to him already. He hit the speed dial number for Lucy.

"Joe, what's going on? We have cops going through our stuff. Our things, our private possessions." She started to cry. "The kids are scared out of their minds. I'm scared. They want to know where you are."

Joe breathed deeply and swallowed hard. Be cool. "Lucy, listen, I'm in a bit of a situation here. I can't go into detail, but they think I did something I absolutely did not do."

Lucy said sternly, "Then you come home right now, and you tell these nasty policemen that they made a mistake."

"I'm afraid it's just not that simple. Listen, I was here seeing a lawyer. He's one of the best."

"Why do you need a fancy lawyer if you didn't do anything? Come home. Okay? Come home, we'll work it out."

"I can't come home until I see my lawyer again. I can't tell you where I am. I should be home in a couple of days, trust me. Put the kids on the phone."

He spoke to Kaylan. "Daddy?"

"Hi, honey, I have to go away for a few days. Daddy loves you. Tell your brother."

Lucy took the phone back. "This detective wants to talk to you." Dooley hung up and turned off his phone.

Now the task was to get his hands on the retainer that his lawyer demanded. He had cash in a private account in the Savannah bank. He also had access to the other account with Victor's name on it. He didn't have quite the cash that Leclare thought he had. His personal joint account with his wife had eleven thousand dollars, the Savannah account about fifty-eight thousand of ill-gotten profits. He was still a little short. The VictorE account had about twenty-five thousand. His personal credit card had ten thousand dollars cash advance. He decided not to touch the account with Victor. That could be dangerous, maybe deadly.

Dooley headed back to the attorney's office on East Bay Street. It was almost 2:00 p.m. Eliana was at her desk. He asked if he could have access to the internet to make some fund transfers. This wasn't the first time Eliana had seen a desperate need by a client to get the money for the retainer or some other purpose before the hammer completely fell. There was a non-network laptop in a desk drawer for clients' various needs.

Dooley sat by Eliana's desk and logged on to his bank account. He was able to transfer the entire fifty-eight thousand into his personal joint account. Now there was sixty-nine thousand. His wife needed some funds for living expenses. He couldn't clear it all out. He handed Eliana his debit card and another card. "I'm paying for my retainer. Take sixty-five K off the debit card and ten off the credit card." That left four thousand for his family, for now.

He punched in his bank card code on the debit card. He pressed the green Yes button when it asked "$65,000.00 Accept?" That along with the charge card would do it.

"Seventy-five thousand, would you like a receipt?" Eliana asked.

May as well, he thought, *might be deductible.*

"Okay, I have to turn myself in. When can I do that?"

Eliana responded, "That you'll have to discuss with Mr. Leclare. He'll be in court till about four thirty."

"Well, I'm a major client now. I have to see him."

"Oh, don't worry, Mr. Dooley, if you're his client he *will* take care of you. Guaranteed. Be here at five. He will see you."

CHAPTER 43

"**A** *nd now the six o'clock news on* Channel Eleven *with Bob Osterwalt.*"
"This evening, we start off with Alyse Hazelwood and some breaking weather news. Alyse?"

"Thanks, Bob. It looks like hurricane Cleo is galloping toward the South Carolina Coast with no further northward movement. The National Weather Service has just issued a hurricane warning for the coast from Charleston to Savannah and a hurricane watch from Myrtle Beach to Jacksonville Florida. No kiddin' around folks, this is a serious storm. I've been telling you about it for the past few days, but most everyone is now in agreement that the storm is headed this way. If you're in coastal areas, it's time to start securing your property and heading toward higher ground. As you can see on satellite, it's a compact system with is a tightly wrapped eye around the center of the storm with a pressure of 950 millibars and sustained winds of 120 miles per hour. She's sitting about 150 miles off shore spinning in the gulf stream, almost like she's sucking up energy ready to strike. Cleo is a fast mover. Conditions are really going to start going downhill in a hurry around sunrise tomorrow, so you have time to make some plans, gather up the emergency supplies we've been talking about, find your pets, and get moving. Right now, Hilton Head appears to be ground zero. Don't wait until morning. If you have friends or relatives inland, I suggest you pay them a visit overnight."

Although Alyse and her meteorology professor friend were calling for the nearby strike for the part two or three days, the other local forecasters were not, nor was the National Weather Service. The locals were lulled into believing the storm would strike north of Myrtle Beach, leaving the low country, if not high and dry, at least not at high risk for damage. At about 4:00 p.m., the various computer models came together, giving low-country residents eighteen hours to prepare for what was at the moment a strong category three to plow directly into the marshes, beaches, barrier Islands, and inlets.

"Rip currents along the beaches are already starting to cause erosion. I know it's hot and sunny right now, but please, please stay out of the water. It's highly dangerous. We may get some of the outer rain bands by sunrise. The storm is moving quickly now, but the exact time of landfall is not precise."

Channel eleven viewers had a leg up on the other coastal residents. Alyse had been warning them for the past two days. The weather was typical midsummer sun and heat, not much breeze, with previous predictions of a storm going somewhere to the north. The State Emergency Management Department was now interrupting television programs.

At 1830 hours, the dispatcher at the security headquarters at Bay Area State Hospital received a telephone call from Elliot Desjardins who had just received an urgent call from the Department of Behavioral Health Services, who had just received a call from the governor's office.

"Hello, this is Elliot Desjardins. Who is in charge right now? Is Garner there?"

"I'm Officer Cynthia Belo. I'm working the dispatch. I believe Sergeant Ralph Gregg is the lead for this shift. He's filling in for Sergeant Dooley, who's on leave."

"Well, get him quickly."

"Yes, sir."

Desjardins was trying to get Garner on her cell, but she wasn't answering his calls. Although she had left the grounds, the security chief has to be available 24/7. After a few minutes, Sergeant Gregg came on the line."

"Yes, sir, this is Sergeant Gregg."

"Gregg, listen, they're talking about a hurricane hitting the area tomorrow."

"Yes, sir, so I've heard."

"Are we executing our hurricane preparedness protocol?"

"Hurricane preparedness protocol?"

"Gregg, don't we have a hurricane protocol or some sort of administrative directive addressing the issue?"

"Well, sir, can you give me the number of the directive and I'll get on it."

"Dammit, Gregg, I don't walk around with administrative manuals in my head, don't you have it?"

"Actually, I've looked, sir, and I can't seem to locate any such directive."

"Well, call Dawkins. He'll know what to do."

"Dawkins, sir?"

"Never mind, I never said that. I'm just a little flustered right now."

"I understand, sir."

"Listen, I guess I'll have to come over and take charge. I'll be there in a half hour."

Bay Area State Hospital, located on a coastal marsh island, about two miles from the sea, was on acreage that had been built up a few feet and graded when it was constructed as a military base in the 1930s. The hospital's infrastructure had not been thoroughly upgraded since the early 1960s. The entire facility did not meet FEMA coastal flood guidelines. Somehow the state officials managed to convince Federal officials that they were going to move the facility "real soon." Millions of dollars budgeted for a new facility became tens of millions of dollars. The blueprints for a new state hospital near Goose Creek were drawn up, stamped by the architect and stuck in a drawer.

In 1989, when hurricane Hugo hit the coast, it was a little north of Charleston. The town of Bayside, which was not nearly as developed as it is now, suffered minor flooding and blown-off shingles. The hospital fared well with no injuries and minimal damage. The executive committee met in anticipation of the storm. There was no major plan then either. When asked what should be done, the executive director responded, "I guess we oughta pray." Which they did with bowed heads. The center of that storm hit a little north of Charleston, then veered farther north into North Carolina. Maybe prayer was the way to go.

Elliot Desjardins was behind the wheel of his SUV, heading back to the hospital, and hadn't been home even an hour. It was a fine evening—what were they talking about? He voiced Evelyn Garner's number into the Bluetooth.

"This is Lieutenant Garner. Please leave a message."

"Evie, dammit give me a call. This is an emergency. It's about the hurricane."

Fifty miles to the north, Sally J received a phone call from Roswell. She was at the *Charley Town* office, working to get this week's somewhat abbreviated issue print ready. The layout was all on computer these days. Various writers were sending in their poems and reviews by way of attachments. She was highly preoccupied. Annie was reading a lot of the contributions. They weren't editing very well, only the most glaring grammatical errors were being caught.

"Sally J, you hear about the hurricane?"

"Yeah, I have a pile of sandbags around the house, but the storm is supposed to slice south, so we didn't stack them up yet. Anyhow Sam is getting some of his buddies to help. I got his number. I hope this doesn't screw up Ash's hearing."

Roswell had been concerned too. "I checked with the court clerk. Everything is go for tomorrow here in Charleston anyhow. The sheriff from Bay County is going to transport Ash here personally. He should be in good hands."

"Hurricane or no hurricane, I got one heckuva homecoming lined up."

"I'm happy for you guys, really, but we have business first. We're looking 10:00 a.m., courthouse, Broad and Meeting."

"Roswell, this is the most important meeting of my life. Don't worry, I'll be there."

CHAPTER 44

Ash was mildly worried. He surely didn't want any hurricane screwing up the plans. The patients' responses were anywhere from apathy to panic. They were in the large dayroom, watching the news. One older appearing male, smelling of cigarette smoke, sporting a long frizzy beard and wearing a worn stocking cap, leaned over and said, "You know this is what I've been talking about. It's the Chinese fucking with us. I know, I've been hearing about this for years. They've captured our nuclear satellites and using them against us."

Another patient spoke out. "Maybe they'll cancel group tomorrow."

Just as long as they don't cancel court, Ash was thinking. Today was a long hot day, his last one here he was sure. There was much to find out. If his plan was to be a patient and find out stuff, the plan worked. Brilliant plan, but it was supposed to last six hours, not six days.

The evening was perfectly fine, warm breezes and hazy sunshine. Supper was done, so the residents could sign out. Curfew was 8:00 p.m. Ash figured that as long as it was his last evening here, it would be a good opportunity to take one final walk around the grounds. Never know who you might meet or what info you might find out. Ash felt he had a book's worth already.

He wasn't going to catch Ernie Joe, who was on lockdown on the old unit. There was no way he was going to interview that guy. The word was that old Dr. Mandlebaum had sedated Ernie Joe into an ongoing stupor so he wouldn't cause any trouble. Ash did have a chance to talk to various staff members, and it was clear they felt disrespected by a system that would send a murderer back to the scene of the crime. There were many victims, victims of soiled spirit and physical fear, now being victimized once again by the same perpetrator and the system.

It was 6:30 p.m., Wednesday, July 6. The sun was still bright. The sky was blue except for some high silvery cirrus clouds reflecting the sunlight. The air was moist enough that there appeared to be a faint halo circling the sun. A pleasant breeze swept across the sweet green lawn. A stronger breeze whispered through the tops of the pines and rattled the fronds of the bristling palmettos. Ash took a tour around the fifty acre enclosed compound. He noticed a middle age black man sitting by himself at a picnic table. Despite the man's solitude, he was talking to himself, or perhaps to an unseen companion. Ash walked closer and decided to engage the man. Ash started the conversation. "Hi, how ya doin'?"

"S'all right, sir. Yes, sir, fine evening."

"I'm Ash. What's your name?"

"Tyler, yes, sir, that's me."

Ash recognized the name, the fellow who got Ash interested in this hospital in the first place. "That's Mr. Goode, right?"

"Yes, sir, that's right. Say you must know my momma."

"No, sir, but I hear she's a fine woman. I hear you're leaving soon, going home, isn't that right?"

"Well, I ain't got no home now. The guvmint stole it from me."

"So where will you be going?"

"The man from TransComm be takin' me out in a few days. He got a place for me to stay."

"Well, that should be nice. Good luck to you."

"I just wanna see my momma."

"That's understandable."

"Yeah, but a lotta people don't see it that way. They punks."

"Tyler, do you pray?"

"Sometimes I actually do, yes, sir."

"Let's pray now for peace for you and your momma and that things work out, okay?"

"That would be nice. You probably a very righteous man. I can tell that. I know about people."

He took Tyler's big hands into his own and closed his eyes. "Dear Lord, see to it that this man, Tyler, finds peace in the community and that he makes friends and listens to his doctor and when You see fit, to bring this man together with the people he loves, especially his momma. Amen"

"Amen." Tyler smiled and very much seemed at peace.

"Good luck, Tyler. Try not to be so mad at people."

"All right then, good night, sir."

CHAPTER 45

The administrator hit his knee on the steering wheel of the SUV, taking the speed bumps on the hospital entrance road a little too fast. He had to give directions to the nitwits who obviously couldn't figure out anything if he wasn't holding their hands. And where the hell was Garner? Safety and security was her baby. That's what she wanted, and now she's got it in spades. It wasn't just security, no—it was safety too.

The regular evening shift sergeant was gone, and now the acting chief was AWOL with a freakin' hurricane dancing around out there off the coast somewhere and no protocol. Was the previous administration just sitting on their thumbs, planning to dump this mess into his lap?

Desjardins jogged into security headquarters, irritable and anxious. He wasn't particularly pleasant when he felt calm either. He snapped at the uniformed officer behind the counter. "Okay, where's the sergeant on duty?"

"Gregg here."

"Okay, Sergeant Gregg. We need to talk. Let's say a hurricane blows in here tonight or tomorrow. How do we ensure safety for the staff and patients?"

"Well, sir, the L wards are in two story buildings. We can move all the patients to the second floor."

"Brilliant! And then I assume everyone is going to sleep in the hallways and floors. What did the hospital do in 1989?"

"I don't know, sir. I was nine years old then."

"It's too late to transfer everyone to the prisons."

"Well, sir, the hospital is on a graded elevation, and we are two miles from the shoreline. I don't think we're at a great deal of risk from major flooding, and the windows are all reinforced with steel mesh."

"Listen, I'll need you and the entire shift to work a double or a triple if need be." You'll need to double up with the night shift. We can't do anything now except hope."

"Will you be here, sir?"

"I guess I'll have to be." Good thing his office has a couch, he thought.

CHAPTER 46

A round 4:00 a.m., the wind rumbled and then screamed loud enough to be heard through the locked reinforced windows. Rain intermittently pelted the roof, sounding like the applause at Carnegie Hall. Flashes of lightning illuminated the tattered curtains, followed by immediate cannon shots of thunder that shook the room. Ash wasn't able to sleep with this enormous racket. He was surprised that both of his roommates remained completely zoned out in their medication-induced stupor.

He sat up and slipped into the blue twill state-issue slacks that were thrown over the back of his desk chair, slipped on the socks on the floor, and walked quietly out to the hallway. The charge nurse for the NOC shift, a heavyset middle-aged white man named Blanton shouted to Ash and the three or four other frightened souls who ventured out of their respective rooms. "Everything's all right. Get back to your rooms. You can't be wandering the halls in the middle of the night."

Ash continued toward the nursing office. "I want to ask you something."

"You just need to get back to your room." The lights flickered, dimmed, and then went out. There was a buzz followed by a loud thump as a spotlight flashed down the long hallway, apparently responding to an emergency backup generator heard whirring beyond the back door.

Ash thought this might not be the best time to ask about transportation. Who signs up to work graveyard shift anyhow? Ash thought he'd be out of here in a few hours. Now it wasn't looking so good. He made his way back to his room. There was nowhere else to go at the moment. The intense storm continued for another forty minutes and then abated. The wind calmed and the predawn pale light gradually filtered through the windows. Ash peered through the crack in the shades and saw a gray blue sky. The large oak in the courtyard had dropped several small branches that were littering the basketball court. The recycling bin had blown over, and plastic bottles littered the courtyard. There were some large puddles but nothing flooded. The lights went back on in the hallway. It was 5:30 a.m. The sky was brightening, but it was a little too early to see the sunrise.

Hmm, that wasn't so bad, Ash thought. Blanton knocked on Ash's door.

"Ash, get ready, the sheriff said he's coming. He'll be here in a half hour. We got you some breakfast." Ash dressed, washed his face, skipped trimming his beard, dressed quickly, and made his way to the dayroom, where there was coffee, the good caffeinated kind. He had somewhat of a headache the first few days because of the caffeine withdrawal. The real brewed high-octane coffee was available to staff, not patients, but sometimes a kindhearted nurse's aide would sneak some real coffee to the oversedated patients. Blanton offered, "If I were you, I'd skip the coffee. They may not stop for a pee break on the way up." That could be an issue. Still, Ash took a couple of wonderful sips of acceptable coffee and enjoyed a reasonably tasty fried egg sandwich with ketchup.

Sheriff Harmon was driving from McMurtree over to the state hospital, listening to the weather radio. He still had some mild swelling of his nose courtesy of Burton Peals a few weeks earlier. The DA told the sheriff to take good care of his passenger. He wanted to get Ash to the Charleston County Courthouse promptly but safely.

"*This is the NOAA weather forecast for the South Carolina coast from Little River Inlet to Savannah to twenty miles off shore. A hurricane warning is in effect for the South Carolina coast. A category three hurricane is just offshore ready to make landfall within the next few hours. Some heavy rain bands have preceded the storm, causing heavy downpours south of Charleston, from Folly Beach to Daufuskie Island. The storm's center is projected to make landfall around Hilton Head Island at approximately 1100 hours. Maximum sustained winds currently close to 125 miles per hour near the eye wall, with hurricane force winds extending 60 to 80 miles from the center. Mandatory evacuation is in effect for the coastal regions of Charleston County South of Folly Beach, as well as coastal sections of Colleton and Bay counties. Please stay tuned for further details and emergency information . . . This is the NOAA weather forecast for the South Carolina Coast . . .*"

The sheriff thought about abandoning the trip, but the radio said the storm was a little south and they were going to head north. There were some tree limbs on the road to drive around, and some shallow puddles. Sounded like Charleston was out of the direct path. He called up to Charleston dispatch. Apparently there was a thunderstorm earlier but just breezy and partly cloudy at the moment. It was too early to contact the court clerk to see if there were going to be closures.

He pulled into the hospital grounds to the portal area. He waved a paper at the attendant officer. "I got a pickup order here."

The officer in the port office said through the intercom, "You sure you want to do this today?"

"Yeah, I hear it's okay up in Charleston."

"You pickin' up that Bridgeman guy? We're bringing him out, just stay put."

Ash appeared in a golf cart driven by a security officer. It was 6:20 a.m., just about sunrise, but the sky was darkening and gusts of wind were blowing trash around the grounds. "Well, I'd like to get moving before things get worse." Harmon commented.

Ash stepped out of the golf cart and stood up. The sheriff brought out a waist chain with shackles. "Sorry, buddy, regulations, you know."

"No sense in protesting, just let's get the hell out of here." His wrists were shackled to the waist chain. He was helped into the backseat of the sheriff's patrol car. The sheriff backed out of the portal area, made a U-turn, flipped on the flashing light bar, and said, "Okay, friend, we're code two, northbound and rollin'."

The flashing sheriff's patrol car actually headed west, away from the coast, over the marsh road that connected Bayside with the main road up to Charleston. It was going on 6:45 a.m.; and although the sunrise was twenty five minutes past, the sky was darkening. Sheriff Harmon flipped on the headlights. There was marsh on either side of the road with tidewater rising. Sturdy bald cypress with wide girth at the water line tapered upward over the roadway. Harmon was learning that hurricanes could move faster than speeding patrol cars.

Although it wasn't raining when they left BASH, fat drops of precipitation splatted on the windshield, slow at first, then more regular, and then pounding. The normally calm marsh was rippling with the rain, and small waves slapped against the shoreline and the edge of the road. The sheriff told Ash, "Don't worry, this is probably one of those rain bands they were talkin' about on the weather radio this morning. It'll pass by."

Ash hadn't had access to the weather radio. "What else did the radio say?"

"They said a hurricane will be moving in later, but . . . why don't I just flip it on?" The sheriff's vehicles were equipped with weather radio. The radio could pick up little but loud static, punctuated with even louder crackles of lightning interference. Harmon tried a few other channels but could receive nothing intelligible from the high-frequency bands.

"Well, anyhow," Harmon continued unfazed, "it's supposed to blow into Hilton Head about eleven."

Ash, as a former military officer, knew something about weather conditions from his training at the Citadel. He was alarmed at the sheriff's cavalier attitude. "What else?"

"They said the hurricane force winds would be 60 to 80 miles from the center, and I know Charleston is about 100 miles up the coast from Hilton Head. You know I've driven it quite a few times."

"Well, sheriff, it's a hundred miles to drive, but it's only about seventy or eighty miles in a straight line."

"Don't worry, son, I'll get you there well before ten. We should be there before nine, even with these road conditions." The sheriff didn't quite understand that hurricanes could cause a lot of damage before the center gets there. Also, they were in the hurricane strike zone, even if not near the dead center. Being on the north side of the hurricane and near the coast, the counter clockwise rotation of the storm would add speed to the already high wind velocity as it moves on shore.

"You know, sheriff, and with all due respect, I think we may run into trouble here. I don't think this is a rain band. I think this is the real thing."

"Well, maybe it is and maybe it isn't, but I promised the DA I would get you to Charleston safe and sound and on time. You must be some kinda big shot. Don't you worry, I've driven in worse weather than this."

The sky darkened quickly. It wasn't daylight anymore, as if the sun came up and decided to set again. The rain drove sideways and splattered sheets of water onto the windows and windshield. Wind groaned around and through the car. High tide was due around eleven a.m. The wipers were on high, working ineffectively. Water was lapping up from the marsh onto the road. The sheriff could make out a reflective sign indicating they reached the main road. "Well, I guess we ain't goin' back."

"Can we stop somewhere?"

"Maybe, but it doesn't look like a coffee shop is open that I could take a shackled prisoner into, if I could see one."

"Could you radio for help?"

"I don't think that's necessary. I've got everything under control. We'll stop here and see if this doesn't let up in a little bit." Harmon kept the engine running so the air-conditioning could operate. He tried tuning in the regular broadcast radio. Lightning static was intense. He found a Charleston station with a strong signal. There was a discussion about the hurricane. A strong gust of wind rocked the car on its suspension.

"...and power outages are already being reported from Kiawah down to

Beaufort, especially along the coast. We have on the phone Alyse Hazelwood from Charleston's WCHA TV, who's been tracking this storm, probably better than anyone else from the beginning. Thanks for joining us, Alyse. What can you tell us?"

"All I can say is it's here. The outer edges of the hurricane are already coming ashore. The eye is expected to hit somewhere between Hilton Head and Bayside a few hours from now. Emergency officials in the South coastal counties say it's too late to evacuate. Try to get to an upper story or to a sturdy shelter at your local fire station or school. Most coastal area schools are built to FEMA standards to withstand flooding, and the Red Cross has been working with local officials to set up shelters. We're expecting some hurricane force winds here in Charleston, but ground zero is fifty to eighty miles down the coast."

"Thanks, Alyse. In related news, all municipal, state, and federal offices will be closed this morning in all South Carolina counties. Stay tuned for all the latest details on your home for radio news in Charleston . . ."

The sheriff flipped off the radio. "Well, I guess we don't have to rush now."

"We can't stay here. It looks like water is coming up over the wheels." Harmon looked out the window as the rain slacked for a few moments. The entire roadway was covered with water.

Ash spoke. "Listen, we're in an emergency situation. We're in the middle of a hurricane, and this vehicle is in jeopardy. You can't leave me shackled."

The sheriff thought about it. "If you escape, y'know it's my ass." *And maybe my nose too.* He thought about his encounter with Burton.

Ash answered, "Would you rather have your knuckles rapped for an escape or possibly be charged with negligent homicide if this car is submerged and I drown with shackles? Besides, you know the DA thinks I'm okay. Also where do you think I'm going? I'm having a hearing to get released." So was Burton Peals for that matter.

The sheriff was silent for a moment and then sighed, "Okay, I might need your help." There was a barrier between the front and backseats. Harmon stepped out of the car onto the roadway and leaned into the backseat with his key. He was standing in ankle-deep moving water; the wind blew the back door hitting him in the rump as he unlocked the waist shackles and cuffs and sprawled across Ash's lap. The rain was picking up again as the lawman righted himself, slammed the back door, and moved his large wet frame back to the front seat.

Ash rolled up the chains and rubbed his wrists. "I thank you. You know,

I'm a decorated combat veteran. I could have grabbed your gun. I could have choked you. I could have done a lot of bad things just now, but I want you to know I'm a decent person, and you can trust me."

"Guess I'll have to," the sheriff replied.

The engine was still running, as was the air conditioning. The rain blasted like sheets of water from a fire hose somewhere in the darkness. Occasional flashes of lightning illuminated the roadway amid the heavily swaying trees. The wind rumbled over the car, causing it to vibrate with a low-pitched hum. The car was stopped on a small bridge crossing the marsh. A lumbering eighteen-wheeler passed by slowly, spraying even more water from the road. Harmon figured he better turn the light bar back on if for no other reason to act as a sentinel for anyone daring to head farther up the road. The water on the roadway rose with the water in the marsh, now up to bumper level. It was flowing from right to left as the tide flowed inland pushed by the fierce wind which was now rocking the car in rhythmic jerks as the low vibration became more intense.

The water rose to the level of the doors, creeping up inch by inch. The tide from the marsh, and the water moving inland started pushing the car away from the edge and toward the middle of the road. The tires left the road, and the car continued to drift aimlessly toward the barrier on other side. The vehicle slowly turned, facing the opposite direction, and then rotated another quarter turn until the trunk lodged against the cement barrier marking the side of the bridge. The lights and air-conditioning stopped, and the engine died. They were in the dark.

"Now we're fucked," the sheriff exclaimed.

"Got a flashlight?"

"Right here on the seat," Harmon said, picking up a long corrugated cop flashlight.

"We gotta abandon the car!" Ash shouted as the water was halfway up the side. The rain was almost as loud as a freight train.

Harmon shined the flashlight out the window. All that was visible was falling sheets of water, which were swirling in the air rippling sideways in waves. There was a loud sustained ripping and cracking noise followed by a thud. Harmon pointed the light beam in the direction of the sound only to see a large pine tree lying across the road, twenty yards from the car. There were no lights from any structures along the road.

"Maybe not, I don't think you want to step out into a rushing river."

"Got any rescue equipment?"

MIKE BARTOS

Harmon shouted back, "I have some rope and a life preserver in the trunk."

There were several more cracks followed by more thuds.

"We'll have to work our way back there. If we pop the trunk, it may take on water and the car will be less buoyant," Harmon shouted.

"That's okay. It'll stabilize the car for a few moments. Got a hammer or something that can smash the window?"

"I got something better. Cover your ears and close your eyes."

Ash got it. Harmon fired a round through the window, shattering it. The water was not up to the window level yet. Ash was still trapped in the backseat. The water was moving like the surf when it sucks back to the sea. The sheriff pulled himself out the window, grabbing the back door handle. He held the back of his weapon up to the window so Ash could see. Ash covered his eyes as Harmon smacked the handle of the gun through the window, shattering it into little beads.

The car was backed into the railing of the small bridge. Ash worked his way out the window and held on to the frame of the car. The trunk was opened a few inches. Ash let go and was pushed against the bridge railing; and as he braced himself against it, Harmon joined him. They found a round cork life preserver, soaking wet flares, and nylon rope. "Now what?" Ash yelled as the rain pelted him in the face, almost blinding him.

"Any ideas?" Harmon shouted back. Ash tied one end of the rope to the bridge railing and the other securely to the life preserver. There was no dry land in sight.

Ash took charge, "Just park yourself here. This railing will keep us here. Hold on to the life preserver." The wind blew white caps on the water on the road, the marsh, and the surrounding land. There was no light or cars, and the tops of small trees were snapping off and landing with a splash. The water rose further until it was up to their chests. The water was warm but moved with crushing force. It pressed them against the railing of the bridge, but now the flood was getting higher than the barrier. Both men had to grab the life preserver to keep from washing over the side of the bridge into the black swirling maelstrom.

Harmon yelled; he was exhausted. He loosened his grip with one hand and was pulled by the current over the barrier and into the swirling flood. Ash grabbed for the sheriff, but he was gone. Ash let out a scream, one that no one could hear, not even himself. He drew his body through the center of the life preserver, allowing his arms to rest as he pulled by the current but tethered in place.

The world diminished to the roar of the wind and the pull of the current as he was weightless for hours, as in a surreal dream. Ash was transported into an alternate universe. All he ever knew, his college, his military service, and loving wife were remnants of another dimension.

CHAPTER 47

At the hospital grounds, the dull gray light of the early morning sky turned to shadow with wisps of lower white clouds racing against the slower-moving blackening sky. Gusts of wind shook the magnolia trees with their fat leaves and oversized flowers, an occasional petal spiraling across the hospital grounds. Somewhere in the distance, a gust slammed an unseen door. A continuous rumble of thunder shook the ground.

The residents of the Bay Area State Hospital lined up for breakfast. Looking out the windows in the hallway, the residents could see an odd darkness tinged with green permeating the atmosphere. The rain pelted the thick reinforced glass with a frightening fury. One of the patients mumbled to a companion, "Guess we ain't getting no grounds passes today."

"No kiddin', Einstein, they don't even let us out in a drizzle" was the reply.

They sat quietly in the dining room until each patient was called by name to come get his meal from the kitchen worker. Everyone had his or her diet ordered by the doctor and dietician. No peanut butter for denture wearers; low-fat meals for the obese, despite unfettered access to tvending machines; Kosher or Halal meals for religious reasons; rice instead of potatoes; and vegan if requested. Then there was the free-for-all stolen off the plates of anorectic patients or slow eaters or anyone not looking.

They usually ate quietly; conversation was not too popular. This morning, the rain, darkness, and thunder engendered fear and fascination. The lights flickered and dimmed in the K wards dining area and then went out completely, followed by emergency floodlights going on in the dining area and hallways.

In cafeteria C-2, where the patients from K3 and some other wards took their meals, they ate in the unnatural light and racket. Martha stood up from her chair and started crying, face contorted in frustration. "I'm scared, I'm scared. I hate this place, I hate it. I want to go home." One of the nursing aides walked over to her and put her hand gently on Martha's shoulder and said, "Don't worry, you'll be safe. We'll be right here."

"I don't care. I hate this place. I hate it, I hate it, I hate it." Martha's tearfulness and anxiety escalated as the rain beat loudly against the windows and the wind roared outside. She grabbed her tray and slung it across the dining room area, slicing through the air like a frisbee and catching one of the nursing aides, a middle-aged black woman named Bernice, behind the right ear. Bernice didn't see it coming and put her hand up to the wound. Blood was flowing out of the cut and was covering her hand. Bernice felt lightheaded and stunned. She suddenly got sick to her stomach and vomited and finally collapsed on the floor.

Martha yelled, "Good for you, bitch." Several of the staff present hit the alarm devices attached to their belts. This would bring available staff from anywhere nearby to contain the situation. But the alarm did not sound. The system was down and unresponsive. Two staff members ran over to Martha, each staff grabbing an arm and moving the uncontrolled patient against the wall. There was no staff assistance to help escort Martha back to the ward, but she had to be moved as she struggled against the physical restraint. Two staff members were now engaged in a restraint procedure, one staff was injured, and one staff was on his feet, watching the melee. There were forty-five patients with one remaining free nursing staff member and the backup system failing. Three kitchen workers, all small foreign-born females, none proficient in English, with hairnets and rubber gloves in place, retreated to the back of the kitchen.

Two patients, one male and one female stood up and came forward. The male, Jorge, offered to assist with the restraint. Bernice was coming around, although still clearly stunned. The female patient, Kathryn, found a clean napkin and applied it to the wound behind Bernice's ear.

The remaining staff member, Brian Lutz, a registered nurse, shouted above the din, "Everybody back to the ward." Several of the patients protested that they hadn't finished breakfast yet. "We'll work that out later," Brian insisted. "In the meantime, we've got to get going."

Bernice was on her feet, shuffling slowly with the assistance of two other helpful patients. "Let's go. We gotta go," Brian exhorted. The two staff members were coaxing Martha along. She had tired of fighting and walked along with one staff now. The hallway back to the ward was slippery as several leaks were noted coming through the hung tile ceiling. It was difficult to see anything out the windows, as the intense wind-driven rain and darkness obscured visibility.

Back on the ward, Brian tried to call security. The internal lines were still working. He needed to report an injured staff and request transportation to the infirmary.

"I'm sorry, sir," the dispatcher said, "but there's nobody staffing the

MIKE BARTOS

infirmary, and the night OD is about the only doctor in the hospital and he really can't get anywhere. Can you possibly apply some first aid on the ward until we can move about the campus? I'm sorry, I have to go."

Several patients were straggling in the hallway, looking out the window at the unworldly scene. The ward itself was starting to leak as tiles were blowing off the fifty-year-old roof. Brian called over to some of the other wards to see if there were dryer quarters. They would have to go outside to get to another building. With the very adverse conditions blowing about, it was decided to stay put and try to deal with the leaking water in the living facilities.

Radio reception was poor in the hospital due to the thickness of the walls. In the core of the nursing office, nothing but static could be heard. Although the hospital was elevated six to seven feet above the surrounding terrain, the storm surge, coming in on high tide, was predicted to be seventeen feet at the shoreline and ten to eleven feet in the nearby marsh. The rising water would still be four to five feet at the hospital itself. The phone at the nursing office on K3 rang. The underground lines remained intact, at least for the moment. The word was coming in from security that remaining on the ward was an unsustainable plan.

The patients had rain gear available: slickers, hats, and mid calf boots. It was time to get the gear ready and make the march over to the L wards, where they could ride out the crisis on the second floor. Doubling the density of the population on a ward was not seen as a great idea, but it was the only idea. The water was creeping up to the level of the hospital grounds, now an island surrounded with foaming angry waves. The anxious nursing staff had to quickly supervise the patients into donning their protective gear. It was almost as dark as night. The water was now several inches deep outside and was starting to seep under the doors. They had to move as quickly as possible to the buildings fifty yards away through the howling vicious wind. If they stayed in the one story K wards, they could end up totally submerged. But now the howling wind and darkness made it too dangerous to venture outside. They could not dare risk leaving the shelter of the building.

Many of the patients and a few of the staff were convinced that they were going to die, right here, right now.

The wind accelerated to a fevered pitch but, within a few minutes, decelerated, slowed, calmed, and ceased altogether. The sky lightened, and the sun shined through a layer of milky haze as some patches of blue sky appeared. The water now at ankle depth was calm and reflecting the warm sun. The quiet was miraculous, but unnatural.

Brian and some of the other staff yelled frantically, "We have to get over to the L wards now." He pushed the door open. "Let's go, let's go." The patients sloshed across the flooded grounds, some falling and picked up by staff, some crying, some helping their fellow patients along. It was up to the nursing staff; there were no doctors, no social workers, and no rehab therapists. The wind was calm, but the sky was darkening again. They had a window of just a few minutes.

There were six steps and a ramp up to the first floor of the L wards which appeared reasonably dry once they were inside the building. For the sake of safety, they made their way up to the second floor. The caravan of patients split up to occupy two separate wards, as did the patients from the first floor of the L building. The second floor wards now had two to three times the normal density of population, jammed into a few steamy day rooms and hallways. They were allowed to dry off wherever there was a square foot to stand or sit and ride out the next few hours.

The light from outside faded and the sky darkened quickly and the relentless powerful wind resumed within minutes, as the eye of the hurricane passed over Bay County.

Four hours passed. The bathrooms were overloaded on the second floor of the L wards. Patients crowded together became irritable or tearful or paranoid. Fights were breaking out. Nursing staff had trouble separating fighting patients on the steamy second floor. Obviously, lunch was not being served. Vending machines in the dayroom were toppled, and bags of snacks were being grabbed and fought over. Staff made runs to the first floor kitchen, which had a variety of dry foods and bread. Staff got busy making peanut butter sandwiches and passing them out along with apples and bananas.

By mid-afternoon, the storm had abated, but rain showers persisted and the outgoing tide dragged the floodwaters back out to sea. Staff were exhausted. Nursing and security staff were wrapping up a second shift with no relief in sight.

At the edge of the confined perimeter, outside the fence, the sturdy oak, forty feet in height, a seedling when the founders of this country signed the Declaration of Independence, unable to flex with the wind and unsteady in the loose saturated soil, started to tilt toward the fence. There was a groan, then a rumble, and then an earsplitting crash as the old majestic oak tumbled onto the perimeter fence bringing its tons of weight and centuries of growth down through the razor wire and chain links, splitting and crushing a complete section. The long graceful limbs splintered on the ground inside the fenced area, while a huge section of stump and roots pulled out of the ground, leaving a gaping hole by the parking lot. It lay there as the storm abated, a fallen tower of strength, overwhelmed by the force of nature.

One security officer was surveying the situation as the disheveled patients were leaving L ward for their return to the home unit. Several of the patients saw the rift. "Do you see what I see?" One young patient spoke to another. All the patients looked in awe at the fallen oak.

A group of about twenty patients in yellow slickers moved toward the fence. The cop yelled, "Hold it right there."

One patient responded, "We're just looking," as he moved toward the fence. The officer grabbed the patient as several others scrambled over the tree and out to freedom. Another officer at the portal ran over to assist as several more made it over and through the broken fence.

Burton Peals was one of the K ward refugees. "Hey, Burton, wanna take another crack at freedom?" a fellow resident asked.

"You know, I don't think so, but go ahead and be my guest. Maybe you can do better than I did."

CHAPTER 48

Charleston was about fifty miles north of the storm's eye when it battered the coast. Heavy rains and high winds blew into the city with force just about hurricane level, which is about seventy-five to eighty miles per hour. While the official recording station in the town of Bayside reported fifteen inches of rain in a ten hour period, downtown Charleston measured a little over five inches during in the same time frame. Streets flooded during the heaviest rains of the day but not much damage as the residents had repaired and upgraded their properties after Hurricane Hugo in 1989. Hugo had been a near direct hit then; this was a glancing blow with the most severe damage farther south.

As afternoon turned to early evening, numerous reports of devastation along the coast were coming in. There were several deaths, significant property damage, people missing, and power remained out. Communication lines as well as cell towers were down, so reports were sent along by police and emergency radio as well as by ham radio operators.

Some power outages remained in the Charleston area, especially south and west of the city. Some streets remained mildly flooded, especially in the marshy neighborhoods along the Ashley River. Water was still knee deep in the area near the Medical University. Telephone landlines were in good shape, with some spotty cellular coverage. Ash and Sally J's Cumberland Street carriage house and Roswell's Tradd Street residence came through the storm well, as they had over the previous century.

Around six p.m., the sun appeared through hazy blue sky, illuminating towering puffy yellow-white cumulus clouds to the west as the tail end of Cleo moved inland. Sally J knew the hearing had been postponed but had no further information. Phone contact with the hospital had been impossible. She did not know if Ash had been picked up but assumed that the sheriff would have the good sense to hold off, especially since heavy rains started before dawn. She had been in touch with Roswell throughout the day, and he was in and out of the sheriff's office, trying to glean whatever word was coming up from Bay County. He had friends in the sheriff's department. They had his cell number; if anything came up, they would let him know.

Around seven, Roswell received a call from a Charleston County deputy.

"Mr. Chamblee?"

"Speaking."

"This is Charleston County Deputy Esterly. Sheriff Gould wanted me to let you know the word from Bayside is that there was considerable damage there. Also Sheriff Harmon apparently picked up Mr. Roper at approximately 0620 hours during a pause in the precipitation activity. The sheriff's vehicle was found abandoned where the marsh road meets Highway 41 on the creek overcrossing. The vehicle was pushed against the side bridge barrier. I'm sorry to report that the body of Sheriff Harmon was found by the side of the creek about two hundred yards from the car. The local authorities have been unable to locate Mr. Roper. Search and rescue teams are being organized, but as you can imagine, the way Bay County and Bayside got blasted, we're over our heads here. We have a problem with moccasins and gators on the roadways and everywhere else where they don't belong."

Roswell felt sickly and faint. "Thanks, please let me know as soon as you find out anything." He hung up. He sat for a few moments, immobilized. He had to let Sally J know what was going on. She was counting on him to be her link. He ran through the information he had so far. Ash and the sheriff were not in the car. They abandoned it when they got caught in the flood. They were by a creek that was apparently a running river flowing inland. At least Ash still may be out there somewhere. He thought about looking himself, but there were roadblocks either by nature or the police. Right now, it would be impossible for a civilian to get into the area. He thought about how he would tell Sally J what he knew so far. It didn't take long. He told himself, *Just go to her. She needs me now.*

The streets and sidewalks were wet with puddles but not flooded. They were littered with branches, leaves, some random trash, and a few roof tiles. The traffic lights were blinking red in all directions. Across the street was a downed electric line blocked off with wooden barriers. Utility men wearing hard hats and bright orange vests were tending to it.

He reached the carriage house and knocked on the door. It was the day of a hurricane, and a reunion foiled. Sally J was tired. She gave Roswell a hug as he entered. She knew something was wrong. She shivered.

Roswell felt ill, but he needed to be strong for her. "Ash is missing. He and the sheriff must have gotten pinned down in the flood along one of the little bridges over a marsh creek. They found the car but not Ash." For now,

MIKE BARTOS

Roswell decided to omit the part about the sheriff's body washed up on the shore of the flooded creek.

"Oh my god. Oh, Roz, do you think he's all right?"

He didn't know. "All we can do right now is hope and pray. Ash is a pretty resourceful guy. How you holding up?"

"Not so well, Rozzie, not so well." Her eyes filled with tears.

"I have my cell phone on. The Charleston County sheriff will let me know whatever he knows." He took her into his arms to comfort her. "Looks like your house held up pretty well."

"Yeah, I guess. I don't really care about the house right now."

"Have you eaten yet?"

"I haven't thought about it."

"You need to eat, sweetie. We need to be strong and ready."

Sally J sobbed deeply. "He's gone. I know he's gone. It's my fault. He needed me. He needed me to love him and support him. I wasn't there." Her breaths came in short gasps.

"Sally J, you were always there. I know you." Her tears soaked through his shirt. She trembled with each breath.

Roswell hugged her silently. She loosened herself from his arms and sat down, trying to compose herself. "Roswell"—Sally J spoke in a measured voice—"I don't think I can see you. I don't think I can be around you."

Roswell was stunned. "I'll leave now if you want."

Sally J composed herself. "Rozzie, I'm sorry. I shouldn't be angry with you, I'm not. I'm upset with me. If only—"

"Sally J, don't go there. There's no point. We can't do anything now. We don't know what happened yet. We're small in the grand scheme of things. Ash is a fighter, and he'll fight his way back to you. It'll take more than a hurricane."

"Maybe. I don't know." She began to weep again. "Roswell, let me be alone tonight. I have food in the house. I'll eat something, I promise."

Roswell stroked her hair, but Sally J gently pushed his hand away. "Not now, Rozzie, please."

"I'm sorry, Sally J, I really am. I'll be here for you."

"I know. I'm so tired now. I just need to rest. Do call me when you find out anything."

"I will, sweetie. You know where to find me." Roswell and Sally J regarded each other silently for a moment before he turned and left, knowing that things have changed between them forever.

CHAPTER 49

A sh was buffeted for hours by the flowing storm tide as he remained afloat wearing the life preserver tied with a nylon rope to the bridge barrier. He could not move in any direction, imprisoned by the moving waters and high winds. He thought about his chances if he could untie the rope and let the currents carry him where they may. If the rope broke, that's exactly what might happen. His choice was to stay where he was and not risk being driven into trees or bushes or mud or rocks or an alligator nest.

As the tide reversed flow, he was exhausted, dehydrated, and cold. The seawater was warm enough but flowing over his body for the past several hours had cooled him, and the saltwater dehydrated him. He couldn't help but swallow some of the salty brine that splashed around him. The water flowed back under the bridge, to the marsh, and back out to sea. Ash had to be careful to avoid hitting his head on the underside of the bridge. The rain continued but the sky was brightening, and the intensity abated. He was able to reach and grab the side of the barrier. It was only about four feet high, and he was able to pull himself over and fall to the road surface. He removed the life preserver, which had fit snuggly around his chest. He sat on the wet roadway on the bridge, exhausted, leaning against the concrete barrier, listening to the water rush a few feet beneath him. It was flowing out with much less speed and intensity than it had moved in. The sheriff's cruiser remained motionless on the bridge, the rear still wedged against the barrier. Ash didn't want to be there when it was discovered and try to explain to authorities why he, a transported prisoner, was alive while the sheriff was missing or most likely dead.

He sat there for moments or hours, he wasn't sure. The sky continued to brighten and the rain abated. The late afternoon sunlight ended the chill as the atmosphere around him became sticky warm. At the edge of the bridge, he saw a six-foot cottonmouth moccasin slither off the road and into the marsh and then another. *Okay*, he thought, *you guys head home. Maybe I will too.*

First he needed water. The ambient brackish water wasn't drinkable. Perhaps he could find rainwater that collected off the ground, but the surge had risen quite high, polluting any immediate source of potable water. He stood up; he felt a little shaky and chilled. Ash headed north along the blacktop road. He was aware he was wearing the hospital blues, soaked as they were.

In the distance he could see a police car moving slowly down the road toward him. The driver was focused on avoiding branches and other obstacles. Police would pick him up. He had mixed feelings about that. It would be a rescue of sorts; but then with no ID, he'd be back in the county jail and the legal processes would begin all over again. Ash moved quickly behind a partially destroyed shed and remained out of view until the car passed.

From the position of the sun, it was around 6:30 p.m., still plenty of daylight. The sky clouded again, and a brief rain shower washed over the roadway, but it cleared again quickly. The highway was covered with branches large and small, fallen trees, and tops of smaller trees that had snapped off. There were trash barrels, wooden shingles, milk cartons, and abandoned cars. A pickup truck was nosed off the road, stuck in pluff mud. Electric lines were tangled and down. Ash knew enough to keep clear of them, although they were probably dead at this point, as the utility company would shut down the power for safety reasons. There were just a few people in sight at first. Apparently, some locals got away from the coast ahead of the storm, but many rode it out in shelters and on second stories. He figured there were probably a number of folks who didn't survive.

Ash needed help, but he didn't want to be too visible. He came upon a small roadside store, apparently gone awash but still standing. There was no one inside. The door was torn off. He stepped over the detritus, boards, papers, and other items on the muddy floor. Crackers remained dry in their cellophane wrappers. Soda cans and bottles were scattered. He found a can of root beer intact. It was warm. He popped the top and quickly downed the drink. The liquid and the sugar revived him. He picked up another can, wiped off the mud, and drank again. His head was clearing, and he felt stronger. He remained dripping wet, but the air was warm, and he was not shivering anymore. He ate a package of peanut butter crackers, which were well protected within the wrapping. One more can of soda and he was ready to continue his trek.

His shoes and socks were soaked through and sloshed like a sponge with every step. Ash pulled off the wet socks and slipped back into the shoes which he would need for protection on the rubble-strewn road. He stayed by the side of the road, which was littered with debris but easily traversed by foot. The roadside structures were in various stages of destruction. Some of the more recently renovated stores were elevated on cinderblock pilings and seemed

MIKE BARTOS

to have experienced the least damage. Many of the old dilapidated wooden structures were severely damaged; some lay in piles of wood and splinters and old shingles.

It appeared that much of the storm surge effect was nearer the creek. As he moved farther up the road, more of the damage to property was apparently due to wind and not the rising floodwaters which traveled up the tidal marsh where he and the sheriff had been stranded. But it was the fierce winds that toppled trees and blew off roofs, and there was plenty of evidence of that as he continued his journey north.

He walked along for an hour or more. There were a few people visible, picking through the remains of their homes and stores and gas stations. A wet hound sniffed at the ground, circling in random directions, searching for scraps of food. It was after 8:00 p.m. and the sun was still visible through the trees. Ahead on the left was a familiar landmark, Ginny's Sea Island Café. The sign was blown away, but the familiar gray wood and brick façade with the window sign was visible. The restaurant stood, battered but intact. The main floor of the building was about six feet above ground on wooden pilings, and it seemed to have escaped flood damage. The residue of the rising water was just about two feet up the pilings, and the floodwaters had spared the main floor and second floor of the structure. Jermaine Smalls was on a ladder, taking down a large plywood board used to protect the front window. Ash approached the young man.

"Hey, Jermaine, Jermaine!"

Jermaine turned to see the man in wet muddy clothing approaching. "Do I know you?"

"Maybe a little. Is Miss Ginny, your mother, home?"

"Who askin'?"

"Tell her it's Ash, the guy from that newspaper in Charleston."

"Oh yeah, I remember you, yeah. You okay, man?"

"I'm alive, that's saying something."

Jermaine climbed down the ladder and shook Ash's hand. "You look like hell, man."

"I feel like it too. I'm not doing too good. How about you?"

"We're okay. Ma and me rode it out on the second floor. The water came up under the restaurant but didn't flood the inside. We're gonna be busy cleaning up."

After a few moments, Ginny Smalls appeared on the front porch of the café and looked at Ash standing uncomfortably in his disheveled state. Her eyebrows wrinkled as she was trying to place the face and then opened her mouth in astonishment. "You're that Ash guy from the *Charley Town* paper."

"Yeah, how's business today?"

She chuckled. "We came through okay. Probably clean up for a month. We got some water leaked through the roof upstairs. The heat pump nearly fell off in the back. I think we can rescue it. What's up with you, boy?"

"Long story. I got stranded on the road coming back from the hospital." He didn't want to go into too much detail. "Car got washed away. I've been on foot, nearly died I think. Happy to be alive. I could use a little help."

"Always happy to help a friend. Come on in. Jermaine, show Mr. Ash here some dry clothes. If the water's runnin', let him shower."

Jermaine was about three inches taller than Ash, thirty pounds less, and twenty years younger. Any of his clothing would be a bad fit. Ash and Jermaine went up the stairs to the small but pleasant two-bedroom apartment with one bathroom.

The water pressure was low in the shower. It was cool, a little brownish, not salty, better than the drying stinky marsh mud he was wearing. Jermaine favored baggy jeans. Ash still couldn't squeeze into them. Ginny asked her son if he could find his basketball warm-up shorts with the stretch waist. With some reluctance, Jermaine found them on the back of a chair and handed them to Ash along with a large blue T-shirt with a picture of Bob Marley against a marijuana leaf background and the words "Angry Man" underneath.

Ginny offered, "Once the water clears up and the electricity goes back on, I'll wash these for you," pointing to the mud-caked hospital blues in the sink.

"Those really aren't clothes I ever want to see again, ma'am," Ash responded. "Please just toss them. And Jermaine, thanks, I'll take good care of your shorts and Bob Marley shirt." A pair of sandals and the outfit was complete.

"Ms. Ginny, any way I can get back to Charleston? I'll pay Jermaine a hundred bucks to drive me."

Jermaine chimed in, "I can get behind that."

"I don't think you can get back tonight, honey. Them roads is all closed up. I don't think you can go anywhere. The pickup got wet too—couldn't start it up. We can try in the morning. You can sleep on the couch. Lights are out. We got some candles, though."

"Do you have a radio?"

Ginny repeated, "Jermaine, where's that radio your grandma bought you?"

Jermaine returned with a portable radio and handed it to his mother, who handed it to Ash. A sharp clear signal was coming in from Charleston. There was music interspersed with news reports about the hurricane's aftermath. There were over a hundred people reported dead or missing in the area. The Hilton Head resort received a lot of flooding damage, as had the town of Bayside, although the high-rise condos stood intact. Both resort areas were fairly new and built to hurricane standards. The Bay Area State Hospital received severe damage with several escapes and at least one death. The inmates were in the process of being relocated. McMurtree was farther inland and escaped most of the effects of the tidal surge. The National Guard was clearing roads and conducting search and rescue. Power remained out along much of the southern South Carolina coast. Charleston was beginning cleanup, although flooding had been minimal.

Ash asked about phone service.

"Well, that's out. We got no cell phone either. I think we just gonna have to wait."

Outside in the approaching dusk, Ash could hear the sound of a helicopter buzzing over the marsh, looking for people to rescue, maybe looking for him. But he assuredly was not the only soul in jeopardy today.

Tomorrow, he would continue his journey back to his life.

THE MORNING GREETED them with a crystal-clear, sunny blue sky. The T-shirt and shorts were comfortable like pajamas. Despite his anxieties, he had slept well through the night given the physical stresses he had endured the day before. He flicked the switch in the bathroom; electricity was still out. It would probably take weeks given the extent of the damage. The toilet, filled with rust-colored water, was able to flush.

Ms. Ginny was in the kitchen, doing her best to serve a houseguest without refrigeration or electricity. "Mr. Ash, we got some cereal. The milk was spoiled, though, and I had to throw it out."

"Whatever you have is fine," he said as he picked through a bowl of dry sugary cereal with his fingers.

CHAPTER 50

A clear peaceful dawn broke the sky as the citizens of Charleston came out of their shuttered houses and repopulated the streets and markets, businesses, and government offices this fine Friday. The phones were working, and the cell towers were reactivating around Charleston.

Sally J had a most fitful night, even as an exhausted Ash slept peacefully on the couch in Ginny Smalls' modest apartment. The phone by her bed never rang. She was aware communications and power were out down the coast. As the morning brightened, she sat and waited, gazing out the window, waiting for some word, any word. Perhaps, for now, no news was good news.

Further south, the sun rose over the wounded coastline.. Crews in tractors with flashing yellow beacons and heavy duty dump trucks rumbled in forward and reverse, sounding shrill intermittent beeps as they backed up, guided by men in hard hats, signaling with flags. The rural area was alive with the reassuring whine of chainsaws cutting through fallen trees. At around 6:30 a.m., the first signs of traffic moved past Ginny's Sea Island Café with splashes and the sizzling sound of tires on a wet road. As the sun lifted into the sky, the roads warmed and dried and became passable, with county workers stopping traffic intermittently with their manually rotating Slow and Stop signs. National Guard transports, canvas covered personnel carriers with visible uniformed guardsmen, moved up and down the roadway. Bay County was bustling with the sights and sounds of rescue, recovery, and healing.

After his simple but very welcome breakfast, Ash decided to give full disclosure to his hosts. He spoke to Miss Ginny and Jermaine together. "You folks have been wonderful, and life-saving for me, but you need to know some complications here. I checked into the hospital a week ago—"

"You checked in, like a hotel or somethin'?" Ginny asked.

"Not exactly. You know I'm a reporter. I had help getting checked in as a patient to find out what's going on there—"

"I don't think I'd want to know what's goin' on there, least not firsthand," Ginny interrupted again.

"Not too many people want to see firsthand either, but I'm a reporter—that's what I do. Anyhow, I got stuck there, and I was on my way up to

Charleston for a hearing to get released yesterday, but the sheriff who was taking me and the car got washed away. I managed to survive, obviously."

"I'm glad you're safe. You must have an angel watching,"

"Anyhow, my wife doesn't know if I'm dead or alive, so I really need to get to Charleston."

"And you want Jermaine to take you up there?"

"Unless I can borrow the truck, but I don't have my wallet or driver's license or anything."

"So they think you an escapee or something like that?"

Ash sighed, "Yeah, something like that."

"Uh-huh." She turned to her son. "Jermaine, you still don't got your license back, do you?"

Jermaine simply raised his brow. "Ma, I got it back last month."

"Mr. Ash, I know you in a fix here, but I need to stay around here. It might take all day on these roads, and with this mess around here, I need him here."

"How about if I pay Jermaine two hundred dollars?"

"That won't work too well cuz we're gonna need the old truck." She thought for another moment. "We could use the two hundred. You buy the gas? And you write that story about my restaurant like I remember you talkin' about."

"Deal, thank you so much, Miss Ginny." Ash was feeling hopeful.

Ginny turned to Jermaine. "See if you can get the truck started." She turned to Ash. "It got pretty wet here yesterday. The water come up a couple of feet, and the engine may be wet."

Jermaine cranked the ignition a few times. The starter churned but couldn't quite turn over the engine. He tried a few more times, with the same result, except the starter was more subdued. "I'll give it a little rest," he decided.

Jermaine opened the hood and tweaked some valves and connections. After a few minutes, he tried the starter again. It sputtered and almost started. He took a deep breath and turned the ignition again. It groaned and shuddered. After one more turn of the key, the engine turned over and vibrated with a deep rumble.

"Got less than half a tank, Ma."

He let the engine run as it smoothed out a little, but it seemed uneven, perhaps it was down a spark plug. Ash decided to hit the restroom once before the journey continued. Ginny made a couple of cheese sandwiches. "This should last you boys. Everything else is spoiled right now."

"Miss Ginny, I'll owe you one, more than one. You too, Jermaine. Thank you."

"Be careful. Jermaine, don't do nothin' to get pulled over," Ginny reminded her son.

"Stop worryin', Ma. I'll be careful." Jermaine took the driver's seat.

Ginny offered a God bless, and Ash returned the wish. The truck rolled cautiously off the gravel driveway in the back, down the muddy entrance, and turned left heading north to Charleston.

It was midmorning, and there was a lot of activity and disruptions along Route 41. They had to stop several times for slow moving tractors. Cut up treetops lay by the side of the road like fresh logs. There were several places where the road narrowed to one lane as workers held up one direction of traffic for a few minutes and then stopped the other lane. After one hour out, they had made about twenty miles progress. The damage seemed a little less dramatic as they continued north.

Jermaine focused on the road. Ash tried some conversation. "Your mom's a good woman."

"That's what everyone says. She raised me by herself—made sure I finished school."

"What's next?"

Probably sign up for the navy this year. Ma wants me out of the house."

"Really? I thought she needs your help."

"I help but she wants me to get my own life. There are some local people who would be happy to work for her."

"How about the army instead of the navy? I could tell you all about that."

"I don't know. I think the navy would be cool. If I could get stationed in North Charleston, then I wouldn't be too far from home."

Ash suggested the marines, right down the road at Parris Island.

"I wish," Jermaine responded. "I'd do it if I could. Don't know if I could get in."

"You never know, Jermaine, not until you give it a try. I bet you could cut it."

"Well, it's somethin' to think about, Mr. Ash."

News talk radio was giving more details of the damage and how the south coast was the bull's eye. He was stunned to hear about the escapees and the one known death at the hospital. A patient was found drowned in his room. Was Ash considered one of the escapees? It was also good to hear Charleston was not badly damaged. The hurricane was now a soggy tropical depression over Central Virginia.

The gas tank was down to a quarter of a tank. Jermaine had a small amount of cash. As they headed farther north, there were some gas stations open.

"Jermaine, how 'bout we get some gas?"

"It's okay. That gas gauge reads wrong most of the time. We're okay."

Ash would have stopped to fill up, but then he wasn't the one holding the steering wheel or the money.

The traffic moved smoothly for the next fifteen miles as they approached the outskirts of Charleston. Damage seemed fairly moderate. Some signs were blown down, branches and trash were scattered, and electric signs were operating. He could probably make a call. "Jermaine, you don't have a cell phone, do you?"

"No, not much use for one down where we live—sort of in a dead spot."

"Any way we could stop and make a call, maybe a gas station?"

"We can try, but I haven't seen a pay phone for years."

They pulled into a gas station with a convenience store. Jermaine relented and agreed he could buy three gallons. Ash asked the cashier, a heavyset middle-aged black man with a mustache, where he could find the pay phone.

"Pay phone? Who has a pay phone?"

Ash was feeling very old school. "I have to make an emergency call. How about that phone right there?" he asked, pointing to a portable phone on the counter.

"Sorry, this phone is for employees only."

"Look, we came up from the hurricane area. Our cell—everything was lost."

"Can't help you. I'd lose my job."

Jermaine was pulling out his last ten dollar bill to buy the gas and intervened with the clerk. "Listen up, my brutha. This here man is with me, and I am asking you man to man for some respect for my friend here who is worthy of all due consideration, and I would personally appreciate it if you would kindly help a man in need. It would be in the best interest of all concerned if you would reconsider your position. Do we have an understanding here?"

The clerk handed Ash the handset from behind the counter. Ash thought, *Jermaine, army, definitely army.* Ash punched in Sally J's number and waited. An automated voice came on the phone, *"All circuits are busy now, please try your call again later.*" He pressed redial, same response. Cell circuits must still be messed up. He looked up Roswell's office number. Three rings. It was lunchtime; the answering service picked up. "Givens, Levin, Pratt and Chamblee."

"This is Ashley Roper. I have an emergency call for Mr. Chamblee. Can you get him on the line?"

"And how do you spell that name?"

"For crissake, R-O-P-E-R."

"Mr. Chamblee isn't in the office now. May I please have your call-back number?"

"Listen, just page him. Tell him I'm on my way to *Charley Town.*"

"I'm not sure when he'll be back in, sir."

"Listen, this is an emergency. Just make sure he gets the message. I'll hold you and your service responsible if he doesn't get it." He hung up.

"Jermaine, let's push on." When they were alone in the car, Ash thanked Jermaine for the intervention.

"No problem, I was just pretendin' to be a marine."

Thirty minutes later, they crossed the bridge across the Ashley River, the river from where Ash got his name. The area they just came through was the urban/suburban area of Charleston sometimes called West of the Ashley or more commonly "West Ashley." There were many Ashleys in Charleston, some male, some female, some first-named, some last-named, and some middle-named, but they all carried part of the geography of their city with them from birth until death, a quality uniquely Charleston.

It was just another mile along Cannon street, and then down King. He was almost home. The *Charley Town* office was ahead on the right. There was a small crowd on the curb outside the office. He could see Sally J, Roswell, Annie and the interns, his glorious welcoming committee.

"This is it Jermaine, this is my family. pull it in right here." Sally J gave out a squeal as she saw Ash waving out the window. Jermaine nosed the old truck into a too small parking space. Ash jumped out before the truck stopped moving.

Sally J was waiting. She ran to Ash and threw her arms around him and buried her head in his chest. "Welcome home, baby, welcome home. Are you okay?" Roswell watched the happy reunion. After a few moments, he walked over to Ash and shook his hand and smiled. He pulled Ash toward him and gave him a hug. Annie and the interns gave a cheer and crowded around him.

Ash freed himself from the hugs momentarily. "Folks, this is Mr. Jermaine Smalls, my escort and road warrior. This is his truck that got me here," Jermaine smiled and nodded his head.

Sally J offered, " Thank you Jermaine, thank you so much," then threw her arms around the young man. catching him by surprise. She let go and looked at her husband. "Ash, baby, you must be starving." He didn't think about it until she mentioned it.

Roswell put a friendly hand on Ash's shoulder, "Welcome home, buddy. We still have some things to talk about."

"Let's talk over lunch. I've got a long story to tell." The dry cereal he had for breakfast was long gone, and his stomach was grumbling. "I want Jermaine to be our guest of honor."

Jermaine politely said, "I need to get home and help Ma."

Ash insisted, "Jermaine, you really helped me. I want to thank you. Anything I can do to help you and your mom—"

"The money will help, and don't forget that publicity you told my ma about."

Ash, Sally J, Roswell, and Jermaine headed on foot up King Street looking for a nearby ATM. There was one within a block. Ash asked Sally J for the card and withdrew the maximum three hundred dollars and handed fifteen twenty-dollar bills to Jermaine. "Get yourself some gas, thank your mom, thank you, and I'll be in touch. We'll talk army, okay?"

Jermaine smiled as Ash shook his hand. He tipped his ball cap respectfully to the grateful crew, then walked back to the sloppily parked pickup, backed out, and headed home toward rural Bay County.

Definitely army, thought Ash as he grinned. *Kid's got a heart as big as South Carolina.*

CHAPTER 51

"Do you think I look okay to dine out like this?" Ash asked referring to his funky shorts and blue T-shirt.

"You never looked better to me," Sally J responded

"Me too," Roswell added.

They took a seat at a round wooden table in a casual barbecue restaurant. "I know it's midday, but I'm havin' me a damn beer."

Sally J jumped in, "I love you, but the only way you're having a beer is over my dead body."

"Yeah, sorry, give me a pass for asking' I could use one though."

Sally J looked at him sympathetically. "Maybe you need to tell us what happened. We want to hear."

Ash then began relating his story of the hurricane, as Roswell and Sally J looked on in astonishment. He told of his transport and hazardous experiences, the near drowning, and the loss of Sheriff Harmon. He had to pause several times, and became teary eyed when he related his feelings of helplessness as the sheriff was washed away and drowned. There was his journey home, hiding from the cops, avoiding snakes, survival, finding food and water, and the kindness of Ginny Smalls and the heroics of Jermaine.

Roswell clasped Ash's hand and sighed. "It's amazing you're back here with us. We were so worried, we had no idea where you were. We knew about Sheriff Harmon, we feared for you, but somehow we knew you would make it. We prayed for you."

Roswell went on, " But I have to tell you your hearing is rescheduled for four p.m. today. Do you think you can handle it? The courts are agreeing to extend their hours today in light of yesterday's cancellations. After I got your message, I called Judge Silberman's chambers. I spoke to him, and he agreed justice delayed is justice denied. He said you could be in my custody for the time being. The state DBHS was contacted. They won't be sending anyone to contest. I've spoken to the assistant DA, and he's going to have no objection. We should have you freed for the weekend. When we're done here, go home and get your act cleaned up, jacket and tie for court."

"I don't own a tie. I think I have a jacket."

"Just do the best you can."

Sally J looked at Ash and put her hands on his shoulders. "All I can say is thank God you're home. That's all I care about. I can't believe what you've been through."

"Baby, being back home with you is the most important thing in the world."

Roswell swallowed a big gulp of chowder and looked up to the higher powers and then at Ash. "It ain't over till it's over. There's still some battles ahead, but I got your back, buddy"

Ash finished off the best double hamburger he ever ate. Roswell continued, "The lunch is on me. I'll drive you two home. You don't have a lot of time, a little over an hour. Be at my office at 1530 hours sharp. You with me?"

They squeezed into the Beamer for the four-minute ride home. "Get your ass in gear, Ash. See you soon," Roswell said as they headed to the front door.

Ash stepped into his quiet, cool, clean home. He felt like he had been gone for years. Sally J stroked Ash's face and looked into his eyes. "I'm never letting you out of my sight again."

"Okay, next time you can come with me."

"Shoo, go shower, and let me burn that awful outfit."

"How about one photo before I abandon these clothes?"

"You can't be serious?"

"Sure, it's part of the story."

Sally relented and snapped a picture with her phone. "Maybe I ought to e-mail it to everyone you know. I'll post it on your Facebook page."

"Ha!" Ash exited to the bathroom. He seemed to be holding up well under the circumstances.

By three p.m., his beard was trimmed, hair washed, fingernails cleaned, and teeth brushed. He wore a navy blue blazer, fresh clean blue dress shirt, and khaki slacks, looking very Charleston. Still, he was looking quite tired. Sally J called a taxi. Ash protested, "It's less than a mile to Roswell's office."

Sally J took charge, "I don't want you workin' up any more of a sweat than you need to, hon. I have our marriage certificate and your birth certificate. I have everything I need including you."

They were right on time to Roswell's office on Broad Street. Roswell greeted them and ushered the couple into his office. "Ash, you look a whole helluva lot better than you did at lunch."

"I feel better too. Everything set?"

"This should be fairly simple," Roswell replied. "I don't think we'll need your testimony, Sally J, but if we do, it shouldn't take very long. It's late afternoon, and I think everyone wants to wrap this up."

Ash said, "Okay, let's do this thing."

Judge Silberman dismissed the jury in his courtroom at 3:30 p.m. for the weekend. He was ready to start at 4:00 p.m. sharp. He had reviewed the writ and had just a few questions. Roswell, Ash, and Sally J were ready. The State of South Carolina, the respondent, was represented by the assistant DA, Dale Hammer. The distinguished Judge Silberman entered the courtroom as all rose. He took his seat at the bench under the great seal of the state of South Carolina and called the hearing to order.

Roswell began, "Your Honor, my client, Ashley Roper has been held at the Bay Area State Hospital for the past week under another identity, that of one Garrison Bridgeman, deceased. It was part of an investigative journalism project. The security chief who brought in Mr. Roper intended to let him spend the day and release him that evening. Unfortunately, Chief Dawkins took ill and expired that day, leaving my client trapped in the hospital despite the knowledge of security and administration. I believe they wanted him released under court order and not just by an administrative decision."

The judge was astonished. "So your client was never actually committed to this hospital in the first place?"

"Correct, Your Honor."

"But he voluntary entered under the pretense of being a patient?"

"Correct."

"And you can document this?"

"Yes, Your Honor. First of all, I have personally known and have had close contact with my client for more than a dozen years. Also his wife is here, and we have his birth and marriage certificate."

Mr. Hammer rose. "If it pleases the court."

Judge Silberman looked at Roswell. "Mr. Chamblee?"

"No objection."

Mr. Hammer declared, "The state is willing to stipulate that this petitioner is whom he says he is, and the state has no interest in keeping him incarcerated."

"Fine, I will rule that the writ is granted and that Mr. Roper be released."

Mr. Hammer continued, "Thank you, Your Honor, but there are a couple of other matters here. Mr. Roper is an eyewitness to a homicide which occurred during his incarceration and is a key witness, and I request the court order Mr. Roper to not leave the state until the matter is adjudicated."

Roswell's objection was overruled.

"And one more thing, Mr. Roper may have committed a felony by assuming the identity of another person, deceased or not. Identity theft is a serious matter."

"Have you filed charges?" the judge asked.

"Not yet, Your Honor, but I did want the state's concerns noted in the record and inform Mr. Roper and his counsel that the matter is under consideration."

"So noted. Is there anything else?"

"Nothing else, Your Honor."

"Mr. Chamblee?"

"No, Your Honor."

"In that case, court is adjourned."

Roswell walked over to Dale Hammer. "Dale, what the hell?"

"You mean the identity theft business?"

"Why would you want to pursue that?"

"Well, your client caused a lot of havoc—"

"He wouldn't have if they let him the hell out when they knew who he was. He tried to come clean and nobody cared. I was down at BASH trying to get him out, and they wouldn't hear of it. Hell, they arrested his wife."

"I suppose I have better things to do, but it'll be up to the state if they want to pursue this."

"Maybe we should have a meeting with the Department of Behavioral Health Services."

"If you want to set one up." Hammer agreed.

"Maybe we will," Roswell responded.

"Sure, have a nice weekend."

Ash and Sally J headed back to Roswell's office with him. As they walked, Ash asked what was going on.

"What's going on is some gamesmanship. No one's filed any charges yet, and I don't know if they will. I'm pretty sure we can work this out. Try not to worry. Anyhow, you're done with BASH."

Ash said, "I'm just getting started with BASH. I have a story here that should make waves locally if not nationally."

Sally J added, "We're calling it 'Ash in BASH', subtitled, 'The Life and Times of the Bay Area State Hospital.'"

Roswell added, "It might be the Life and Death of Bay Area State Hospital because they're moving people out of there and maybe closing it down. It was apparently out of compliance with FEMA regulations and is not inhabitable."

"So who's still there?"

"I don't know for sure. I've just heard some reports on the news. Ernie Joe Plumm, the murder suspect, was found drowned under his bed. Ash, that's something you might need to look into while you're doing your story. Why don't you give your buddy, Kerrigan, a call? Find out some stuff and let him know you're all right."

"I will, but right now, my muscles all ache. I feel like I was run over by a truck."

Sally J chimed in, "I think you just need to rest and relax this weekend, eat, sleep, maybe a little recreation, huh? Don't worry about that place for a while. I'll take care of you."

Ash added, "Roswell, I really owe you here. You really stuck your neck out for me."

"You're welcome. I did this for the both of you. Anyhow, we're not done yet. Those dicks at DBHS have something up their sleeve. Don't move on your story yet, there ay be some complications here."

"Maybe you could start billing us at this point?"

"Ash, buddy, you can't afford me. This is what friends are for. I know you guys will be there for me if I ever need you. That's good enough. Now go get your butt home and reacquaint yourself with your charming bride. Stay out of trouble and keep Sally J happy—that's payment enough for me."

"How about a lawsuit?"

"Lawsuit?"

"Sure, I may have shown up uninvited, but they kept me falsely imprisoned, even when they knew I didn't belong there, exposed me to violence, arrested Sally J and roughed her up, exiled the doctor who tried to help me. And then they transported me under hazardous conditions even when forewarned and almost cost me my life."

"We'll talk about it Monday. In the meantime, get some rest, go home. You look like hell."

"I thought you said I looked great."

"I lied, but I expect you to look great after the weekend."

Sally J was curious. "You seein' Kimberly?"

"Oh you betcha, so I'm getting out of this office as soon as I wrap up a few details. Anyhow, we'll talk next week." Kimberly was helping Roswell keep his mind off Sally J.

After thanking Roswell and exchanging good-byes, Ash and Sally J and left hand in hand. They took the long way home, circling down East Bay Street, through the waterfront park lined with tall palmetto and young oak. It was a typical hot, sunny July afternoon busy with strollers, joggers, and couples playing with their young children on the somewhat muddy green. Large puddles remained as a memento of the storm the day before. Sally J took Ash's hand as she saw young parents with a toddler laughing and awkwardly throwing a tennis ball as an enthusiastic mutt dog chased it, returning the slobber covered ball to the youngster. Ash gazed at the child with the tennis ball.

"What are you thinkin', hon?" Sally J asked.

"I was thinking this is the way life ought to be."

"Sally J smiled. "I was thinking that too."

CHAPTER 52

Another Saturday Morning. This one was a bit busier than most. The hurricane brought in quite a surge in the neighborhood. Grover and I didn't evacuate and rode the storm out here in Marshlandia. It was worse than I expected. Thursday, the water rose about five feet here and the bungalow is nine feet above ground level, not much room to spare. The wind shook the house for hours, and I thought for a while we were going to be blown away to Oz. Many of the roof tiles flew off, and I had water leaking onto the parquet floor, which buckled and will have to be redone. The yard was a muddy, debris strewn mess. Grover really wanted to run out there, but he got quite a bit of mud when he tried, and I had to hose him off on the back deck.

Most of the neighbors in new construction did okay; but the poor neighbors in run down homes, not so well. My nearest neighbors, the Simmons family—husband, Gil; wife, Violet; and their two young kids—spent the day in the house with me.

Most of my neighbors are rural blacks who have been in this part of the coastal Sea Islands since the end of the Civil War. Former slaves were granted property rights, which in various areas is known as "heir's land." The land titles, if there ever were titles, are not traceable, but they still live in their humble homes on the marsh side of these coastal islands. The homes and lots pass from generation to generation without much in the way of formal documentation. In the century and a half that these families have been here, there have been hurricanes and floods. Very simple wooden homes come and go, but the people stay. Some homes have been built up above the flood lines; others like the very basic home of the Simmons' do not handle a flood tide. As far as I know, my bungalow may have once been on heir's land; I don't really know, but I was the interloper in their world, and they were welcome to shelter in my storm resistant home.

As the flood tide rose, they had nowhere to go. They knew I lived in an elevated house, and it was a life and death situation. They weren't here long when the water started to rise under the house. There is a second floor bedroom we could have retreated to, but the water didn't reach the main floor. The lights went out; we were all in near darkness throughout the day.

We huddled together in the living room until the water receded in the early evening.

Gil and Violet Simmons, whom I had only previously nodded to on occasion, gave me a hug and a blessing, and then left. One could say they lost everything, but I don't think so. They would be back, and their neighbors would help them rebuild on the exact same spot. After all, it is their land. I donated a pickup truck's worth of lumber to the cause. I'm not much of a builder or handyman, but I would do what I can do. I was one of the fortunate ones.

I decided to clean up and patch up and then head back up to Charleston until all the services were restored in Bay County. I went to the building supply store, but it was a zoo and supplies were limited. After I put in an order for the lumber for the Simmons', I managed to find some blue plastic tarp and then came home and climbed upon the roof myself and nailed it down over the leaking and denuded areas. The ladder sunk a bit in the mud but seemed stable. Anyhow, no one was going to find a handyman the day after a hurricane.

My cell phone was not able to locate service and electricity was out. It was near noon. With the house as secure as I was going to get it, I packed a suitcase and hosed off and towel dried Grover, and we headed up to Charleston. It was two days since the hurricane struck, and according to the news, most of the roads, the main roads anyhow, were open.

I was curious to know what was going on over at BASH. Radio reports indicated that patients were dropped emergency supplies and being transported to county jails, some to prison psych units and some to other state hospitals. There was one patient death reported, that being the infamous Ernie Joe. I was waiting for the details on that one. Also, about twenty escaped, but most had been found or willingly returned. There was still about half a dozen out there somewhere, fending for themselves. The National Guard had been mobilized, and all their business was urgent.

I was quite sure that the administration was on the scene looking up protocols, special orders, and "opportunities for improvement." Desjardins had spent the night there and was there during the day of the hurricane. But nurses, doctors, social workers, kitchen workers, janitors, cops, and over a thousand employees were without a workplace. Not without a job, just without a workplace, sort of like I was for the previous week.

The roads were not in bad shape. There was one annoying detour where a small bridge was washed out. That added about a half hour to the journey.

Road crews, utility crews, business, and homeowners were now out in force. The chain saws were growling; bulldozers were backing up and moving forward on and off the roads.

What was striking to see was a grove of young trees all snapped in half like a stand of broken toothpicks, treetops dangling or scattered in tangled brush, and tree limbs piled on the forest floor. It will take years, but they'll recover.

The damage lessened as I approached Charleston from the South. According to the news, this was a powerful but compact storm, and the only other good thing about it was that it moved quickly over the coast and did not linger. If it had, I might not be here to tell the story.

Grover and I arrived on Market Street mid afternoon on Saturday, July 9. The Market was busy with tourists and some locals looking for lunch. Lunch! Now there was a capital idea. A couple of days of soggy sandwiches and I was ready. I realized I haven't checked in with Cassandra for a few days, no phone service. I checked my phone which was charging during the drive—low battery but good old four bars of signal. Back in civilization.

I parked the car around the side of our building, grabbed my suitcase, and entered the bar with Grover at my heels. "Doc! You son of a bitch, we thought you were dead," Brad called out. He gave me a hug. "Bet you need a drink."

"That's a bet you would win." It was good to see friendly faces.

Brad poured me a shot of Houlihan's. "How are ya? What happened?"

I went into a long tale about the storm, the mud, the roof, the neighbors, and maybe no place to work, at least no place from which to be administratively suspended.

"So you'll be hanging around here for a while? Maybe we'll put you to work behind the bar. Great place for a shrink, don't you think?"

"I don't mind." Actually true. I downed the whiskey, really smooth and rich. That settled things fairly well. "Let me and Grover get settled and we'll catch up."

When I got upstairs, I saw Brad had closed the skylight during the storm, thank heavens. I saw a voice mail message on my cell from Ash, which was sent around 10:00 a.m., when I was out of reach. It was brief. He said he was in Charleston, doing okay, and he wanted me to call back. That was good news. I was so wrapped up in my own and my neighbors' survival during the storm that I had only a few passing thoughts about Ash. It was good to hear from the man.

I punched in his number, and he answered after two rings. He obviously saw my ID. "Doc, thanks for calling. How are you? Where are you?"

"I'm at my place in Charleston. Had to bail on rural Bayside. The question is how the hell are you? Where are you?"

"I'm at home. Had a writ hearing yesterday after almost drowning in the sheriffs car during the peak of the hurricane the day before. It's a long story."

"We both have a long story. One thing, you have some of the most devoted friends I ever met and a great wife."

"That I know."

"Listen, since you live in the neighborhood, why don't you and Sally J make your way over here around seven. Kerrigan's Bar and Grille, you know the place. I think I told you it's the family business. You'll be my guests."

"Well, Sally J wants me on ice this weekend, but I think I can sweet talk her into it."

"You do that. I know you're writing about everything that's going on, and I have some tidbits for you to add to the stew. How about your lawyer friend?"

"I think he made it clear that he had some hot plans for tonight that doesn't include shootin' the breeze with us."

"Okay, we'll catch him next time. We had an agreement to all get together when you were free."

"We will. There's still unfinished legal business, and there were some traumatic events that I'm trying to deal with. I'll tell you about it. Once we clear that up, we'll celebrate."

"Anyhow, we'll have a table around seven. We'll swap stories, listen to some music, and have some fun."

"I'm there. I want to hear things from your perspective." Ash sounded eager.

I WAS PLAYING a little blues, passing the time, nursing some straight up whiskey when they arrived. I didn't really know these people very well; but at some level, it seemed I did, as I became part of their struggle. I wanted to meet them under less stressful circumstances.

I motioned to a table, and they found their way across the bar room. I was surprised when Sally J greeted me with a hug, followed by a hug from Ash. I like warm, open people.

The last time I saw Sally J, she was scared and angry, her hair was mussed, and her dress was torn with a little blood, but she ultimately held it together. Tonight she was prettier than I remember, with her reddish blond hair down over her shoulders instead of the pigtails I remembered. Sally J began the conversation. "I wasn't wanting to go out tonight. Ash really needed a rest."

Ash cut in, "I had all the rest I needed by ten a.m., if not before. I understand you met our friend and attorney, Roswell."

"Yes, I did. Fine fellow indeed. By the way, what are you having?"

"Whatever is non-alcoholic—recovering, you know," Ash replied.

I didn't know, but I can respect that. "How about you, Sally J?"

She surprised me. "I'll have what you're having, Doc."

"Paul," I called out, "Houlihan's straight up for my friend here."

"You got it, Doc."

Now we were properly prepared for an evening of conversation. Cassandra was planning to drop by around nine. She might enjoy this couple. I was disappointed that Roswell and Kimberly weren't going to be here. I ordered some of the evening specialties but no reason we couldn't start with fried clams.

Ash told me much of what went on in the past week while I was cruising the internet in the library. He found out a lot more than I had in four years. The story of the death of Jesse, the open drug dealing, and the intimidation were things I knew about but not with this clarity and detail. Then there was the journey through the hurricane, the death of the Bay County sheriff, and the nearly lethal journey back to Charleston. I listened with some degree of disbelief, even though I knew the story to be true.

We were both somewhat curious about the fate of BASH and the patients and employees. Ernie Joe was dead. I was in touch with Morty Frizell, who informed me that Ernie Joe was apparently in a doctor induced semi-coma to keep him quiet. He drowned under his bed, unable to make the trek to the neighboring dry ward, and somehow was missed in the patient count. The covering doctor was under investigation for patient abuse. A nurse reported Dr. Mandlebaum for punitively oversedating Ernie Joe, leading to his death. Dr. Mandlebaum would have been reassigned to the library to keep me company if the library were still open. I didn't know where he or the patients were relocated.

My story was not so exciting. Sally J thanked me profusely for my minimal help. I'm sorry I couldn't have done more. Ash wanted to ask some more pointed questions. He was dipping some French bread in onion soup when he asked, "Do you think they suspended you just to neutralize you? To get you away from me?"

"Who's 'they'?" I asked.

"Maybe the security, because they were involved with some of the drug stuff going on, maybe to leave me isolated. I was assaulted twice, and if another patient hadn't intervened, we might not be having this conversation."

I recalled administration was none too helpful in getting me back to my ward.

"Then another thing," Ash added, "and this has been bothering me. Captain Dawkins drops dead at his desk the very day I get smuggled in. Coincidence? I think he was clean, just a feeling I got talking to patients and staff. He even told me he knew a lot of skullduggery was going on but couldn't track it, couldn't prove a thing. Did they do an autopsy? Toxicology? I don't know, do you? I mean, here's a guy who knew too much and, with my presence, wanted to find out more."

I had to admit I was in the dark about that, but interesting question. I asked Ash, "You're the reporter here. I guess you know ways to find these things out."

"I got friends," Ash smirked. And then he asked me, "When you first met me, did you think I was mentally ill? I mean after you interviewed me? Did you think I was full of shit?"

I had to think about that. "Well, Ash, you came with a chart that detailed mental illness and violence. If you ask what you're asking, the only other assumption I could make is that you were not a real patient or spontaneously cured, and why would I think that? Anyhow, you know that I let you have your say, and of course, none of the patients here believe they are mentally ill. I'm glad I took the time to check out your story, and you know I put my ass on the line to help you out, and I would do it again."

"I believe that. I just had to ask. Do you think I'm mentally ill now?"

I had to laugh. "Just about as much as I am."

Ash retorted, "That serious, huh." The three of us laughed.

"Yeah, and I got the cure." Sally J and I had another round as Ash looked on enviously. We put our suspicions and doubts on hold. Especially since Cassandra just arrived to join us.

I introduced my new friends. Cassandra said, "I've heard a lot about you. I feel I already know you. I'm glad you're home safe."

Sally J replied, "I'd love to share a drink with you. It looks like somebody finished off this whole bottle of Houlihan's. Omigod, forgive me, I'm so drunk."

I intervened, "Once we get all this nonsense settled, we'll have Roswell and Kimberly join us at some fine place, not this dump, and we'll celebrate in a righteous manner. Cassandra shook hands with both Ash and Sally J before they headed toward the door. I told Cassandra this was going to be a great weekend and, since I wasn't planning to be at work on Monday, or Tuesday for that matter, a very long one.

MIKE BARTOS

Ash felt a bone-deep fatigue after the first several days following his return to Charleston. Muscles ached, muscles that he never knew he had. The physical stress of fighting the currents and the emotional stresses were catching up with him. In the military, they called it post traumatic stress disorder, or PTSD, which involves painful intrusive memories of conflict and battle. He had been attacked several times and almost killed once at the hands of another man and once by the forces of nature, perhaps more than anyone would have expected on a tour of military duty. Then he watched his wife being manhandled and was helpless to intervene, then helpless to rescue Sheriff Harmon. The relief of freedom was being replaced by anxiety and nightmares. Then there was the issue of unresolved legal charges.

Sally J worked on the newspaper story for the following week. The "Ash in BASH" series was taking shape, although Ash was staying in the background. Sally J and the other staff writer, Jolene Caldwell, were piecing together the information. Ash wasn't ready to work on the retelling of the story, not yet. He was excited at first but was not fully recovered nor ready to throw himself into the mix. He still needed time to work everything out in his head.

Sally J pushed him somewhat but decided that she needed to back off which Roswell ordered anyhow. The story could wait a little. Ash wasn't eating very well and dropped a few pounds during the weeks since he had returned home. It's not that he couldn't have stood to lose a few pounds but not this way, not by default.

Against her better judgment, she called Roswell. Maybe she needed advice, or maybe she just wanted to hear his voice.

ASH SAT ON a well-worn couch in the living room of an old restored frame house on Wentworth Street. He heard a sudden outburst of laughter from a room upstairs, followed by some animated muffled conversation. A few minutes later, eight or ten people filed down the stairs. One woman detoured into the kitchen, opened the refrigerator door, and took out a clear pitcher and poured water into a paper cup and drank. She replaced the pitcher in the refrigerator.

All the members of the group were adults, male and female, ranging in age from late twenties to sixties. Two of the women hugged and talked about looking forward to next week's session.

A few minutes after the group filed out, a tall portly man, sixtyish, gray beard, hair pulled back into a short ponytail, wearing a red plaid flannel shirt, sleeves rolled up, and blue jeans, came down the stairs and walked over to Ash.

"You must be Ashley. I'm Scotty Powell."

"Nice to meet you. I've heard about you."

Powell gave out a boisterous laugh. "I hope you haven't heard that much."

"Trust me. It's been mostly good."

"Mostly? I'll settle for that," Scotty mused, "Can I get you something?"

Ash declined. They ascended the stairs and entered his rather large office. There was a large window facing east with a partial view of the harbor. A chockablock assortment of couches, wicker chairs, and even a rocking chair were arranged in a circle around the periphery of the room. The large upholstered easy chair was reserved for the good doctor himself. He dropped into his chair with an exhalation, put his feet up on a non-matching footstool, and took a coffee mug and rested it on his ample belly. "It's decaf tea. I have to cut back on the caffeine—blood pressure, you know. So Ash, what's up?"

"What's up?" Ash repeated. "A lawyer friend advised me to see you."

Scotty placed his feet on the floor and leaned forward. "Is this your first time seeing a psychiatrist?"

Ash laughed. "You can say I've seen a lot of psychiatrists lately. Not as a patient, just seeing them, like you see cattle when you drive through Nebraska."

"Sounds interesting."

"I had a therapist at the VA years ago for PTSD and drinking. I thought I was fine."

"So what's the story now?"

"Okay, this is a long story."

"I don't particularly like long stories."

"What do you like?"

"I like what's going on today, here and now, this minute,"

"This minute, I'm not so sure I like being here."

"That's okay. That's a start. That's honest."

Ash asked, "What do you do here?"

"We talk. We're two men having a conversation. We eventually go where you need to go."

"Like a journey?"

"That's one way of looking at it."

"Why do I need to go anywhere?" Ash asked.

"Because you don't like where you are."

"How do you know that? I don't know that."

"No one comes to Scotty's Café if he's not hungry. So let's go back to the beginning. What do you think you need?"

"I need to get my old self back."

"Is that a good idea?"

"The new me isn't working out so well."

"What's going on?"

"Can't sleep, I'm losing weight, having nightmares."

"Are you depressed?"

"That's what my wife says."

"So she knows how you feel better than you do?"

"She does tune in. Sometimes it's a gift, sometimes a burden."

"I know the feeling well. Okay, what's going on in your life?"

"You know the paper *Charley Town*? That's mine. We can't keep up with the competition. I investigated BASH, and like you said, you don't like long stories but a lot of things happened. I was down there for what was supposed to be a few hours, and it turned into a week right before the hurricane, almost got killed a couple of times, almost drowned in the hurricane, couldn't get out, saw too many things. The sheriff who was driving me got killed. It's like Kuwait all over again. The whole BASH experience was more than I expected or bargained for."

"I used to work at BASH. It was quite a few years ago."

"It's quite a shit hole, don't you think?"

"I hope you didn't go through a lot of trouble to find that out." Scotty laughed

"That's where I ran into a lot of psychiatrists."

"I think I'd prefer to hang out with the Nebraska cattle you were talking about."

"Well, that's one reason I wasn't so hot about seeing a psychiatrist professionally."

"Ha! That's a perfectly sane attitude," Scotty observed.

"The only one who tried to help me got his ass booted out of there the day I arrived."

"That's the way they work at BASH. Keep your mouth shut, follow the state directives, and they might let you work until retirement. The fact that you're having nightmares about it is troubling."

"My wife thought you might prescribe an antidepressant for me."

Scotty raised one eyebrow, which he did so well. "That's something we can consider. For now I think that would get in the way."

"That's actually reassuring."

"Let me tell you something else." Scotty leaned forward, "What's going on with you is a normal process. People suffer. I see this every day. Burdens can be wearing, but they can prod you to get you moving on to the next step. You started this whole trip, investigation, whatever, because you had to up the ante. Your *Charley Town* isn't working. You tried to make a change. And change is what you're getting, not the change you thought you were looking for, but change. That's not a bad thing. Love your misery right now. It's a gift."

"Okay, so what do I do in the meantime?"

"Just be aware, aware of how you feel, of where you've been. Don't think too much about where you want to go. There are forces taking you there now. I feel that coming from you. You can't control everything."

"You know I was a platoon commander in the first Gulf War. That was a battle. I saw some awful stuff. I thought I could handle everything. It wasn't until I got back—"

"Okay, you're a warrior, and thank you for your service, but this is a different battlefield now. Tell me, how's your marriage?"

"I think it's fine. My wife is a sweetheart, creative, pretty. She's had this thing for her lawyer friend going back twenty years. I don't think she's cheated, but she's not always completely there. Then again, I haven't been the easiest husband in the world. She's made sacrifices for me. Sometimes I think she's resentful."

"But you both keep growing."

"I guess so. When we first met, she said she could help me stop drinking. It took a couple of years."

"Did she have anything to do with that?"

"Probably so. She didn't tell me what to do. I sort of just started doing it. I don't drink anymore. Sometimes I order a beer just to look at it. I drank one only once."

"Kids?"

"Not now, not yet. Maybe." Ash was vague.

"What else?"

"I have some legal problems too."

"I've had a few in my day myself."

"The DA might want to file some charges relative to my being in the hospital under false pretenses."

"You have a lawyer?"

"Yeah, one of your patients, Roswell. He referred me here."

"Oh? He's the lawyer friend?"

"Yeah, he is. Anything you can tell me?"

"Don't even go there, Ash."

"I think you're right. I'm afraid I'm going to owe him way too much. He's helped me a lot so far and won't take a dime from me."

"Here's the deal. When you are offered a gift, whether it's from a friend or from the universe, you take it and honor it. That is your gift in return."

"Good thought." Ash reflected.

Scotty pulled out an appointment book. "I want you to come in weekly for a while."

"Can I afford you?"

"Sure you can. It's $275—"

"A session? I don't think my insurance—"

"That's $275 per month total, not counting today's session. You'll be coming to a group. I see everybody in groups. It's cheaper and you learn more and you'll get done what you need to get done. How about Tuesdays? I have an opening in my 3:00 p.m. group. Mostly professionals, plus one or two schizophrenics."

"Do I want to be in group therapy with a schizophrenic?"

"Don't worry, you'll learn something. Can you make it?"

"I'll try."

"Trying sucks."

"Okay, I'll be here."

Both men rose and shook hands. Ash walked downstairs to see a room full of people, presumably the next group. Scotty yelled from the top of the stairs, "Okay, let's get started," as the assorted group members filed up the steps.

Ash stepped outside then walked along the old cobblestone street heading home and feeling oddly optimistic.

CHAPTER 54

"How are things working out with you and Scotty?" Roswell asked Ash on the phone.

"I'm sleeping better anyhow."

"How are things at the paper?"

"Could be better, a lot better if I could get the BASH series going, but you said it would be best if I didn't yet."

"I did say that, and there's a reason, mainly, as I've told you, I don't want you antagonizing the state officials if they are considering pressing identity theft charges against you."

"So when do we settle this?"

"I've been talking to an assistant DA from Bay County, Sarah Wong, nice gal. Don't tell anyone but we dated a few years back."

"Oh yeah? Who dumped who?"

"Don't worry about that, we're still friendly. Anyhow, she's in charge of the whole BASH investigation from the local perspective. This story has the attention of the state attorney general too. Sarah wants us to meet Wednesday. She has a deposition with that security sergeant from BASH scheduled for tomorrow. He has a high-powered attorney at his elbow who will probably help him cut a deal. We may as well catch her as long as she's in a deal-making mood."

"Do I really need a deal?" Ash asked.

"From what I'm getting, the state wants you to think so. I haven't shown my hand as to what type and how much damages we're asking for. Now that you're in psychotherapy, heaven only knows how much oomph that can add to our case. So we're set to go Wednesday ten a.m. in my office conference room. I need to let you know that someone from the state attorney general's office will be there. But no one has filed charges yet, so that's a good sign. But I'm telling you, keep your BASH story under wraps. Don't dig your own grave."

"I'm still writing it."

"Write whatever you want, but sit on it. Please."

"Okay, for now. I think I get where you're coming from."

"I don't know what the state and the county have up their sleeves, but I'll guess we'll find out." Roswell concluded, "In the meantime, keep your wife happy."

"I'm working on that too."

"This Wednesday, buddy, come around nine thirty."

CHAPTER 55

The following excerpts are taken from the transcript of the deposition of Sergeant Joseph Dooley at the office of David Leclare, Esquire, on August 2, 2011. It has been edited to provide the reader with the most salient information.

Present: Mr. David Leclare, counsel for the witness; Ms. Sarah Wong, assistant district attorney for Bay County; Sgt. Joseph Dooley, witness; Ms. Juliana Holsopple, court reporter; and Mr. Phillip Seale, videographer.

(On record 0932)

Mr. Leclare: The witness has been sworn. Are we on the record?

Ms. Holsopple: Yes.

Mr. Leclare: Thank you. Mr. Dooley, please state your full name, age, and place of residence for the record.

Witness: Joseph Dooley. I'm 33. I live at 265 Dorchester Road in the township of Wadsworth.

Mr. Leclare: Mr. Dooley, you have waived your Fifth Amendment rights against self-incrimination, am I correct?

Witness: Yes, sir.

Mr. Leclare: And you understand that you are to answer questions, which may or may not be incriminating?

Witness: Yes.

Mr. Leclare: Mr. Dooley, where are you employed and in what capacity?

Witness: I am a sergeant in the security force at Bay Area State Hospital. My employer is the State of South Carolina Department of Behavioral Health Services, or DBHS for short.

Mr. Leclare: How long have you been employed there?

Witness: Um . . . four, no, five years in October. That's right, it'll be five years.

Mr. Leclare: And what did you do before that?

Witness: Well, I went to the state police academy.

Mr. Leclare: No, I mean what did you do for a living?

Witness: I was in the navy for three years, then I worked as a private security guard for a company in Columbia, then I decided to try being a real cop, so I got into the academy.

Mr. Leclare: How did that go?

Witness: It was all right. I liked it. I did okay.

Mr. Leclare: Why did you choose to work at the state hospital?

Witness: They were hiring and I like the area and I had a young child and another on the way and the benefits were pretty good. It's easier than being a city cop.

Mr. Leclare: But the pay is less?

Witness: That's a tradeoff, I suppose.

Mr. Leclare: So what did you do about it?

Witness: We lived within our means. My wife worked part time too, but that's rough with two small kids. I was home in the mornings because I worked in the afternoon and evenings.

MIKE BARTOS

Mr. Leclare: What else?

Witness: I put in for a promotion from officer to sergeant. There was an opening. I took the exam. I became a sergeant about two and a half years ago, about 600 bucks a month more.

Mr. Leclare: And did your duties change?

Witness: I became shift lead for the swing shift, five days a week, sometimes on weekends.

Mr. Leclare: What did that entail?

Witness: I led the change of shift reports, made some minor assignments. I reported to the captain.

Mr. Leclare: That would be Captain Dawkins?

Witness: Yes, sir.

Mr. Leclare: And Captain Dawkins is now?

Witness: Deceased.

Mr. Leclare: You also maintained and participated in security patrols, safety. I mean you performed normal security office duties yourself as well.

Witness: That's right.

Mr. Leclare: So you were quite busy?

Witness: I'd say so.

Mr. Leclare: So you decided you needed more income?

Witness: Uh . . . yes, I did.

Mr. Leclare: Tell us about that.

Witness: Word got around, I mean everyone knew there was meth and weed in use at BASH. That's because it was confiscated. We'd get it. If it was weed, we'd throw it away. We had better things to do than worry about who was smoking marijuana. Sometimes it would disappear.

Mr. Leclare: Disappear?

Witness: You know, just disappear.

Ms. Wong: Could the witness be a little more specific?

Mr. Leclare: Sergeant, please explain.

Witness: People, staff, would take it home and smoke it or sell it.

Mr. Leclare: People? You mean?

Witness: Security staff.

Mr. Leclare: Did you take it home and use it?

Witness: (pause)

Ms. Wong: Your client agreed...

Witness: Yes, I took it home.

Mr.: Leclare: Did you sell it?

Witness: I started to. I found I could make easy money, like a few hundred bucks a month, tax-free, really.

Mr. Leclare: And you gave some away.

Witness: Sometimes.

Mr. Leclare: Like to whom?

Witness: The administrator used to drop in and ask about contraband, asked to see it.

Mr. Leclare: That would be?

Witness: Mr. Desjardins. He would drop by, said he wanted to see contraband. We had some evidence, broken CDs, black-market cigarettes, bags of marijuana and meth, X-rated DVDs, and the like.

Mr. Leclare: He had no right to touch any of the stuff, did he?

Witness: No, not really. I mean he's the overall boss of the place, but this was part of the law enforcement department, and we are part of the state law enforcement system.

Mr. Leclare: So what happened?

Witness: Well, he—

Mr. Leclare: You mean Mr. Desjardins?

Witness: Yes, Mr. Desjardins would come by and say he was going to expedite the investigation.

Mr. Leclare: Did Captain Dawkins ever know about this?

Witness: Not to my knowledge, sir.

Mr. Leclare: So how was the investigation expedited?

Witness: Mr. Desjardins never did take anything. He sent Lieutenant Garner by, and she did pick up some stuff.

Mr. Leclare: What stuff?

Witness: Some meth, some marijuana, maybe a couple of small bags each.

Mr. Leclare: So what happened to this so-called contraband?

Witness: I really don't know.

Mr. Leclare: And you took some home yourself?

Witness: I did. It was a mistake.

Ms. Wong: Could the witness clarify what he took home?

Mr. Leclare: Go ahead and answer.

Witness: Well, I started off with marijuana, but then I started taking some meth as well. I figured I wouldn't get in trouble. I figured the lieutenant wouldn't hassle me if I didn't hassle her. Like we had something on each other.

Mr. Leclare: Then what?

Witness: About a year and a half ago, Lieutenant Garner told me that she was looking into the source of some of these drugs and wanted me to investigate further. She said I shouldn't do any paperwork, nothing official, just ask around.

Mr. Leclare: For the record, that would be Lieutenant Evelyn Garner.

Witness: Correct.

Mr. Leclare: So what did you do?

Witness: She gave me a name. I should check out this guy who she said was suspicious.

Mr. Leclare: Did she say why?

Witness: Nope.

Mr. Leclare: Who was it?

Witness: It was a patient, name of Victor Enale.

Mr. Leclare: Did you follow up?

Witness: I did within the week. I came on the ward and talked to him in the private conference room.

Mr. Leclare: What did he say?

Witness: I was really surprised. He said he said that he was expecting me to call.

Mr. Leclare: Why?

Witness: He didn't say why, but I guess Garner told him.

Mr. Leclare: Go on.

Witness: He said he knew I would be interested in helping him out, and I could help myself at the same time.

Mr. Leclare: What if you didn't want to? I mean how did he know you wouldn't bust him?

Witness: He knew a lot of stuff. He never mentioned Garner's name or her rank or anything, but he said he had sources that knew I took contraband home from the evidence room, and he just knew I'd be interested. He didn't actually say so, but he hinted that there were videos of me stealing drugs.

Mr. Leclare: So you believe you were being blackmailed somehow?

Witness: I was sort of stuck.

Mr. Leclare: So why do you think you were put in this position?

Witness: It seemed that people owed people favors, and I believe the higher ups all got some kind of cut, including from me, and they didn't want to get their hands dirty.

Mr. Leclare: So that would be your job?

Witness: Turned out that way. I mean, I did okay. I started dealing inside the

Confined Perimeter. I worked out a good financial deal with Enale. I think everybody was making money.

Mr. Leclare: Which brings us to the question of why you are coming forward with this information?

Witness: Well, you know, one of the meth providers was killed on July Fourth, must have been minutes after I made a purchase and drove off. I left all kinds of evidence of my presence. I'm a cop. I got sloppy. I should've known better.

Mr. Leclare: Were you under arrest or charged with anything when you came forward?

Witness: No, I was not.

Mr. Leclare: For the record, why are we here today and why are you waiving your Fifth Amendment rights?

Witness: Well, we all spoke, including the DA here, that if I cooperated, I would receive due consideration and leniency should I plead guilty and cooperate. Also, I wanted to make it very clear that I had nothing to do with the demise of Plato Ballinger. To be honest, I thought I would be a suspect.

Mr. Leclare: So you felt evidence was going to point to your presence at the murder scene?

Witness: I guess that's one way of putting it.

Mr. Leclare: And you're providing this testimony knowing that there are other suspects being pursued and you are not a prime suspect at this time?

Witness: (sighs) I am.

Mr. Leclare: Is it okay with everyone if we take a break now and go off the record?

Ms. Wong: Sure.

(off record 1024)

CHAPTER 56

The group was gathered around Scotty, like a king holding court. Ash sat in one of the wicker chairs. After some initial greetings, Scotty parked his cup on his belly and waited for anyone to start up.

"Scotty!" It was Ann, the wife of a prominent local physician. "I still think my mother-in law is running my husband's life, and she runs my life too. So I told her what we said in role play last week, and she says, 'Oh is that what your psychiatrist says?' and then my husband hides in the other room."

"So I guess you're on your own?"

Peter, one of the younger adults chimed in, "Why don't you just tell your mother-in-law to go fuck herself?"

Scotty looked at Peter and raised one eyebrow. "Peter, you're bringing your own anger issues into Ann's situation."

Peter replied, "Maybe she should borrow some of mine instead of being a depressed wimp."

Ann complained, "Scotty, why don't you do something about Peter's rudeness?"

"Because you don't need me to."

"What do you mean? You're running this group."

"Okay, I'm running it, and you're a competent adult, so you handle it."

Ann turned to Peter, "Peter, shut the hell up."

Scotty looked at Ann. "Try an adult interaction this time."

Ann turned to Peter again. "Peter, I don't appreciate your rudeness and your interruptions. I'm working on something important here."

Applause from the group. "Good work, Ann. I'm going to move on. Ash, how have you been? What's going on?"

Ash sighed, "I'm sleeping better, eating better. I'm writing more."

"Okay, what's with the legal situation?"

"Well, I can't go into great detail here, you know, but I'm having a big meeting with all the lawyers tomorrow, and I don't know what's going to happen."

Kyle, a young schizophrenic in the otherwise well functioning group, volunteered, "Yeah, I get nervous when I'm around lawyers. You never know what they're going to do."

"It's something I was involved with, I can't really talk about, nothing really criminal, but apparently I pissed the wrong people off. It'll be some kind of negotiation."

Scotty asked, "Will you have any control of the situation?"

"I might."

"Then do the right thing. You're at a crossroads now. Remember we talked about new directions in your life? Tomorrow's one of those signature days."

One middle-aged woman, a teacher, added, "I get the feeling you'll be okay. I think that people respect you and like you. This is just your second time in this group, but you're calm."

There were some scattered comments generally along the lines of "Good luck, Ash." Kyle stood up and walked over to Ash and gave him a hug.

CHAPTER 57

Ash was at Roswell's office at 9:30 a.m. There were pastries on a serving plate. Ash took a chocolate frosted cake doughnut and a cup of espresso.

Roswell was busy thumbing through a sheaf of documents and then looked up at Ash. "I think we can wrap this up by lunch. I asked the judge to push back another hearing I had until one thirty. Just remember, let me do the talking. I know they want something, probably drop the lawsuit, and they won't prosecute."

"You think so?"

"They didn't say that, but that's the vibe I'm getting."

"Aren't these charges just a bunch of BS anyhow? Aren't they stretching it?"

"I think so, but then again, if the state machinery wants to go after you, they'll pursue you into the next decade. I'm a good lawyer, but not good enough to take on the state by myself."

Sarah Wong knocked on the conference room door and entered, pulling a two-wheeled cart with several boxes of files. "Hi, Roswell, are we ready?"

"We're still waiting for Mr. Williams from the attorney general's office. Have a doughnut? How are things down in McMurtree?"

"They're still fixing some water damage in my office, I hope to be back in by the beginning of next week."

"How's the courthouse?"

"There was roof leak, and the walls of courtroom 1A got warped. It looks like they're finally going to have to renovate."

Mr. Jackson Williams of the state attorney general's office was shown into the conference room. He was a tall middle-aged African American man, wearing a pinstriped suit, wire-rim glasses, and sporting a graying goatee. He shook hands with everyone, including Ash.

Roswell started, "Shall we begin?"

Mr. Williams started, "As we agreed this is an informal meeting. No records or transcription. Are we all in agreement?"

Mr. Williams continued, "First of all, we have received notice of your lawsuit for however, what was it? Four million dollars?"

Roswell asked, "So you're here to settle?" knowing full well that wasn't the case.

"Not hardly, no. We're negotiable, though."

Roswell interjected, "Well, as you know, my client suffered documented physical and psychological trauma through not only the negligence of the state but through the willful disregard of his rights and well being. He was locked up despite the knowledge that he was there wrongfully and then negligently extradited to Charleston County during a dangerous and lethal hurricane, which regretfully took the life of the sheriff who was transporting him."

Williams responded, "Keep in mind he voluntarily presented himself for incarceration under false identity. We don't mean to impugn the departed, but if Chief Dawkins were alive, he would be indicted for conspiracy to commit fraud, and your client is still alive."

Roswell asked, "Are you planning to take this to the grand jury?"

"Well, this would be a complicated and protracted case, which we would like to avoid and I'm sure your client would like to avoid. I mean it involves conspiracy and identity theft, both serious felonies."

"And you're very well aware any lawsuit would also be very involved and complex," Roswell added. "I'm getting that you would prefer not to pursue this."

"There are a lot of legal complications here that would cost everybody a lot of time and money, including the taxpayers. So let me get to the point, okay? Our position is that the state is willing to stipulate, by way of a sealed agreement, that your client, Ashley Roper, was never incarcerated at Bay Area State Hospital or any other facility. He just was never there."

"So that means he never committed any crime because he wasn't there," Roswell surmised.

"And likewise, the state could not have committed any negligent acts against your client as he was, as we agreed, never there," Williams countered.

"So there is no lawsuit, correct?"

"No charges, no lawsuit."

"Interesting offer." Roswell was not surprised. "Let me consult with my client for a moment, okay?"

"Before you do, there is one more thing," Williams added. "If he was never there, then your client can't publish any exposé of what went on at BASH and cease all further investigation."

Ash blurted out, "You want to kill my story?"

Williams looked at Ash coolly. "You were never there. There is no story."

Ash was turning red. Roswell excused the two of them as they left the conference room to go to Roswell's private office.

Ash paced back and forth, obviously agitated, and said in a strained voice, "What the hell, Roswell, I risked my life to get this story, and you want me to throw it away? No freakin' way. I don't care if I go to jail." He kicked a wastebasket across the room.

Roswell put his hand on Ash's shoulder. "I don't want you to do anything, Ash, except stay out of jail and be a free man and get on with your life. The state is apparently dead serious about avoiding embarrassment and taking down their bureaucracy. They could give you ten years. Take the goddamn deal, Ash. Otherwise, you won't have a life, even if by some chance you get acquitted. Your lawsuit isn't a slam dunk either. I can't spend my career fighting your battle. This isn't just about you. Think about your wife too.

Ash took a deep breath and sat down. "I need a drink."

"Not now. Just take some deep breaths and calm down. Let's get back in there, and end this now."

Ash and Roswell returned. Ash was still red faced but doing his best to keep from cursing. Roswell spoke. "What do we need to do?"

Williams already had the papers on the table. "You and your client sign these documents. Ms. Wong and I have already signed them. We each keep a copy. There is a gag provision here. If you or your client violate it, you are open to prosecution. Otherwise, the lawsuit is dropped, we agree there is not enough evidence to prosecute. This all goes away. Both sides keep the documents sealed as part of the agreement."

Sarah Wong looked at Roswell. "It's a good deal. I helped draft it. Take it."

Ash glowered at Williams, took a deep breath, and signed both copies of the agreements, muttering under his breath, "Son of a bitch."

"Any questions?" Williams asked as he was slipping the sealed manila envelope into his briefcase.

Roswell asked, "Yes, what about that deposition with the security officer yesterday?"

Williams smiled as he turned to leave. "What security officer?"

CHAPTER 58

EIGHT MONTHS LATER

"**C**an I cop another feel?"

Roswell leans across the table at my famous bar and grille and caresses Sally J's round tummy. She says, "Oh! I can feel him kicking. Can you feel it, Rozzie?"

"Maybe, yeah, there it is. I think you got a lively one on board. Hey, Ash, how's the nursery coming along?"

"We just bought the crib. What else do I need to do?"

"Yeah, I think you've done plenty already," Roswell snaps back.

Sally J smiles and says, "I wish I could have a drink."

Ash asks, "Hey, Doc, you're a doctor. A little taste of wine at six months won't hurt anything, will it?"

"I'm off duty folks, but I won't tell if you have a small glass, just make it red."

Sally J backs off. "I don't really need it."

This is the monthly meeting of the BASH Memorial Marching Club and Chowder Society at Kerrigan's. We raise our glasses to the men and women who lost their lives in the line of duty, those who escaped—including Ash and me—and those who threw a wrench into the wheels of the bureaucratic machine. We remember Chief Dawkins—somebody has to, and Sheriff Harmon, and Doug Riley, too. Then there are those who turned their backs on the truth, manipulated the system, and intimidated those who came forward. We don't drink to those bastards.

Ash had a story to tell, but he can't. I don't blame him. Life has to go on. And as we are gathered here tonight, we share that truth and love with each other. As Ash learned, and I agree with him, you have to choose your battles carefully.

Roswell is here tonight with a gal he's been dating for the past two months, even though she is fourteen years his junior. Alyse has shared her story of tracking the hurricane with us, and I have shared it with you. Roswell is representing her in negotiations with a major media outlet in Atlanta. Alyse is a hero, and she had been nominated for the award of Broadcast Meteorologist of the Year, not bad for a rookie. And she is eye candy to be sure, although I see Roswell making quick but heartfelt glances at Sally J while she's yakking it up with Alyse and Cassandra, Sally J gaily tilting her head back and laughing, not aware of Roswell's attention.

Charley Town, well, that's history, at least the Ash and Sally J version. Without the BASH story to boost the distribution and interest, there wasn't much left. Ash didn't have his heart in running an internet town and gown site. The big media conglomerate, which ran the competition, bought him out, mainly for the name that they now use. *Charley Town* has grown from sixteen to eighty-four pages, but it belongs to someone else. Ash remains as a paid consultant. He has been able to transition to his new role as employed writer and soon to be dad with the help and support of Scotty Powell, whom he still sees in the Tuesday group.

Ash wants to do a story on Alyse. She is more than willing. The article about Ginny Smalls' café brought her more business than she can handle. Charlestonians are making the hour drive for her now famous shrimp and grits, and her recipe was featured in the *Southern Styles* magazine. Two weeks ago, Ash got a letter of thanks from Ginny Smalls, and she enclosed a copy of a letter she received from her son, Private First Class Jermaine Smalls, United States Marine Corps. Ash is also doing some freelance writing for several other magazines as well.

BASH, that's history too. Some of the pricks who ran it and implicated in closed grand jury proceedings simply faded away with the hospital, transferred to other state facilities. Lieutenant Garner? She's in the women's prison but not as an inmate, just working as a run of the mill corrections officer. Sergeant Dooley was sentenced to residential drug rehab and made a deal with the IRS, which let him avoid jail, but he'll be working overtime to pay his tax bill for years to come. He's still a state employee. That never changes.

Victor Enale—they threw his ass in jail for drug distribution. There was no more easy state hospital time for him. Somebody's head had to roll. He was fingered by Dooley, who hopes old Victor doesn't get out anytime soon.

Then there is the matter of the Silver Swords murder of Plato Ballinger. It seems Reggie left a variety of prints, including footprints, fingerprints, and even lip prints. He wasn't the trigger man, but he sang like a canary to avoid the death penalty. Beau Rippington, not so lucky, as he will go on trial next month, facing capital murder charges. And, oh yes, Ash sent a check for sixty dollars to Burton Peals, now at a psychiatric unit at the state prison, awaiting transfer to the Goose Creek facility once it is completed. Tyler Goode now lives at a halfway house in McMurtree, is clean and sober, and staying out of trouble.

The bulldozers and cranes are down at Bayside, demolishing that sad facility, and I hear a golf course and resort will be going in. The town of Bayside itself got smacked pretty hard by the hurricane with several million dollars of damage. Since Bayside has mostly relatively new construction, it held up well considering the severity of the blow. I've been down to the shoreline just to check things out. A lot of the beach washed away. I suppose the developers will be dredging up sand for years to come. The town is filled with the sounds of hammers and circular saws, blue roof tarps, and the smell of freshly sawed two-by-fours.

My old house, Marshlandia, is repaired and on the market. There is no reason for me to live there anymore. If anyone is looking for a 1600 square foot renovated marsh home on a half acre, with three bedrooms and two baths, for the bargain price of $425,000, let me know or send them over to Bayside Resorts Realty.

So now I'm living upstairs from the pub, which is okay for now, but Grover and I are getting a little cramped, not to mention Cassandra, who is spending more time in my happy little penthouse.

I officially left state service and worked out a gentleman's agreement with DBHS; that is, I have an unblemished record, and I just leave. I cleared out about forty thousand from my state retirement fund, rented a small office on Queen Street, and started a cash only psychiatry practice. So now I have a grand total of eleven therapy cases, and I don't see them every week. That's okay. I have time to work on my piano blues technique. I'm playing more often.

My friend Ash couldn't tell his story, silenced by the bureaucratic thugs. But it's a story that needed to be told. There's always something to be learned from a good story, if you listen. I hear lots of good stories listening to patients or friends like Ash and Sally J or patrons at the bar, as I'm getting more involved in Kerrigan's Bar and Grille. Maybe I'll just work in the family business and forget about psychiatry altogether.

So as I'm wiping down our lovely mahogany bar, a customer steps up and says, "Hey, bartender, can you get me a beer?"

And I say, "Don't call me bartender. Call me Doc."

Mike Bartos is a physician, psychiatrist, and amateur jazz musician who lives with his wife Jody in Napa, California.

Made in the USA
San Bernardino, CA
08 May 2014